VENGEANCE FROM ASHES

HONOR & DUTY 1

SAM SCHALL

ALSO BY THE AUTHOR

E-book ISBN: 978-1-949901-26-9

Print ISBN: 978-1-949901-27-6

Hunter's Moon Press

Cover art: Space Battle © by Julia Kovalova.

If you enjoyed this novel, please visit my website for more information.

Thank you for your support.

To Sarah, for pushing me to finish this.

———

Vengeance from Ashes

———

They took away her rank and freedom.
They left her only honor and duty.

1

_____

"Prisoner Four One Niner Baker One-A, prepare for transfer," a disembodied voice said from the overhead speaker.

Lips pulled back, teeth bared in an animalistic sneer, the prisoner sat up and swung her legs over the side of her bunk. As she stood, she turned away from the cell door. Her hands automatically went behind her head, fingers lacing. Almost without thought, she sank to her knees, legs spread, ankles crossed. Then, realizing what she had done, she cursed silently, hating herself and those responsible for bringing her to this state.

Two years. Two very long years in Hell had taught her how to act. Her body responded automatically to the commands barked at her. Only when she allowed her mind to surface, to let herself fully experience what was going on around her, did she hesitate. But not this time. There was no reason to disobey, no threat yet to meet.

Those years may have taught her all too painfully how to act, but they hadn't broken her. Not yet at any rate. Even so, they had come close. Two years cut off from those she cared for, from almost all human contact. Stripped of even the most basic of human rights and dignity, she knew she was little more than an animal to break and tame to those in charge. She knew it just as she knew she could do nothing about it.

Just as she knew she'd been betrayed by the government she'd served and had been ready to die for.

What she didn't know was why. Why had she been betrayed? Worse, why had those who'd served loyally at her side been targeted?

The soft *swoosh* of the heavily armored door sliding open broke the silence of the small cell a few moments later. With her back to it, she couldn't see who entered, not that she wanted to. One of the first lessons she had learned after arriving at the Tarsus military penal colony was not to look. That had been a very painful lesson, one that landed her in the prison's infirmary for several days. It was also a mistake she'd never repeated.

That had been one of many *lessons* she'd been forced to endure since arriving there. With the commandant's tacit – hell, as far as she knew it was his overt – approval, the guards could be as sadistic as they wanted. Correction for even the most insignificant infraction might take the form of a rifle butt to the ribs or kidney, and that was if she was lucky. If not, the beating that followed would leave her hurting so badly she could barely move. Even then, the guards wouldn't send her to the infirmary. After all, it was so much more fun to watch her suffer, reminding her that she alone was responsible for what had happened.

Fortunately, she'd heard the horror stories before arriving at the penal colony. Even though she hadn't been ready to believe them, they had helped prepare her for what she'd face. Even so, it had been a shock the first time one of the guards beat her down for asking what would have been a simple question on the outside. That had been enough to convince her that the best course of action was to remain silent unless it was imperative that she speak. That wasn't to say there hadn't been times when circumstances forced her to break that rule and she bore the scars to prove it. All she wanted now was to live through the remainder of her prison term. Survival was the first goal. Vengeance would come later. Not for her, but for those brave and loyal souls who had followed her despite her protests and who had paid the ultimate price as a result.

She swallowed hard, forcing her mind away from past horrors, as boots clomped across the small cell in her direction. A rough hand grabbed her right arm, twisting it painfully behind her back. She flinched as a security cuff was locked tightly around that wrist. Her breath hissed out as the process was repeated with her left arm. Moments later, similar restraints were fastened about her ankles. Then a gloved hand closed around her left arm and jerked her to her feet.

Guard-captain Gavin Haritos spun her to face him, grinning sadistically. His fist caught her with a vicious backhand. With a sharp cry of pain, she staggered back. The short chain connecting her ankles tripped her. Only the man's quick grab at the front of her jumpsuit kept her from falling. He pulled her forward and, with the ease of much practice, draped a heavy hood over her head before she could react.

Haritos' cruel grip on her arm kept her on her feet as he hauled her out of her cell and down the long corridor. Blood pounded in her ears, almost deafening her. Fear and hatred raced through her, sparking every fiber of her survival instincts. She *knew* this was going to be bad, very bad. It always was when the guard-captain came for her. But she could do nothing to stop him, at least not yet.

"This is your lucky day, bitch." Haritos shoved her into one of the three lifts at the end of the corridor and she heard him slam his fist against the control panel. A moment later, the lift gave a slight lurch and she felt the car start downward. "You're being transferred, Shaw. But don't get your hopes up that it means the rules no longer apply because they do. If you're smart, you'll remember those poor bastards sentenced here with you. Everything you say and do from now on impacts them."

A soft moan escaped her lips before she could stop it and fear raced like an open current through her. No matter how many times she'd been in this position before, she couldn't help it. A transfer could mean almost anything, none of it good. Not as long as the survivors of her unit were still on Tarsus.

Bile rose in her throat as the lift came to a sudden halt. But it wasn't that which caused her breath to catch. The guard-captain's low chuckle sent a shiver of fear down her spine. Once before he had stopped the lift short of their destination. He'd told her then it was time to deliver a warning.

Warning!

He had beaten her so badly that day she had prayed for death. Was he about to repeat that performance? If so, why? She had done nothing to break the rules. She hadn't been out of her cell in weeks, her only contact had been with the guards who checked on her three times a day.

Without warning, Haritos' fist connected with her stomach. Pain doubled her over. Tears filled her eyes beneath the hood and she fought the urge to vomit. The neck of her jumpsuit tightened uncomfortably at her throat as the guard-captain's hand fisted in the material. Using it to hold her in place, he continued his assault. Her head snapped back and she tasted blood. She lost track of the number of times he struck or where each blow landed. All she could do was stand there, held in place by the hand at her collar, and pray the beating ended soon.

Suddenly, Haritos released her and she fell to the floor of the lift. Before she could struggle to her knees, his heavy boot caught her in the ribs. Once, twice, he struck, each time forcing her to cry out in pain. Her ribs ached and it hurt to breathe. Her face, especially her nose, throbbed with each beat of her pulse. From the stuffiness of her nose, she knew Haritos had broken it – again. Her right eye felt puffy, swollen. It had been a long time since she had been beaten this badly and why?

Why now?

"Listen carefully, bitch," Haritos growled as he once more hauled her to her feet. "This is only a temporary respite for you. Sooner or later, you will be sent back. Remember your people are still here and we can do whatever we want with them. So keep your mouth shut. We'll know if you do or say anything about your time here."

To her surprise, Haritos said nothing more. That was unusual. Whenever he'd come for her before, he'd taken perverse pleasure in detailing what horrors awaited her. The fact he'd gone silent worried her. And what did he mean by this being a respite and she would be back?

Dear God, what was happening?

Haritos remained silent as he forced her off the lift. Doors opened and then closed behind them. She didn't know how to react when, for the first time in months, she felt the sun beating down on her. They were outside. But why? Where were they going?

It didn't take long to find out. Haritos led her up a ramp. The hood obscured her sight, but she could hear the muffled sounds of a crew working to prepare a shuttle, maybe even a courier ship, for launch. Haritos pulled her to a halt and told her to stand still. Then he released his hold on her arm and she sensed that he had moved a short distance away. There were soft voices. Straining to hear, she only caught a few words. *Transfer . . . prisoner . . . dangerous . . . tried to escape . . . take no chances . . . don't listen to anything she says. . . .*

Dear God, was she actually being transferred out of the Tarsus penal colony?

Hope flared only to die as quickly as it had been born. She remembered Haritos' warning. Her people, those few who had survived the ambush only to be betrayed by those who should have stood for them, were being left behind. That meant she had to do as the guard-captain said. Otherwise, her people were as good as dead.

No!

Before she could do anything – not that there was much she could do, bound and hooded as she was – Haritos was once more at her side. She stumbled forward as he grabbed her and led her further up the ramp. He hissed one last warning not to do anything foolish. Then he turned her over to someone else. Flanked on both sides by unseen guards, she was led into another lift. A few minutes later, her restraints were removed and then her hood and she found herself standing in the center of a small cell. She didn't need to hear the announcement for all hands to prepare for departure to know she was on a ship. But a ship to where?

And what about those who'd been sent to the penal colony with her? Why weren't they being transferred with her?

Now, almost a week later, she stood in yet another cell, this one planetside, and worry warred with anger. She'd overheard enough from the guards on the transport to know her fears were true – the others had been left behind on the penal colony.

That's when an anger so great it overrode the fear of the unknown had flowed through her. For the first time in two years, she'd been separated from the survivors of her unit, those poor, brave souls who had followed her into hell and back only to find themselves brought up on charges right along with her. It didn't matter that the commandant of the penal colony hadn't let her see her people. She'd managed to get word of them from time to time and that had been enough to let her know they were all right – or at least as all right as anyone could be after being sentenced to the Tarsus penal colony.

It still amazed her how the prison grapevine managed to keep tabs on everyone and pass along information. It might be inconsistent, but it was there, and it had been all that kept her sane. She'd never thought herself a social animal, but two years of rarely seeing anyone but her jailers had been almost more than she could handle. Thank God for the grapevine and the bits of information it brought her.

During transport from the penal colony, no one had told her anything. Held in the transport ship's brig, she had no opportunity to learn anything about their destination or why she had been taken from Tarsus. A guard brought her food and drink at regular intervals, but he never said a word that wasn't necessary. He certainly hadn't volunteered any information. Still, she'd managed to work out that she was alone in the brig by the way his steps never stopped before he appeared at her cell door and because no one had responded when she'd tapped out messages using the code learned on Tarsus.

She had just noticed the slightest change in the rhythm of the ship's engines, indicating it had assumed orbit somewhere, when another guard arrived with a change of clothes for her. She'd looked at the plain black jumpsuit with suspicious eyes. Nothing about it marked her as a prisoner. It could have been something worn by almost any worker on the docks or in a warehouse. That should have reassured her but for one thing. There was nothing about the guard's manner to indicate she was about to be freed. In that moment, she'd come the closest to breaking her rule of "never ask a question you don't know the answer to" than she had been since her first few days on Tarsus.

Half an hour later, she'd been seated on a shuttle. The guards had secured her hands behind her back before locking her safety harness in place, but they hadn't hooded her. They obviously weren't worried about her recognizing where she was. Of course, the only way she could do that was if she could actually see something of the lay of the land. So she'd craned her neck in an effort to see into the shuttle's cockpit. One corner of her mouth lifted ever so slightly at the sight of the high rises ahead of them. Her heart beat a bit faster and her breath caught as she recognized the skyline of Fuercon's capital city. New Kilrain. She was home. But why?

Now, after being processed into the same military brig where she'd been held during her trial, she still didn't know why she'd been brought back home. It couldn't be good. They may have taken away her prison issued jumpsuit, but she'd still been brought there shackled and had been processed into the brig as quickly as humanly possible. It had almost been as if FleetCom was afraid word of her return might leak out. But why?

Damn it, what was going on?

Of course, there'd been no explanation. Nor had she asked for one. It would be a long time before she forgot that lesson. Too much talking, too much curiosity was a bad thing that almost always resulted in painful punishment. She might not be on Tarsus any longer but that didn't mean things would be any different here. After all, who policed the jailers? No one, at least not on Tarsus and she wasn't willing to risk it now that she was home. That was especially true after the way she and the others had been betrayed by those they'd been loyal to

Freed of her restraints and alone, she looked around. One cell was pretty much like any other. Across from the door was a narrow bunk. Hygiene facilities were at the foot of the bunk. It was almost exactly like her cell back on Tarsus. There was nothing she could use to escape and nothing she could use to kill herself, not that she planned on taking that route out. At least not anymore. No, there were others who needed to die before she did.

"Prisoner is secured," the guard who had brought her to the cell radioed as he stepped back.

Ashlyn Shaw, former Marine captain, didn't move. Instead, she stood in the center of the small cell, her brown eyes focused on some point beyond the guard, her hands behind her back even though the restraints had been removed. As the security field across the cell door activated, she gave no sign of realizing it even though the faint, high-pitched hum was something she'd learned to listen for over the last two years. That sound, like a distant bunch of angry bees, meant she'd fry her nervous system long before pushing through the field. Freedom might look close, but she'd be dead – or worse – before she actually found it.

At least the guard didn't close the physical door. For the first time in what had to be months, she could look beyond the confines of her cell. It might not be the same cell she'd occupied since her conviction. Hell, this wasn't even the same planet. That didn't matter. All that did was the fact that the open cell door gave her at least some semblance of not being completely cut off from all other life on the planet.

As the guard disappeared from sight, Ashlyn remained where she was, motionless except for the rise and fall of her chest and the slow blinking of her eyes. She listened, counting his footsteps as they slowly faded away. When she'd been escorted to the cell, she had focused on what was directly in front of her. She had not wanted to give the guards on duty the satisfaction of seeing her look around in curiosity. Now, with only silence filling the air, she allowed herself to relax just a little.

Once convinced the guard was gone, she moved to the door, careful not to get too close to the security field. Looking to her left, she couldn't tell how far away he might be. All she knew for certain was that her cell was located at the end of the corridor, the door situated so she couldn't see much beyond the far edge of the cell. So there might be any number of other prisoners close by but, for all intents and purposes, she was alone – again.

That was fine. Alone meant fewer chances for anyone to figure out what she planned. But it also meant she had to keep up appearances. She couldn't let them guess what she had in mind. So she lay on her bunk, her back to the doorway. She wouldn't let those she knew were watching over security monitors see her curiosity or her concern.

This was as close to home as she was likely to get in a very long while. If the opportunity to escape presented itself, she'd take it and be damned with waiting on the military courts to finally get it right. Once free, she'd deal with everyone who had betrayed her and then she'd find a way to free those who had been sent to the penal colony with her. After that, she really didn't give a damn about what happened.

––––––

THE TWO FOLLOWED the guard down the long corridor. Bare white walls intersected by six reinforced doors on each side marked their path. Silence, broken only by the sounds of their steps, enveloped them. This wing of the security complex felt deserted – which it was with one notable exception. There hadn't been a need to use the high security cells for a long while.

As far as the tall redhead was concerned, there was still no need to – even considering just how special this particular prisoner happened to be.

Admiral Miranda Tremayne (ret.) and Admiral Richard Collins were there with one purpose. They had to find a way to convince Ashlyn Shaw to trust them enough to listen to what they had to say. That was their first hurdle. The second would be harder. Somehow, they had to persuade her to work with them again. If she agreed, they'd secure her immediate release. It was a long shot, Tremayne knew, but they had to try. Not only for the prisoner's sake but for the sake of so many more.

Their escort stopped before the last cell and nodded. Like every other cell along the corridor, this was a high security cell. Thick, reinforced walls with one narrow opening, just wide enough for a single person to step through. That opening could be secured with a reinforced door that slid firmly into place when activated. But for now, that door was open, the security field active.

Directly across from the door was a single cot. On it lay the prisoner. Her back was to them and nothing about her revealed whether she realized she was being watched. But Tremayne knew better. She'd known the prisoner for years, most of the younger woman's life in fact. She had no doubt Ashlyn Shaw, decorated Marine captain and now convicted war criminal, was well aware of the fact someone was there, even if she might not know who.

"On your feet, prisoner!" the guard barked. "I said, on your feet!"

Tremayne watched Shaw as the guard pounded his stun baton against the cell wall once and then again. Not that it seemed to phase the young woman. Only the slight tensing of her muscles, so slight Tremayne almost missed it, betrayed the fact Shaw even heard the guard. Interesting. The young woman had always possessed great self-control. Clearly, she'd honed it to a new level during her incarceration.

"Damn it, Shaw, on your feet. Don't make me come in there," the guard all but growled.

Tremayne frowned. The last thing they needed was to further antagonize the young woman. Besides, were their roles reversed, she'd probably be doing her best to show as much indifference as was the young woman. Even so, she could understand the guard's frustration. He was under enough pressure just escorting the two of them through the security wing. Collins was First Fleet's commanding officer. Then there was Tremayne herself. So-called war hero, not that she thought of herself as such, and now a member of the Senate. To have a mere prisoner ignore his order in front of such "luminaries" had to be not only frustrating but humiliating as well.

Of course, there was nothing *mere* about Ashlyn Shaw and there never had been.

"Ma'am, I can go inside."

The guard sounded unsure, not that Tremayne blamed him. She doubted there was anyone on the planet who didn't know who Ashlyn Shaw was. Her war record had been stellar up until the time she'd been court-martialed. Whether they believed the charges that had been leveled against her or not, they'd know she wasn't someone you wanted to cross.

Tremayne frowned and shook her head. This wasn't the way to proceed. If the prisoner wouldn't respond to the guard, it was time to try something else.

Carefully judging the distance, Tremayne stepped forward, coming so close to the barrier that she could feel the energy dancing across her skin.

"Out of that rack, Marine, and on your feet!" she snapped in her best command voice.

Her order met with a more pronounced physical reaction from Shaw. This time there was no mistaking the way the young woman's muscles tensed, as if preparing to sit up. Holding her breath, Tremayne waited. Would Shaw respond or would she force herself to return to her relaxed pose on the bunk?

Several long seconds passed as they waited but to no avail. The prisoner continued to ignore them.

Damn it.

"Admiral, let me call for backup and then we can go in." Before the guard could reach for his comm, Tremayne's hand closed over his arm.

"No." Most definitely not. But they had to get through to Shaw somehow. Maybe it was time to put aside rank and go to the personal.

"I know you can hear me, Captain Shaw, so I'm just going to talk. I hope you'll listen."

God how I wish the last two years had never happened. Everything would be so much easier.

"Things have changed since you were brought up on charges. Those responsible are no longer in power, either in the government or in the military chain of command. That includes those who found you and the others guilty at your court-martial." She paused, watching, hoping for some reaction. Was there a hint of tension easing in the prisoner's body? She wasn't sure. All she could do was continue and hope for the best. "Some things haven't changed, however. We are still at war. It doesn't matter that we've technically been sharing a truce with the enemy. All it did was slow hostilities. The fact is things are about to get bad again and you know what that means."

Surely that would get through to the young woman. In all the years she'd known Ashlyn Shaw, there'd been one thing she could rely upon – Shaw's sense of duty. She just hoped the last two years hadn't destroyed it.

"Shaw – Ashlyn." She reached out, the palm of her right hand almost touching the security field separating them. As she did, she sensed the guard tensing, ready to pull her back before she made contact with the field. "We need you. Please."

Finally, a reaction. A slight tremor ran down the prisoner's back. Then a bitter laugh filled the cell. Tremayne bit her lower lip to hear it.

"You seem to forget, *Admiral*, not only that I've been stripped of all rank but that I still have three years to serve on my sentence. There's not much I can do for you while I'm a prisoner. So, unless you've brought a pardon – for not only me but for my people as well – you can go straight to Hell."

"That's enough, Shaw!" Collins snapped. "You may be a prisoner but you're still a Marine and you'll respect the rank, if nothing else, and listen to what we have to say."

"Respect the rank!" Fury filled the young woman's voice as she rolled over and surged to her feet.

Tremayne gasped in shock. Gone was the promising young officer she'd known. In her place was a hard, scarred woman, a veteran of battles that had killed so many on both sides. But there was more. Her face showed scars that hadn't been there when she'd been sentenced to the Tarsus military prison. Worse, Tremayne saw the unmistakable signs that Shaw had been beaten, and badly, in the not too distant past. Anger flared and the redhead forced it down as she continued to take in the young woman's appearance.

A band of white ran from her left temple back, stark against the otherwise dark hair. Thin, not quite gaunt, Shaw had lost a great deal of weight over the last two years. Her once healthy tan looked wan and Tremayne wondered how long it had been since she'd seen the light of day. What in the hell had happened to her in the last two years to bring her to this?

And would it prevent her from helping them, even if they managed to arrange for everyone to be pardoned?

"Ashlyn, please, just listen," Tremayne said softly.

"I listened once before, Admiral, and it cost most of my people their lives. Those that survived found themselves brought up on phony charges, just like me, and sent to that hellhole of a military prison. But maybe you've forgotten that."

Tremayne closed her eyes and breathed deeply, struggling for calm. She hadn't forgotten. She'd kept the memory of that betrayal close to her. It had been why she'd resigned her commission to run for office. She'd known she needed to work the system to get those brave souls freed and their names cleared. Unfortunately, she hadn't expected it to take this long.

She still remembered all too clearly the events that had led up to Shaw's court-martial. Shaw had done nothing wrong. She'd done her duty. She'd followed orders despite her misgivings – misgivings she'd voiced not only to her immediate commanding officer but to the sector commander and to Tremayne as well. And what had it gotten her? Her company decimated in an ambush and the rest of them, Shaw included, court-martialed and imprisoned and all in the name of face-saving by some damn-fool politicians and senior officers.

Worse, Shaw's family – and the families of the other survivors – had also paid the price. Those in government service who hadn't been willing to condemn their relatives had seen their jobs disappear. There had been other pressures brought to bear on those in the private sector. That could no more be forgiven than what happened to Shaw and her people, as the next round of elections had proven.

"Ashlyn, I can't undo what happened. I wish to God I could." Tremayne waved Collins back as he stepped forward. The last thing they needed was him losing his temper. She understood why he'd reacted as he had. It was his fleet about to head to the front lines. His people would be the first to die. Even more would die if they couldn't convince Shaw to work with them. "All I can tell you is that things have changed since then. Fleet leadership has undergone a turnover the likes of which you wouldn't believe. What happened to you and your company became a rallying cry at the last elections and those politicians responsible were voted out of office. There is no chance of a repeat of what you went through ever happening again."

"At least until the next election." Shaw shook her head and ran a hand through her short cropped dark hair. "Sorry, Admiral, unless and until you can tell me my people have been pardoned and are safely away from Tarsus, I've got nothing more to say to you."

"Ashlyn, at least listen. Please."

"Not until I know my people are free."

With that, she returned to her bunk and once more turned her back to them. There'd be no getting through to her. Between past betrayals and whatever Hell she'd been forced to endure the last two years, she'd changed. But she'd given them a lever they could use, one Tremayne had already considered.

"Ashlyn–"

"Admiral, all I want is to finish serving my sentence. Then, maybe, I can finally bury my dead."

"Please just think about what I've said."

Tremayne turned and retraced her steps down the corridor. She'd known it would be difficult to convince the young woman to trust them. As far as Shaw knew, they had accepted the way she and her people were offered up as political sacrifices just as most of the military leadership had. She didn't know everything Tremayne and so many others done to clear their names and win their freedom.

What she hadn't anticipated was the change in Shaw. Something had happened to her during her incarceration. The physical scars were proof of that. Those visible scars were bad enough, but how deep did the psychological scars run? Obviously, she had a great deal of homework to do before she next tried to talk with Ashlyn Shaw.

"Miranda," Collins began as the lift doors closed behind them, his frustration clear.

"Later." She needed to think before discussing what happened even with him.

———

THE SOUNDS of footsteps grew fainter. Part of her wanted to call Tremayne and Collins back, to ask all the questions she'd had no answers to for so long. But the other part, the part that had learned how to survive in the military prison, held her back. She'd trusted once and that trust had cost her and her command dearly. It would take more than Tremayne's assurances that things had changed for her to trust again.

Despite that, it was so very difficult to stay where she was, to stay quiet. Swallowing hard, she squeezed her eyes shut and willed herself not to react. Just because the admirals were gone didn't mean she wasn't being watched and she'd be damned if she'd let anyone see how badly their visit had shaken her. She might not have known what to expect when she'd been brought back to the capital, but this certainly wasn't it.

A moment later she drew a shaky breath and held it. When she slowly exhaled, she forced herself to relax. So many emotions raged within her, too many. Among them was hope, something she hadn't felt in a very long while. But she couldn't allow herself the luxury of experiencing any of them and especially not the latter. Emotions were a weakness to be exploited. She might not be at the penal colony any longer, but she was still a prisoner. She'd give her jailers nothing they could use against her. Indifference was her best defense just then.

But it was hard. When she'd heard Admiral Tremayne's voice, she'd thought for one moment she'd finally lost her mind. Tremayne had been the one person in the military she'd always been able to count on. She knew Tremayne had tried to speak on her behalf at that farce of a trial, but the military judges hadn't let her. Tremayne had been on her side then, just as she'd always been.

But now the admiral was asking her to help them despite how she and the remainder of her unit had been betrayed. Had she been wrong all this time in believing in Tremayne? Or had the admiral really been telling her the truth when she'd said things had changed?

She couldn't think about that, couldn't hold out hope. Not when her people were still on Tarsus. At least she'd been able to warn the admirals – if they understood. They had to understand. Or they had to at least wonder enough about what she'd said to start digging.

Dear God, let me be careful though.

Otherwise, she'd be joining those dead she'd talked about and, despite everything, she wasn't ready to die. Not yet. She still had vengeance to mete out first.

2

_____

Major Rico Santiago stared at the image on his screen. He couldn't believe it. There was no way she could be on-planet, much less be just three floors below his office. But, as the ancient adage went, a picture was worth a thousand words. In this case, it was worth a hell of a lot much more and it raised just as many questions.

He leaned back and shook his head. Even after watching the scene in the cell for approximately five minutes, his mind refused to accept what his eyes saw. The prisoner, dressed in the standard issue black jumpsuit that the JAG euphemistically called "persons of interest", was moving through an increasingly more difficult set of push-ups. First had been five standard push-ups. Then five knuckle push-ups followed by five fingertip push-ups. He'd continued to watch, even after catching the line of her jaw and the tilt of her head. That had been enough to confirm her identity. Even so, he still wondered if it wasn't all a dream. No other explanation made sense.

His fingers moved over the virtual keyboard as he typed in a series of commands. He paged through the readouts, moving them into order, his eyes quickly scanning the results. Then he leaned back and blew out a breath. There was no doubt about it. Not only was she on-planet but someone had managed to get her there and into the security complex without him getting wind of it.

And that most definitely was not good.

As one of FleetCom's top intelligence officers, it was his job to know everything before it happened. The fact this had almost slipped by him spoke volumes about who had issued the orders to bring her back to New Kilrain. He had no doubt those orders had come from well above his pay grade. No one else had the pull to not only send a ship for the woman but to get her released to local confinement. Who and why he didn't know – but he would.

Frowning, he drummed his fingers against the synth-wood of his desktop. Could it be there were others besides himself looking into the circumstances surrounding Ashlyn Shaw's court-martial and conviction? If so, what was their motivation and why had they brought her back? More important in some ways, who were they and why had they acted on their own instead of through his office?

He hated not having the answers. Any intelligence officer would. Unanswered questions could easily mean death, if not for the "spook" then for others, usually innocents.

Damn it, what the hell was going on?

First things first. He needed to identify the ship that had returned Shaw to Fuercon. That would tell him a great deal. It would also give him an idea of how she had been slipped into the security complex without fanfare. But would that information be something he could work with or would it be one more thing to investigate and pray did not present yet another potential danger for Fuercon and her allies?

Before he could start his search, his comm-link sounded. Impatient at the interruption, he glanced at the incoming code. A slight smile touched his lips as he recognized the code. Interesting that she should be calling him just then. He reached out to activate the link with his right hand while, with his left, he input a search command for the video feed from the security wing of the brig.

"Santiago." He didn't activate the video feed. The code might be one he recognized but that didn't guarantee it hadn't been cloned by someone. That suspicious mind had kept him alive for years and he wasn't about to be careless now.

"Rico, it's me." The caller waited a slow count of three before activating the video feed on her end. He carefully studied the image that appeared before him, checking his readouts to make sure it wasn't a composite.

"Good morning, Admiral, or should I say Senator?"

"Admiral will get you an answer quicker, old friend," Miranda Tremayne replied. "You know I'll never consider myself as a politician."

"You should have thought of that before you resigned your commission, ma'am. You know we were working on other alternatives," he reminded her. As he did, he fought back a smile. Never one to believe in coincidence, he felt confident about he knew why Tremayne had called. If he was right, it would also explain how Shaw came to be on-planet without even the faintest whisper about her arrival reaching him.

"You don't have to remind me, and I don't have to like it."

No, she didn't, but it had been her decision.

"I take it this isn't a social call, ma'am." He leaned back and wondered how long it would take her to get to the point.

"Unfortunately, no. Let me start by saying that Admiral Collins is here with me."

Interesting and, now that he thought about it, not all that surprising. In the years he'd known Miranda Tremayne, Santiago had been aware of the friendship and respect she held for Richard Collins. He'd suspected for a long while that the two had been lovers, but he'd never found any evidence to support that suspicion. The fact that they were working together on whatever it was that had brought Ashlyn Shaw back from the Tarsus military prison made sense.

"I have to admit you're beginning to worry me, ma'am."

"Good because I'm already worried, Rico." She paused and he could see how she searched for the right words to explain the reason behind her call. "Rico, I need you to do something for me. It has to be off the record and it has to be done now."

"I'm listening."

"I need to know what's been happening at the Tarsus military prison over the last two years."

He tried not to smile but it was hard, especially since it always felt good to have his suspicions confirmed.

"Is there anything in particular you want me looking into, ma'am?" Not that he had to ask, not with that *reason* sitting in a cell below his office.

"I need to know if anything out of the ordinary has been happening."

Oh, she was being very careful with what she said. For some reason, she wasn't ready to tell him that Shaw was back on-planet. Maybe it was because she trusted such information over a comm-link no more than he did. But it could be there was more to it. If that was the case, he needed to know.

Of course, he could be wrong. She could be asking for his assistance because the prison administration refused to allow any contact with Shaw and those sent there with her. He'd run into that very same roadblock each time he'd tried to reach out to the former captain. He'd even made a trip to the prison, only to be told on his arrival that he should have checked before coming. According to the prison commandant, Shaw had been in the infirmary for days with some sort of virus and couldn't see anyone. No, there was no time-frame on when she'd be cleared for visitors.

That could be why Tremayne had contacted him, but he didn't think so. He'd bet his next two paychecks that she'd been behind bringing the captain back to Fuercon. As a senator, she'd have the resources to find some legal reason for bringing Shaw back and she certainly had the contacts within Fleet to arrange for Shaw's transport on the QT. She certainly had the contacts to do so without any but a handful of select members of FleetCom knowing about it.

Perhaps it was time to cut through the verbal sparring.

"Ma'am, does this have anything to do with a certain mutual acquaintance of ours, one who shouldn't be on-planet, much less in the capital, but is?"

Tremayne shook her head, one corner of her mouth quirking up. That confirmed it. She had been involved with bringing Shaw home. "It does and I'm very interested in hearing how you happen to know her whereabouts."

"Ma'am, I've been looking into certain events concerning this individual for months now. I can't tell you why, not over the comm. But I can tell you I was very surprised when I discovered that she was no longer on Tarsus and was, in fact, just a few floors below my office in the security complex."

"Then I think it is past time for two old friends to get together," Tremayne said.

"Agreed, ma'am. I'd be mighty appreciative if you'd send the invitation through my admin with the time and location." That way no one would think to look too deeply into why they were meeting. Fortunately, they already had the habit of meeting every month or so for drinks.

"I'll do that," she assured him. "I look forward to our meeting."

And so do I, he thought as he ended the call.

He leaned back and shook his head. The morning had certainly been filled with surprises and that was something he didn't like. No intelligence officer did. Now he had to find out how Shaw's transfer had slipped under his radar. Then he needed to get ready for his meeting with Tremayne. It was clearly time for them to compare notes.

But there was one thing he wanted to do first. He wanted to see Shaw and he wanted to do it without anyone else in the office knowing.

Well, that was easy enough. Santiago smiled to himself as he entered a code into his desk link that would forward any messages to his personal link. Then he pushed to his feet and crossed to the bookcase against the far wall. It might not be the most original method he could have chosen to hide the secondary exit from his office, but it sufficed and no one had asked any questions yet. Of course, they had looked at him more than a bit strangely when he'd had the bookcase installed and when the books had been delivered. He had no doubts some of his staff had never held a real book before. But he was a throwback. He loved the feel of a book in his hands. So, he'd let his passion also be his cover.

His fingers found the right pressure points to activate the release for the bookcase. It swung silently away from the wall to reveal a narrow door. Next to the door was a security panel coded only to him. He pressed his palm to the panel and then stood still as the scanner activated. Facial and biometric recognitions passed, the inner door opened and he stepped through, pausing only long enough to make sure the bookcase swung shut behind him.

Every senior intelligence officer in the capital knew about the passages that ran throughout the security complex, but he doubted many had used them. Too often the men and women in his position had been put there through family ties and had never seen battle nor run a covert operation. He'd been an exception. For more than fifteen years he'd been one of FleetCom's best intelligence operatives. Much of that time had been spent behind the lines, gathering intelligence to help win the war. For the last seven years, he'd trained the next generation of intelligence officers, making sure they learned from his experience. For the last year, he'd been FleetCom's senior intelligence officer in the capital and had been doing his best to make up for all the mistakes his predecessors had made.

Three floors down, he paused before another door and waited. The video pickup indicated the corridor beyond was clear. Satisfied, he entered the code that unlocked the door and he stepped out, closing it before anyone appeared. A quick look over his shoulder and a slight smile touched his lips. If someone didn't know where to look, they would never know a door was there.

"Major, we didn't receive word you'd be coming down," the corporal in charge of the current watch said as Santiago rounded the corner, surprising him and the two privates manning desks near him.

Monitors along the wall showed a dozen cells, only one of which was occupied. As Santiago watched, the prisoner continued to move from one exercise to another, each more difficult than the one before it. The Marine in him approved and so did the intelligence officer.

Shaw was not only keeping herself in shape but it wouldn't surprise him one bit to discover she used the exercises to keep her guards from guessing she was planning something. At least that's what he'd do and he had helped train her.

"I need to see the prisoner, Corporal."

"Sir, we haven't received authorization-"

"Shall I contact Senator Tremayne and Admiral Collins for you?" His tone bit and his eyes were hard as he reached for his comm-link.

"N-no, sir." The corporal swallowed hard. Then he nodded to one of the privates. "Escort the major-"

"That won't be necessary." Santiago waited until realization dawned on them. As an intelligence officer, he had every right to be there. He was also one of the very few people who would be able to activate and deactivate the security field for the prisoner's cell without assistance from the guards.

The corporal nodded and entered the security code to let the major through the door into the cell block. As the door slid shut behind him, Santiago allowed himself a slight smile. There were some benefits to having the reputation of not suffering fools kindly. Of course, the three would soon learn first-hand that reputation had been well earned. The fact they had simply taken him at his word and hadn't contacted either Tremayne or Collins meant they'd soon be standing before their CO explaining why they'd violated procedure.

But that was for later. He had something much more important to see to first.

A few moments later, Santiago stood before the door to Shaw's cell. She was executing a set of perfectly executed fingertip pushups. He waited, wondering if she'd acknowledge his presence. When she didn't, instead moving on to sit-ups, he nodded in approval. She'd maintained the discipline he'd come to expect of her when she was a young officer fresh out of the Academy. In fact, she'd honed it until it was not only her weapon but her armor as well.

Even as a part of him regretted the fact she'd had to do it, another part approved. Of course, if it kept her from listening to him and trusting that he had her best interests at heart, they'd all be up the proverbial creek.

Without a word, he deactivated the security field and stepped inside. The first indication Shaw gave that she was even aware of his presence was a startled glance in his direction when he didn't reactivate the field. Then the mask was back in place and she went back to her sit-ups.

He waited until she finished her set before speaking.

"All right, Ash, you've put up a good front, just as I taught you. But you can drop it now. Believe me when I say the guards are looking at a video loop of you exercising and me standing outside the cell watching." He waited, wondering how much time would pass before she responded.

Ashlyn Shaw slowly stood and then dropped onto the edge of her bunk. Her eyes were wary, her mouth tight. Santiago felt his own mouth harden as he saw the scar marring her left cheek and another bisecting her right eyebrow. She looked pale, as if she had not been in the sun for a very long time. Worse, she was thin, too thin, even if she had managed to maintain muscle tone through her exercise regimen. It was no wonder Tremayne had called him.

"What do you want, Major?" Shaw's voice seemed harsher than he remembered, almost as if she'd been screaming for a long while and had strained it.

"I just had an interesting call from Miranda Tremayne." Before she could say anything, he shook his head. "No, she didn't tell me what you talked about and I didn't ask. But she did ask me to look into what has been happening on Tarsus for the last two years. Since I was already doing so, I told her I thought it was time she and I shared information. But now I want – no, I need – to ask you some questions."

"Sorry, Major. I'll tell you exactly what I told her. Until I know my people are safely away from Tarsus and have received full pardons, I'm not talking. If you can't accept that, then you might as well just send me back so I can finish out my sentence."

Santiago drew a breath, held it for a long moment and then blew it out. Her response didn't surprise him, but it did frustrate him. There were too many possible reasons for her reluctance to talk and none of them were good. So he had to find a way break her silence, at least enough to give him a clue about where to start looking for answers.

"Kid, I know something's going on. Anyone taking a look at you would. But I need to know what it is so I can put an end to it." He'd always been honest with her and he wasn't going to stop now. "I need you to listen to me, Ash. I've known you for a long time. I helped train you, make you into the Marine you are–"

Her lips peeled back in an almost feral snarl and her eyes flashed dangerously. For one moment, she looked as if she might say something. Before she could, Santiago held up a hand to prevent her from interrupting. He understood at least a little of what she must feel. The court-martial had stripped her of her rank and had ended her career. He doubted she'd allowed herself to even consider the possibility she might one day be able to rejoin her beloved Corps.

"You are a Marine now and forever, kid. Don't forget that. Don't you ever forget that. It's in your blood. But that's not what I want to talk about.

"I've reviewed your reports from before your court-martial. I've seen your correspondence with Admiral Tremayne, Rear Admiral Sorkowski and Major O'Brien. I've also seen the *original* copy of your orders. I know you did your best to keep your people from being caught in the backlash caused by those orders. I have also discovered evidence proving Sorkowski had those orders altered after the fact. Further, I can prove O'Brien knew and didn't say anything. I know they did it to cover their own sorry asses. I know and can prove they were responsible for the loss of most of your unit as well as the civilian deaths that were the result of your orders as well as enemy reprisals. I can also prove you not only warned Sorkowski and O'Brien about what could happen but that you also officially objected to your orders as being unlawful – not to mention stupid – and how you forwarded copies of your objections to Admiral Tremayne and others. Finally, I can show how those messages were delayed or miscoded so they wouldn't be admissible at your trial. In other words, *Captain*, I can prove you were set up."

Shaw's head snapped up, anger flashing in her eyes. Santiago nodded slightly. He understood. She'd sworn over and over again that the copy of the orders that had been introduced at her court-martial hadn't been the orders she'd received. Now there was proof of that and more.

"Then why in hell haven't my people been brought back here and cleared?" Her hands gripped the edge of her bunk so tightly her knuckles shone white.

"I just found the information last night, Ash, and I have to make sure I can prove its validity." God, didn't she know how badly he wanted to do exactly what she asked? He wanted to clear all of them. Their convictions were a black eye to the Corps and to the military as a whole. He'd like nothing better than to be able to correct the miscarriage of justice. "That's why I need you to talk to me."

He hoped thought she might actually relax enough to answer his questions. Instead, she shook her head, her expression closing again.

"Damn it, Ash, I've been looking into what happened since before your court-martial. But Sorkowski isn't stupid. He covered their tracks well. It's taken time to break through and find evidence corroborating your claims." Frustrated, he waited, watching for any sign she believed him. What was it going to take to get through to her?

"Major, whether you want to admit it or not, you already have what you need. If you need more, check my personal files. If the admiral – sorry, senator – doesn't have them, my parents will. But that's all I will say, at least until my people are freed."

"I'm doing my best, but it would be a hell of a lot easier if you'd help me." He took a step forward, stopping when she shook her head. "Ash, please."

For a moment it looked like she might change her mind. Then she pushed off her bunk and moved as far away from him as she could. When she turned and looked at him, the anger reflected on her expression rocked him.

"You want to know what's happening at Tarsus, *Major*?" Her words were clipped, her voice harsh. "Take a look at the prison records. Compare the stats for the current leadership there to earlier administrations. How many people are sentenced there and how many actually manage to survive their sentences? Of those who do, how many are still sane?

"If that's not enough to answer your questions, then look at me. Take a good look, damn it!" She waved a hand at her scarred face. Before he could say anything, she grabbed the left sleeve of her jumpsuit and pulled. The sound of the shoulder seam ripping filled the cell. She dragged the material off her arm and tossed it onto the floor.

"Look at this, *Major*. Look at what they did and know it is only a small example of what they've done to all of us."

Santiago's stomach churned and bile rose in his throat. The skin of her bicep had been torn away from the underlying muscle and it looked as if it had been left to heal without proper medical treatment. Rough, discolored scar tissue hid the definition of the underlying muscle. Worse, he knew what had been on her arm where now there was only ugly scarring. His own right hand reached up to touch his left arm and the Devil Dog tattoo he proudly bore. Every member of the Devil Dogs, past and present, had one. Shaw had as well – at least until someone had so cruelly removed it.

"Do you want to see more?" she demanded, tears pooling in her eyes. All he could do was shake his head. "Now think about this. Every day I'm here is another day those bastards are figuring out new ways to torment my people. I was warned before I left Tarsus not to say anything. If you've lied to me, if there is someone listening in on what I've said, my people are dead. If that happens, I promise you'll die a very slow and painful death."

Santiago dragged his hand over his close-cropped hair. He had no doubts she meant every word she said. If her people were hurt because she'd talked to him, she'd find a way to hunt him down and kill him and he wouldn't blame her. It was exactly what he'd do if their situations had been reversed. Well, he hadn't lied to her and somehow he'd just have to prove it.

But that would wait. It had to. He had other things to see to, things like making sure nothing else happened to her or to her people. Then he'd gladly help her avenge all that had been done to her and the others.

"Ash, I promise, no one has heard a word of what we've said." He spoke softly, knowing she wouldn't believe him. "I'll return when I've figured out how to keep you from going back and how to bring your people home. I swear it."

She didn't say anything. Instead, she returned to her bunk and stretched out, turning her back to him much as she had to Tremayne and Collins earlier.

Damn it, just how deep was this can of worms going to turn out to be?

———

EVAN MOREAU TOUCHED the recessed button on the wall near her elbow and an almost inaudible *swish* sounded as the lock slid into place. At the same time, the lights came on. She blinked once even as she quickly scanned the room. Something was wrong. The sequence should have been lights and then lock. She ought to know. She'd programmed it that way the day she moved into the apartment. Damn it, she was getting sloppy and that could get her killed!

As her eyes sought out the intruder, a knife dropped into the palm of her right hand. Security in most buildings in the capital was such that it would pick up any sort of weapon, but she'd learned long ago that certain alloys could pass undetected through the security fields. This knife was made of one of those alloys and it had served her well over the years. Hopefully, it would do so again.

Senses alert, knees bent slightly, she waited. There! The faint sound of a breath. Her eyes cut to the far corner of the room where shadows still hung heavily. The intruder, whoever he was, wasn't as smart as he thought. The fact he'd killed the light there and nowhere else in the room betrayed him. Well, he'd soon find out just how foolish it was to try to ambush her on home ground.

"Relax, Moreau."

Abel Kannedy stepped out of the shadows. Hands away from his body, fingers splayed to show he wasn't holding anything, he waited. For a moment, Moreau simply stood there, anger darkening her expression. He, of all people, should know how foolish invading her home could be. Over the last few years, she had worked several special "contracts" for him so he should know what happened to those who crossed her. He had hired her often enough to deal with his own enemies to know better than to try to surprise her. The fact that he'd taken this tack to meet with her meant trouble.

But for whom and would she have to kill him before the night was over?

With a smile she really didn't feel, Moreau slid the knife back into its quick release sheath on her forearm and moved past him to the bar. She needed a drink. In fact, she needed a drink very badly. Not that she would allow herself more than one until she knew exactly why he was there.

Then she'd have to consider changing her place of residence. She never should have let him know where she lived. The only reason she had was because he'd gotten suspicious the last six months, worried she might one day decide to deal with him on a very permanent basis. He had insisted the one way to prove her loyalty was to finally allow him to not only know where she lived but to invite him up to see her apartment. She'd known better but she still had need of him. Even so, she should have arranged for him to see another apartment, one far from here. She knew now that had been a mistake, a potentially fatal one, and no one in her line of business could afford such things, not if they expected to live for long.

"I'm assuming there's a good reason for you to have risked both our lives by coming without warning." She tossed back a shot of whiskey before pouring Kannedy a brandy. That gave her time to settle. Never would he know how badly his presence had shaken her.

"There is."

"And?" She handed him a brandy and motioned for him to be seated on the sofa. That put his back to the door and hers to the wall. That way, no one else could enter without her seeing them.

"Tremayne and her lot have pulled a fast one." He spoke softly. Nothing in his voice or on his expression betrayed his thoughts. But his hands told the story. His left hand held the crystal brandy snifter so tightly it was a wonder the snifter hadn't shattered. The fingers of his right hand clinched into a fist that beat not so lightly against that thigh.

"We've known since the election that it's only been a matter of time before someone in the new administration did something that could upset our plans." She shrugged with a nonchalance she didn't feel and leaned back. "What happened to upset you so?"

Now that she was over the immediate shock of finding Kannedy, she could think. She needed to put him at ease and find out why he'd risked both their lives by coming to her. Then she could figure out what her next move should be. She'd regret it if the time had come to move on, but it wouldn't be the first time she'd left one life to start another. Giving up an identity, even one she enjoyed, was a small enough price to pay to stay alive.

For a moment, Kannedy remained silent. Moreau waited. Experience had taught her not to rush him. He would tell her what happened in his own time. As she waited, she sipped her drink and tried to recall if she had heard anything during the day that might be of concern. But there was nothing. So what had Tremayne done, or what did he think she had done, to cause him to risk so much?

"Several things happened today that caught myself and our colleagues off-guard."

With that, Kannedy stood and moved to the bar, pouring himself another drink. Moreau frowned but remained silent. His actions were so much in character that they didn't surprise her. Wealthy and powerful, at least in his own mind, Kannedy did what he wanted, when he wanted and then hired others to clean up the mess. That was probably why he was there now. He'd made another mistake and wanted her to ensure no one ever learned about it.

"To start, I received word not long ago that Harper is about to carry through with his campaign promise to disband the Defense Council. He will appear before Congress in less than three hours to inform them of his decision. Notice has already been sent out to the members of the Council, formally notifying them of the council's dissolution."

Moreau blinked in surprise. The Defense Council had been created by executive order more than three decades earlier. During the last war, President Boothe Markham had filled the Council with those he owed political favors to. He'd effectively managed to use the Council to cut Congress out of almost all decision-making when it came to the war, even finding ways to pass on budgetary issues to the Council. That had served him well until FleetCom had changed tactics and started giving nothing more than lip service to the Council. The resulting victories caught the public's attention and approval. The average citizen was tired of all the years of war and all the atrocities committed by the Callusians. Nothing short of a full surrender by the enemy would satisfy them. Nothing Markham said or did swayed them and it had led to his defeat in the last election.

But for Harper to disband the Security Council so soon after taking office . . ..

And why hadn't the media picked up on it yet?

"Again, not that surprising. I'll admit, he did it sooner than I expected but we've discussed how it was inevitable, especially considering the platform he ran on."

"That's not the worst of it, Evan."

Now every internal alarm she possessed sounded. Kannedy never called her by her given name. Even though they'd known one another for years, it was a line he never crossed, partly because she was an employee – albeit one with very special skills – and partly because he would never see her as his equal. Not that it bothered her. She'd learned very early in her career that it was best not to form attachments with those she worked for. They might be her employer one day and her target the next.

"Tell me."

"Ashlyn Shaw is back on-planet."

For a moment, she looked at the man. Surely, she hadn't heard right. Shaw and the others were on Tarsus. Hopefully, they would stay there, never again seeing a moment's freedom. Yet there was something about Kannedy's expression. No, it couldn't be. Not now. Not when everything was finally falling into place.

Disbelief fled and Moreau's anger spiked to almost uncontrollable levels. She couldn't believe it. Of everything he could have said, this had to be the worst. It was certainly the most unexpected. So much effort and so many months of planning, bribing, and blackmail had gone into the effort of making sure Captain Ashlyn Shaw had been taken out of play. Moreau had done everything possible not only to make sure Shaw was convicted but also that those involved in the set-up never suffered an attack of conscience.

Kannedy had paid extremely well to ensure Shaw had been discredited. What he didn't know, and never would, was that Moreau would have gladly done the job for free. Shaw had been a thorn in her side for years, an irritant she hadn't been able to get rid of. Then Kannedy had offered her the opportunity to do exactly what she'd spent so many nights dreaming of. It might not have meant the bitch's death, but it had been almost as good. She could still see that haunted, stunned expression on Shaw's face when the guilty verdict had been read. The only thing that would have made it better was if Shaw had known who'd been behind her downfall.

But now, without warning, that irritant was back and her return could bring an end to it all, including Moreau's own life. Somehow, she had to find a way to ensure Shaw never learned the true circumstances behind her court-martial. If that meant more lives had to be taken and more bodies made to disappear, fine. That was her job after all.

"How? More importantly, why?" Thank the saints her voice didn't betray her emotions.

"I don't know." There could be no mistaking his anger. Good. She had to keep him focused on that. Maybe then he wouldn't think too much about her own reaction.

"Then how can you be sure she's back?"

"Because one of my contacts in the security complex saw her."

She closed her eyes, thinking hard. If Shaw was back, why hadn't the media picked up on it? They'd be running the story non-stop, especially if the bitch had been pardoned. So, she had to assume that hadn't happened, not yet at any rate. Not that it made her sudden reappearance any easier to accept.

"Was she in custody?" She had to know everything he did. Only then could she plan her next move.

"What?" He looked at her in confusion and then nodded, a slow smile spreading across his face. "Yes. My contact said she was chained."

She nodded, relieved. Perhaps things weren't as bad as she feared. "Good. That means they don't know what happened." She got to her feet and crossed to the bar. It might not be smart, but she needed another drink.

"But why bring her here?"

Moreau heard the hint of fear in his voice and understood. His life, even more than her own, lay on the line should FleetCom realize the true circumstances behind what happened on Arterus. "She's still technically a member of the military. It could be that she committed some sort of offense at the penal colony and they brought her here to face additional charges. It could be any number of other reasons, none of which are bad for us." She poured herself another whiskey and then turned to face him. "But it could also be that Tremayne is holding true to her campaign promise to look into the charges against Shaw and has convinced others in the government to play along. If that's the case, you could be in for some trouble."

"I think you mean *we* could be in for trouble," he corrected, eyes flashing dangerously.

"Of course." Let him think that. She had back up plans to her back up plans. If this should suddenly turn bad, she'd have a new identity and be off-planet within the hour.

"This is your mess to clean up, Moreau. I don't care how you do it, just make sure it doesn't wash back on me." He stood, all but tossing his now empty snifter onto the table next to the sofa. "I don't want that bitch saying anything that might cause Harper and his supporters to start sniffing in my direction."

"How much collateral damage are you willing to accept?"

"I don't give a damn if the entire capital city goes up in flames as long as it doesn't harm any of my holdings."

"Then consider it done."

"Don't fuck this up, Moreau." He jabbed a finger in her direction. "You're as deep in this shit as I am. Our partners won't accept anything that might put their plans in danger."

She inhaled and forced herself not to react to his none-too-subtle threat. "And I suggest you remember just who brought whom into this little deal, Kannedy. *Your* partners will look at you long before they do me." She waited, smiling slightly as he blanched at her words. "Remember this as well. I do *not* take kindly to being threatened."

Even as she pinned him with a firm look, she hoped he didn't realize just how badly his last comment had shaken her. Those *partners* he spoke of didn't accept failure from anyone. She'd known that when she first agreed to deal with Shaw for him. Even then, she'd known better than to get involved but the chance to finally get Shaw out of her life had been too tempting. Damn it, that bitch could still be the end of her.

The end of all of them, unless she figured out how to deal with her once and for all.

"Don't worry, Mr. Kannedy. I'll make sure she never sees the light of freedom."

And I'll be finalizing my own escape plans just in case.

———

For the next two days, Ashlyn Shaw ate, slept and exercised. Her routine in the brig was much the same as it had been in her cell at the military prison. There was comfort in routine, something she'd never really understood until her freedom had been ripped from her. But it was also a defense mechanism. No one worried about what she was doing as long as she did nothing out of the ordinary.

Besides, following routine meant she had the freedom to think about what was going on and why. More importantly, it gave her the chance to observe her jailers and to plan. She was always planning. It was all that kept her sane.

The only problem with that was she still didn't know why she had been brought back to the capital. After the rather disastrous meeting with Tremayne and Collins and then the visit from Major Santiago, she had seen no one but her guards. While they were a bit more talkative than those at the prison, they were no more likely to answer her questions – were she to ask them.

Not that she would. Her questions could, and would, give someone like Santiago an idea of what was on her mind and she didn't dare risk that happening.

What troubled her, though, was the concern, possibly even worry, she sensed in them. There was a grimness to them that reminded her all too clearly of how those she'd fought side by side with during the war had felt during those dark days. Were things really as bad as Tremayne had alluded to?

Did she really care?

As she moved from pushups to sit ups, she frowned slightly. One thing the last two days had taught was how much she had come to rely on the prison's grapevine. Even when she didn't see anyone but the guards, word still reached her about how her people and others in the penal colony were doing. She had none of that here. The only thing she knew for sure was that she seemed to be alone in this wing of the brig and that did nothing to reassure her. Why would they have brought her back and yet continue to keep her in isolation?

What still surprised her, what she was having a hard time wrapping her mind around, was the one change she knew had occurred since she'd last been on-planet. When she'd heard the guard addressing Tremayne as "Senator", she'd been sure she'd misheard or that it had been yet another trick by the commandant of the penal colony to break her. Then, when she'd finally lost control and had rolled off the bunk and confronted the newcomers, she'd been forced to admit it was her former mentor standing before her. Had

Tremayne been drummed out of the Service or had she voluntarily left? More important, what did it all mean?

She finished her sit ups and climbed to her feet. Three steps and she stood in front of one wall of her cell. She bent at the waist, placed her palms on the floor and kicked up into a handstand. Slowly, carefully, she bent her elbows, lowered herself toward the floor, her heels lightly scraping the wall as she did. Then she straightened her arms again. Think. She had to think.

She couldn't forget the worry she'd seen reflected in Tremayne's eyes, heard in her voice as the senator asked her to just listen to what they had to say. It had been more than worry for her. That had been there, plain to see, when she first faced Tremayne and Collins and they'd seen the effects of the last two years on her. But she knew there was more to their worry and that is why she'd been brought back to the capital. What it was and what it ultimately meant for her and her team was still something she couldn't guess.

Her team. God, that was her one regret. They'd followed her into Hell and most had paid the ultimate price. The rest might as well have. But she'd avenge their loss and their families' pain. She didn't know how, but she would.

Of course, that assumed she ever saw freedom again.

3

Miranda Tremayne paced the small conference room like a caged animal. With every step she took, her anger built. She'd been furious for the last two days, ever since her futile meeting with Ashlyn Shaw. She was angry with Shaw for being such a stubborn pain in the ass. She was furious with the military tribunal that had convicted Shaw and the others simply because it had been politically expedient to do so. Most of all, she was furious with herself. She should have found a way before now to break down the so-called evidence against her protégé and get her and the others out of that hell hole.

The evidence! What a laugh.

No, not evidence. Innuendo and the need for a scapegoat because the former Secretary of Defense and his political cronies hadn't wanted to admit one of their own had not only issued illegal orders but had then covered them up. They had willingly sacrificed Shaw and so many others in the process, not to mention how they betrayed all those still willing to lay their lives down to keep Fuercon and her allies free.

Tremayne's fury had turned into something she'd barely been able to contain after meeting with Rico Santiago the night before.

The major had arrived at her home, exactly as her admin had arranged, his wife on his arm. To anyone who might be watching, they were nothing more than a happily married couple coming to spend an evening with friends. What those potential spying eyes wouldn't have seen was how Anna Santiago had retired to the game room with Tremayne's grown daughters while Tremayne and the major disappeared into her study. There they'd stayed until well after midnight, reviewing what they knew about the so-called evidence against Shaw and all that had happened since her court-martial.

Tremayne had suspected all along that Sorkowski and O'Brien not only lied in their reports about what happened that fateful day but had actually altered Shaw's original orders and then made sure her protests were "lost". But to see actual proof of it and then to remember how many people had died, Marines and civilians. . . Damn it, she should have pushed harder to find out what happened the moment she got Shaw's message and realized just how concerned the young woman had been about that last assignment. By the time she learned Shaw and the others were being brought up on charges, the damage had been done and records had been altered.

Damn them!

Worse in so many ways was learning what had been done to her after her arrival at the penal colony. She remembered how excited Ashlyn had sounded when she commed to tell her about her assignment to the Devil Dogs. Not long after that, the young woman sent a picture of herself with her new Devil Dog tattoo. How proud Ashlyn had been and now that, just like her career, had been torn away from her.

Someone had to pay.

Now, in the light of day, Tremayne's fury continued to grow. She had not only failed her protégé but also the members of Shaw's unit who had survived that fateful mission only to be brought up on charges and sent to the penal colony with Shaw. Then there were the dead. They would haunt Tremayne for the rest of her life.

So many had died during that last mission. The survivors had been made into scapegoats just to save a few political and military careers. She'd sworn two years ago that there would be justice for them, just as there would be for Shaw. Now that justice was close to becoming a reality. But it wouldn't be easy, especially not if Shaw continued to be such a stubborn pain in her ass.

And where the hell was the guard with Shaw?

Before she could reach for her comm-link to demand – yet again – that Shaw be brought to her, the door slid open with a soft *whoosh*. Tremayne turned. Her expression hardened to see Shaw, shackled and sullen. Her wrists were secured behind her back. The chains about her ankles forced her to take short, shuffling steps. If that weren't bad enough, the guards escorting her held her firmly by her upper arms, so firmly Tremayne knew they would leave bruises. It was no wonder Shaw looked sullen.

Well, that was something Tremayne could deal with now.

"Remove the restraints, all of them!" she snapped and was rewarded with the sight of Shaw looking at her in surprise for one quick moment before the younger woman had herself under control again.

Good. Hopefully that meant she was in more of a mood to listen.

"Senator," one of the guards began.

"I said to remove the restraints," she repeated firmly. "And then leave us alone."

"Senator, we can't!" the second guard protested. "Regulations—"

"Regulations be damned," she countered. "I suggest you remember that I am not only a senator but I am also an admiral in the fleet, even if retired. That means I outrank you by several orders of magnitude. If that isn't enough, where do you think Captain Shaw can go? There's only one entry to the room and you two will be on the other side. As for worry that she might try to harm me, let's take care of that right here and now." She turned to Shaw and prayed the young woman understood what she needed to say. "Captain, are you going to try to do anything foolish like attack me the moment the guards leave the room?"

For a moment, Shaw said nothing. Instead, she looked from the guards to Tremayne and back again. Then she shook her head, a slight smile – bitter and bemused at the same time – touched her lips.

"No, ma'am, I won't try anything. You have my word as a Marine."

"There. You have your answer. Now release her and leave us alone."

"We'll have to report this to our CO, ma'am," the first guard said as he removed the cuffs from Shaw's wrists.

"You do that – from the other side of the door."

She waited, her expression hard as the guards finished freeing their prisoner. If possible, her expression turned even harder as the second guard leaned in close to Shaw and warned her what would happen she even thought about doing anything to the senator. Instead of reacting, Shaw simply stared through him. Tremayne shook her head, not sure whether to be amused, impressed or worried.

"Ashlyn, please have a seat," she said as the door slid shut behind the guards.

Instead of waiting to see if she did, Tremayne moved across the room and poured water for both of them from the pitcher sitting on the narrow counter against the far wall. By the time she returned to the table, Shaw had pulled out one of the chairs and was seated, her hands resting on the table. Well, that was one small victory. Now, hopefully, others would come.

"Ash, I know you have no reason to trust me, but I'd like you to listen for a few minutes. I want to explain why we brought you back here," Tremayne continued as she sat opposite the younger woman and handed her a cup of water. "And then I'd like you to explain a few things to me."

"Permission to speak, ma'am?"

Tremayne closed her eyes and willed herself not to react. Except when they'd been on duty, they never stood on this much formality. Was this another indication about what her life had been like at the penal colony?

"Ash, you never have to ask me for permission to speak," she answered. "I wish you'd believe me when I say you're safe now."

"Ma'am, that may be but it won't last, not if I have to return to Tarsus." Shaw reached up and touched the scar marring her left cheek and then the streak of white at that temple. As she did, Tremayne wondered if she even knew she was doing it. "I meant what I said the other day. Unless whatever you want me for includes freeing my people, my answer's no. I have no other choice. You can ask Major Santiago to confirm it for you if you like."

Tremayne's mouth tightened as Shaw confirmed one of her suspicions. She'd been sure Rico Santiago knew more than he told her the night before. When she'd tried to press him on it, he sidestepped the issue. He'd done his best to convince her she knew everything he did, but she hadn't believed him. Now, sitting across from Shaw and seeing the determination mixed with fear reflected in her eyes, she realized why. Santiago never said he'd gone to see Shaw after learning she was on-planet. There was no way he wouldn't have and, judging from what Shaw had just said, he'd not only seen her but she'd given him some sort of explanation for why she refused to cooperate.

He'd better be ready to explain because, if Shaw continued to be obstinate, Tremayne would be paying him a visit very soon. Even if Shaw cooperated, she would be making that visit. She did not appreciate being kept out of the loop, not when so much could go wrong.

"Ash, you have to believe me. I haven't forgotten your people any more than I forgot you."

———

SHE SAT THERE, watching the admiral – *no, the senator*, she corrected – weighing what the woman said. She wanted to believe Tremayne. There had been a time when she never would have doubted the woman. But that had been before she'd been brought up on charges and found herself, and the surviving members of her command, sent to Tarsus. The last two years had done a great deal to destroy her ability to trust anyone.

Still, there was a ring of truth to what Tremayne said. Besides, it did fit with the urgency she had sensed to her guards since her return to New Kilrain. But what if she was wrong? So many things she'd once thought inviolate had proven to be false. Did she dare trust her former mentor now?

Did she dare not?

More importantly, she had trusted Santiago with at least part of the truth. Surely, she could do the same with Tremayne. But, before she did, she needed information. She needed to know why, after so long, FleetCom suddenly seemed to remember her and the others.

"Ma'am." She paused and licked her lips. It felt strange to speak except in response to a direct question. "Ma'am, will you tell me what's going on? Please."

Damn the desperation in her voice. That was weakness. Even if Tremayne didn't use it against her, there was no guarantee those listening in wouldn't. She had to remember her place. She could not let her guard slip again.

"Ash." Tremayne's voice choked and tears swam for a moment in her blue eyes. That emotion did more to reassure Shaw than anything else had in a very long time. "I'll be more than glad to answer any questions you have. But I need you to answer a question for me first."

"W-what?"

"If we were to guarantee that your people would be freed immediately, would you accept a full pardon?"

For a split second, hope flared. Could justice finally be served?

But just as quickly that hope was extinguished. Tremayne hadn't said they had secured the release of her people. She had asked if they were able to do so. Nothing had changed, nothing at all!

"Ma'am, until I know my people are safely away from the prison and have been pardoned, I can't do anything." She stared at her hands where they rested on the table, fingers interlocked so tightly it hurt. "I'm sorry, but I can't."

"I think I understand, Ash, and I want you to know that is exactly what we're working on right now."

"Thank you." Now she looked up, knowing her expression

revealed too much. But she didn't have a choice. She had to trust this woman to help and be damned with those who might be watching. "Ma'am, I have to ask. Why did you bring me back here after all this time?"

She hated asking, especially since Tremayne hadn't answered when she first asked the question. But, suddenly, she didn't want to return to her cell. She wanted – no, she needed – the small sense of freedom being in the conference room gave her. Anything was better than being alone again.

Oh, God, she didn't want to go back to her cell.

————

"MA'AM, I have to ask. Why did you bring me back here after all this time?"

Hearing the question, seeing the need for an answer reflected in Shaw's brown eyes, Tremayne relaxed some. Finally, a chink in the younger woman's control, a chink she'd hopefully be able to use to get through to her. Anything was better than returning to the stand-off they'd had two days before.

Still, after all she'd seen and read, Tremayne didn't blame Shaw one bit for reacting as she had. Life in the military prison must have been hell for her. The record, such as it was, that she'd seen had revealed how the commandant of the penal colony had basically isolated Shaw and her people not only from the rest of the prison population but from one another as well.

Then there had been the punishments for what were, at best, minor infractions. Most were within the letter of the regulations, barely. But others, the punishments that were hinted at in the records but not actually detailed, were what truly bothered the senator. She had a good idea that was how Shaw received the scars marring her face. What else had happened during the last two years she could only imagine and she didn't like it one bit.

She couldn't let herself think about that though. Not yet. There would be a time to investigate what went on at the penal colony.

But that would come later, after the current situation was dealt with.

"Ash, I'll be honest. What I said the other day is the truth. You were right when you predicted that the truce would be nothing more than farce. That's putting it mildly. The politicians pushed it through in the vain hope it would keep them in office. They sacrificed you, your people and so many others for their own petty ambitions. What they didn't expect was how it would backfire on them. After you and your people were brought up on charges, the voters revolted and took the government back. Almost every person holding office at the time of your court-martial who didn't publicly come out in support of you and against the truce was voted out in the next election. Once President Harper took office, he made a clean sweep of the Cabinet and the military and it trickled down from there.

"This is all a roundabout way of telling you that things have changed, not only politically but also on the front lines. The truce didn't work. The enemy wasn't interested in negotiating a peace. Instead, they continued raiding the outer colonies. At first, before the elections, the administration and military command explained it away as pirates and slavers. They learned fairly quickly that they couldn't keep the rank and file quiet. Those fighting these so-called pirates and slavers were talking to friends and family and they, in turn, talked to others. Then the media got involved. Once President Harper cleaned house and people like Rico Santiago started looking into what had been happening, it became clear that the Callusians had been behind the attacks all along. The public knows and is demanding we quit honoring the treaty terms. They want us to act. They want us to stop the enemy once and for all. More than that, they want the wrongs of the previous administration righted.

"That's where you and others come in, Ash. We want – no, we need you back. No one knows better than you how the enemy operates groundside. Hell, kid, you know their space tactics better than most of our naval COs. We need that knowledge and experience to help us finally defeat these bastards."

As she spoke, Tremayne kept her eyes on Shaw. All expression left the younger woman's face and her mouth firmed. It was as if she suddenly turned to stone. She heard what was said, the senator could see that from the way her eyes dropped to stare at the table before lifting to stare at some unseen point beyond Tremayne's head. But Shaw never said a word.

God, had she lost Shaw again, just when it looked like she had finally been getting through to her?

Fortunately, Shaw hadn't told her to go to Hell. Not yet. That was a good thing, at least she hoped it was.

"Ashlyn, I don't blame you for not trusting me," she continued, praying she found the right words to get through to her companion. "But I want you to remember something. I've never broken my word to you. I promised you when I found out you'd been brought up on charges that I would do everything in my power to clear your name and the names of your people. I gave up my commission to do so because I knew that was what was needed.

"All I'm asking is that you think about what I've said. Think about what a black eye it would give those who so willingly sacrificed you and the others. They've lost their political clout. Now the best thing you can do is show that they haven't beaten you. Prove to them that they haven't broken you."

God, what was it going to take to convince her?

When Shaw pushed back from the table and stood, Tremayne waited. One part of her was glad the guards weren't present. The moment Shaw moved, they would have been on her, sure she'd been about to attack. But Tremayne knew better. She remembered how her protégé would pace when thinking. Maybe there was hope.

So she waited, aware of pain from her fingernails as she clinched her fists under the table. So much might rest on what happened in the next few minutes. If she failed. . ..

"Ma'am – Miranda, I want nothing more than to get a bit of my own back from those responsible for sending us to Tarsus." Shaw stood across the small room and shook her head. "But I can't agree, not unless I know for sure that my people are safe. I can't leave them there. I just can't." Tears welled in her eyes and she reached up to scrub them away.

"Ash, I'm doing my best. I promise." She stood and hurried to Shaw's side. The young woman stiffened as she pulled her close. Then slowly, hesitantly, Shaw wrapped her arms around her and held on, for all the world as if she was holding onto a lifeline. "Shh, Ash, shh," Tremayne soothed, her right hand gently rubbing the young woman's back as she cried.

Dear God, she'd known Shaw all the young woman's life and had never seen her break like this.

"Please, Miranda, you've got to understand. I can't leave them there."

"Come, sit." She gently led the young woman back to the table. "I can guess why you feel that way. But it would help if you'd tell me." Now she held up a hand, hoping to ward off her companion's protest. "I know Major Santiago visited you the other day. I have no doubt he worked his magic and made sure your conversation wasn't monitored or recorded by the guards. Believe me, I have the same precautions in place. So you can tell me without fear that anyone will overhear and report back to Tarsus."

She waited, watching as Shaw considered what she said. Fortunately, it had been the truth. She might not know for sure what Santiago did to insure no one listened in on their conversation but she had a good idea. After all, she had seen him do much the same thing before. He simply hadn't told her about it this time. Besides, she hadn't lied when she said she had made sure no record would exist of this meeting.

Shaw closed her eyes and drew a long, shaky breath. Tremayne waited, knowing her companion was carefully weighing her words. That alone told her more than she'd known a few moments before. Shaw was used to her every movement, every word being monitored and used against her. It was no wonder she'd learned how to exercise such careful control over herself. What hell it must be to know that anything you did or said, no matter how minute or inconsequential, could be used against you or those you cared about.

"Ma'am, let's just say that life at the prison has been something of a nightmare. I never really thought of myself as a social animal, but I've learned to value any human contact, no matter how brief. I've also learned that it's not wise to ask questions or to speak without first being given permission." She opened her eyes and reached up to lightly touch the scar cutting across her cheek. "I got this during a lesson in proper attitude. I'd questioned why I was being held in solitary and wanted to know if my people were being treated the same way. The hell of it was I didn't ask anyone. I'd simply voiced the question in my cell. I was alone and the security door shut. I thought I was safe from being overheard. I was wrong. The next morning, I was taken to the commandant's office where he personally administered my *lesson* in proper prisoner behavior. I spent three days in the infirmary after that."

Tremayne's anger spiked again as Shaw spoke. No wonder the young woman found it so hard to trust any of them.

Damn it!

"Ash, I promise we're doing everything we can to not only bring your people home but to get pardons for them." And sooner, rather than later. "I'll need a full report from you, when you know they're safe, about everything that's been going on at the prison."

"Understood." She paused for a moment and Tremayne waited, hoping she was about to ask another question. Anything that kept Shaw talking was good at this point. "Ma'am, what about Sorkowski and O'Brien? What's happened to them?"

Now the senator smiled. She'd not only approved of the action taken against the two when President Harper took office, she had been the one to recommend it. It hadn't been enough, not by a long shot, but it had been a start. Hopefully Shaw would agree.

"Alec Sorkowski was one of a number of senior officers forced into retirement almost immediately after President Harper was sworn into office. The President and Linden Klingsbury, the new Secretary of Defense, have cleaned house in all branches of the military. As for Thomas O'Brien, General Okafor was even less forgiving than Secretary Klingsbury was with Sorkowski and his cronies. The general, who is now Commandant of the Marine Corps, brought O'Brien back to the capital and he's been assigned to escort the children of diplomats other dignitaries around the city."

That brought a smile to Shaw's lips, a smile Tremayne echoed. No Marine wanted that duty. The fact that someone of O'Brien's rank had been was a sure sign of the Corps' disapproval. Hopefully that would help Shaw understand that things really had changed.

Tremayne knew there was more to why Shaw smiled. Early in her career, Shaw had served under then Colonel Okafor. Over dinner one evening before Shaw reported to her new assignment, Tremayne had told her that Okafor accepted nothing but the best from her Marines and wouldn't hesitate to bounce anyone out of the Corps if she thought they were slacking. Shaw later told Tremayne that she'd quickly learned Okafor was a dedicated officer who asked nothing of those under her command she wasn't willing to do herself. The fact that Okafor was now Marine Corps Commandant meant Shaw could at least hope her beloved Corps was returning to the greatness it once held.

"Ashlyn, I'm not going to push. I know you have to be sure your people are safely away from that hellhole. But I do need to know the answer to my question. If we manage to get them freed and pardons issued, will you accept your commission back?"

"Ma'am – Miranda, I want to say yes. But I can't. Not yet." Now it was her time to hold up a hand to prevent interruptions. She once more climbed to her feet and started pacing. Tremayne waited, worried by how troubled the younger woman's expression had become. "You have to understand that this is almost more than I can take in. For more than two years, from the time I was first informed of the charges being laid against me, I've been cut off from the Corps, from friends and officers I respected. Since being sent to Tarsus, I haven't had any contact with the outside. No visitors and no messages. I don't even know how my family is. Hell, I don't even know where they are."

Once again, the younger woman's voice broke and it was all Tremayne could do not to curse. She'd known Shaw's parents had gone to the prison and had been forbidden the opportunity to see their daughter. The excuse had been that Shaw was ill and unable to see anyone. Neither her parents nor Tremayne, when she found out what happened, believed it. That had been the final deciding factor in Tremayne's decision to resign her commission and run for office.

But to hear Shaw had been denied all messages from home as well . . ..

"Ashlyn, they're fine. Believe me. I would never lie to you, especially not about this. Your parents are here in the capital and they've been instrumental in leading the campaign to not only vote out the old guard but to find whatever evidence we could to free you and the others." She moved to where Shaw stood, wishing there was more she could do or say to reassure the younger woman. "I'll make sure you see them before the day is out. I promise. The only reason I haven't already done so is because I've been working to gather all the evidence the President needs to sign your pardon."

"Thank you." Shaw's voice was so soft Tremayne could barely hear her.

Before Tremayne could say anything, her comm-link beeped. She pulled it from her pocket and studied the small display. As she did, relief filled her. Finally, all the hard work and sacrifice had paid off. More than that, she had good news for Shaw, news that would, hopefully, help the younger woman make up her mind.

Without a word, she led Shaw back to the table. Then she took her seat. She waited as Shaw followed suit. A moment later, she typed in a quick command and watched as the holo-display came to life above the 'link.

"Ashlyn, you need to read this." She pushed her 'link with its holo-display across the table. Then she leaned back, waiting.

Dear God, please let her realize this is no trick.

"Ma'am – Miranda – please." So much hope, and so much pain, filled her voice. "Is this true?"

"It is, Ash. The pardons for your people are now official and the *Breitman* is being dispatched to pick them up as we speak." She paused to give Shaw time to digest what she'd said. "So I have to ask again, will you accept a full pardon, complete with all references to the court-martial being expunged from your record, no hits being taken regarding time in grade, back pay being credited to you, and will you return to duty?"

"I—"

Shaw paused, a look of concern crossing her expression. As she did, a sudden shower of dust cascaded down on them from the ceiling. The floor vibrated beneath their feet and the water in their glasses sloshed slightly. As the overhead lights flickered, went out and then returned, Tremayne pushed her chair away from the table. Fear was quickly replaced by determination as the instincts honed by years of command kicked in.

One corner of the senator's mind wondered if the capital had just been rocked by an earthquake. To be felt this far up in the in the security complex, it had to have been a major quake. That meant damage and casualties. It also meant aftershocks that could cause even more damage.

But that didn't make sense. There hadn't been a quake in this region for more than a century. Besides, the geological service would have issued a warning, wouldn't it? Wasn't that what it was for?

So, if this wasn't a quake, what was it?

Before she could voice her concern, a muted rumble reached them. There could be no mistaking it. The building rocked on its foundations. Bits of ceiling broke free and fell, filling the room with dust. Tremayne's stomach rolled and she grabbed the edge of the table for support. Then she was being dragged under the table, Shaw's hold on her preventing her from crawling out.

"Stay still, damn it!" Shaw rasped.

Tremayne winced as her earbud came to life and chatter from a number of different sources assailed her. Ignoring Shaw's protests, she rolled out from under the table. Her eyes searched for her comm-link. For the first time since retiring, she missed the communications implant that would have tied her instantly into both the military and government com-nets.

"Say that again!" she barked over her 'link a moment later as Shaw joined her.

The building rocked once more. This time there was no mistaking the sounds of an explosion. From the chatter coming through her earbud, it was obvious someone had attacked the building. Whether it was a full-scale attack on the capital or just an isolated incident, she didn't know and, frankly, she didn't care. Either way, they had to get out of the room and down to the ground floor. If the building should start to collapse before they did . . ..

"This is Tremayne. Secure the immediate area and get fighters in the air now!" she ordered. She didn't care that she no longer had the actual authority to issue the orders. All that mattered was launching a counter-strike to turn back the attackers. "And find Major Santiago!"

Even as she barked out orders, Tremayne watched Shaw race to the door. She pounded on it, ordering the guards to open up, reminding them they had a member of the Senate inside. It was their duty to get her to safety.

"Admiral, we have to get you out of here!" Shaw said, turning to face her.

"Ashlyn, give me your answer. Now!"

"Yes. Now let's get you out of here."

Tremayne was aware of sounds beyond the door but she had no time to worry about it. Instead, she reached for the terminal on the table and quickly input a series of commands. Then she grabbed Shaw by the arm and drew her close. Even as the guards yelled something about standing back from the door, she told Shaw to read what was on the screen. There was no time to lose and, damn it, she wanted Shaw in the position to act if necessary.

"All right. Now let's get the hell out of here!" Shaw said as she "signed" the pardon and added her thumbprint via the gen-lock next to the terminal.

———

EVAN MOREAU WATCHED from her table by the window of the restaurant. The last thing she wanted to do was to call attention to herself. But it was hard not to lean forward, expression intent, as she watched the first of several young men approaching the main entrance to the security complex. There was nothing about them to raise any alarms. At least she hoped not. If this part of the plan failed, she'd have no choice but to go to her backup plan and get off-planet just as quickly as possible. No, to the plan would work. It had to.

All around her, men and women went about their business, unaware that in a few short moments their lives would change dramatically, perhaps even end. She didn't care. They were all expendable, pawns in the greater game she played at every day of her life. A few deaths and the ensuing panic were what she needed just then.

Still, she couldn't help but feel more nervous than usual. Most jobs she handled herself. She didn't like relying on others, but this was one of those rare exceptions where she had no choice. She'd worked hard, and in record time, to set this up. If she played her cards right, not only would she manage to appease Kannedy, but she'd manage to make sure Shaw never bothered her again and no one would ever be able to trace what happened back to her.

So much rested on whether or not everything went off as planned. She had put plans into motion that hadn't been set to occur for months yet. She knew there were problems with moving the timetable up without proper preparation. But she had no choice. Besides, it wasn't as if she had any particular loyalty to Kannedy and his "partners". If this failed, she had no doubt Kannedy would turn on her just to save his own skin. What he didn't know, and never would, was that she'd planned for that contingency as well. She had disappeared before and she could do so again. Except this time, she would return to settle the score – with Kannedy and with Shaw.

Hopefully, however, those plans would not become necessary. For now, all she could do was watch and wait.

Another glance at the time and she finished her coffee. She couldn't stay there any longer. There was no need to risk getting caught in the panic that was about to happen. Still, it would be so satisfying to see her plans finally come to fruition.

There!

She almost missed the signal between the young man she'd been watching and the two others she knew were with him. It had been nothing more than a quick flash of a hand signal and then a nod. It was time. If she didn't leave now, it would be too late.

She tossed a handful of credits onto the table before climbing to her feet. Anyone looking in her direction would see just another businesswoman hurrying to get back to work. No one would remember her in the aftermath of what was to come.

A quick look to the east as she stepped outside and a slight smile touched her lips. She picked up her pace and turned the corner. If her estimate was right, she had less than two minutes before all hell broke loose. That was enough time to be safely away.

Another corner turned, more distance between her and the security complex. Just another few moments and she'd be safe.

An explosion sounded in the distance and she quickened her pace, smiling gaily as she did. Damn but she loved it when a plan worked.

4

The building seemed to rock on its very foundations. Dust fell from the ceiling, drifting down like snowflakes. Ashlyn reached out and steadied herself against the table. The windows, reinforced to prevent anyone from breaking them-or anyone in an aircar from shooting them out – suddenly sprouted spider web-like cracks. This was no earthquake. No, someone had attacked the building. Terrorism or an all-out attack? It didn't matter. Nothing mattered beyond getting out of there before the building came down around their ears. She hadn't struggled to survive the hell of the penal colony only to die within days of coming home.

"Admiral, we have to get you out of here!"

"Ashlyn, give me your answer. Now!" Tremayne barked.

"Yes. Now let's get you out of here."

The door slowly slid open, stopping after only a few inches. Tremayne ignored it. Instead, she worked quickly at the terminal on the table. Biting back a curse of frustration as Tremayne told her to read the display, Shaw did as the woman instructed. She quickly scanned the document that appeared on the screen, the pardon she had prayed so long for. But she didn't have time to really register all it said, much less relish the moment. Instead, she picked up the stylus and scrawled her name at the bottom of the document and pressed her right thumb against the gen-lock beside the terminal. Then she turned her attention back to the senator, determined to get her out of there before either of them was hurt – or worse.

"Admiral – Miranda, you've got to get out of here. NOW!" she said as the building rocked yet again.

No matter what had happened over the last two years, this was still the woman who had watched her grow up, who had been her mother's best friend and her own mentor. She was also one of the sharpest military minds alive. There was no way could they risk her now.

That sense of duty Ashlyn had done her best to bury since her court-martial kicked in full force. Frustrated because the guards had yet to open the door, Shaw rushed to the window and looked out. They were too high to see what was going on in the streets below. But she could see the strikeships streaming to and from the spaceport not that far away. Her pulse quickened and she recognized the movement in the sky as a dogfight.

Holy hell, was the capital actually under attack?

For several long moments she stood riveted as she watched the battle in the skies over the city. Then, as two fighters broke away from the pack and bore down on the building, she turned. Her pulse pounded as she raced across the room, upending the table as she did. Before Tremayne could react, much less ask what was happening, she'd shoved the table against the far wall and pulled the woman down behind the meager protection it offered. Then she threw herself on top of the senator, holding her down even as the sounds of rounds striking the side of the building filled the room.

Ashlyn's ears rang from the sounds of the window cracking and the fighters veering off just before impact. But she couldn't think about that any more than she could think about how scared she was. She had to get Tremayne out of there before the fighters made a second pass. They wouldn't survive another assault like the last one and she was damned if she'd just lay down and die. Not when she finally had her freedom.

"Come on!".

Ashlyn's hand closed around the senator's arm and dragged her out from behind the table. The door was open. That meant they could finally get out of this deathtrap. Instinct kicked in. Scrambling to her feet, she dragged Tremayne up after her. There was no time to lose. She turned and took a step toward the door. As she did, she came face to face with one of the guards.

Without warning, the guard slammed his rifle butt into her side. Before she could react, her head snapped back as a second blow landed, a solid strike to her cheek. Pain exploded, thrusting her momentarily back to the hell she had known on Tarsus. Darkness swam before her eyes and her stomach pitched dangerously. A third blow, followed almost instantly by the unmistakable sound of her nose breaking, threatened to send her under. She fought to stay conscious, to stay on her feet. She couldn't black out now. Not if she wanted to live.

Moaning, she climbed to her knees, unaware of the fact she'd fallen. Her stomach pitched and she tasted blood. She hurt so badly that she knew they had broken several ribs as well as her nose. Damn, but she thought she had left this sort of thing behind her on Tarsus.

"Stand down!" someone ordered. Tremayne? "Goddamn it, stand down!"

This time Tremayne pulled her to her feet instead of the other way around. Fury suffused the senator's face as she quickly checked to be sure Ashlyn was all right. Then, to Ash's surprise, the woman reached out and grabbed the nearest guard's sidearm and handed it to her. Ashlyn took it with her right hand even as she used her left to wipe tears and blood from her face.

"Captain Shaw has received a full pardon from President Harper and has been returned to duty. Touch her again and I'll see you up on charges," Tremayne said quickly, before the other guard could react. "Now get us the hell out of here."

That was all the encouragement Ashlyn needed. By God, she'd get Tremayne out of there somehow. She could ignore the pain and blood. After all, she'd had lots of practice doing just that on Tarsus. Besides, the guards would help, at least until they had to report to their own stations. Once she knew Tremayne was safe, she could slip away. She'd make sure her family was all right. She'd make sure her people really were on the way home. Then she'd make those responsible for the last two years of hell pay and pay dearly.

But that had to wait until they were out of this grave just waiting to happen.

For a moment, she thought the guards would protest. Instead, the first one merely nodded. Then he motioned for his companion to take the lead. As they started off down the corridor, the first guard fell in at the rear. Ashlyn did her best to ignore the unease she felt having him behind her. Hopefully, he wouldn't try anything with Tremayne present. She had to trust in that.

But it was hard, so very hard.

At the end of the corridor, the point guard motioned for them to wait as he checked ahead. Eyes alert, her fingers tightening around the butt of the pistol, Ashlyn stood ready. She wasn't even aware of the fact she'd moved forward slightly, positioning herself between the corner and Tremayne, until the redhead gently reached out and pulled her back. Before she could protest, Tremayne simply shook her head and lifted the gun she'd produced from somewhere.

A moment later the guard returned, one hand to his ear as he listened to his comm-link. He nodded once and turned to face Tremayne. As he did, his discomfort was clear. Stiffening, knowing trouble lay ahead, Ashlyn waited.

"Senator, I've been ordered to make sure you get to safety. My partner will take care of Shaw."

Fury, cold and hard, raced through her. She had no doubt how the guard was supposed to "take care of" her. She was damned if she would stand there and let them kill her. Not when freedom was so close. Not when she'd believed Tremayne and had finally allowed herself to hope.

Before she could act, Tremayne did. Her pistol was suddenly aimed squarely at the guard's chest. His partner, caught off-guard, was slow to bring his weapon to bear. Instinct kicked in again and Ashlyn knocked his arm to one side. Her left hand closed over his gun and she quickly disarmed him. Then she waited, her finger tightening on the trigger. She didn't want to kill him, but she would if she had to.

"Stand easy, kid. I'm not about to leave you. Nor am I about to let anything else happen to you," Tremayne assured her before addressing the guards. "I'm only going to say this once. President Harper has pardoned Captain Shaw. She is no longer a prisoner and she most certainly is no longer in your custody. So you can either continue to stand in our way and get us all killed or you can help us get out of this hellhole to safety. I will handle whomever issued your orders to 'deal' with Captain Shaw as soon as this is over."

Ashlyn waited, knowing how precarious their position was. Time was running out. If they didn't move soon, before another attack run against the building, they'd be dead. But did the guards realize it or were they so scared of disobeying orders they'd risk everything, even their lives, over this?

"Aye, ma'am," the first guard replied and then, much to Ashlyn's surprise, he snapped to attention and saluted. "Captain Shaw, I'm counting on you to help keep the senator safe." With that, he turned and started off around the corner, yelling back to them that he'd clear a path and to keep up.

There wasn't time to think or to feel. It was as though the last two years had never happened. Once more she was fighting for her life and the lives of others. One corridor at a time, one corner to be taken carefully to make sure they weren't running headlong into a trap. All the while they made their way closer to the ground before the building collapsed on top of them.

The sounds of fighting were like memories of the nightmares that had plagued her for so long. Weapons firing, people screaming, orders being shouted out even as cries for help filled the air. Ashlyn had done everything she could back then to save her unit but so many had died. More had been injured and she'd been unable to do anything to help them. She'd lived with the dying screams of her people for two long years. Would she ever be able to put them behind her?

She couldn't think about it, couldn't let herself remember that last battle and what happened afterwards. Not now. Not until she was sure Tremayne was safe. Then she could begin figuring out how best to get vengeance for her people.

Finally, after what seemed an eternity, they reached the ground floor. Marines worked feverishly to make sure all non-essential personnel were moved out of the fire zone. Others laid down carefully controlled cover fire. Ashlyn took it all in, her mind racing to catch up with what was happening. They couldn't stay there, not as long as there was fighting going on. But where were they going? Was anywhere safe just then?

Damn it, she wished she knew what was going on.

"Admiral Tremayne." A Marine in light armor slid to a halt before them and sketched a quick salute. Even as he did, he checked to make sure they weren't in the direct line of fire. "Gunnery Sergeant Kevin Talbot, ma'am. I've been assigned by Major Santiago to make sure you and Captain Shaw get to safety."

"What's the current situation, Gunny?" Tremayne asked. Gone was the senator. This was the admiral and Ashlyn hoped Talbot realized it.

"Ma'am, I can't tell you much. FleetCom is still scrambling to respond. Enemy short-range fighters have launched attacks against the security compound, the presidential palace and other governmental buildings. We have enemy boots on the ground and what appear to have been at least half a dozen suicide bombers at various points across the city. Our forces have scrambled to secure the capital and fighters are in the air."

"First Fleet?"

"Is on station and launching LACs to make sure there are no enemy ships on approach. That's about all I can tell you, ma'am. Communication to First Fleet is limited right now but FleetCom is working to restore full comms. As for groundside, we have snipers as well as assault troops trying to breach our defenses."

"Who's in command?" Ashlyn asked.

As she did, she fought down her emotions. Seeing Talbot was yet another reminder of all the lives lost and all that had been taken from her. She had served with the gunnery sergeant before her last assignment. He'd taught her more about battlefield tactics than any of her courses at the Academy and he had pulled her ass out of the line of fire on more than one occasion. Of course, she'd returned the favor almost as many times. After all, that's what Marines do.

"Major Santiago, ma'am, and his orders to me were quite clear. I am to make sure you and the admiral – sorry, ma'am, the senator – get safely out of here. If we get the all-clear, a shuttle will take you to rendezvous with First Fleet's flagship. Otherwise, I'm to get you to the FOB. The major assured me that he'd have my hide, literally, if I let anything happen to either of you."

"Then you'd best lead the way, Gunny," Tremayne said. "But, before you do, make sure these two are secured somewhere safe. I'm going to want to have *a chat* with them once the current situation is under control."

Talbot looked from the senator to the guards, concern momentarily clouding his expression. Then, glancing at Ashlyn, he nodded. Without asking for an explanation, he called another Marine over and *suggested* he escort the two to a secure location where they were to remain until further notice. Then he turned back to the guards.

"Corporal, you and your companion will hand your weapons over to Captain Shaw and then you'll go with Corporal Henson." The look he gave the corporal when the man balked brought a quick smile to Ashlyn's lips. If they lived through this, she'd buy the gunny a drink. It was worth it to see the guard's discomfort. Besides, she had a feeling Talbot would be more than happy to help her with her *other* plans. He had lost friends on that last mission as well. "Captain, I also have these for you," he added after she'd taken their weapons and checked them.

Ashlyn's right hand automatically reached out to catch the dog tags he tossed in her direction. Her chest tightened and she swallowed hard as she stared at them. How he'd gotten them, she didn't know. They had been taken from her when she'd been processed back into the brig after the court-martial panel returned their guilty verdict.

"How?" she asked softly, staring at the dog tags nestled in the palm of her hand.

"Major Santiago had them, ma'am. You'll need to ask him where he got them."

She nodded, unable to say anything just then.

"Welcome back, ma'am. You've been missed."

"It's good to be back, Gunny." She slid the chain over her head, relishing the sound of the tags hitting against one another. Surprisingly, it was good to be back, at least it would be once she'd dealt with a few matters. "Now, let's get the senator out of here."

"Yes, ma'am."

With that, Talbot turned and started toward the rear of the building. As they pushed through the crush of others attempting to get to safety, Shaw thought hard, trying to remember the layout of the building. Unless things had changed since her court-martial, there was a small landing area at the rear of the complex. When she'd been on active duty, it had been used for fleet officers and government officials. But was it secure enough to allow for a shuttle to land and take off without becoming easy target practice for the enemy?

They turned another corner and she saw daylight. For a moment she paused. It would be so easy to slip away into the confusion and disappear. But she was free. She had to remember that. She was free, her name cleared. The rest would come.

Assuming any of them lived out the day.

———

TREMAYNE BIT back a curse as the building was rocked again. Before she could stop and look, Ashlyn's hand closed over her arm and dragged her forward. The young woman had to be acting on instinct now. She'd not worn the Marine uniform in more than two years. It had been even longer than that since she had been on duty. Blood from her broken nose and a fresh cut over her right eye covered most of her face and stained the front of her jumpsuit. Tremayne winced as she imagined the pain Ashlyn must be in. But no one would guess it from the way she moved, carefully checking each corner before allowing Tremayne forward and not letting the senator stop and see what was going on.

Veteran that she was, Tremayne knew this wasn't her kind of fight. She was a space jockey and always would be. Put her on the bridge of a ship and she was in her element. But this up close and personal sort of fight was why she'd chosen to go Navy instead of joining the Marines like her parents. At least she knew to put her trust in those who knew how to fight this sort of battle. Not that she liked it.

But if she'd had any concerns, any doubts about how Ashlyn would respond to a combat situation after all she'd been through, she no longer did. The young woman might not look like an active duty Marine in the black jumpsuit she'd been issued but she certainly acted like one. The rifle the gunny secured for her was slung across her back. The pistol she'd taken from the guard was held at the ready. Her eyes constantly scanned their surroundings, looking for danger from any source.

If that wasn't enough to prove she was ready not only to return to duty but to trust her fellow Marines, the fact Shaw hadn't demanded to be linked into the com-net did. She listened carefully to the reports Talbot gave from time to time, occasionally asking questions. But she didn't demand he turn over his earbud, something Tremayne knew a number of other officers would have. Hell, she probably would have made the demand had she been in Ashlyn's place. Maybe there really was reason to hope the last two years hadn't turned the young woman against them.

God, let it be so.

"Any update on Fleet status, Gunny?" Tremayne asked as they slid to a halt as the corridor ended in a T.

The gunny snuck a peek around the corner and then ducked back. His expression was serious as he checked his weapon. Then he lifted his left hand to his ear, listening to the reports coming in over the battle-net.

"FleetCom says we are to make our way to the FOB, ma'am. They'd like to get you and the captain as far from the fighting as possible, but there are still enemy stingers in the air. So, for the moment at least, you're stuck groundside."

Tremayne nodded. She'd feel better with a deck beneath her feet but that wasn't to be. Not yet, at any rate. A quick glance at Ashlyn showed she didn't feel the same. Not that it really surprised the senator. Ashlyn was a Marine, born and bred. Despite everything that had happened to her, everything that had been done to her, the last half hour proven that much at least.

"Ash," she said softly.

"I'm all right, ma'am." The younger woman gave a lopsided smile that didn't touch her eyes. "Right now, we need to get you to safety. So let's get to the FOB."

———

"ALMOST THERE, SENATOR," the gunny said as they raced through the doors and burst into the sunlight.

A moment later, they slid to a halt behind a makeshift barrier. One of the three Marines stationed there gave them a quick glance before turning her attention back to the area ahead of them. This might be the center of the security complex, but there was still a lot of open expanse to cross, too much when you considered all the buildings surrounding the complex. Buildings that could be hiding snipers, waiting to take their shot.

Ashlyn peeked around the edge of the barrier and blew out a breath. Any other time, a shuttle would have rested on the landing pad not fifty meters from them. If one had been there when the attack began, it would have taken off as soon as its engines had been brought online. No one would have wanted it left there, an easy target and nothing more than a huge bomb waiting to be detonated.

Across the clearing was a second building. A twin to the one they'd just vacated, it housed a number of governmental agencies. Civilians and easy targets. Not that whoever was behind the attack cared. It was obvious they had chosen the timing of the attack very carefully. Not only was the workday well underway, but the streets of the capital would have been filled with tourists and businesspeople going about their daily activities. God, this was a nightmare. How many lives would be lost before the attack was over?

"Where's the FOB, Gunny?" Tremayne asked.

"Three buildings over, ma'am, in the old Cap City Bank building. Major Santiago has set up there and is in contact with FleetCom."

"Why there?"

Ashlyn didn't like it. The bank building had been vacant for years. She doubted it had been kept up during that time and that meant a direct hit against it could bring the building down around their ears. That assumed they even made it there. First, they'd have to cross more than one hundred yards of open area. The threat of snipers, not to mention the possibility of one of the enemy stinger ships zeroing in on them, increased the more open area they had to cross.

"The major will have to tell you that, ma'am. All I know is that's where he was ordered to set up the FOB." Talbot didn't look any happier about than did she. In a way, that made her feel better.

Even so, it was so close and yet too far away.

She leaned against the barrier and closed her eyes, catching her breath. The sounds of fighting at the front of the building reached her. Screams of agony mixed with the unmistakable sounds of gunfire. This wasn't supposed to happen in the capital. Hell, it wasn't supposed to happen planetside. It had been more than two centuries since there'd been a real battle on Fuercon and that had been civil war. Even during the last war, the Navy had been able to keep the enemy out of the home system. How the hell had they managed to get through now?

That was a very good question, one she didn't have time to worry about. The fighting hadn't reached this part of the complex yet, but it would before long, especially if the enemy ground troops continued to press forward. If the enemy actually coordinated their efforts with their air support, Ashlyn knew they'd be overrun. That meant they had to move, snipers or not.

Ash glanced skyward and frowned. Smoke billowed from the side of the building in the general area of where she thought her cell had been. A few minutes more and both she and Tremayne would have died. Wouldn't that have sucked? Brought back to the capital to be offered a full pardon only to be killed in a sneak attack on the planet.

"Gunny, we need to get the senator out of here. We can't wait any longer on the off-chance FleetCom will decide our best bet is the shuttle."

"I'm just waiting for the word, ma'am," he said and cocked his head as he listened to something coming in over his earbud.

"Any word on enemy air support?" She looked up again, relieved to see only their own fighters in the air for the moment.

Damn, it felt like she was fighting blind. She didn't know who the enemy was, what they wanted or what their current position happened to be. She'd been in this position too often during the war, but she'd thought those days were behind her. Of course, she'd also thought she'd be spending the next three years at the penal colony which, just now, sounded pretty damned good. But she was a Marine and she'd be damned if she let anything happen to the woman next to her.

"Looks like their birds have withdrawn, at least for the moment, Captain. But there's no guarantee they won't make another run against us soon."

"How in the hell did they get troops on-planet, much less bring in air support?" Tremayne demanded.

"A very good question, ma'am, and one I'd love to know the answer to," Ashlyn replied, once more peeking around the barricade.

As she did, she felt Tremayne shift restlessly at her side. Her hand flashed out, grabbing the senator before the woman could move forward. That was always the problem with Navy types. They thought about battle in terms of thousands of kilometers of space, not in terms of someone being close enough to put a projectile between your eyes or a knife between your ribs.

"Gunny, recommendations?" Ashlyn looked at the man, nodding as she did. She'd learned early in her career to trust her gunny, especially on the battlefield. Talbot had proven himself one of the best, at least in her opinion. She'd trusted him during the war and she'd trust him now.

"We don't dare wait any longer, Cap. When I say go, you get the senator across the clearing. I'll cover you. Duck into the walkway between the two buildings at the northwest corner. Wait for me there. Then we'll regroup and make the last run for the FOB," he said, his eyes raking the open area before them.

"You'd better be right on our heels, Gunny. I'm not leaving anyone behind, not this time." Even as she said it, she thought about her people back on Tarsus and prayed she'd not imagined the notice of their pardons.

"Understood, ma'am. Believe me, I'll be on so close behind you that you'll think I'm your shadow." An explosion followed by a fresh burst of gunfire sounded to their rear. "I recommend you get moving if you don't want to be caught smack in the middle of the fighting."

Ashlyn glance around, her mouth tight. How in the world had she gone from military prisoner to active duty Marine in the middle of a firefight in less than an hour?

"Senator, you're going to do exactly as I say." She turned to Tremayne. "When I tell you to run, you are going to run like the hounds of Hell are on your heels. You don't stop until you're in the walkway, no matter what happens. Do you understand?"

"I do. You'd better understand that I expect you to be right there with me."

"Gunny, stand ready." Ashlyn checked her weapons one last time. "Now, Captain. Go!"

Shaw nodded and, grabbing Tremayne's arm with her left hand, raced out from behind the barricade. They hadn't gone three steps when the shots she'd been expecting rang out. The staccato of projectiles hitting the pavement at their feet filled the air. Pain like the sting of hundreds of insects registered. One part of her mind identified it as shrapnel and slivers of pavement, possibly even ricochets. Not that it made the pain go away. However, one thing her time at the penal colony had done was given her the ability to ignore such things. She'd have time to worry about it later.

She hoped.

Two armed and armored Marines appeared from the shadows of the walkway as they neared. Their covering fire joined that of the gunny and the others at the barricade. Shaw all but threw Tremayne at the nearest Marine before turning to lay down cover fire for the gunny.

"Keep the senator back and comm the major that we're on our way!" she yelled as she fired in the direction of the last shot to hit the ground near her.

"Captain, get your ass back against that building!" Talbot ordered as he ran across the open area. "Get her back!" he added to the Marines covering her.

Snarling, Shaw jerked against the hands that reached for her. She was damned if she ran before she knew the gunny was safe. She had been forced to leave the others behind on Tarsus. She wouldn't do that here. She couldn't.

Once she knew the gunny was safe, she sank to her heels, breathing hard. The so-called walkway they huddled in was nothing more than a tunnel hollowed out between the two buildings. Barely six feet wide and seven feet tall, it offered them at least temporary cover from an aerial attack. But that limited safety wouldn't last for long if the enemy ground troops managed to close in on them.

"Are you all right?"

She heard the worry in Tremayne's voice and nodded. If this felt a bit too close to what happened on her last mission, she couldn't dwell on it. No, she had to focus on the here and now. Otherwise, she might as well just walk out into the open and let the enemy put a bullet in her skull. That would be easier than having to relive the last few years.

"Yeah." She blew out a breath and then coughed. Smoke filled the air, bringing with it all the smells of battle. "Ma'am, you'd better make sure those folks at the FOB know I'm supposed to be with you.

I'd really hate to be shot as an escaping prisoner." She tried to make it a joke but failed. It was too close to the truth.

"Don't worry, Ash. They know." Tremayne's hand reached over and gave hers a quick squeeze.

"They do, ma'am," Talbot assured her. "Besides, that's why I'm here. I'm your bodyguard right now even more than the senator's and, as you know, I'm very good at what I do."

She couldn't help it. She smiled slightly and nodded. Talbot was good and he'd proven time and again over the years that he would do whatever was necessary to get the job done. It might not keep a sniper from getting off a lucky shot but hopefully it would keep one of her own side from doing something she'd regret, assuming she lived that long.

Without a word, she climbed to her feet and moved to the end of the "tunnel" before crouching again. Her right palm rested against the side of the building as she leaned forward. She took a quick look around the corner in the direction of the old Cap City Bank building before ducking back into the walkway. The sounds of fighting here were a bit more sporadic than at the security complex but she wasn't about to let her guard down yet.

"One more time, Senator." She drew a deep breath, held it for a moment, and then released it. God, the last thing she'd expected when she'd been escorted from her cell was to be fighting for her life and the life of her mentor. "You will stick with me. You will not stop for anything. If I go down, you will keep running until you are safe inside. Do you understand?"

"I'll repeat what I told you earlier. I'll do it as long as you remember to stick with me as well."

"And I'll kick both of your asses, ma'ams, if either of you do anything stupid. Respectfully, of course," the gunny added, grinning slightly. "Cap, when you're ready, give the word and I'll let them know at the FOB to cover you."

"Let's do this." She stood and checked her pistol one last time. Then she said a quick prayer and nodded. "Go!"

She stepped into the street, gun ready and waved for Tremayne to move. As the senator broke into the open, gunfire erupted around them. Ashlyn's hand closed over the senator's arm and together they raced in a zigzag across the street. Marines appeared from the FOB to lay down cover fire. The sounds of the battle echoed off the sides of the buildings, masking Ashlyn's thundering pulse and the sounds of Tremayne gasping for breath as they ran.

"Go, go, go!" Ashlyn yelled as she raced through the door of the bank building a moment later, the gunny on her heels.

One of the Marines pulled the door closed behind them and then pounded his gloved fist against a panel next to the doorway. Almost instantly a heavy security door slid into place. Ashlyn bent, hands on her thighs, and fought for breath. It was one thing to do several hundred pushup and sit-ups in her cell each day, but it was something very different to be running for her life in the middle of a firefight. Her heart pounded, sweat covered her and her breath hitched. But they had made it and, so far at least, no one had shot her. That had to count for something.

"Senator, Captain, if you'll follow me, I'll take you to the major," Talbot said a moment later.

As she followed the gunny and Tremayne deeper into the building, Ashlyn couldn't help wondering what was going to happen next.

5

Major Rico Santiago stood next to a small table, carefully studying a holo display. As Talbot escorted Tremayne and Ashlyn into the room deep inside the building, he looked up. Relief lit his expression and he stepped around the table to greet them. As he did, Ashlyn felt the years of training forcing her body to snap to attention even as her mind suddenly decided to stop working.

Reaction. She knew that's what it was. She had been operating on instinct, adrenaline and training since first realizing the security building was under attack. But now, deep inside the old bank building, inside what had once been the vault, the danger was over, at least for the moment. The need to fight to survive was gone. Now came the waiting and the wondering.

God, she hated the unknown.

"Well done, Gunny," Santiago said. "Any problems?"

"Nothing we didn't expect, sir," Talbot replied. "However, there is a matter the senator needs to brief you on. She had me take the two Marines escorting her and the captain down from the security block into custody."

Santiago frowned and turned his attention to Tremayne. "I know you well enough to know you wouldn't do something like that without good cause, ma'am."

"A very good cause," she assured him, her voice cold. "Who ordered them to escort us down?"

That was a question Ash wanted answered as well. Just as she wanted to be the one to deal with the person who issued that order.

"I'd have to check, but I would assume the Officer of the Day. Why?"

"Because, before we were off the security floor, I was told that one of the Marines would escort me to safety and the other would *deal with* the captain."

Talbot's reaction almost mirrored Santiago's. Both stiffened, their expressions turning thunderous. Watching them, realizing they had nothing to do with the order, Ashlyn relaxed a little. She wasn't ready to completely drop her guard but seeing how angry they were helped.

"Did they explain how they were to deal with the captain?" Santiago ground out the words.

"They didn't need to. The implication was clear."

For a moment, Santiago didn't say anything. "Captain, my apologies. Neither I nor any member of my staff issued such an order. I promise I will find out who did and there will not only be an investigation, but charges will be brought. You have my word on that."

"Thank you, sir." She took his outstretched hand in hers. His promise might not have been enough to reassure her but that, combined with his reaction to hearing what had almost happened, most certainly was.

"Now, before we compare notes about what's going on, there are a few things I need to deal with." For the first time since their arrival, Santiago looked a bit unsure. Then he smiled and there was a twinkle in his eye that had Ashlyn watching him closely. He was up to something and, from the way he looked at Tremayne, it had to do with the senator and not with her. Fortunately. "Senator, I've been instructed by FleetCom to inform you that you have been recalled to active duty for as long as this current state of emergency is in effect. You should be receiving formal notification shortly. Until it is safe to transport you to the *Intrepid*, you will be stationed here to help coordinate our ground forces with our air strikes."

"I can't say I'm surprised. Who is the senior officer groundside right now?"

"For the Navy?" Santiago waited until she nodded. "Senior officer is Admiral Liat. SecDef has been evacced to safety along with the President, Vice President and the Cabinet."

"I'd best report in then." She nodded and stepped to one side, pulling her comm-unit as she did.

"Gunny, escort the captain to the medic. I want her checked over ASAP," he continued. "Ash, by the time they're done with you, we'll have gotten something for you to wear other than that damned jumpsuit. Get your injuries treated and then get your ass back here for a briefing."

"One thing first, sir." She reached up and her hand closed over her dog tags. "How did you get them?" She didn't explain what she meant. She didn't need to, not when he looked at her hand fisted around the tags.

"When your parents realized I was looking into what happened, they gave them to me and asked that I return them to you. They said they figured I'd see you before they would."

She swallowed hard and nodded. Tears burned in her eyes. Her parents had trusted him to help free her. He had managed to carry out his part. But what about them? Were they all right? She couldn't let herself think about them being in the middle of the attack, but she couldn't deny her worry either.

God, she had to get out of there and find them.

"Sir, I'm fine, really. Just give me a few minutes to get out of this jumpsuit so no one mistakes me for an escaped prisoner and then I'll be ready to do whatever needs to be done."

"Medics first." He took a step closer and dropped his voice. "Ash, right now you look like hell. It's more than the smoke and debris from the fight to get here. I can tell you're hurt and hurting. You know as well as I do that you need to get treated before anything else happens."

She wanted to protest but didn't. For one, now that they were away from the fighting, she felt every ache and pain, especially those from her broken nose and ribs. For another, she knew he was only doing what the regs required. They weren't in immediate danger of being attacked. So, as the senior officer until Tremayne assumed that role, he had to make sure all the people under his command were at their best. She didn't have to like it, and she didn't, but she did understand it.

"Yes, sir."

"Good." Now he smiled again, his relief plain to see. "Gunny, stay with her and let me know what the medics have to say."

"Understood, Major."

"Go on, Ash. The sooner you let them do their magic, the sooner you can get back here."

She nodded and turned to the gunny, indicating she was ready to follow orders.

"Captain," Talbot began a few moments later as they moved through the lower level of the building. "Before we get to the medics, I have a couple of things to say," he continued and Ashlyn tensed.

Was he about to damn her for what happened back on Arterus? He'd known many of those who had been lost or injured. Surely, he understood that she'd done everything possible short of mutiny to prevent having her company sent into that Hell.

"Ma'am, don't." He reached out and touched her arm. It was so brief as to be almost non-existent, but it was enough to reassure her. "I want you to know that none of us who served with you believed that line of bullshit the brass tried to feed us. We knew you wouldn't have purposely disobeyed orders, much less put your command in jeopardy like they said. More than that, we knew you'd never do anything to harm innocent civilians. I'd also like to say it's good to know that the injustice done to you and the others has finally been corrected."

"Thank you, Gunny." She blinked back the tears suddenly burning in her eyes. "When this is over, I owe you a drink. I know you went out on a limb and tried to testify for me at my court-martial and the Board wouldn't let you."

"Ma'am, there were more than two dozen of us who were on-planet and who tried to do just that. Dozens more who were off-planet at the time sent their recorded statements supporting you and the others in your command."

Ashlyn swallowed hard. Her attorney had told her that he'd received a number of requests to testify on her behalf from former squadmates. What he hadn't said was just how many. It wouldn't have changed the outcome of her trial, but the knowledge that so many of those she'd served with had come forward to testify on her behalf might have helped her cope with her conviction. At least then she'd have had hope that someone might have been working to free her and the others.

"And you don't need to buy me a drink. I know for a fact that every one of our former squadmates are just waiting for the chance to buy you a drink, myself included." Now he smiled down at her and laid a reassuring hand on her shoulder. "You're home now, Cap, and you're safe. The others will be soon."

"They'd better," was all she said, her voice rough with emotion. "Now, let's find the medics. I don't think either of us want to keep the major waiting."

The next hour was a blur of medical tests. Ashlyn's protests that she was all right fell on deaf ears. Nothing she said swayed the Navy doctor or the two medics working with him. In fact, the longer the doctor worked on her, treating her broken nose and ribs, as well as other injuries she hadn't registered, the grimmer he looked.

Had she been hurt worse than she thought?

Then realization dawned on her. It wasn't her new injuries that upset him. It was the scars she bore from the last two years on Tarsus. Well, that was just too bad. She neither wanted nor needed anyone worrying about what happened in the past. Not right now, at any rate.

Not when the capital was under attack and she didn't know if her family was safe.

"Doc, just give me a painkiller and let me out of here." She sat up on the makeshift examining table and looked around the small room for her clothes. Then she remembered how one of the medics assisting the doctor had taken the black jumpsuit and left with it almost as soon as they'd had her stripped. "And find me something to wear or I'm walking out of here in the clothes I was born in."

She climbed to her feet, convinced her bluff would work. Instead the doctor drew himself up to full height – meaning he now came up to her shoulders – and crossed his arms. His expression reminded her of any number of her teachers at the Academy when she'd said or done something extremely foolish.

Damn it.

"Go ahead, Captain, if you want the Marines here to mutiny."

Mutiny? What the hell was he talking about?

"You really don't know, do you?" His expression softened and he motioned for the others to leave them alone. As the door closed, the doctor pointed to the examining table and waited until Ashlyn sat. "Captain, the Devil Dogs, at least the core unit, are here, in this build-ing. If they saw you and saw the scars you bear, nothing could keep them from haring off to Tarsus to exact their revenge. I'd even join them. I might be Navy, but I spent time as a corpsman for the DDs. That makes you mine almost as much as you are theirs."

The Devil Dogs.

Her heart skipped a beat and memories washed over her. If she'd been thrilled to be selected to join Special Forces, she had been much more than that the day she'd been tapped for the Devil Dogs. To know they were here, in the building . . ..

Relief filled her. Marines looked after their own and Devil Dogs went even further. She was safe now. She could relax and trust the DDs to make sure nothing else happened.

"Point taken, Doc, but you have to know none of my injuries are serious enough to keep me from reporting back to Major Santiago."

She shook her head, a bitter smile touching her lips. "Believe me, they're nothing compared to what I've suffered the last two years."

"I know, Captain, but you have to understand that I need to document everything." His voice was hard, flat, and she looked at him in time to see the flash of anger in his pale eyes. "I have my orders. I am to make sure every injury you suffered after being transported to the penal colony is noted in my records. FleetCom and the major have been very clear on that. Just as they've been clear that I'm to treat what injuries I can right now. I only wish I had the equipment here to bring your implants back online and get them calibrated."

"You and me both, Doc." She'd feel a great deal better when that happened. "But, as you said, we don't have time. Now, if I promise to be good, will you hurry up and finish?"

He shook his head, a slight smile touching his lips, and told her to lie back. As she did, he reactivated his medi-scanner. Ashlyn closed her eyes, willing herself to relax and let him work.

Half an hour later, Ashlyn stared at her reflection in the mirror over the sink in the small bathroom that connected to the room where she'd been examined. For the first time since her arrest, she wore the daily uniform of the Fuerconese Marine Corps. The pattern of colors had been optimized to help them blend into any background. But, just then, those muted colors were the most beautiful she had ever seen.

Maybe it wasn't all a dream after all.

"Ma'am," Talbot began from the doorway. "As soon as you're ready, the major sent word asking if you would join him and Admiral Tremayne now."

"Thank you, Gunny. Please tell him I'll be there shortly."

Ashlyn took a moment to study her reflection one last time, shaking her head as she did. Santiago had surprised her again. When Talbot arrived at the examining room a few minutes earlier with a change of clothes for her, she'd been happy to have something, anything that wasn't prison issued. Then, when she'd recognized the pattern for the BDUs, she'd smiled slightly, relief filling her. There was no way she'd be allowed to wear the uniform if she hadn't been pardoned. So the document Tremayne had her sign before they'd fled the security complex had been real. Hope filled her because surely that meant the other pardons had been real as well.

But that relief had blossomed into something else as she shook out the BDUs once in the privacy of the bathroom. This set looked like it had been made for her, down to the proper rank insignia and name tab. There was no way Santiago could have gotten them from the quartermaster, not in the middle of a firefight. Had he been so sure he'd be able to win her freedom that he'd had them made up ahead of time or was there another explanation? Not that it mattered. What did was once again being able to wear the uniform that had meant so much to her. It was almost as if the last two years had never taken place.

Almost.

All she had to do was look in the mirror to know those horrible months had been all too real. The scar marring her cheek and the other bisecting her right eyebrow had been acquired early into her imprisonment. Other unseen scars marred her body. There was a haunted look to her brown eyes that had never been there before, not even when she'd been about to go into battles she knew she might not return from. Her face was thin, almost gaunt, and her complexion pale from lack of sun. The swelling and bruising to her nose and left cheek made it worse. At least those newer injuries had been properly treated and would soon be nothing more than a bad memory.

Still, all those hours spent exercising in her cell to keep from going mad had given her arms a definition they'd never had before, something she hadn't realized until she'd rolled the sleeves of her BDUs.

"All right." She drew a deep, bracing breath and winced as pain lanced through her ribs. This was real. She had to remember that.

"This is yours, ma'am," Talbot said as she stepped into the treatment room once again.

Ashlyn's fingers closed tightly around the datapad he handed her. For a moment, she just held it, then she swiped a finger across the screen, waiting for it to activate. The first document in the queue was one that meant everything to her: her pardon. Following it were copies of the documents reinstating her to the Corps and removing all mention of the charges leveled against her, her conviction and her sentencing to the Tarsus military prison from her file. Then came the pardons for those convicted with her. Attached to it was a copy of the orders being sent to the commandant of the prison, instructing him to release her people and see they were well cared for until transport arrived to bring them to the capital. Everything was there, everything she had spent so long hoping for and knowing she could do nothing to bring it about.

Then the gunnery sergeant was there, his expression concerned as he handed her a tissue. Until then, she hadn't realized she was crying. Tears ran down her cheeks and she swallowed hard. It was over. Finally. Or at least it would be as soon as she'd seen for herself that her people were safely away from Tarsus.

But this was a start – a damned good start.

"Ma'am, I can't begin to understand what you've been through. But I've seen the scars you bear, scars I damn well know you didn't have when you were brought up on charges." The gunny's voice was a low growl. His anger slowly penetrated and she looked up, brushing away her tears with her right hand. "Ma'am, I promise you this isn't a trick. You are free. Your name and the names of the others have been cleared. I wish there was time for you to accept and adjust to everything that's happened. Unfortunately, we've got a damned battle to win right now and we'll win it a lot quicker now that you're back."

"Sorry, Gunny." She slid the datapad into the pocket at her left thigh and scrubbed her face, doing her best to pull herself together.

"No, ma'am. You've got nothing to apologize for. But we should get on our way before the major and Admiral Tremayne start to worry."

"All right. I'll be just a moment." With that, she ducked into the bathroom to wash her face. She might not totally feel like a Marine yet but, by God, she'd look like one. After all, her parents had always told her the looking the part was often as important, if not more so, that acting the part.

———

MIRANDA TREMAYNE LOOKED up from the small holo-plot she'd been studying as the door to the room Santiago had appropriated as the control room for the FOB opened. For one moment, she was transported back in time almost four years. That day, the newly promoted Captain Ashlyn Shaw entered then Admiral Tremayne's ready room for her first briefing as Marine CO onboard the *Pegasus*. Shaw had worn the same expression of disbelief and determination then that she wore now. The only difference were the scars that now marred the young woman's face and the band of white in her dark hair. Those scars, if anything, made her look more determined. Of course, she probably was. She had reason to be. Her family lived in the capital. Also, unless Tremayne missed her guess, Ashlyn was determined to prove not only to those who had so willingly thrown away her career and her freedom – as well as the careers and freedom of her people – but to herself that she was still one of the best Marines around.

Ashlyn stepped forward, Gunnery Sergeant Talbot a step behind her. She stopped before Major Santiago and braced to attention. Her right hand snapped up in a perfect parade ground salute which she held until Santiago returned it. Then, still braced at attention, she stared forward, waiting for his command.

"Stand easy, Captain," Santiago said before dismissing the gunnery sergeant. Talbot executed a perfect about face and then took up a position beside the door. "I have to admit, it's good to see you in uniform again, Captain."

"Believe me, sir, it is even better to be back in uniform." Ashlyn paused, her expression clouding. "Sir, I want to apologize for my behavior the other day–"

"No need, Ash." He waved aside her protest. "I – we-" He nodded to Tremayne – "should have done our homework better. For that you have my apology."

"And mine," Tremayne put in. There was so much more she wanted to say, but it had to wait until the current crisis was over.

"Ash." Santiago surprised both of them by reaching out and lightly touching her scarred cheek. "I wish there was time for you to adjust to everything that's happened, but there's not. Just as there's no time for your injuries to heal and your implants to be brought back online." Anger filled his voice now, an anger Tremayne shared. They'd had a few minutes to study the doctor's report before Ashlyn joined them. Those in charge of the military prison had a great deal to answer for.

"However," Santiago continued. "I have managed to get you assigned to SpecOps, at least for the time being. Until Major Pawlak gets here and carries you off to prove to the rest of the Devil Dogs here that you're really back, let's go over what we know of the situation."

Ashlyn nodded and stepped toward the plot. As she did, Santiago entered a command into the control panel and a three-dimensional display of the center of the capital appeared before them. From where she stood to Santiago's left, Tremayne watched as her former protégé studied the plot, her brow furrowing as icons lit to show the current locations of the enemy.

"Do we have any live feeds from the fighting?" Ashlyn asked, her eyes moving from one blinking icon to the next.

"We have the feeds from our troops' suit-cams," Santiago answered.

"Not enough," she muttered, moving around the plot's holo display. "This doesn't make sense, sir. I can understand why the enemy would attack the security complex. That's the nerve center for the military. It makes sense as well that they'd attack the governmental offices and the presidential palace. But why here? Isn't that a residential complex?" She pointed to the area in question.

"It is and we don't know why it has been targeted," Santiago admitted.

For a long moment, Ashlyn didn't say anything. Her lower lip caught between her teeth, she continued to study the holo display. Watching her, Tremayne had a feeling Ash was missing nothing as she looked from it to the monitors across from them that showed some of the video feeds from the various areas of fighting from around the city.

"It doesn't look like the enemy is attacking by air any longer," she commented.

"They haven't for the past hour," Tremayne answered. "Our best guess is that we managed to shoot down their birds, but we are still in a no-fly zone until we're sure. First Fleet has sent out additional patrols and Second Fleet has been ordered to move closer to the home system in case we need additional back-up."

"Do we know yet how the enemy managed to get air support through our defenses? Or how they managed to get boots on the ground here?"

"Yes and no. The long-range scans showed several unidentified ships jump in-system approximately twelve hours before the attack began. FleetCom ordered several of our cruisers to investigate. Before they could get close enough to get an ID, the ships jumped back out. We picked up nothing on scanners to show they'd done anything but jump in and then out. Still, we went to alert status and shifted Div-1 closer to the coordinates where the bogeys had been," Tremayne said. As she spoke, she expanded the area shown on the plot and high-lighted Div-1's current location. "What we didn't anticipate was that the ships might have dropped troops and in-system fighters before jumping out. That's a mistake we won't make a second time."

"As for what's happening now," Tremayne continued and once more adjusted the plot so it showed the groundside fighting. "The enemy has dug in in areas where we can't risk air strikes. There are too many civilians in the fire zone. Because of that, and because we don't know how many may be holed up in the surrounding buildings, it's going to be slow going as we retake the areas of the capital where there's been fighting. Then we'll have to make sure none of the enemy is hiding elsewhere."

Ashlyn nodded, her expression grim. "A ground fight then."

"Unfortunately." Santiago paused, his eyes focused on the plot. "Ash, we're fighting blind in a lot of ways here. Yes, we've managed to take out most, if not all, of the stingers the enemy used in their initial attack. That's the good news. The bad is that we haven't been able to get to them in order to examine the wreckage. The fighting has been too intense. So we don't know for sure who they belong to."

For a moment, Ashlyn didn't say anything and Tremayne studied her, watching as she processed the information. "Have we managed to capture any of their fighters or recover any bodies?"

"No." Santiago shook his head, his frustration clear. "To be honest, during the early stages of the battle, we were too busy trying to make sure the President and other key members of the administration didn't fall into enemy hands to worry about it. Now we're trying to retake the areas where the enemy has gone to ground but, so far, they are dug in too well."

Before anything more could be said, the door opened once again and Major Paul Pawlak, the commanding officer of the Devil Dogs, stepped inside. Like Talbot, he wore light battle armor. His graying hair was mussed and his green eyes troubled. But that disappeared the moment he saw Ashlyn standing by the plot. After giving the briefest of salutes to Santiago and Tremayne, he marched across the room and stopped before the captain. To Tremayne's surprise, he grabbed Ashlyn in a bear hug that lifted her off her feet. Then, for the first time since before her trial, Tremayne heard the younger woman laugh. She beat a playful fist against the major's armored shoulder and told him to put her down.

"Damn, Major, what will the others think?" Ashlyn grinned as her boots hit the floor.

"That I'm a wise man to know how lucky we are to finally have you back in uniform, kid," the gravel-voiced major replied. "Hope you weren't expecting to be pampered your first day back."

"Hell no, Major. I'm a Marine. We don't know pampered."

If there was a bit of bite to those words, Tremayne didn't hear it. Watching Ashlyn respond to Pawlak, she swallowed hard. This was the first natural reaction, outside of how Ash had responded when they'd been fighting to get safely away from the security complex, she had seen from the young woman since they'd brought her back from Tarsus. For a moment, Tremayne wished she had been the one to be able to elicit that sort of reaction from the younger woman. After all, she'd known Ashlyn for years, had watched her grow up. But that wasn't enough and she knew it. Like it or not, she represented those who had turned their backs on the young woman even if she hadn't been one of them. Pawlak was a Marine, a Devil Dog, and there was a special bond between them because of it. She had to accept that and be glad someone had been able to break that final barrier of self-control Ashlyn had erected over the last two years.

"That we don't," Pawlak agreed with an approving smile. "Sorry, Major, Admiral. It's just that I'm so damned glad to see Ash and have her back in uniform." He stepped back and looked the young woman over with a critical eye. "Even if the fit isn't quite what it should be." The undercurrent of anger in his voice had Ashlyn shaking her head slightly, her expression darkening.

"I know I speak for all of us when I say we understand, Major." Tremayne watched as Ashlyn straightened her shoulders, as if that alone was enough to negate any concern they might have.

"I take it you were going over the current situation," Pawlak said.

Tremayne nodded slightly. She could trust him not to push Ashlyn about what happened to her and the others, at least not yet. The time for that would come later, after they secured the capital and turned back the attack.

"We were," Santiago confirmed. "Do you have anything to report?"

"Negative, Major. I have our teams ready to move out to support the ground troops." Now Pawlak turned his attention to the plot. "I've designated this as Target Alpha." His gloved hand pointed to the presidential palace "It has one of the largest forces trying to take control of it, but it is also the most easily defendable by our side. The security force there reports that they have been able to dig in and should be able to hold out until we get reinforcements to them. At least that's the case as long as the enemy doesn't bring in more air support.

"Target Beta is the security complex and the area immediately surrounding it. There is a smaller enemy group there. That's probably because they thought the initial air strikes against it would decimate the security force stationed there. Fortunately for us, the complex did what it was supposed to – it stood up to most of the attack. So not only were we able to evac most of the civilians to secure areas but our troops have been able to hold the building.

"The third area of concern, designated Target Delta, is here." He pointed to the area Ashlyn had previously identified as a housing complex. "The enemy is dug in at the front of the building. They've been attempting to breach there but, so far at least, have been unsuccessful. My concern is that they also have a smaller force that has moved to the rear of the building. They're trying to make entry there as well but, so far, the occupants of the building have been able to hold them off."

"Your plan?" Tremayne asked. She knew the question probably should have come from Santiago but SecDef had recalled her to active duty. That made her senior officer. How easy it was to slip back into the role. Command was something she had trained hard for and had been a part of her life for decades. The only problem was this was not her kind of fight and she would do well to remember that.

For a moment, Pawlak didn't say anything. Then, when he looked away from the plot, he focused on Ashlyn instead of the others. There was something in his expression, something that spoke volumes that Tremayne hoped Ashlyn understood because she didn't. Not that there was a lot about the Marines she did understand. Why anyone would prefer fighting groundside, up close and personal to the enemy when they could be kilometers above the surface in a well-armed and armored ship was beyond her.

"Admiral, I recommend that we send three units to Target Alpha and another three to Beta. That should be enough to help the current forces on station to start the push-back. The rest of FirstDiv will drop from First Fleet just as soon as FleetCom gives the word.

"The Devil Dogs will converge on Target Delta. We'll be supported by Lt. Tsui's and Lt. Sanchez's platoons. They'll clear the surrounding buildings of any hostiles as well as protect the civilians while we deal with the main force. We'll have to move carefully to keep from tipping our hand too soon. I don't want to risk the enemy deciding their only option is to destroy the complex with the civilians inside."

Tremayne nodded, watching Shaw as she did. She'd seen the way Shaw looked quickly at Pawlak before looking away when he mentioned the Devil Dogs. By all rights, it was the battalion Shaw should be assigned to. Whether Santiago had already seen to it when he'd arranged for her to be assigned to SpecOps or not, Tremayne didn't know. Seeing the expression on Shaw's face, she hoped he had.

But, before she found out if he had or not, there was one thing Ashlyn needed to know. Tremayne just wasn't sure she wanted to be the one to tell her. Unfortunately, she also didn't have a choice, at least not in her mind.

"Ash, there's something else," she began, her voice soft, almost hesitant. Seeing the concern in Ashlyn's eyes didn't help. "Target Delta is important for another reason. A number of government officials and employees live there, as well as active duty and retired military." She paused, swallowing hard. This was so very hard, mainly because she didn't know how Shaw would respond to what she had to say. "Ash, your parents live there."

———

FOR WHAT SEEMED LIKE AN ETERNITY, all she could do was stare at Tremayne in shock. Then the admiral's words penetrated her mind and Ashlyn swallowed hard. Her parents lived in the building where so much of the fighting was focused. If her parents were there, that meant her younger sister probably was as well, maybe even her brothers. God, why was Pawlak waiting to do something? Didn't he understand how important it was to get troops there *now*?

She clinched her fists, ignoring the pain as her fingernails bit into her skin. She knew better than to let her emotions take control. If she'd learned nothing else at the penal colony, she'd learned that. She had to think. There had to be a reason why Pawlak hadn't dropped his troops yet. But what?

What could be more important that protecting that building?

"Ash." Pawlak's voice seemed to come from a million miles away. Then she felt his gloved hand touch her arm and she forced herself to look at him, to see the understanding reflected in his dark brown eyes. "Ash, the Devil Dogs will move out just as soon as we join them. But you need to get into your battle gear first."

"M-my battle gear?"

God, her brain didn't seem to want to work. Not that it surprised her. She'd been more than halfway convinced she was living some sort of sick dream for the last week. She expected to wake up and find herself back in her cell on Tarsus. But the last few hours had been all too real, even if they too had been a different kind of nightmare. Maybe she'd finally reached her breaking point. Had so much happened that she could no longer think or understand?

"Ash, look at me. I need to know if you can do this," Pawlak continued. "No one will hold it against you if you can't." Now he held up a hand to ward off the protests she wanted to make but couldn't figure out how to. "Ashlyn, you've been through hell the last two years. This last week has seen that hell, the only world you've known for too long, turned upside down. You've been asked to trust a system that betrayed you. Then you were thrust into a battle zone without warning. I know I couldn't process it all and certainly not as well and as quickly as you seem to have. So, if you need time, you have it. You can stay here and advise Admiral Tremayne and Major Santiago. But, if you are up to, I'd be honored to have you at my side as the Devil Dogs make sure those bastards don't get control of that complex."

She drew a deep breath and then exhaled. She had to do this. She just had to.

"Then I guess you'd better tell me where my gear is, Major." She didn't sound as calm as she'd have liked, but it was better than grabbing him by the shoulders and shaking him out of pique.

"Wait a minute," Santiago began unsurely.

Ashlyn spun toward him, her expression darkening. "Major, I'd hate to be brought up on charges of insubordination and failure to obey an order on the same day I finally received my pardon, but I will risk it if you try to keep me here." She stepped away from the plot, both to put some distance between them and to give herself a moment to think. "Sir, that's my family out there. Family I haven't seen since my trial because the commandant wouldn't let me have visitors. Hell, sir, you know he wouldn't even let me have communication of any sort with them or anyone else. Now that I'm this close, there's no way I can just stay here and wait for word if they're safe or not. I can't. Please understand."

For a moment, he didn't say anything. When he looked to Tremayne, she simply shrugged and nodded. Seeing it, Ashlyn relaxed some. At least her mentor understood. She might not approve – hell, there was no way Tremayne approved. Ash could see the worry reflected in her eyes. But Tremayne knew her well enough to know better than to argue. Hopefully, Santiago did as well.

"All right. Major Pawlak, I don't need to remind you that we need Captain Shaw alive and well." Now it was Santiago's turn to shake his head so she wouldn't interrupt. "Like it or not, Ash, but you are a symbol. Not only to the Marines but to everyone. So don't do anything foolish. Please."

"Yes, sir." She meant it. After so long wondering if it might not be easier to just kill herself and stopping only because she wouldn't be able to help her people if she were dead, she had no desire to die now. Tremayne had been right when she'd talked about what it would do to those who'd been so quick to betray her to see her back in uniform and taking the fight to the enemy. Besides, there were a few people she planned to have a *discussion* with when the fight was finally done.

"Don't worry, Major. I'm sure Ash understands that if she is suddenly possessed by the urge to do something foolish, I'll stun her myself and throw her on the first transport back here." The look Pawlak gave Shaw spoke volumes. No one present doubted he'd do exactly what he said. "Gunny, I believe you know where to go to get the captain outfitted. Once you have, we'll head out. I'll get the other units on their way while you do."

"Aye, Major." Talbot shot Shaw a quick grin and then braced to attention. "Ma'am?"

Shaw took one last look at the plot display and then turned to leave. One thing at a time. Get outfitted for the assault on the residential complex. Then do whatever it took to make sure her family was safe. After that, she could worry about what her next move should be.

6

Half an hour later, Ashlyn stood beside Major Pawlak in a makeshift command center approximately one kilometer from Target Delta. The six-story building usually housed a variety of shops and restaurants. Within minutes of the first explosion, the Marines moved in. They'd evacuated employees and customers to a safer location. Then they set up the FOB. The fact the building lay barely more than a kilometer from them Devil Dog's target made it the perfect location for one last briefing.

Ashlyn did her best to ignore the sounds of fighting just down the street. Those sounds brought back memories of her last mission, memories she couldn't allow to distract her. Worse, they reminded her that she didn't know if her parents were in the building or somewhere else. Instead of dwelling on what she didn't know, she forced herself to focus on the portable plot that displayed the target area. For several long moments, she studied the different approaches. Then she looked from the plot to the plans displayed on her datapad and back, a frown playing at the corners of her mouth.

"This doesn't make sense, sir. They're focusing their efforts on the front of the building. That puts their forces in a pincer if we manage to get troops into the building across from them. They have sent a smaller squad to the rear of the building, but is it to simply prevent anyone from escaping or are they going to try to make entry there? If it's the latter, why? The front of the building is must less secure. Either way, it doesn't look like they are doing much more than digging in. Do we have any idea as to why?"

Pawlak chuckled almost evilly before answering. "Seems the folks inside figured the enemy might try to come in that way and set up defensive positions. They've managed to hold the bastards off with what look to be nothing more than hunting rifles, small arms and homemade boomers. For now, at least, it appears that the enemy is satisfied with just making sure no one tries to come out that way."

Ashlyn nodded and entered a quick command into her datapad. A moment later, the list of tenants for the complex began to scroll across the small screen. Another command and things began to make more sense, at least in one way. Whether by intention or not, the enemy had chosen to attack a building with a higher than average number of military-trained occupants. At least one quarter of those living there were either active duty or retired military. A number of them had been career military. It wouldn't surprise Ash one bit if those retirees, not to mention those still on active duty, had at least light armor and service weapons on hand. It was no wonder the enemy had been unable to make easy entry.

But would an enemy organized well enough to quick hop into the system and off-load troops and stingers make such a serious mistake? Or was there someone or something in the building worth the risk? If so, who? Or what?

"Sir, nothing about this feels right. Either this whole thing has been an exercise to see how we react or it's some sort of botched snatch and grab. If it's the latter, then something went wrong and now they're trying to mask their original target so they can try again later. If it's the former, FleetCom has a very tough job ahead of it."

Either that or these were the most inexperienced, ineffective soldiers she'd ever seen. Unfortunately, that didn't make them any less deadly. Quite the contrary, in fact. It made them unpredictable and that made them harder to anticipate and defend against.

"Talk it out, Ash. Let's see if we're on the same page," Pawlak said.

"While they haven't withdrawn their ground troops from the security and government complexes or the presidential palace after their air support was neutralized, they haven't really pressed their cause in any of those locations either. They have dug in. It's as if they are either waiting for reinforcements or orders to withdraw. Hell, sir, for all we know, they are waiting for us to kill them. They sure don't have a way off-planet now.

"And let's face it, despite the fact they took us completely by surprise and have used a variety of attack methods, they haven't been very effective. None of the buildings have been taken. Yes, there have been casualties and even deaths, not to mention the property damage they've caused, but it's nothing like what either of us have seen in battle before.

"But there's more to it. Attacking the residential complex doesn't make sense. It doesn't follow what we – well, what I – know of Callusian tactics." God, those two years in prison meant her knowledge of the enemy's tactics were out of date. "When they attacked our outposts and allies during the war, they focused first on government and military targets. Take out the leadership and the ability to defend the planet. Then they moved in against soft targets. Has that changed?" She tried to keep the anger and bitterness out of her voice, but it was hard.

"No. Not that they've done many direct attacks since the *truce*." Pawlak spat out the word. Obviously, he felt about the so-called truce the same way Tremayne and Santiago did. "Most of their tactics have been masked as pirate attacks on commerce and remote trading posts."

"Then this really doesn't fit." She closed her eyes and thought for a moment. "If I didn't know better – and I don't – it's almost as if they came with specific targets in mind. Targets that are either human, tech or code. Targets worth risking a direct attack on the capital. More than that, whatever it is they're after, they can't risk destroying it. Otherwise, they'd be more aggressive in getting into their target building or buildings."

"Agreed."

Once more she studied the tenant list for the residential complex. So many of the names were familiar and any of them could be a target. How were they supposed to narrow it down? And what if they were wrong?

What if her parents were there instead of at their house outside of the capital?

"Sir, would you happen to know my mother's current assignment?"

That would tell her a lot. Growing up, she'd learned quickly that they stayed at the house whenever her mother was on leave or when she was stationed off-planet. But if she had a duty station in the capital, they stayed in town. After she and her siblings were grown and out of the house, their parents sold the townhouse they'd owned and settled on the first of several apartments in town.

When Pawlak didn't reply right away, Ashlyn looked at him in concern. His expression was enough to tell her she wasn't going to like what he had to say.

"Ash, I'm sorry. I thought you knew." He ran a hand over his face. "Ash, your mother's been beached since shortly after your court-martial."

For a moment Ashlyn stared at the man. Surely she'd misunderstood. Then, seeing the truth reflected in his eyes, her lips pulled back in an almost feral sneer as anger, cold and hard, filled her. Wasn't it bad enough they'd tried to ruin her and her unit? Hell, they had almost killed them all. Those they hadn't, they'd sent to Tarsus and all to cover the corruption and ineptitude of a couple of political appointees and a few officers who never should have made it out of the Academy.

"Who?" she ground out. Forgotten was the battle going on around them. Now she was simply a daughter wanting to avenge the wrong done her mother and who knew how many others. "Who, damn it?"

"No one who is still in the Corps, our chain of command, or even in the military," Pawlak said softly. "And no one who won't feel the full force of our vengeance once we are done here and we have the rest of our people home from Tarsus. You have my word on that."

She believed him, or at least she wanted to. In all the years she had known him, Pawlak had never broken his word to her or lied to her. If he told her he'd do something, he did it. She had to be satisfied, for the moment at least, with his assurance that the wrongs done to her mother and others would be atoned for. She could trust him on that. Couldn't she?

Breathing deeply, she fought for control. She couldn't let her anger take away her focus. Not when enemy troops were just down the block. That not only could but would be disastrous. And that brought her back to the question of why they seemed so interested in the residential complex. There had to be someone in it they wanted. Someone or something. But who? Or what?

Or she could be completely wrong. Two years ago, she never would have doubted her instincts. But that was before she'd been betrayed and before so many of her unit had been killed. She'd been on her own, not in a combat situation since then. Did she – did Pawlak – dare risk even considering her concerns?

"Let it go for now, Ash. I promise those responsible will pay," Pawlak said softly. "But right now we have more immediate concerns and, as you said earlier, all this could be a feint to see how we respond and how long it takes us to do so."

"A feint or a decoy."

She looked again at her datapad. Nothing in the reports coming in from across the system seemed to indicate another attack was about to take place. Fortunately.

Of course, looking at the datapad reminded her of yet another major disadvantage she operated under. When she'd been brought up on charges, her combat implants had been taken off-line. That meant she was no different from those civilians holding out against the enemy. There'd be no medical implants to control pain or enhance muscles and reaction times. No ocular implants to aid in sighting on the enemy. No communication or HUD implants to have instant access to data coming in real time. It was a handicap, but one soldiers had lived with for centuries before the implants had been invented. She would do her duty with or without them.

Hopefully.

"I know, but we can't worry about that right now." Pawlak paused and listened to the latest report from Captain Wilkinson. Wilkinson and his company were in place and ready to reinforce the troops at the security complex. Pawlak told him to stand ready. As soon as the Devil Dogs were at Target Delta, he'd give the word. "Your recommendations?"

"I'd take a small squad to the back, pick off the enemy stationed there before they can give the alert to their cohorts out front. Then that exit can be used to evacuate the civilians. Lieutenant Tsui's people could oversee the evacuation while the DD's clear the building of hostiles before making their way to strategic points near the front of the building to support the rest of our people as they commence the frontal assault."

"Agreed." Now Pawlak smiled. "Pick yourself six members of the DDs to accompany you, Captain. I figure you've more than earned the right to lead the infiltration team."

For a moment, all Ashlyn could do was stare at the major. Doubt warred with relief. She wanted to lead the smaller party, knowing it was the one way she could be sure everything possible was being done to not only save her family but also the others who lived in that building. But there was that confidence-shredding doubt, reminding her that she'd been on the sidelines for more than two years. Did she still have what it took to lead this sort of a mission?

More importantly, would any of the Devil Dogs follow her orders after everything that happened?

"Sir–"

"Ash, you can do this. All I want is your word that you won't do something foolish like get yourself killed. Admiral Tremayne would have my hide and that doesn't scare me nearly as much as what the Marines would do to me if anything else happened to you."

"He's right, ma'am," Talbot put in. "With the major's permission, I'd like to join you."

"Thanks, Gunny." Now she smiled slightly. She'd feel better with Talbot at her side. "Major, I'll leave the assignments to you. You know your team." She closed her eyes for a brief moment and forced down the pain. There had been a time when she'd known every Devil Dog. Maybe she would again, but she didn't dare let herself hope – not yet at least.

"I know my team well enough to know they'd all jump at a chance to follow you on this mission, Ash." He grinned. "I'm sure the gunny can help you if you want. But be quick about it. I want you in place ASAP."

"Understood, sir."

Less than ten minutes later, Ashlyn held up her right fist, signaling for the others to come to a halt. Crouching, she peered around the corner of the building, checking first the streets and then the area ahead. They were less than two hundred meters from Target Delta. But it was a long two hundred meters with little cover. So they had to move carefully to avoid tipping off the enemy.

"Suggestions?" she asked Talbot as they crept back from the corner.

"Put Sievers up high. He can take out anyone who happens to look our way."

"Sievers?" As she looked at the sniper, she wished she knew him. The other members of her squad were men and women she'd served with before. But Sievers was new to the Devil Dogs. Both the major and Talbot had assured her he was one of the best, but he was still an unknown.

The man inched forward and scanned the area. Then he moved to stand with Ashlyn and Talbot. Scratching his chin, he thought for a moment before speaking. "Cap'n, I reckon I could find myself a perch and keep an eye on things, make sure none of them bastards gets a bead on you or the others."

"Do it. Comm me just as soon as you're in position." She didn't like not knowing exactly what he had in mind but she reminded herself he was a member of one of the most elite units in the Corps. Pawlak's Devil Dogs had made a name for themselves during the first war and almost any Marine who tried out for Special Forces wanted to be a member. That had to count for something where Sievers was concerned.

"Once Sievers is in place, we move. We go in fast and hard. Don't give the enemy a chance to contact their companions at the front of the building. I'd like at least one of them to stay alive long enough for us to question him, but don't risk yourselves or the civilians to do so. Understood?" She looked at the rest of the squad and waited as they each nodded in return.

"Understood, Cap," Talbot said for the rest of them. "What about entry into the building?"

"Let's hope the civilians really are monitoring the back door and let us in. Otherwise, Dumont, you'll have to work your magic."

"Aye, Cap," the small demolitions expert replied. "Just give the word."

She nodded and turned her attention back to their target. The residential complex was new, at least new to her. The briefing information Pawlak had downloaded to her datapad confirmed that the complex had opened to tenants and select merchants less than a year before. That worked in their favor because it meant they had accurate plans for each floor. Even more important, at least to Ashlyn's mind, was the fact that the complex had been built with the realities of war in mind. The structure was reinforced to withstand anything short of a direct hit from heavy ordinance. It was obvious the attackers hadn't taken all that into consideration.

"Cap'n, I'm in place," Sievers reported over her earbud.

"Stand ready." She turned her attention to Talbot. "Gunny, let's move."

Talbot nodded and motioned to their point man. Sergeant Yancy Puckett shouldered his rifle and crept forward. At the corner of the building he paused. Ashlyn watched as his gaze raked the area between their position and the target. Then he gave a nod and started off, moving quickly and silently despite his battle armor.

Ashlyn waited as Puckett's partner followed close on his heels. They moved almost as one, betraying not only the fact they'd trained long and hard together but that they'd also seen more than their fair share of battles together. There was something about having to rely on your partner to make sure you both returned safely at the end of a mission that no amount of training could teach.

When the two were ten meters away, Ashlyn looked at the gunny and nodded. Talbot nodded in return and signaled for the rest of the squad to move out. Without waiting for the gunny, Ashlyn shouldered her assault rifle and started off. She moved quickly and as quietly as possible across the open area. Her eyes were locked on the assault vehicle parked less than ten meters from the rear entrance to the building. Their readings indicated at least half a dozen enemy were in place around the armored vehicle. She guessed at least one more was inside, monitoring communications. That meant they had to deal with the vehicle quickly, before whomever was inside managed to warn his companions or those attempting to breach the front of the building.

A single shot rang out from above and behind the half dozen armored Marines racing toward the residential complex. Ashlyn stopped for a split-second, her eyes sweeping first her people and then the enemy ahead. One corner of her mouth lifted slightly to see a light armored enemy trooper topple over ahead of her. Sievers was definitely as good as the gunny had said.

"Move!" she yelled as another head popped up from behind cover only to explode in a splash of red and gray as Sievers picked him off.

Idiots. You don't come to a fight and not wear full armor.

"Take out that armored vehicle!" She watched as two of the squad peeled off. The lead man laid down suppressing fire for his partner as she zeroed in on the vehicle. The corporal shouldered her grenade launcher and fired. The sounds of the explosion filled the air and echoed off the surrounding buildings. If the poor sods inside the vehicle cried out before they died, no one heard.

Serves 'em right. They should have kept better watch. Then they might not have been caught in that death trap.

As if suddenly alerted by the explosion that their position was compromised, the enemy turned away from the housing complex and began firing at the approaching Marines. The first two went down quickly, easy targets for Sievers and his sniper rifle. Another screamed in agony as Talbot swung his assault rifle in his direction and opened fire. Three more died quickly as the Marines continued moving forward, carefully choosing their shots.

Ashlyn held up a fist to stop her squad as the last enemy fighter dropped his rifle and started running away from them. Sievers' voice came over her earbud, asking if she wanted him to take the coward down.

"No. He's mine."

She snugged her rifle against her shoulder and took aim at the retreating figure. The scope zeroed in on the target. Slowing her breath, she focused. Damn, what she'd give for her ocular implant to be online. For that matter, she'd really like to have been able to put in some target practice over the last two plus years. She hated relying on just the scope and her very rusty skills. But she had to do this. She had to be careful and hopefully she'd get lucky and they'd take him alive.

Her finger tightened on the trigger. There was a slight kick as she fired. She continued to watch through her scope. The fleeing soldier – if he really was a soldier and she was beginning to question whether the attackers were soldiers or mercenaries or even some-thing else – staggered, his arms flailing. Then, as if in slow motion, he took two more stumbling steps before falling face first to the pave-ment. A slight smile touched Ashlyn's lips as she lowered her rifle. The shot might not have been as good as she would have liked and it had taken her longer than it should have to get the aim, but she'd done it without her implants.

Not bad for her first shot in more than two years and with an unfamiliar weapon.

Before she could say anything, Talbot dispatched two of the squad to retrieve the fallen man. Then he signaled for the rest of them to get under cover. There was no guarantee more of the enemy might not come around the corner at any moment to try to re-secure the position.

Ashlyn knelt behind the remains of the armored vehicle and watched, her rifle at the ready, as the two Marines dragged the wounded man forward. As she did, she commed for a corpsman to join them. Then she keyed in the code for Pawlak.

"Major, we're in position. I'm keeping Sievers up top to cover us," she reported. "No casualties and we have one prisoner. Shot while trying to flee." She glanced at Corporal Dumont who was kneeling next to the wounded man. The demolitions expert nodded, his mouth grim. "He should be able to answer questions if we get a medic here to patch him up so he doesn't bleed out."

"Lt. Tredennick is on her way to you now, Captain," Pawlak said. "Can you make entry into the building?"

Before she could answer, the rear door slid open. The Marines moved as one in that direction, their weapons coming to bear. As far as they knew, the building hadn't been breached but they weren't taking any chances. Then, even before the door was open all the way, a white piece of cloth was shoved through. That ancient signal of truce might or might not be a trap. Since they had yet to see who had thrown it, Ashlyn wasn't about to risk any of her squad.

But that didn't mean she wasn't above risking herself.

"Major, we have movement from inside. Someone just tossed out the proverbial white flag," she reported.

"One of our people?"

"I don't know, sir. I'll report as soon as we have an answer for you."

With that, she stood and stepped out from behind the wrecked armored vehicle sliding her assault rifle into its scabbard over her right shoulder. As she did, her left hand rested on the butt of the pistol at her left thigh. If it was a civilian trying to let them know it was safe to come in, she didn't want to spook him into doing something foolish. But, if it was a trap, she wanted to be able to act before anyone got a lucky shot off at her.

"Step out so we can see you!" she called, motioning Talbot back when he started in her direction. "Gunny," she said over the secure channel. "Stay there and keep me covered."

"Captain, damn it, get back here!"

"Gunny, I'm the weak point in the team and you know it. I'm more than two years out of practice and my implants are offline. So cover my ass and make sure no one gets a lucky shot off at me." She keyed off the comm and turned her attention back to the door. Then she frowned when no one appeared.

Damn it.

"Sievers, can you see anything?" she commed.

"That's a negative, Cap," the sniper replied.

"Tran, Dumont, go!"

She motioned the two forward and ducked back behind what was left of the armored vehicle. As she did, she nodded slightly to see the promised medic kneeling beside the wounded prisoner. With the medic was a member of Tsui's unit. The burly Marine touched his battle helmet with his right hand in what could almost be called a salute – something that would most definitely be a breach of regulations. You never, ever do anything on a battlefield to single out for the enemy who your commanders are.

"Corporal Gould, ma'am," he said. "I'll keep an eye on the LT and prisoner."

"Good." She nodded. "Dumont?" she commed.

"All clear, Cap."

Ashlyn moved carefully out from behind the wreckage, Talbot on her heels. As she moved toward the door, the rest of the squad ranged around them. No one was taking any chances.

Good. That was good. She didn't want to lose anyone now.

"Major," she began as she once again opened a comm channel to him. "We are about to make entry."

"Leave the channel open, Captain. We'll hold position out front until you have secured the building and have started the evac."

———

"WHAT THE HELL WAS THAT?"

He raced to the window looking down on the area behind the complex. Plastering himself against the wall, he carefully peeked out. Smoke rose from below. The sound of gunfire, faint but there, reached him. As it did, his mouth drew tight. That had been their first warning something was happening and they'd almost missed it because it had been muted by the almost perfect soundproofing of the building. The same damned soundproofing that had almost cost them everything by not letting them know earlier they were the target of an attack.

Now he watched in disbelief as a squad of Marines moved forward, their assault rifles making short work of the attackers. A bittersweet smile touched his lips as he recognized the unit markings on the battle armor of the nearest Marines. The Devil Dogs. Well, if anyone could get through the attackers and help evacuate the occupants of the complex to safety, it was the DDs. But they weren't the same DDs he'd known.

Hell, it wasn't the same military he'd known although, thanks to the last election and some changes at the top, it would be again.

He hoped.

But he didn't have time to worry about that now. He had more than a hundred people – men, women and children – to keep safe. At least there was a large number of both former and active duty military, as well as military dependents, living in the complex. It was amazing how many of them had, at a minimum, either their old service weapons, hunting or sports weapons. Others, like he and his wife, had what could only be termed a small arsenal at hand. It hadn't taken them long to get everyone armed and into position to hold the building until help came.

Fortunately, the attackers hadn't been very good at their jobs. All it would have taken was a carefully placed blast to the rear doors to get in. The front, with all its crystalcrete, might hold against small arms fire but a direct hit from a grenade launcher or something similar would breach the building. That was why he'd stationed snipers on the upper floors. Between them and the firebombs some of the others had made, they'd managed to keep the enemy from moving in too close.

But why had the enemy targeted their building and why hadn't they made a more concentrated effort to make entry? It didn't make any sense.

"Abe, what now?"

He turned and smiled slightly at the brunette who was now plastered to the other side of the window frame. She wore the light armor of a Marine and her assault rifle was slung across her back. She had secured a long bladed knife to her right calf and past experience taught him she had at least two more secreted on her person somewhere. Then there were the two pistols, one at each thigh. No one looking at her would mistake her for anything but a well-trained Marine, ready for anything the enemy might throw at them. There might be a few more wrinkles on her face and some gray in her hair, but it was hard to realize they'd been together for more than thirty years. First, they'd been partners on the battlefield. Now they shared their lives. How easy it had been for them to fall back into old habits when the first shots rang out more than three hours earlier.

Thank God.

And thank God she hadn't left her armor and weapons behind when they came to the capital more than a week ago. She might not be on active duty, but she still insisted on carrying her gear with her wherever they went "just in case".

There had been a time when he would have done the same. But that had changed more than fifteen years ago. By then, their four children needed at least one parent home, or so he and his wife believed. Fuercon had been at war and neither of them wanted to risk leaving their children orphaned. He knew his wife's career potential outweighed his own. He had left active duty, exchanging his battle rifle for stock quotes and investment prospectuses.

"It looks like we're about to get reinforcements." He nodded out the window to the squad of Marines. "Have Herve open the back door. Tell him to toss out a white flag. Then he's to fallback to the secondary position. I don't think this is a trap, but let's not get careless now."

"All right." She glanced out the window, her expression troubled. "I'll go down and make sure everything's okay. If it is the Marines, I'll bring the CO up and we can figure out how best to get our people out."

He didn't like it, not one bit. If she went downstairs, she'd be closer to the enemy and that meant closer to danger. Then he shook his head, memory of other times he'd felt this way coming to mind. They had been younger and still in uniform. She'd been headstrong then. But she'd also been smart enough not to put herself in danger's way without a damned good reason. He had to trust her now as he had then.

Besides, she'd be able to handle just about anything that might happen. Two years beached had done little to take the edge off of her abilities as a marksman or tactician. She might not have a duty assignment at the moment, but she had kept her abilities honed as she waited for the day she'd once more be called up for active duty.

"Do it." He ducked under the window and moved to her side. "Just be careful, Liz."

She nodded, gave him a quick hug and then turned, pulling her rifle from the scabbard slung across her back. The years and the four children she'd born hadn't robbed her of her ability to move quickly, gracefully and silently. He had to believe it hadn't robbed her of her ability to stay alive.

He sighed heavily and then moved away from the window, activating his comm-link. "What's the status out front?"

"We've got movement behind the enemy, Abe. It looks like friendlies, but we're holding station until we're sure."

"Excellent, Marc. We are doing the same at the rear." He raced through the apartment and into the hall. He wanted to see for himself. The door across the hall stood open and he moved quickly into the apartment that was a mirror to his own. "Keep an eye out for any reaction from the attacking force. If we do finally have reinforcements on-site, the enemy may decide they have nothing to lose."

"Understood."

"Keep me informed."

———

"CAPTAIN, YOU WILL STAY BEHIND ME," Talbot said seriously as they neared the doorway.

"Gunny," she growled.

"I mean it, Captain." He looked down at her. His expression, what she could see of it through the visor of his battle helmet, was serious. "Ma'am, please. You heard Major Santiago. We need you. Besides, Major Pawlak will skin me alive if anything happens to you on my watch. Then I'd have to face Admiral Tremayne. Believe me, they scare me more than you do."

"Only because you don't know me, Gunny." She held up a hand to prevent him from interrupting. "I'm not the same officer you served with, Talbot. But I'll try not to get you in trouble. However, you'd best remember that I am in command of this squad and you will do what I say. If I give you an order, your only response is 'yes, ma'am'. I'm not going to risk a repeat of what happened on Arterus. Is that understood?"

God, she'd order a full retreat before allowing that to happen again. Too many of her people died needlessly on that last mission. Then, when she ordered the survivors to withdraw while she lay down cover fire, they'd refused. They would all retreat or no one would.

"Yes, ma'am. However, you need to remember that you are our CO. That means we're tasked with keeping you safe even as we carry out our orders."

Ashlyn drew a deep breath and then exhaled. They could stand here and argue for the next hour and she'd never get Talbot to back down. She'd seen him like this before – on more than one occasion. So she knew he had a stubborn streak a kilometer wide. Besides, she had no doubt Pawlak was on a secure com-channel even as they spoke, telling the gunny to make sure she didn't do anything foolish. Well, she could play nice – for the moment.

"All right, Gunny."

He looked at her for a moment and she knew he was trying to decide if she meant it or not. Then he shook his head and stepped in front of her. As he did, two members of the squad took up positions behind them, their weapons at the ready. Talbot nodded to the point men and they began moving slowly toward the rear entrance of the building.

Ashlyn raised her right fist and her squad halted. Dropping to her right knee, assault rifle snugged against her shoulder, she focused on the door. The security panel to the right of the doorway showed signs of tampering. Perhaps the attackers had tried to bypass security to make entry. Obviously, they'd failed. Just as obvious, at least to Ash, was the fact that Callusian-trained troops wouldn't have worried about bypassing security unless they were trying for a silent entry. That begged the question of why, when they hadn't taken precautions not to be seen from the building, they would want to try for a silent entry. Had the plan been for the enemy troopers at the front of the building to make enough of a distraction that they could enter, grab their target was and leave before being discovered? If so, they'd failed and they were now extremely dead – the usual result of stupidity on the battlefield.

Ashlyn motioned the point men forward. Sweat pricked out on her forehead and she fought the urge to remove her helmet to wipe her brow. But seeing how Sievers had made quick work of the attackers, easier because of their carelessness in not being fully armored, she decided not to repeat their stupidity. Instead, she concentrated on keeping her breathing even, her attention focused on the doorway.

Most of all, she did her best not to compare this mission with that last disastrous one on Arterus. But it was so hard. Then, like now, they'd been fighting in the middle of a city. They'd been tasked with taking out the enemy without causing unreasonable collateral damage. At least this time they didn't seem to be up against an enemy willing to kill hundreds, even thousands, of innocents.

Swallowing hard, Ashlyn fought against the demons of her past. It didn't help that the squad was exposed, easy targets if the enemy decided to start fighting smart. But these were some of the best of the Devil Dogs. They'd keep a sharp watch out for enemy movement. She knew it. All she had to do was trust them.

When the door slid open a few moments later, she tensed. Her finger twitched toward the trigger guard. Then Marino and Dumont appeared, Marino signaling for the rest of the squad to move forward.

"Report," Talbot said.

"Open area just beyond the door. There's a second door at the northwest corner which leads into a corridor. The corridor, according to our schematics, leads to the elevator banks, stairs and then on to the front of the building. It's not a straight shot. There's a ninety-degree turn about ten meters past the door. The building occupants have set up a series of barricades," Marino reported.

"Did you make contact?"

"No, Cap. We figured it might be best for you or the gunny to assess the situation first." This from Dumont.

"Reason?" Ashlyn asked.

"Ma'am, the way we see it, we've got ourselves some very nervous civilians around that corner. They're going to react better to rank than to us, even if some of them are former military."

"All right." As she spoke, she could almost feel the gunnery sergeant fidgeting at her side. He'd know Dumont was right, but he wouldn't like it. He wouldn't like it because, knowing his captain, he'd know she meant to be the one to make first contact with the civilians. Well, too bad. It was her job to do just that.

She reached up and removed her helmet. Before Talbot could protest, Marino took it from her. Ashlyn nodded in appreciation, glad to be rid of it. She'd never admit to any of them just how much it had shaken her when she'd first secured the helmet in place. Something that had once been such a normal part of her life now reminded her too much of all those times she'd been hooded by the guards on Tarsus before being taken to the commandant for her latest *lesson*. There'd been a moment of panic, of memories best forgotten, before she'd gotten herself under control. Hopefully, it would get better. It had to get better. But, for now, she was glad to be rid of the helmet.

"Gunny, I trust you to have my back," she said softly before approaching the door.

"Your back and I'll have your head if you do anything foolish, Cap," he replied just as softly.

A smile touched her lips, not that she'd let him see it. Then she nodded to Dumont and waited as the door slid open. With a deep breath, she stepped inside, wondering what she'd find when she rounded the corner ahead.

7

"Someone's coming."

The comment, given in what could best be described as a stage whisper, was unnecessary. She'd been monitoring the vid-feed from the rear entrance since her arrival at the makeshift barricade almost five minutes earlier. Part of her had been surprised the Marines – if that's what they really were – hadn't already made entry. But another part of her, the Marine in her, knew that was a good sign. It meant they were well-trained and even better disciplined than the attackers. It also meant the squad probably was what it appeared – Marines – and not poor copies meant to trick the defenders into lowering their guard.

Not that she was going to let any of the five men and women manning the barricade with her do that. Instead, she opened her comm-link, knowing her husband was listening in, ready to send reinforcements if necessary. Then she lifted her rifle into position. She held it ready, her grip firm but loose enough to let her adjust her aim as needed. If these really were Marines, they wouldn't come waltzing around the corner. Unless, of course, they were as stupid as the attackers had proven to be. If they were, well, they weren't Marines. At least not *their* Marines.

If they weren't *their* Marines . . . Well, she'd make sure they quickly learned how foolish they'd been to attack the complex. If the current Marine commandant didn't approve, to hell with her. Elizabeth wasn't going to let her people, her friends and neighbors, down.

"Stand ready but do not – I repeat, do *not* – fire unless I give the order," she said softly, glancing at each of her companions to be sure they understood.

"Liz?" Abe's voice, as it came through her earbud, sounded worried and she frowned. He knew better than to distract her. She needed her full attention on the corridor ahead of the barricade.

"Not now, Abe," she snapped. "I'll leave the link open so you can listen in."

She pictured him grinding his teeth in frustration. She'd make it up to him later. But this wasn't the time for spousal concern. Not when so much could go wrong if they weren't careful. Hell, it could go wrong even if they were careful and they both knew it.

The seconds stretched out at an agonizingly slow pace. It had been years, too many years, since she'd had to man such a post. Doing it with nothing more than an assault rifle, her combat knives, two pistols and five men and women she'd never fought with before and who were armed with hunting rifles or old service weapons didn't help. Nor did the knowledge of what would happen if the approaching squad was the enemy. She'd had friends die before. She'd held them in her arms as it happened. But that had been before she'd been promoted out of the field. Those men and women had been brothers-in-arms, not her neighbors, many of whom had never seen combat.

"Stand ready," she said as the vid-feed showed the Marines in their battle armor nearing the corner. A few more steps and they'd be visible from the barricade.

Her heart beat faster and she drew a deep breath, willing herself to stay calm. It would soon be over, whatever "it" was. All she could do was wait.

ASHLYN SIGNALED for the squad to come to a halt. Less than two meters ahead was the bend in the corridor. Just beyond that lay the barricade. She hoped the residents manning it were former military. That gave the squad at least a chance of making it around the corner before one of the civilians did something exceptionally stupid like open fire on them.

Talbot stopped next to her and slid his rifle into the scabbard on his back. "May I make a suggestion, ma'am?" he asked softly.

"Of course."

"Let me announce our presence. Once I have, I'll advance with Dumont. As soon as we're sure no one is going to do anything foolish, you can join us."

Ashlyn shook her head. She'd been waiting to see how the gunny would try to keep her from being the first to make entry. As they'd slowly progressed to this point in the building, she'd felt his frustration growing. He no more approved of her being at the head of the squad now, when they were fairly sure there was no danger, than he did of her being the first to show herself to those behind the barricade.

"You can call out, Gunny, but I'll be the first to appear. Dumont was right about that. They need to see an officer." She held up a hand to cut off his protest. "You'll be right there with me, watching my back. But I need to do this." For more reasons than she would ever admit.

She waited, watching closely as he processed what she said. He didn't like it. She didn't need to see his expression turn thunderous to know that. But he also seemed to understand. He nodded once and then turned to the rest of the squad.

"You heard the captain. The two of us take point. Marino, Puckett, you'll be right behind us. The rest of you after them. Let's do this by the numbers. Marino, you have one duty. If this goes south on us, you are to get the captain out of here and to safety. If anything happens to her, you will answer first to me, then to Major Pawlak, then to Admiral Tremayne and then to the rest of the Devil Dogs." Now it was his turn to hold up a hand to keep Ashlyn from speaking. "Captain, you know I'm right."

She tried to stare him down and lost. Damn it, he was right, but she didn't have to like it. Instead of speaking, she nodded and reached up to remove the helmet she'd put back on once inside the building.

"Captain!"

"They need to see us, Gunny, *us* and not just the armor. Quit acting like my nanny and think. You know I'm right."

"I swear to God, ma'am, if you get yourself killed, I will find a way to resurrect you just so I can kill you myself."

It wouldn't surprise her if he managed to do just that. So she'd have to make sure she didn't get herself killed.

Besides, she still had a few things she needed to do before Death finally found her. There were some people who needed to pay for what had happened to her and her command back on Arterus.

"Then let's do this. Stow your helmets but keep your weapons ready." As the others complied, she moved closer to the bend in the corridor, Talbot on her heels. "All right, Gunny. Let them know we're here."

"Attention at the barricade. This is Gunnery Sergeant Kevin Talbot, First Marine Division, Devil Dogs. Stow your weapons. I repeat. Stow your weapons. We're moving forward."

Ashlyn waited long enough to hope the civilians heeded what the gunny said. Then she nodded. With Talbot all but glued to her and radiating his displeasure, she moved forward. One step at a time. That's all it took. Let the civilians see they were who they claimed and then she could figure out how to get everyone to safety.

Still, as she neared the corner, she drew a deep breath. Her fingers itched to pull the pistol at her right thigh. She knew how dangerous her actions were. All it would take was one overly nervous civilian pulling the trigger and either she or Talbot could pay the ultimate price. The problem was she didn't see any other way. These might be some of those residents who were ex-military. But she couldn't count on it. That meant they had to see for themselves that the squad was friendly, not part of those who'd been trying to kill them.

"We're coming out!" she called.

————

ELIZABETH SHAW'S head snapped up and her eyes went wide. No! It couldn't be. Damn it, this was a trick after all. There was no way, absolutely no way, the person she'd heard could be there. Lips pulling back in a snarl, she signaled for her companions to stand ready. She'd damn well show those bastards that they'd screwed with the wrong woman.

The sound of a step focused her attention on the corner. Her rifle snugged against her shoulder. Her finger rested next to the trigger, she waited. If this was a trick . . . .

It had to be a trick. There was no other explanation.

It would also be the last trick those responsible ever played. She'd make sure of it.

But if it wasn't . . . .

She couldn't think about that now. She couldn't let hope make her sloppy. Others, too many others, were relying on her to protect them.

Breathing deeply once, twice, she steadied her nerves. It might have been years since she had seen action, but she hadn't forgotten her training. She knew exactly what she had to do.

"Stand ready," she said softly. "Be prepared for anything, but do not fire unless I give the command."

————

ASHLYN PAUSED and listened to the sounds coming from around the corner. Was she doing the right thing? She knew Talbot wasn't the only member of the squad unhappy with her orders. Unhappy? That was putting it mildly. They were pissed and, if she were honest with herself, she would be too if their places were reversed. The CO wasn't supposed to expose herself to danger, not like this. But this was one situation where she had to. Surely, they understood that?

The problem was she didn't need to do it, at least not tactically speaking. She could easily send Talbot in as her second. Once he was sure the situation was secure, he'd stand down in her favor. That's what she ought to do. That's what Pawlak would tell her to do if consulted. But she couldn't. Maybe she was being foolish but, after what happened on Arterus, she wasn't letting anyone take chances for her, at least not if she could help it.

She exhaled, drew another deep breath to steady her nerves and stepped forward. As she did, she forced her fingers to relax the grip they'd taken around the butt of her pistol. Holding her hands out from her body, she moved around the corner, her eyes sweeping from side to side. So far, so good. No one had taken a pot shot at her and nothing had gone boom.

That had to be a good sign, right?

Then her eyes focused on a tall, slender woman with brunette hair sprinkled with gray and she came to an abrupt halt. In that moment, nothing existed except the woman in light battle armor, rifle snugged to her shoulder, crouching behind the barrier. Of all the shocks she'd been dealt over the last few days, this one rocked her the most. Yet one small part of her brain told her she should have expected it, especially after what Pawlak had said earlier.

Shaking her head, trying to still her emotions, Ashlyn prayed this wasn't a dream from which she'd soon awake.

All thought of safety and protocol suddenly forgotten, she took a quick step away from the gunnery sergeant. His hissed protest fell on deaf ears. Her entire focus was on the woman slowly rising to her feet, disbelief and even anger reflected on her expression.

"Mom?"

Tears filling her eyes, Ashlyn took another step forward. Then the world exploded and all went dark.

———

"Hold your fire!" Elizabeth yelled. "Goddamn it, hold your fire!"

Without thinking, she slid her rifle into place across her back and vaulted over the barricade. She felt her implants kicking in, giving her added speed even as they released high doses of gamma amino butyric acid to stop the panic rising in her. Her heart pounded and fear rose in her throat as she raced to where the young woman had fallen. As she dropped to her knees at the captain's side, the gunnery sergeant knelt opposite her. Her eyes went wide with recognition. Then she flinched under his withering look as he barked out for someone to find a medic. Before she could open her mouth to say they had a doctor, he glared at her again and she clamped her jaws shut.

Not that talking was much of an option as she gazed down at the face she'd missed seeing for so long. Her heart clinched at the sight of the scar marring her daughter's cheek. Another scar bisected the young woman's right eyebrow. From the bruising and swelling around her nose, it was easy to guess she'd broken it very recently. But worse was the blood at her left temple. Had Ashlyn somehow managed to make it home only to be killed by friendly fire?

Then she was aware of Abe yelling at her through her earbud, demanding to know what was happening. She reached up and tore the device out of her ear, tossing it to the ground. She couldn't talk to him, couldn't deal with him, until she knew more. Wasn't it enough that her own heart had just been torn out? She couldn't let that happen to him, not again.

"Who fired that shot?" the gunny demanded as he looked up from his captain, his eyes fierce.

"Answer the man!" Elizabeth ordered without looking up from her daughter's face.

It was Ashlyn. It couldn't be anyone else. But how?

"Gunny, let me," a young blonde in light armor said as she slid to a halt at his side.

For a moment, it looked as if he might argue. Then he nodded and slowly climbed to his feet. Elizabeth caught the hand signal he sent the rest of his squad, putting them on guard. They weren't going to risk anything else happening to their captain or anyone else.

"I asked who fired that shot." He ground out each word. Elizabeth knew she needed to do something, say something, but she couldn't. She couldn't pull her attention away from her daughter.

Get it together, Liz. You can't do anything for Ash, not now at least, and you have to make sure no one else gets hurt.

"Stand down, Gunny," she said firmly as she forced herself to her feet. "We'll deal with that later. But for now, I need to know what's happening and then we need to get the civilians evacuated."

She waited, wondering if he'd argue and press the point. She wouldn't blame him if he did. Hell, he'd asked exactly what she wanted to know. Not that she didn't have a damned good idea, especially considering the way Ramsey was doing his best to hide behind the others at the barricade.

"Yes, ma'am." He visibly got himself under control. "Colonel Shaw, our squad took out the enemy at the rear of the building. Major Pawlak and the rest of the Devil Dogs, as well as support troops, are in place to deal with the attackers out front but the major wants to make sure all civilians have been evacced first. Once we have a clear picture of how many people you have here, we can get started." He paused and glanced back to where the medic busily worked to treat Ashlyn. "LT?" His concern was clear.

"She's going to have a hell of a headache when she wakes, Gunny, but she should be fine," the blonde assured him. "It would help if we could get her off the floor."

"Gunny, detail two men to carry her. We'll move her down to the basement where the children are. Then you'd better be prepared to tell me just what the hell is going on and how my daughter happens to be here," Colonel Elizabeth Shaw, former CO of the Devil Dogs, said.

And I'd better let Abe know what's going on before he blows a gasket and comes down to see for himself.

———

Oh, God, Gunny is going to kill me.

Ashlyn lay still, assessing how she felt. Why in hell had she agreed to take part in the mission without first having her implants brought back online? At least then she wouldn't hurt so badly. Without the implants, her battle armor didn't know to release the pain killers that would have kept her head from pounding so.

Not that it was anything like the headache she'd likely get after Talbot finished yelling at her. Then there would be Pawlak to deal with and a simple headache wouldn't come close to what she'd feel then.

Keeping her eyes closed, she listened to what was going on around her. Voices, some sounding much too young, were talking. She caught snatches of conversation. Fear that the enemy would move in before they were ready. Another voice, a woman's, reassuring someone that his mommy was all right, that she was just sleeping for a bit. Then she heard Talbot saying they were just waiting for Lieutenant Tsui's people to get there to help with the evac. Another voice, the woman's again, told everyone to get ready to move. When Talbot gave the word, they wouldn't have any time to waste.

God, she wished her head didn't hurt so much. It made it hard to think.

She must have moved without realizing it because she sensed someone bending over her. A moment later, a hand tilted her head to the side. "Lie still, Captain. You're going to be fine. Let me give you something for the pain."

There was a sting at the right side of her neck as a pressure syringe was applied. Almost instantly, the pain eased. Ashlyn opened her eyes and found herself looking up at the young medic who had been dispatched to treat their prisoner. The blonde gave her a slight smile and nodded before looking over her shoulder. Ashlyn followed her gaze and gasped. Standing across the room, a very large room she guessed must be part of the basement, were Talbot and . . ..

"Mom?" It hadn't been a dream after all. Or, if it was, she hadn't awakened.

Ignoring the lieutenant's protests, Ashlyn pushed into a sitting position. For a moment, the room swam around her and her stomach protested. She ignored it. Hell, she'd felt worse too many times on

Tarsus for this to really bother her. Besides, nothing mattered just then besides the fact she was just a few feet from her mother.

But where was her father? Her sister?

Then, without warning, she found herself almost thrust back into a prone position as someone launched himself at her. A small some-one. Arms and legs wrapped around her armored torso and a soft, warm face burrowed in against her neck. Her arms automatically wrapped around the child and held him close. Then, recognizing the dark hair, the shape of the head, her heart clinched, and tears filled her eyes.

"Mommy!" her five-year-old son cried.

"I'm here, baby. I'm here." She held him close and sat up, rocking back and forth as she did. Then, with the lieutenant's help, she care-fully climbed to her feet. This was too much to take in. She'd known it was possible her parents might be in the complex. But not her son. He was supposed to be halfway across the system with his father. Her bastard of an ex-husband had made sure he gained full custody of their son once she'd been convicted. What in the hell was Jake doing here? Not that she'd object, at least not once she'd made sure he was safely away from the fighting.

Then her mother was there, enveloping them both in a hug. "There's a lot to say and even more to ask but it can wait, dear heart," Elizabeth Shaw said a moment later, tears glistening in her eyes.

"Dad and Katie?"

"Your father's upstairs making sure the others are ready to move. He'll be down once Lieutenant Tsui's people relieve them. Your gunny is right. We don't want to do anything to tip the enemy off about what's going on.

"And your sister's safe. She's off-planet right now. She left more than two weeks ago and isn't due home until next month."

"My brothers?"

"Off-planet and on ships."

A shudder of relief ran through Ashlyn to know none of her family had been harmed during the attack and she held tightly onto her son. There were so many other questions she wanted to ask, but they could wait. They had to wait, at least until everyone was safely away from the fighting.

"All right." Ashlyn carefully shifted Jake to her left hip and then nodded to Talbot. "Gunny, status?"

"The LT is one his way with our relief, Cap. Once they are in position, the civilians will be moved out and we'll put the screws to the enemy."

"Excellent." Now she nodded. "Lieutenant, what about our prisoner?"

"He's been moved back to the FOB, Captain."

"Cap, the major is on the horn for you," Marino reported.

She nodded and activated her suit's comm unit. "Shaw here, Major."

"Captain, what part of *don't do anything stupid* do you not understand?" Pawlak demanded. She winced slightly as his words echoed through her earbud.

"Sorry, sir, but it was a necessary risk. I'm sure the good lieutenant has already assured you that I'm all right. Besides, my head is very hard, as you've told me on more than one occasion," she countered easily. Although, she did plan to have a *discussion* with whomever had been the one to fire at her. She'd been lucky and she knew it.

"And you're still as cheeky as ever," Pawlak said. Fortunately, he sounded more amused than angry. "Report."

"We're ready for the next phase as soon as Lieutenant Tsui arrives."

"Good. You'll be returning to the FOB with the civilians, Captain. I want to see for myself that you aren't seriously injured. After you've given your report, I'm turning you over to the medics so they can do their magic with you. After that, well, I'm sure FleetCom and the Commandant will have orders for us all."

She wanted to argue but knew better. She was lucky they hadn't hauled her out of there already. It had been a damn fool stunt. But there was one thing she wouldn't take "no" on. She wanted – no, she needed – for her family to come with her. After so much time away from her and the shock of learning her darling son had been in the middle of the fire zone, she needed time with them and if it had to be at the FOB or on a ship or somewhere else, so be it. All that mattered was spending some much needed time with them.

"Ash," Pawlak continued softly, almost gently. "Don't worry. Your family will be going with you. I promise."

"Thank you, Major."

"Now, make sure everyone's ready to move."

"Aye, sir." She turned to Talbot. "Gunny, you heard?"

"Yes, ma'am. We're ready."

"Mommy?"

"It's okay, Jake." She smiled at him. She ought to put him down, but she couldn't. Not yet at any rate. "We're going to get out of here real soon and then you're going to get to meet some of the nice Marines Mommy has been working with."

"Ash?"

"Mom, I'll explain everything just as soon as we're out of here. But believe me when I say this has been an even bigger surprise for me than it has been for you. A certain family friend has a lot to explain to both of us." She didn't need to name Tremayne for her mother to nod, a look of understanding lighting her hazel eyes.

"You home now, Mommy?" Jake asked.

"I hope so, baby. I sincerely hope so."

8

"You can sit up now, Captain."

Careful not to move too quickly, Ashlyn levered into a sitting position and swung her legs over the side of the examination table. As she did, Dr. Samuel Ahern watched closely. She didn't need to be a mind reader to know what he was thinking. She'd heard it often enough over the last few days. He didn't think she needed to be anywhere except in the hospital where all her injuries, old and new, could be treated.

And where the head-shrinks could delve into her darkest nightmares and decide if she was fit to return to duty.

Not that he had ever come right out and said that last part. He didn't need to. She had seen too many of her fellow Marines face the same situation during the war. It usually happened after they had been seriously injured or their unit had suffered major casualties. Sometimes it happened after a particularly bad battle. Full psych evals were always required if a Marine, or any member of the armed forces, fell into enemy hands and then somehow managed to get free. After all, no one – meaning no politicians – wanted to risk them going rogue and hurting innocents or damaging government property because they cracked under the pressures of being held captive or had been indoctrinated or changed loyalties.

What none of them seemed to realize was that forced inaction was the last thing a soldier or Marine needed after falling into enemy hands – and, as far as Ashlyn was concerned, that's exactly what she and her people had done. They needed to be on duty, fighting those who wanted to destroy the very government and people they were sworn to protect. Action, preferably direct action, always trumped too much introspection.

Duty and honor. Family and the Corps. That was all a Marine needed.

At least her mother understood. Elizabeth had been there for her in the dead of night when the nightmares came. She had fought to not only keep Ashlyn out of the hospital but involved in analyzing the attack on the capital. She'd promised to do everything she could to make sure Ash was on the ship sent to Tarsus to bring her people home. Most of all, Elizabeth had assured her that if the powers-that-be didn't soon hand over the results of the investigation into the charges brought against Ashlyn and the others, she'd go to the media with what she knew.

Unfortunately, none of that would matter if Ahern didn't agree to let her return to duty.

"How do you feel?" he asked. He may have been looking at the monitors on the wall behind the examining table, but Ashlyn knew he wouldn't miss even the most subtle hint she wasn't telling the truth if she tried to hedge the question.

"Better."

That was certainly the truth. A few days of a well-balanced diet and enough water – and other fluids like coffee, something she hadn't had since her conviction – had done wonders for her. Add to that the fact the low-level pain that had become a way of life was gone. That alone was worth all the long sessions she'd endured at the medical facility each day.

"Good." Now he smiled at her, his expression softening some.

"Your knee is healing nicely. You'll need to wear the brace another week or so until the nanites finish doing their work. If you have to armor up, be sure to make the necessary adjustments so you don't undo all the good work that's already been done."

She frowned as she remembered the events as they evacuated the tenants from the residential complex. Talbot had looked at her and told her that for once she was going to take orders from him. She was not going to lead the tenants out. In fact, she was going to be in the second wave. This wasn't his order but Major Pawlak's. Before she'd been able to argue, the gunnery sergeant had nodded to where she held her son at her hip. That had been enough to get her to agree. After being separated for so long from the boy, she wasn't going to give him up, even if only for a few minutes.

With her mother at her side and her father behind them, they'd started out of the building. Lt. Tsui's squad waited for them at the rear of the building. The lieutenant's people led the civilians out and down the road in the direction of the FOB in groups of half a dozen or so. Unfortunately, the evac took longer than anyone liked. But doing it that way also meant it was less likely one of the enemy would see a large group of people and signal for an attack.

Because her parents refused to leave until the last of their people were safely away, Ashlyn hung back. She knew Talbot and the rest of her squad didn't like it, but she didn't care. Besides, as she reminded the gunnery sergeant when he tried to protest, the DDs were with her. She'd almost laughed at the look of frustration the gunny, as well as the rest of the squad, wore when she said it. Then she had turned her attention to the rear of the building and watched as Lt. Tsui's people once again assumed their positions near the doorway, ready to escort the last of them to safety.

And it almost worked. The last group was out of the building and moving quickly and relatively silently down the street, doing their best to keep to the shadows. Once they were outside, Ashlyn handed Jake to her father. She knew he'd keep the boy safe. More than that, she and her mother were better armed, and armored, than he was. So it made sense that they would guard their rear as they moved away from the residential complex.

Only, like so many plans in the heat of battle, things went to hell with little warning. Ashlyn heard a shout and, as she swung in its direction, she realized her mother and Talbot did as well. Then both reacted almost instantly and dove for cover. At the same time, they shouted for everyone to move, to run. Ash turned and saw her father, his right arm wrapped around her son's waist and his left hand holding Jake's head pressed to his shoulder, sprinting toward a barricade where several of Lt. Tsui's men waited. A moment later the world exploded – again – and Ash flew through the air. Then she slammed to the pavement and slid on her back into the side of a building. Her light armor prevented her injuries from being serious, but she could feel pain in her left knee and her right shoulder throbbed.

Pushing down the pain, she rolled to her good knee in time to see her mother and Talbot open fire. A moment later, the enemy trooper who fired the RPG in their direction fell, fatally wounded. With that worry dealt with, Ashlyn looked around, fear for her father and son almost choking her. Then, seeing them appear from behind the barricade, she heaved a sigh of relief and slowly climbed to her feet. The rest of the trek back to the FOB was painful but worth it to know she was finally reunited with her son and parents.

"As for your other injuries, time to recover is all you need. Well, time and not doing anything foolish." Ahern pinned her with a firm look.

"I promise to be good, Doc."

Could all that possibly mean he was going to clear her for duty? Surely it wouldn't be that easy. Not that she'd argue if it were.

"As for the tissue regeneration on your arm and face, that's done much better than I dared hope for, especially where your arm's concerned. Dr. Li's new procedure has yet to disappoint. That means I want to start treatment on the rest of your scarring as soon as possible."

Ashlyn couldn't help looking at her left arm as he spoke. Just a week ago, her upper arm had been a mass of angry-looking scar tissue, a stark reminder of what had been and all that had been lost. Now, in its place, was soft, supple skin. It had even lost the slightly pinkish tint it had those first few days as the skin regenerated after the scar tissue had been excised. She could see the definition of the arm's muscles and, as she ran the fingers of her right hand over the new skin, she wondered if she would once more be allowed to wear the traditional inking of the Devil Dogs.

God, she hoped so. That, more than almost anything else, would prove everything she had been promised was true.

"Thanks, Doc, for everything."

"Don't thank me yet." He held up a hand before she could voice the worry that suddenly filled her. "Captain, you have done remarkably well with all the treatments we've put you through. A lot of that has to do with your motivation. I know you want nothing more than to go with the Marines being sent to Tarsus."

When he paused, she nodded. He was working up to something and she had a feeling she wasn't going to like it. "But?" she prompted.

"But I know you have also been doing your best not to let on to anyone just how much you've been through and I don't mean just on Tarsus. Nor have you talked about how it has affected you. So far, you're managing to cope remarkably well. But that's not going to be enough, not in the long run and certainly not if you get to Tarsus and find things there are as bad as you fear. Because of that, I can't, in good conscience, certify you fit for duty. So, I'm going to make you a deal."

Her eyes narrowed and she looked at him suspiciously. "I'm listening."

"I will sign off on you returning to very limited duty for the mission to Tarsus. But you will have to continue our treatments with the ship's CMO. She can help with rehabbing your knee and your shoulder. I'm still not happy with your range of motion where they're concerned."

"What do you want in return?"

And what would she do if it was more than she was willing to agree to?

"I want your promise that you'll return here once you're back on-planet. I get two weeks with you to finish any treatment I feel needs to be done, including upgrading your implants. It will also include the psych evaluation I know you want to avoid." He waited, as if expecting her to protest. "Captain, there will be no negotiation where that's concerned. Trust me on that."

"Will you activate my implants now if I agree?" That alone would do a great deal to reassure her this was not just another ploy to get her to drop her guard before the trap was sprung.

"I will. In fact, I insist upon it if you are returning to Tarsus."

His voice turned hard and she looked at him in surprise. She'd known he'd been upset to see the many scars she sported upon her return from the penal colony. But she had never seen this level of anger in him and it shocked her.

"Captain – Ashlyn." He took a step away and she watched as he struggled for calm. "I may be a Navy doctor now, but I had the extreme honor and privilege of serving as a medic for the Devil Dogs early in my military career. I spent two years with them and those are the years of service I'm most proud of. That makes you one of mine and it's why I'm not grounding you. I *know* you need to go to Tarsus. You need to for your people and you need to for yourself. But I will, by God, do everything I can to keep you safe not only now but in the future."

For a moment, she just looked at him. She heard the emotion in his words and, thinking back on the medics she'd served with, knew he meant what he said. More than that, he was giving her a chance if she would trust him enough to take it.

Besides, what choice did she have?

"All right, Doc. I'll do as you say."

Seeing how he relaxed a bit, she shook her head. The memory of a snippet of discussion with the medic who treated her immediately after she and Tremayne had escaped the fighting at the security complex returned. He'd been a medic with the Devil Dogs as well.

Now that she thought about it, it couldn't be a coincidence that the two doctors she'd seen since returning to Fuercon happened to have once belonged to her beloved DDs. Someone, probably the Commandant of the Marine Corps, had issued orders to make sure she didn't have to deal with anyone who she couldn't trust completely and that pretty much meant only people who were Marines or who had served with the Devil Dogs.

Not that she was complaining, at least not too much.

"Good." Another smile, this one the smile of a man who realized how close he'd come to losing the battle. "Lie back and I'll bring your implants back online and get them calibrated. We should have enough time to do that before you have to meet with the powers-that-be."

"Don't remind me."

She grimaced. The one thing she had never expected was having to spend so much time not only with Pawlak but with an endless stream of military personnel and politicians. They wanted to know all she could tell them about the events leading up to her conviction as well as her thoughts about the attack on the capitol. The only good thing about it all was that she had, so far, managed to avoid having to face the media.

For now.

"All right, Captain. That's the best I can do right now." Ahern stepped back and gave her a reassuring smile. "I will let the brass know that I've authorized your return to limited, very limited, duty."

"Thanks, Doc." Even limited duty was welcomed if it meant she'd be allowed to finally return to Tarsus for her people. "I promise I'll be good."

"No, you promise you'll be as good as you can," he corrected with a smile.

Ashlyn grinned in response and nodded. He really did understand what it meant to be a Marine. Fortunately.

"But I meant what I said earlier, Captain," he continued, this time his voice serious. "As soon as your return from Tarsus, you are to report here for two weeks."

"Doc—"

"Let me rephrase that, ma'am. I don't mean you have to come here as soon as you return. I know you will need to debrief and then you'll need to spend some time with your family. However, as soon as that is done, I expect you here. I'll be putting that in my report as well."

"Understood and thanks."

She slid off the examining table and stretched, wincing slightly as her right shoulder caught. Still, it was better than it had been the day before and none of her hurts were as bad as what she'd lived with on a daily basis back on Tarsus. Hopefully, her emotional wounds would heal as quickly as the physical ones were. Unfortunately, if her nightmares were any indication, that wasn't going to happen. But she'd lived with them this long. She could a bit longer, at least until the others were home.

"Your implants should all be fully operational now, Captain," Ahern continued. "I'll update them when you return. I promise."

"Doctor, that sounds a bit like blackmail to me." She grinned again. It didn't surprise her one bit that he would use the promise of new implants to make sure she returned for further treatment.

"Why, Captain, I'd never stoop to blackmailing a Marine, much less a Devil Dog, with the possibility of new combat implants just to get her to return for some much-needed medical treatment."

Damn, butter wouldn't melt in his mouth. She bet he was a great poker player.

"You're an evil man, Doc, but I take your point. I promise I'll be back for treatment just as soon as I've done what I need to."

"I know you will, Captain. You are a woman of your word, even when you don't like it," he said confidently. "Now get out of here. I have patients waiting who actually want the treatment I can give them."

With a grin, she finished dressing and did as he said. As she stepped into the corridor outside the examining room, Gunnery Sergeant Talbot fell into step behind her. He had been waiting for her that morning when she left Tremayne's house where she, as well as her parents and her son, had been staying since the attack on the capital. Without a word, he'd handed over his datapad with a copy of his orders displayed. Ashlyn had quickly scanned them, fighting the urge to sigh as she did. FleetCom was taking no chances. It had assigned Talbot as her escort, aide and guard -- of course, she didn't know whether he was guarding against someone trying to hurt her or her going after those responsible for sending her and her people to the penal colony. Not that it mattered. He would be with her until she received her orders, orders that would hopefully send her back to Tarsus for her people.

"All right, Gunny. Where to next?" she asked as they emerged from the hospital a few minutes later.

"Your presence is requested at a meeting with General Okafor, ma'am," Talbot replied as he signaled the driver that had been assigned to them. "It's my understanding that after meeting with her, you are to report to Major Pawlak."

"All right, Gunny. Thank you." She waited as the aircar pulled up next to them. Talbot opened the door and checked inside, making sure no untoward surprises awaited them. Then he stepped back and motioned her inside.

"FleetCom HQ, Corporal," he told the driver as he climbed into the back with Ashlyn. As soon as the driver confirmed their destination, Talbot activated the privacy shield.

"Ma'am, before we get there, I've been hearing rumblings that FleetCom is about to send a ship to Tarsus for our people. Word has it that the Devil Dogs, at least a good sized contingent of them, are to be assigned to the mission."

"I see." She looked out the window and thought hard. Over the last few days, she and Talbot had played this game several times. He would pass on information he'd "heard", and she would act as if she didn't know he was using every resource he had to ferret out the information for her. "And have you, by any chance, heard what ship and what members of the DDs might be going?"

"Sorry, ma'am, but no. I heard the rumor just before you were done with the doctor." He frowned and she knew he wished he had more to tell her. Well, truth to tell, so did she.

"And did your sources suggest that this meeting we're going to might just happen to be about what you've just learned?"

"I believe so, ma'am, but that's just my gut feeling."

She nodded and once more turned to look out the window. God, could FleetCom finally be ready to send a ship after her people? She understood why a ship hadn't been sent before now. No one wanted to leave a hole in planetary defense. The attack had badly shaken everyone, most especially the military. As it should have, at least as far as Ashlyn was concerned. They had gotten too comfortable in the safety of Fuerconese space. Just because the Callusians hadn't launched an attack against the home system during the last war didn't mean they wouldn't.

And that lesson had been driven home all too well.

"Well, I guess we'll find out soon enough."

But would the news be what she wanted to hear?

————

"I UNDERSTAND you're somewhat of a stubborn patient, Captain," General Helen Okafor, Commandant of the Fuerconese Marine Corps, said with a smile as she motioned for Ashlyn to take a seat in front of her desk

"Not really, ma'am. It's just that the good doctor has a different set of priorities than I do right now."

"I understand and I happen to agree with you. I'd be telling him exactly the same thing you did if our positions were reversed." The general moved around her desk and took the seat next to Ashlyn's. "However, you will report to him after your assignment and you will submit to any testing and treatment he prescribes. At least you will if you wish to return to active duty."

"Understood, ma'am."

At least she thought she did. This was the first time anyone had directly mentioned the possibility of her actually returning to active duty. She wanted to hope it meant she'd not only be allowed to go free her fellow Marines from Tarsus but that she would then be able to return to the Devil Dogs. But after so many months and years of not being able to trust anyone but herself, she didn't dare let herself do so. Not yet, at any rate.

"Gunny, why don't you go check in with Major Pawlak and let him know that your captain and I will be busy for the next several hours. Return here at 1300 hours to escort her to the major."

"Aye, ma'am." Talbot braced to attention for a moment and then left, the door sliding closed behind him.

"Now, Ash, before we get started, let's get a couple of things out of the way." Okafor leaned back and smiled. Gone was the imposing commandant. Now she was the concerned senior officer, not quite a friend but someone who understood what Ashlyn was feeling.

"All right."

"You and I are going to talk, just talk, for a few minutes. Then we'll be joined by some other folks who need to hear what you can tell us about Tarsus and about what happened on your last mission."

"Ma'am." She swallowed hard and then licked her lips. Didn't any of them understand that she couldn't say anything until her people were freed?

"Ashlyn." Okafor waited until she blew out a breath and nodded for her to proceed. "Nothing you say will leave this office. I promise you. Nor will anyone present say anything until I give them the okay to do so. But, if that's not enough to convince you, think about this. Every one of the four who will be joining us worked tirelessly to prove your innocence and to bring you home. You and the others have a number of champions. Some gave up their commissions. Others were beached and others, like myself and Major Santiago, managed to work behind the scenes while staying on active duty.

"We have built very solid cases against some of those involved in bringing you and the others up on charges. However, we need to know what you can tell us to help put the final nails in their proverbial coffins. It isn't enough that we've managed to clean house under the new Administration. We need to bring those responsible to justice, a justice they denied you and those who served with you.

"But it is more than that." Now the general got to her feet.

Worried, Ashlyn watched as Okafor crossed the office. She stopped at the window and looked outside. Even with her back to her, Ashlyn could see the anger and worry in her former CO's posture. "I won't get into all of it right now. It can wait until everyone is here. But know that this is necessary, not only to protect you and your people but also everyone you were each willing to lay your lives down for." She turned back and there could be no mistaking just how serious she was.

"As long as you understand that, right now, my loyalty has to lie with those who were sent to that hellhole with me, ma'am."

Okafor nodded and returned to her seat. "Since they are at the center of everything right now, let's get this out of the way." She leaned forward and reached for a leather folder resting on her desktop. Without opening it, she placed it in her lap and folded her hands on top of it. "I've spoken with Dr. Ahern and it's my understanding that he's agreed to release you to limited – in his words, very limited – duty."

Ashlyn nodded. As she did, her heart beat a bit faster and she hoped her nerves didn't show.

"And I assume you still wish to return to Tarsus with the Marines we're sending to bring your people home."

Another nod because she didn't trust her herself to be able to speak just then.

"Then be prepared to report to the *Magellan* day after tomorrow as part of the Marine contingent assigned to secure our people on Tarsus and transport them back home. Hopefully, it will be a quick turn-around. However, while there, the records for the prison are to be secured and examined by members of the JAG who will be accompanying you on the mission. The senior JAG will make the determination of whether or not any members of the prison staff should be returned here to face charges, military or civilian.

"And that brings us to part of why you need to tell us what you can about Tarsus. If there are any you know who should be brought back, help us start building the case now. That will let the JAG issue sealed warrants to take with them."

Ashlyn sat back in her chair, not sure whether to be relieved or not. She couldn't deny that she'd had her doubts since Tremayne first raised the possibility of her people being pardoned. After all that had happened, it was all too easy to believe her people were being used as pawns to get her to agree to help fight the Callusians. After all, they'd used against her before. She would have fought harder to prove her innocence if they hadn't been involved – and if the JAGs prosecuting her hadn't threatened to try for the death penalty against her people if she didn't basically let them convict her. Now she was being asked to trust the same system that had done its best to betray and then forget about her and her people.

But it was more than that. After the attack on the capital, she'd tried to believe that FleetCom would keep its promise to return to Tarsus for the others. But part of her had known how easy it would be to use the attack as a reason not to send a ship. Her people could have been written off as acceptable losses. Hell, that's what the previous administration had done. But now, hearing how the *Magellan* would be heading out in two short days – and that she would be on it – she could almost allow herself to finally accept everything her parents, Tremayne, Pawlak and even Talbot had been telling her.

But the presence of the JAG officers bothered her. She couldn't deny it. The JAG rarely sent officers into space. Ships' commanders could hold disciplinary boards or could confine anyone under their command until the accused could be returned to a spaceport to stand trial. That not just one but several JAGs would be accompanying them on this mission was worrisome.

"Ash, look at me."

Until Okafor spoke, Ashlyn hadn't realized she'd turned away from the woman. Now she turned back, not trying to hide her thoughts from the woman she'd once served under. Next to her mother and Tremayne, there were few in the Corps she trusted as much as she did Okafor.

"I can't imagine what you must be feeling right now. I've been a POW. I've had to live through that hell. But I've never been betrayed by my own like you and the others were. You have to believe that those responsible will pay for what they did. You have my word on it, not only as Commandant of the Corps but also as your friend and as a fellow Marine. I promise the only reason the JAGs are going on the mission is so all the legal ins and outs are followed."

"Ma'am, I do trust you. I just don't have a hell of a lot of trust for the system right now."

And that was putting it mildly.

"And I don't blame you. That system betrayed you. Now let it work to get a bit of vengeance for you and the others."

"Yes, ma'am."

She'd at least try to do what the general said.

"There are a couple more things before the others join us," Okafor continued. "We have all been making assumptions where you're concerned and I apologize in advance for that."

"Ma'am?"

"We've assumed you'd want to stay in the Corps and that you'd want to return to the Devil Dogs. I even had orders drawn up to that effect. But it dawned on me this morning that no one has asked you what you want to do."

For a moment, all Ashlyn could do was look at the general in disbelief. She had been so afraid they wouldn't let her return to duty. Now Okafor was telling her that they'd assumed all along that she not only wanted to remain in the Corps but wanted to return to the Devil Dogs. The way it sounded, they had even cut her orders to that effect. Now Okafor wanted to know if they'd been wrong.

"General, I'm a Marine. One of my biggest fears since being returned to the capital and having Senator Tremayne ask me if I'd be willing to accept a pardon and return to duty has been that this was all a trick. Three things kept me going while I was on Tarsus. The first was the knowledge that as long as I lived, the guards focused most of their sadism on me and not on my people. The second was the need to survive so I could see my family, especially my son, again. The third was the determination to do nothing to bring shame on the

Corps or the Devil Dogs, no matter what the court-martial results had said.

"When the attack on the capital happened, I knew I had to do whatever was necessary to keep the senator alive. I think the only thing that kept me going was instinct, at least at first. It would have been easy to slip away during the confusion to either hide or go after those responsible for sending me and my people to Tarsus. I'll even admit I considered the latter on more than one occasion. But I didn't. I couldn't. The system and the Corps didn't betray us. The people who manipulated them did."

And maybe one day she'd really believe all that.

"So, the answer to your question is to ask another question. If I stay in the Corps, will I have some time after returning from Tarsus to spend with my family? My son has suffered enough as it is. I can't leave him for long, not so soon."

"Ash, I'll be honest. We need you. We need you on the front lines again, leading our people just as you did before that last mission. But, that said, the doctors are adamant that you have the time you need to receive treatment and fully recover from what happened to you. You also need to be brought back up to speed, not only on the current state of affairs but on your training. So, unless something else unexpected happens, I can pretty much guarantee that you'll be on-planet for at least a couple of months."

"One more question, if I may."

"Of course."

"Ma'am, no one who has ever been a Devil Dog wants to move on to another unit. You know that."

Okafor nodded, a smile touching her lips. She'd been a Devil Dog earlier in her career. She understood what it meant to be chosen to join the First Marine Division.

"But I will not return to the division unless I know for sure that Major Pawlak and the rest of the Devil Dogs want me."

Shaking her head, a smile touching her lips, Okafor got to her feet. Wondering what she was up to, Ashlyn watched as the general moved to the door to the outer office. Once there, Okafor paused and turned back, motioning for Ash to join her. Knowing better than to keep a senior officer, much less the Commandant of the Corps, waiting, Ashlyn climbed to her feet and hurried in her direction.

Okafor opened the door and stepped through, Ashlyn on her heels. Without a word, the general moved through the outer office. She ignored her aide asking if she needed anything. Instead, she left her suite of offices and walked purposefully down the long corridor. When she paused before a set of double doors, Ashlyn looked past her and swallowed hard. She didn't know what waited behind the doors and wasn't sure she wanted to.

Without knocking, Okafor opened the doors and stepped inside. The moment she did, a man's voice snapped out the order for everyone to come to attention. Ashlyn followed the general, her eyes going wide. The conference room was filled with more than a dozen men and women, all of them Devil Dogs.

"General Okafor, were we right?" Major Pawlak asked once she put the group at their ease.

"We were." Now she grinned at Ashlyn and motioned her forward. "I'll paraphrase but basically she said she wouldn't rejoin the Devil Dogs unless she knew each and every one of them agreed to it."

Pawlak looked past the general to where Ashlyn stood. "Is that correct, Captain?" he asked, his expression as neutral as she'd ever seen.

Damn, she wished she knew what he was thinking. Unfortunately, he'd always had the best poker face in the outfit.

When in doubt, fall back on protocol.

"Yes, sir."

"So, Major, can you think of any way to convince her that her return to the Devil Dogs is exactly what the outfit wants?" Now there was no mistaking the humor in the general's voice.

"I believe so, ma'am."

A broad grin replaced his perfect poker face. Then he turned and signaled to someone. Almost instantly, six men and women stepped forward. Each face was more than familiar. Ashlyn had served with each of them, had hit the battlefield with them, mourned their losses and celebrated their victories. Non-coms and officers, they had helped shape her into the officer she'd been until her court-martial.

"Captain," Gunny Talbot began. He marched forward and stopped. His right hand snapped up in a perfect parade ground salute that he held until she returned it. "We represent each squad, platoon, company, battalion and regiment of the division. It is our pleasure to inform you that the Devil Dogs not only want you back but we demand it, assuming you wish to return. You are one of us. You are one of the best of us. No way do we want to lose you to another division or, worse, to civilian life."

"Captain, I'm here on behalf of First Regiment," a dark-haired woman continued as she stepped forward.

Like most of those present, she wore BDUs and combat boots. Her hair, so dark it was almost black, was pulled back into a braid. Her green eyes danced with excitement. Seeing her, Ashlyn's throat tightened and her eyes burned with unshed tears. Damn, Pawlak and the general weren't pulling any punches.

"Your boots have been impossible to fill," the woman continued. "I swear if you don't say yes right now, I'll have the Gunny hit you over the head and we'll hold you in the barracks until you come to your senses."

"Ah hell, Luce, you probably would." She laughed and shook her head. Then she suddenly found herself standing in the middle of those who had been waiting for her. These men and women had been some of her closest comrades. They'd been family in a way most would never understand. Now, it would seem, they wanted her back.

"I most certainly would. You'd be wise to remember that," Captain Lucinda Ortega said simply. "Better yet, remember what I used to do to you back in the Academy when you tried to do something foolish."

"Me? You're the one who kept getting in trouble and trying to pull me into it with you." She grinned, remembering their days together as roommates. Then she sobered some and turned her attention to Okafor. "General, you sandbagged me. That's not nice to do to someone who is still trying to figure out which end is up." She grinned to take any sting there might have been out of her words.

"I figured it was the best way to convince you that the Corps and, most especially, the Devil Dogs want you back, Captain."

"And, in case you still have your doubts, Ash, I think I know just the thing to convince you." Pawlak signaled to someone else.

At the sight of the small, bald man who stepped forward, Ashlyn laughed gaily. Pawlak was right. Reinhold Gerhardt, a former Devil Dog himself, was the tattooist who had inked every member of the DDs for years. Could he actually be there to redo her inking?

"Mr. Gerhardt, her doctor has cleared her for you to work your wonders on," As she spoke, Okafor patted Ashlyn's shoulder and then urged her forward. "Major, I'll need you and Ash back in my office in an hour."

"Not gonna be long enough, General," Gerhardt said. "I'll be needing at least two hours."

"Come on, old man. I know your tricks. You can have it done in an hour and a half. That's how long you have. Otherwise, you'll have to finish later."

"Always were a pushy thing," he muttered before turning his attention to Ashlyn. "Off with that top, girl, if you're wanting me to get to work."

Laughing, feeling as if at least some of her fears had finally been removed, Ashlyn complied. After handing her uniform blouse to Talbot, she took the seat Gerhardt indicated.

"I assume this means you'll be accepting your new assignment, Captain?" Okafor asked.

"Yes, ma'am."

She looked around at the familiar faces, all watching her with expressions of approval and welcome. Now she could believe she was truly home. The only thing missing were those still left behind on Tarsus. But that would be corrected soon. She had to remember that.

"Good." Okafor gave a satisfied nod. "I'll finalize your orders then. Major, Captain, I'll see you in my office in an hour and a half. In the meantime, someone get the captain a beer and show her just how glad we all are to have her home." With that, Okafor pivoted on her heel and left the room.

"You heard the general, Gunny. Get the captain a beer and let's get this party started," Pawlak said. "But this is just a taste, Ash. The real party will be when we return from Tarsus with the rest of our people."

And that was the best thing she'd heard in a long time.

9

"You're sure?"

Even as he asked, he felt the color drain from his face. He had to have heard wrong. Or the information was wrong. Or he was having a nightmare, a very bad nightmare. That had to be it. That was the only thing that made sense.

"Do you think I'd be here if I was mistaken?" Major Thomas O'Brien demanded before tossing back his whiskey. "You may be retired and out of the loop, Admiral, but I was escorting yet another bunch of brats through the security complex when the attack hit. I saw her." He shook his head, as if by doing so he could erase the memory. "Damn it, I saw her. She was with Tremayne and Talbot and she most definitely wasn't being treated like a prisoner. If anything, she acted like she'd returned to duty. She was armed, for God's sake."

Alec Sorkowski forced himself not to react. He couldn't let his former Marine CO see how much of a shock his news was. Nor could he let on to those around him that they were anything more than two former shipmates who'd run into one another and decided to grab a drink. The problem with that was O'Brien. The man could not control himself where Shaw was concerned. Now that inability could very well work against him unless Sorkowski did something. There were too many people around and that meant too many ears listening in. Damn it, what he would give for a bit of privacy.

O'Brien was right about one thing, however. Sorkowski was out of the loop. Like so many others, he'd been given two choices after the last election. He could retire and accept limited benefits and pay or he could face a full investigation into his command and the probable loss of his commission. Because he didn't dare risk an investigation, he accepted the chance to retire. Since then, he'd become *persona non grata*. Oh, whenever he was forced to deal with anyone on active duty, they treated him with the respect his rank deserved, but that didn't fool him. He knew they laughed at him. At least they did it behind his back instead of to his face. Damn them all.

And damn Shaw. It was all her fault. She had been a thorn in his side from the moment she stepped foot onto his flagship more than two and a half years ago. She hadn't fooled him one bit with her false respect and smug attitude. He'd been able to ignore her, thinking her O'Brien's problem, until she began questioning their every order. She never let anything go, no matter how mine.

The fiasco of that last mission had been her fault. Everything had been so carefully set up. It had taken time and more than a little money had passed hands to make sure everything was the way he wanted in the sector. Then she'd come onboard and had started asking questions. Worse, she'd insisted on following their orders from FleetCom to the letter, no matter what he or O'Brien said.

If she'd just done as she'd been told, if she hadn't questioned him and then tried to send her objections further up the ladder, none of them would be in the mess they were now. More importantly, he'd still be where he belonged, on the flag bridge of a destroyer. But no, she had to be a royal pain in his ass and the downfall of his career.

Well, he'd shown her. Fortunately, O'Brien had no more love for the woman than had he. Shaw might have been a thorn in his side, but she was worse than that for O'Brien. Shaw could have been the recruiting advert for the Marines while O'Brien was just putting in his time until he could retire. O'Brien was a good enough CO in peace time, but when the war broke out, the powers that be decided he needed someone as his XO who could get the job done. Shaw had been the last of a long line of officers assigned to him and the most stubborn.

So, when the mission on Arterus went bad, neither he nor O'Brien had any qualms about offering up Shaw and the survivors of her unit as sacrificial lambs. Someone had to pay for the fiasco and Sorkowski knew exactly who it should be. After all, if Shaw had spent as much time preparing for the mission as she had opposing it, she might not have led her people into the trap that had killed so many of them and even more civilians. Okay, maybe he and O'Brien hadn't given her access to all the intelligence they had, but she'd had enough to complete the mission and get out without too much collateral damage.

Emphasis on *too much*. Unfortunately, she hadn't even managed that the way he'd hoped. She'd come back alive. So, when FleetCom demanded answers and wanted someone to pay for the civilian deaths, Sorkowski never paused before offering her up to them.

Hindsight being what it was, he cursed his own lack of foresight for not realizing she'd have reported her concerns not only about the mission but about him and O'Brien to Admiral de la Cruz, Third Fleet's commanding officer. More importantly, they should have realized she'd have sent copies of her messages to de la Cruz to that thrice damned Miranda Tremayne. When he'd learned what she'd done, it had been a mad scramble to alter Shaw's orders and information downloads. Even now, almost three years later, Sorkowski wasn't completely sure he and O'Brien had managed to cover all their tracks. Maybe that was why he'd been wondering how long it would be before Fleet Intel pulled him in for yet another "debriefing".

And now, finding out that Shaw was back on-planet, it was as if his worst nightmares had come to life. But maybe he was overreacting. There had been nothing on the news reports about Shaw being on-planet, much less having been pardoned. But, after the attack on the capital, nothing would really surprise him.

God, if they had pardoned her, he was as good as dead. He had no doubts that bitch would come after him. She had said as much after her trial and one thing he'd learned about her was that she was a woman of her word.

He had to think. Just because O'Brien thought saw her during the attack didn't mean he actually had. Even if he was right and it had been her, the fact she hadn't been treated like a prisoner really didn't mean much. The Marines manning the security complex would have armed anyone they felt could help protect the building and its occupants. No, he wasn't going to worry about Shaw being put on the front line in the fight.

At least not yet.

First, he had to find out was why she'd been brought back from Tarsus and why no one warned him of the possibility of her return.

"Do you know if the others are here?" He forced himself to look and act as unconcerned as if they were discussing the weather. O'Brien might still be on active duty, but Sorkowski had long ago figured out it was simply so the Marines could keep an eye on the man. Frankly, he was surprised some of Shaw's supporters in the Marines hadn't already dealt out their own form of punishment for what they saw as his betrayal of one of their own.

"Not that I know of, but then I didn't know Shaw was here until I saw her." There could be no mistaking the bitter anger in the major's voice.

"Have you seen or heard anything about her since the attack?"

"Negative. It's not like I can go around asking people if they've seen her or if they know why she's back."

For a moment Sorkowski said nothing. A faint glimmer of hope appeared. Could he actually be lucky enough that the bitch had been killed in the fighting? The only thing that would be better than that would be if she died before talking to any of his enemies about the events leading up to her conviction.

"Good. That means she either managed to get herself killed or she is back in custody." *At least I hope it does.* "Either possibility works in our favor."

"But why bring her back?"

"That's something we'll have to find out."

And the sooner, the better.

Sorkowski leaned back, studying his companion. O'Brien had never been the model of what one expected of a Marine. On the short side and carrying a few extra pounds, it wasn't too far of a stretch to guess that someone in his family had the political connections needed to get him into the Academy as a young man. From there, they'd made sure O'Brien had secured postings that wouldn't task his mediocre leadership skills. Then war had broken out and nothing could keep him, or most of the rest of the Corps, from the front lines.

And that was another cross Sorkowski had had to bear. If O'Brien had been even halfway competent as a Marine CO, Shaw never would have been assigned to the ship in the first place. Then she would never have been a problem. But, once she'd been assigned to the ship, O'Brien should have been able to handle her – or get rid of her somehow – without anyone ever questioning why.

Well, he'd had to clean up after O'Brien before and it looked like he would have to again. Of course, if things got too hot, he'd offer O'Brien up just as easily as he had Shaw. The only question was if he'd be able to before O'Brien turned on him.

Damned stupid Marines.

"Well, I must say you're looking better than you did a couple of hours ago." General Okafor smiled as she escorted Ashlyn into her office, closing the door behind them.

Ash didn't need to look in a mirror to know the general was right. It was amazing what a couple of hours with people she cared about and a tattoo she never thought she'd wear again could do to raise one's spirits. It might not have eased all her doubts, but it had helped – even if her arm stung despite all Gerhardt had done to prevent her from hurting any more than necessary. In fact, now that she thought about it, he'd been much more gentle as he worked this time than he had been when he first tattooed her so long ago.

Of course, if she were to be absolutely honest, the three beers she'd shared with her fellow Devil Dogs probably hadn't hurt any either.

"I feel better, ma'am." She reached up and lightly touched her arm in the area of her new tattoo. "Thank you. For everything."

"Don't thank me yet, Ash."

Okafor motioned for her to take a seat on the sofa against the far wall. As she did, Ashlyn's eyes narrowed and that all-too-familiar seed of doubt once more appeared. What did the general mean? Why shouldn't she be thanking her? Had she let her guard down too soon?

"Ashlyn, don't look so worried." Now the general smiled in reassurance and once again motioned for her companion to be seated. She waited until Ash complied before continuing. "It's just that there are some things we need to discuss first."

"Ma'am?"

"I have hard copies of your orders here as well as a few other official documents you need to review." Okafor patted the file she'd held during their earlier meeting. "If you're still willing to return to duty."

"If it means being able to bring my people home, I am."

"Good." There could be no mistaking the general's pleasure with Ashlyn's answer. She opened the file and pulled out the top set of pages. "Here are your orders, Ash. You are now officially reattached to the Devil Dogs. You will accompany Alpha Company to Tarsus to retrieve our people. Major Pawlak is going as CO. Remember, however, that you are on restricted duty status."

"Understood, ma'am." A flicker of relief began to replace the suspicion. That flicker turned into a flame as Okafor handed her the hard copy of her orders.

"This next is a copy of the official notice of your pardon and reinstatement as an officer of the Corps. It will be released to the press an hour after the *Magellan* breaks orbit. I figured you would want to avoid the press as much as possible."

"Thank you." Ash heard the relief in her voice and felt her cheeks color as the general smiled in understanding

"The rest of it is pretty self-explanatory. The paperwork is there to assure that you get credit for your time-in-grade for the last two and a half years as well as back pay. It should be credited to your account by the time you get home."

"General, that's not necessary."

Not that it wouldn't help.

"It is and you won't argue with me."

"Yes, ma'am." Ash nodded once.

"Good. Now, we have a briefing to attend and then you'll need to meet with Major Pawlak. Spend tomorrow with your son. Your orders don't require you to report to the *Magellan* until the morning you break orbit."

Ashlyn swallowed against the lump in her throat. The fact the general had thought about her son meant a great deal to her. "Thank you, ma'am. I'll not argue with you about that."

"I know it's going to take time, Ash, but you need to realize just how glad we are to have you back. I wish I could say there aren't at last some ulterior motives because you know there are. We need you and the others in this war to help us win once and for all. But that's only part of it. A small part when considered against the rest of it. We're glad to have you back because you were wronged and we're glad that is being corrected. Most of all, we're glad because it means you will have the chance to help us find out why you were set up and then you can see justice, real justice, done."

"I hope you understand that I know that, at least where the Devil Dogs – past and present – are concerned, General." And, surprisingly, she finally had come to accept it. Perhaps the rest would come with time. She hoped so. "May I ask one question, ma'am?"

"Of course."

"I know my mother was beached after my conviction. I even have a pretty good idea why. She's never been known as one to stay silent when she feels a wrong has been committed."

When Okafor threw her head back and laughed, Ashlyn felt herself responding. From what little her parents had told her, it was clear her mother made life miserable for a number of senior officers before she'd been beached. If they thought that would silence her, they'd been wrong. No longer worried about chain of command, Elizabeth had gone public with her campaign to not only free Ashlyn and the others but to clear their names as well.

"And you want to know why she hasn't been returned to duty. Right?"

"Yes, ma'am."

"I've tried to reactivate her from the first day I assumed my duties as Commandant of the Corps." Gone was the humor from a moment before. "She refused. In fact, she threatened to resign her commission if I pushed. She wasn't going to return to duty until you and your people were cleared of all charges against you and brought home. At least she wasn't against working with me to do just that."

Ashlyn nodded.

"But, after the attack on the capital and learning you were home, she finally agreed to return to duty. If you don't mind, I'll be sending hard copies of her new orders with you when you leave today."

Another nod. One simply didn't tell the Commandant of the Corps to find another messenger. Not that Ash wanted her to.

"I don't want you to worry, however. For the immediate future, she will be stationed here in the capital. She's being assigned to FirstDiv."

Ash smiled, pleased for her mother. She knew the Corps meant as much to Elizabeth than it did to her. But more importantly, her mother would still be there for Jake. That was important, especially with Ash about to leave for Tarsus. Jake didn't understand why his mother had been gone for so long and Ash didn't want to think about how he'd feel when he found out she'd be leaving again so soon.

"I seem to be saying this a lot today, General, but thank you."

"No need, Ash. You know me. I demand the best of all my Marines, myself included. That means I insist the best people fill command positions. And, now that you're home, it's time for your mother to get back to duty." Okafor handed the file with the rest of its documents to Ashlyn, telling her to study them and let her know if she had any questions. "Now, let's get to the briefing so you can get home to your son."

Grinning, Ash tucked the file under her arm and stood. Maybe things really were going to work out. At least she was finally beginning to believe it.

———

ASHLYN NODDED in appreciation as a young steward poured her a mug of coffee. As he handed it to her, she smiled slightly to see the Fuerconese Marine Corps crest on the side of the mug. Then she leaned back, cradling the mug in her hands. When General Okafor said it was time for their briefing, she'd expected it to be about the attack. Looking at the others gathered around the conference table, she had a feeling there was more on the agenda than that.

Okafor sat at the head of the table. To her right sat Miranda Tremayne. No longer the senator, Tremayne wore the daily uniform of the Fuerconese Space Navy. Her head bent, she appeared to be studying something on her datapad. Then, as if sensing Ashlyn's eyes on her, she glanced her way. Tremayne nodded and smiled in encouragement.

Ash lifted her mug slightly, wishing as she did that it was that easy. She had a feeling by the time the briefing ended, she might wish she hadn't agreed to return to duty.

Also present were Rico Santiago and Secretary of Defense Linden Klingsbury. The former's presence made sense. If Okafor planned on debriefing them about the attack, Santiago had been one of the senior officers on the ground during the initial phases of the attack. If they were to discuss why Ash had been brought back to Fuercon, he'd played an instrumental role in that. His presence made sense.

Klingsbury's, on the other hand, did not. Never before had she been in a briefing where SecDef, no matter who held the position, took part. Her mouth turned desert-dry even as her palms began to sweat. The uneasiness that plagued her most of the day returned in full force. What did Okafor have in mind and what did she expect from Ash?

More importantly, was it something Ash could give?

"Let's get started." Okafor reached for her own mug and took a sip before continuing. "Secretary Klingsbury, may I present Captain Ashlyn Shaw?"

Before Ash could stand, Klingsbury waved for her to remain seated. "Captain, it is indeed a pleasure to finally meet you."

"Thank you, sir, but the pleasure is mine."

As is the paranoia.

But was it paranoia or a healthy dose of self-preservation after all she had been through? She didn't know and, at the moment at least, didn't care.

"Before we get started, this is an informal meeting between the five of us and nothing said in this room is to leave it. I've given Captain Shaw my word on that. After all she's been through, she needs to know she can trust us."

Ash's breath caught and she swallowed hard. "General, I've never doubted that I could trust you – or Admiral Tremayne or Major Santiago. None of you betrayed me or my people."

She couldn't say the same about Klingsbury, however. She didn't know him. What little research she had done on him indicated he believed much as she did but how much of that was truth and how much spin? Until she had an answer for that, she'd have to watch what she said. The lives of her people back on Tarsus depended on it.

"Let's start by everyone agreeing since this is an informal meeting, we aren't going to stand on rank or formality. We're simply going to talk. Agreed?" Okafor glanced around the table, waiting until everyone nodded in agreement. "Ash, let me begin by saying we understand your desire to do or say nothing that might endanger your people at the penal colony. What we are going to ask about today is so we can protect them and bring them home sooner, rather than later. It is also to help us start putting into place everything necessary to bring those responsible for what happened to justice. That includes bringing charges against those at the penal colony responsible for injuring or abusing you and your people."

Ashlyn nodded once and waited. This was the general's show, at least for the moment.

"If you don't mind, I'd like to get us started." Tremayne gave Ash a smile of encouragement. "I've shared your messages to me, both from before that last mission on Arterus as well as leading up to your court-martial. Some of us have also seen your original orders and have compared them with what the prosecutor presented. It is clear from those, as well as evidence Rico turned up, that you and your people were set up. Hell, kid, I know I speak for all of us when I say you were set up, both on the mission and when you were brought up on charges."

She cleared her throat before answering. "Thank you."

"That brings up my first question. Why in the hell didn't you fight harder to prove your innocence?" Anger roughened the admiral's voice. "I was there for most of your trial. Throughout it, you looked like you had given up and that's not you. So, what happened? Why weren't you shouting your innocence at the top of your lungs?"

She didn't care if it was a breach of protocol. Okafor said they weren't standing on ceremony. Besides, she needed to pace. If she answered Tremayne's question, she knew it would lead to others. Did she dare relax her guard now? Did she dare not?

"Admiral – Miranda, I couldn't." She returned to the table and sat, reaching for her mug. What she wouldn't give for a stiff drink right then.

"What do you mean?" Klingsbury asked.

"Sir, you're aware of the fact I was held in custody after charges were leveled against me?" She waited until Klingsbury nodded. "Several days before the trial started, I had a visitor. I was told in no uncertain terms that I was to do nothing that might prevent a conviction from being handed down. If I didn't do as they said, they would see to it that my people received the death penalty." She took a deep drink of her coffee more to give her a moment to calm her emotions than because she wanted it.

"Who?" Santiago asked. "Ash, who told you that?" Even as he asked, he reached for her datapad and she had a feeling he was calling up the visitor's log for when she'd been in custody. Not that she expected it to tell him anything. If they'd been smart enough to alter her orders, surely they'd been smart enough to erase any mention of the prosecuting attorney visiting her in her cell.

"Rico, I can't."

Damn it, he knew she couldn't tell him what he wanted to know, not yet. Not as long as her people were still on Tarsus.

"Ash, look at me." Okafor waited until Ashlyn complied. "As a Marine, I swear I will personally cut off the balls, literally and figuratively, of anyone who violates your confidence. Then I will turn them over to Gunnery Sergeant Talbot and the rest of the Devil Dogs with instructions to do with them as they will."

They were asking so much.

"Captain Jerrold Burnside." One of many who had haunted her dreams for so long.

Santiago made a quick note and then gave a decisive nod.

"Rico?"

"Burnside is one of those who was shown the door after the election, Ash," Tremayne said before Santiago could respond. "There were enough questions about his conduct, not only with regard to your trial but to other things as well, to have the CNO give him the choice of serving on the front line or resigning. He chose the latter."

"I have to ask this, Captain. If Burnside hadn't said what he did, would your defense have been different?"

Ashlyn glanced at the Secretary of Defense and then down at her hands where they rested on the table. "I doubt it, sir." She shook her head before anyone could interrupt. "Talk to Joseph Anders, my defense counsel. He can give you more details than I can. But I know he tried calling others from the Corps, especially the Devil Dogs, and the presiding judge wouldn't let him. He also wouldn't let him introduce evidence that my orders had been altered. There's more but Anders can give you a more complete answer than I can."

For a moment, no one spoke. Their anger filled the room. For the first time in much too long, such emotion did not scare Ashlyn. In fact, it reassured her. They were angry for her, not with her. That made all the difference in the world. It also helped convince her they had no hidden agenda, at least not one that would come back to bite her or her people on the ass.

"I'll take a closer look at both the prosecuting attorney and the presiding judge to see if they have any ties to Sorkowski or O'Brien," Santiago commented.

"I can answer that for you, Major. Or at least part of it." Anger roughened Klingsbury's voice.

"Sir?" Ashlyn looked at him in concern.

"I've been doing my own investigation into what happened, Ashlyn." He smiled almost apologetically. "I'm sorry, Captain. I've been working to find out what happened to you and why for so long, I feel as if we've known one another for years. May I call you Ashlyn?"

"Of course, sir."

"Linden or Lin," he corrected. "As I said, I have some information where that's concerned. Burnside's father was best man at Sorkowski's wedding and Sorkowski is the man's godfather."

Ash ground her teeth. How had they missed that?

Because they weren't looking for it.

Damn it.

"If they had any contact before or during the trial, I'll find it," Santiago promised. "They'll pay, Ash. I swear it."

"We all do," Tremayne said. "Will you tell us now about what happened to you once you arrived at the penal colony?"

"Miranda, I can't." She shook her head. Her hands gripped the coffee mug so tightly she worried it might shatter in her grasp. "Please."

"We need to know, Ash." Okafor's voice, gentler than she had ever heard, drew her gaze to the general's face. "Please."

For a long moment, Ashlyn said nothing. Even though she wanted nothing more than to get up and pace – no, she wanted to run, as far and as fast from there as she could. If she never thought about the penal colony and all she'd been forced to endure, it would be too soon. But Okafor was right. They needed to know. But she needed to know her people were safe first.

"I." She closed her eyes. There had to be a way. Maybe there was a way without her actually saying anything. "You've seen the medic's report after the attack?"

For a moment, no one said anything. Then, one by one, they nodded grimly. Several of them reached for their datapads and, unless she missed her guess, pulled up the doctor's report. Instead of watching as they did, she climbed to her feet and crossed the conference room to stare outside. So many secrets could be discerned by comparing her medical reports from before her court-martial to the one upon her return to Fuercon.

"Rico, you saw what they did to my tattoo. When I say that wasn't the worst done to me by far, it wouldn't be a lie."

"Is there more besides what the doctor documented?" Okafor asked.

"I-I don't know. I haven't looked at his report." She wouldn't look at it, not yet at any rate. She didn't need a medical report to tell her everything that had been done to her. She would never be able to forget her "sessions" with the guards or with the penal colony's commandant.

"All right." A chair scraped against the floor and, a moment later, Okafor stood next to Ash. The general's hands were gentle as she turned the younger woman to face her. "Ash, look at me." She waited until their eyes met. "Was it more than beatings?"

She couldn't answer. She wasn't sure she could even breathe. So, she nodded, just once. "Please, don't tell my parents." She spoke softly, barely more than a whisper.

"I won't." Okafor rested a hand on her arm and then let it slide down until she grasped Ashlyn's hand. "They'll pay for it, Ash, for every single thing that happened to you and yours. I swear it."

"We need more details," Klingsbury reminded them from where he, along with the others, sat.

"And we will get them, after we bring the rest of our people home."

Ashlyn looked at the general and mouthed a silent "thank you".

"Until then, we have more than enough to start with. Rico?"

"We have more than enough, ma'am. I'll get started on it as soon as I leave here."

"Ash, thank you. We'll have to talk some more about this, but it will wait until the others are home." Okafor smiled at her in reassurance. "Now, you'd best report to Major Pawlak before he sends a search party out for you."

"Thank you, ma'am."

"Ash." Tremayne stood and moved around the table in her direction. "Comm me before you leave for the day. If I'm done, we'll ride home together."

Ashlyn nodded. She knew why Tremayne said to comm her. The admiral wanted to be sure she was all right before Ash arrived home.

"I will. If you aren't ready, I can wait."

Tremayne nodded and gave her a small but reassuring smile. It wasn't much but it was enough to let her know her mentor would make sure no one tried to do anything else to compromise her or her people.

"Go on, Ash. We have a briefing in the morning at 0730 to discuss the attack on the capital. I want you, as well as Major Pawlak and Captain Ortega here for it."

"Understood, ma'am." She gave a quick salute and then turned to the door. As she left, she hoped the time it took her to find Pawlak was enough to get her emotional equilibrium back in place.

10

─────────

"Come!"

At Pawlak's call, Ashlyn opened the door. The moment she stepped inside, Pawlak rose and moved around his desk. His expression concerned, he studied the captain. Then, before she could brace to attention, he waved for her to stand easy. Relieved, she did as he said. Hopefully, this meeting would not be as emotionally draining as the last.

"You look like you've been through the wringer, kid," he said. "You okay?"

She nodded. "They had some questions I wasn't ready to answer." She didn't say anything more, knowing she wouldn't have to. One thing she learned very quickly about Pawlak was that he understood loyalty. Even though she knew he wanted her to explain what happened during the Arterus mission, not to mention during her time on Tarsus, he'd never pushed. He trusted her to tell him when she was ready. Hopefully, that day would come soon.

"But?" He escorted her to one of the chairs before his desk and then sat in the other, turning so he could watch her.

"But I managed to give them at least some information, specifically about the trial, they hadn't known. In return, SecDef had an explanation, at least a possible one, for what I told them. Santiago is going to look into it."

"Then we will let them deal with that. We have something more important to concern ourselves with." He stood and patted her shoulder before moving around the desk. Before sitting, he activated his comm and sent for Lucinda Ortega. Then, as he settled onto his well-worn chair, he looked at Ashlyn in such a way that she fought the urge to squirm. "There is one thing we need to clear up before Luce gets here."

Her eyes narrowed and she wondered if she had made a mistake coming straight to her CO's office. "What?"

Pawlak threw back his head and laughed. Then he sobered. "You may have bent a little, Ash, but those bastards didn't break you. But we will, by God, break each and every one of them. When we do, you will be standing with me as my XO. The position's yours again if you want it."

Ashlyn didn't dare respond. Earlier, when Lucinda Ortega and the others told her they not only wanted her back with the Devil Dogs but that they wanted her back as the XO, she couldn't believe it. That alone had meant more to her than they would ever know. Even so, she had not seriously considered returning to her role as Pawlak's XO. Not only was she acutely aware of the impact the last two years had on her, she wouldn't do that to Ortega. Her friend deserved the role, a role she'd held since Ashlyn had been relieved of duty.

"Major – Hammer, you have an XO."

"I have an XO who would much rather return to her role as the battalion's intel officer. Something you'd realize if you thought about it for a moment."

He smiled to take any sting out of his words. Then, when a knock sounded at the door, he called out for the newcomer to enter. A moment later, Lucinda Ortega took the seat next to Ash and looked from her former roommate to their commanding officer and back.

"Well, what did she say?" Ortega asked as she once again turned her focus to Pawlak.

"She said I already have an XO."

For a moment, Ortega looked at Ashlyn. Then she smiled slightly even as she shook her head. "Ash, I meant what I said earlier. Your boots have been very difficult to fill. Now that you're back, you are the XO. I will gladly go back to my role as the intel officer. You know that's what I love doing and it's what I'm good at. The Devil Dogs will be better served with us back in our former roles."

"You've got to be sure, both of you."

No matter how badly she wanted to return to her former role with the battalion, she wouldn't insist, not if it put the Devil Dogs at a disadvantage.

"Ash, we are," Pawlak said. "Before you think of any other reasons why you shouldn't be my XO, hear us out. First of all, the Devil Dogs want you as their XO. If you refuse, you are going to have to explain it to them because Lucinda and I sure as hell aren't going to."

She couldn't help it. She chuckled softly. Then she motioned for him to continue.

"Hammer's right, Ash," Ortega took up. "We also know you will worry about being out of the loop when it comes to everything that's happened since your court-martial. So, to help you start catching up, I've pulled together some briefing materials. It's pretty extensive but it should bring you up-to-date with not only what's been happening with regard to the so-called truce but also with regard to the investigation into what happened to you and the others. Look it over and let me know if you have any questions." As she spoke, she handed Ash several data chips.

"Any other objections, Captain?" Pawlak arched one brow and grinned.

"All sorts of them, sir, and they all come down to one basic thing. How can you trust me to do what needs to be done when I'm not sure I can trust myself?"

"Ash!" Ortega looked at her in concern. "What do you mean?"

"Luce, I worry that what happened on Arterus will act as a distraction. You know how dangerous that is." She ran a hand over her face. "Then there's the fact it's taken every ounce of self-control since the attack not to slip away to pay a visit to Sorkowski or O'Brien. They owe me and the others for what they did."

Neither Ortega nor Pawlak said anything. Worried, Ashlyn glanced from one to the other. Instead of seeing condemnation or, worse in so many ways, pity, she saw understanding. More than that, she saw the same need in them that she felt. They understood. More than that, they agreed and quite possibly approved. That should have made her feel better, but it didn't. One of the last things she wanted was for either of them to get into trouble because of her.

"Ashlyn, don't." Ortega all but glared at her before standing. She paced the length of Pawlak's office several times before turning her attention back to her friend. "You don't get it, do you?"

"Don't get what?"

"Hammer?" Ortega looked to their CO and, when he inclined his head, continued. "Ash, we never once believed the charges against you or the others. None of us, officers, NCOs and enlisted, thought you guilty. We know you too well. We also knew someone behind the scenes was manipulating things to make it look like you had done everything those bastards Sorkowski and O'Brien said. Believe me, once they were grounded here on Fuercon, it was all Hammer could do to keep some of us from paying them a visit and having a little *chat* with them."

"Luce!"

"So, when you say you've wanted to slip away and do the same, we understand. Hell, Ash, we'd go with you and hold them down while you got some of your own back if that's what you wanted or needed." Ortega dropped onto her chair and leaned forward, elbows on knees. "But we aren't going to let you do that because we aren't going to risk you ever being taken from us again. Yes, we feel that strongly about it and about you. I swear, if you don't agree to be the CO again, I'll march myself over to Major Santiago's office and ask to join his staff. I am not going to have the other Devil Dogs thinking for one moment that I wanted to stay in the role."

"Angel." Pawlak's use of her call sign had her looking at him in concern. "You are one of us and I thought you understood that."

"I do." She shook her head and then blew out a breath. "I'm damaged, Hammer. How badly damaged, I don't know. Hell, I don't know if I will ever be back to the Marine you knew."

"Bullshit!" He frowned and she swallowed hard. In all the years she had known the man, she could count on two hands the number of times she'd heard him curse and never, not once, had it been aimed at her. "You're hurt and hurting. I'd be lying if I didn't say anyone could see that. Damn it, you may as well have been a POW these last two years. So yes, it will take you time to recover from that. But that doesn't make you any less of a Marine, or a Devil Dog. In my book, it makes you a better one." He waved off her objections before she could make them.

"Angel, I've seen your psych evals as well as your medical records. Both Sorceress and I have." Now he nodded to Ortega. "I wish half the battalion was as well-adjusted as you are. What you're feeling is natural and the best way to deal with it is to go get our people from Tarsus and then to take the fight straight to the Callusians. What say you?"

She wasn't going to win this argument, so why fight it?

"I say that sounds very good, Hammer." She even managed a slight smile. "So, yes, I will officially accept the role of XO."

"Good!" He reached across his desk to shake her hand. As he sat, he grinned as Ortega gave Ashlyn's shoulder a light punch. "Now that that's settled, let's get to work."

By the time she left Pawlak's office three hours later, Ashlyn felt more like the Marine she remembered than she had since her return to Fuercon. The major's briefings hadn't changed much since her court-martial. He'd gone over the major points, often anticipating her questions. Between the two of them, he and Ortega brought her up to speed on the battalion as well as what they knew about the attack on the capital. She'd been given full access to battalion records and Ortega promised to be moved out of the XO's office by morning, giving her a place to work.

What surprised Ash the most had been learning the Devil Dogs had been kept in the home system since the election. When she asked about it, Pawlak explained FleetCom wasn't as trusting as the previous administration had been. With the Callusians playing fast and loose with the terms of the truce, there were those in FleetCom who expected the enemy to strike, if not at the home system, at one of their close allies. As a result, the Devil Dogs had been kept close so they could respond without delay.

Fortunately for everyone, that meant they had been on hand when the capital was attacked.

The attack still bothered Ashlyn. It helped to know her CO, as well as her best friend, worried about it as well. The more she thought about it, the more convinced she became that there had been a two-fold reason for the attack. The first had been to test their response. It wouldn't surprise her at all to learn the enemy had left sensors in-system to monitor what happened. When she said as much, Pawlak agreed and said he had already suggested FleetCom order a full sweep of the system to be sure. The last thing they needed was the enemy watching everything they did.

When she asked if they had learned anything from the enemy soldier she'd shot, she knew before they said anything what the answer would be. Both Pawlak and Ortega turned grim and she saw the quick flash of anger in her former roommate's eyes. She understood both when Pawlak said the man had died, not as a result of his injuries but because the security team and medics missed the suicide capsule implanted in his cheek. Once the man regained consciousness after the medics treated him, he bit down and released the poison. He was dead before anyone could react.

Worse, no others from the attacking force had been captured alive. Not that it surprised Ash. The Callusians long ago proved they would not allow themselves to be captured. She had seen ships that could have surrendered activate their self-destruct codes instead. The Fuerconese Navy, as well as its allies, had learned not to come too close to the enemy for that very reason. They'd lost several ships that way and weren't going to lose any others, not if they could help it.

There had been more, and she knew there was much more for her to review in the briefing materials Ortega had prepared for her.

But they could wait. All she cared about just then was getting home to her family, especially to her son. In little more than twenty-four hours, she had to report to the *Magellan*. Soon she would return to Tarsus, this time to free her people instead of to become a prisoner. She could hardly wait to see the look on the faces of those who had taken such sadistic pleasure in tormenting her and the others, especially if she had the chance to give them even the smallest taste of what they had done to her.

———

"Another story, Mommy," Jake said as she finished reading him the third story of the night.

"Not tonight, baby. It's your bedtime."

She bent and kissed his cheek, pulling the sheet about his shoulders. As she did, she swallowed against the lump in her throat. How she'd missed being able to do something so simple and so wonderful as reading her son a bedtime story. Tears pricked at her eyes and she blinked them back. He had grown so much in the time she'd been imprisoned, time she'd never be able to get back. That was one more thing to add to her list of reasons to get revenge on those behind her conviction.

"But you're going away."

Tears welled up in his eyes. It broke Ashlyn's heart to see them roll down his cheeks. She wanted to stay with him and make up for all the time she'd been gone. But she had to return for those sent to the penal colony with her. He would understand, she hoped, when he was older. But right now, he was still so young. All he knew was that she had finally come home only to leave again.

"I won't be gone long, sweetie. I promise." She bent and kissed his cheek again. As she did, a thought came to her and she quickly produced her datapad from her thigh pocket. A moment later, the calendar appeared on the screen. She shifted, drawing her legs onto the mattress and holding the datapad so Jake could see it. "Grandma tells me you know how to use one of these. Right?"

He nodded his head, one small hand reaching for the datapad.

"Then you know that this–" She pointed to the entry for the next day – "is tomorrow. I leave then. And this–" She tapped the entry for three days later – "is when I will reach my destination. I'll be there for a couple of days probably. Then I'll come home."

Now he looked up and grinned, his finger pointing to a date a little more than three weeks away. "Will you be home then?"

"I'll be home then. I promise. I won't miss your birthday."

Even if I have to hijack a ship to be here.

"Can we have a party?" Excitement lit his face as he looked up at her.

"Sure, sweetie. I'll talk to your grandma and grandpa about it before I leave."

He grinned and snuggled up against her side. "Mommy, can I see your ship?"

"You'll have to get up real early."

"I can do that." He nodded vigorously.

"Okay. I'll talk with Grandma and Grandpa about it." She held him close and hugged him tightly, her heart soaring as his arms went about her and squeezed back. "But that means you have to go to sleep now."

He planted a wet kiss on her cheek and snuggled down in bed. Ashlyn brushed his cheek with the fingers of her right hand and stood. He watched, his brown eyes, so much like her own, following her as she backed toward the door to his room. Then, just before she switched off the light, he blew her a kiss. Her right hand flashed out, as if to catch it. She winked at him, reminding him that if he didn't get to sleep, he wouldn't wake up in time to go see her ship. Then she switched off the light and left the room.

"Is he asleep?" Elizabeth asked, handing her a beer.

"If not, he will be soon." Ashlyn smiled her thanks and took a sip. "He wants to see my ship before I leave."

"I'll take him when I go in in the morning," her mother said.

"Thanks."

She settled on the sofa, pulling her feet up under her. As she did, she realized she'd positioned herself so her back was to the wall and she could see all entrances into the room. Damn it, how long would it take for her to be able to let her guard down in her own home?

"How long will you be gone?" Abe asked.

Ashlyn glanced at her father where he sat at the opposite end of the sofa and shrugged. "This shouldn't take more than a week, but it wouldn't surprise me to be delayed there a few days longer. However, I will be home in time for Jake's birthday. Nothing will keep me from that." Not when she remembered the joy reflected on her son's face when she promised she'd be there. "By the way, he wants a party."

Elizabeth chuckled. "Of course, he does. A party means more presents. Shall I take care of setting it up?"

For a moment, Ashlyn didn't answer. Anger flared as did resentment. Then she shook her head. Getting upset with her mother did not good. Elizabeth wasn't trying to take her place in Jake's life. Quite the opposite, in fact. Her mother was giving her the chance to do something she needed to in order to close a very bad chapter in her life. Besides, she didn't know Jake's friends and her mother did.

"Please, Mom. Set up something fun for him. I don't care how much it costs. All I want is for this to be the best birthday he's ever had."

"Don't worry about that. All he really wants is for you to be here."

"Believe me, I'll be here, even if I have to hijack the *Magellan* to get home in time."

"I still don't like the idea of you going back to that hellhole, Ashlyn." Her father's concern was clear.

"I know, Dad, but I have to do this. I have to see for myself that my people are not only freed but that they are all right." She took another sip of her beer and then leaned over to grasp his hand. "They are there because of me, because they chose to follow me and to voice the same objections to the mission I did."

"And when you return?"

"I have no idea beyond knowing I've been ordered to report back to the doctors. I need to have my implants updated and, while they do that, they'll deal with the rest of my scars. They'll also run me through all the psych evals. From what I've been told, those of us sent to Tarsus are being treated like former POWs where that's concerned." She still didn't like the idea of having to put herself in the hands of the shrinks, but she knew it was necessary, at least if she wanted to return to active duty. "General Okafor has already told me that, between the time I'll be spending with the medics and the time I'll need to bring my training back up to where it needs to be, I'll be planetside for several months at least. After that's done, we'll see what FleetCom wants to do with me."

An uneasy silence fell over the room. Too many ghosts and too many fears haunted them. Ashlyn knew her parents relived the last time they sat here before she left on a mission. That had been before the fiasco on Arterus. She also knew until those responsible for what happened were brought to justice, none of her family would rest easy.

But that was only one of her concerns. Before her court-martial, she had always known she might not return from a mission. That fear had been an abstract one, however. In the back of her mind, she'd always thought she'd come home. She wouldn't leave her son without his mother. The foolishness of that belief had been driven home with her court-martial and her time in the penal colony on Tarsus. Because of that, she had taken certain precautions and, like it or not, she needed to discuss them with her parents.

"I, uh, stopped by the lawyer's on my way home today." She tipped up her beer and drained it.

"Ash, has something else happened?" Concern sharpened Elizabeth's voice.

"No, Mom, I swear it." She cursed herself for not anticipating her parents' reaction. Both Abe and Elizabeth looked at her in concern, in fear. Damn it, after all that had happened, of course they thought the visit had something to do with what happened on Arterus.

"Then what?" her father asked.

"Let's just say the last couple of years have taught me not to take anything for granted." She leaned over and set her beer on the low coffee table in front of the sofa. "Being brought up on charges and convicted was bad enough but knowing my bastard of an ex took Jake from you was worse. I knew he didn't love Jake but was doing it to get back at me and at the two of you for not taking his side in the divorce. Nothing made me happier after learning you were all safe was learning you'd gotten Jake back. As soon as I could, I contacted the attorney and made sure everything was in place to prevent his father from ever having any legal claim on him again. I know you had his rights terminated but I took it a step further. I had the paperwork filed on Midlothian as well. That covers all our legal bases, at least I hope so.

"I also updated my will and associated documents." She shook her head before either of her parents could interrupt. "I know you would always look after Jake. Mom, Dad, I'm trusting you to do that. All I did was make it legal. If anything happens to me on this mission, you become his legal guardians. My estate will be put into a trust for him, to help pay for his education and anything else you think he needs. Dad, you're the trustee because, let's face it, you're the best person I know when it comes to understanding and growing invest-ments. I named Katie as a substitute guardian in case anything happens to the three of us.

"I've also left small bequests to the two of you, as well as the brothers and Katie. My death benefits will go into the trust for Jake. Dad, I named Miranda as backup trustee for the money. Mom, you're executor of the estate with Dad as your backup. Miranda comes next, just in case."

She leaned back, waiting. A moment later, Elizabeth knelt in front of her. "Ashlyn, nothing is going to happen." Her hand shook slightly as she reached out to lightly touch her daughter's cheek.

"We can't know that for sure, Mom."

"This time, I do." A slight smile touched Elizabeth's lips, but it didn't reach her eyes. They remained somber. "But I – we – under-stand why you did this. I know I speak for your father as well when I say we will never let you down where Jake is concerned. You have my oath on that."

"I know." She kissed her mother's cheek before leaning over to do the same to Abe. "Let's say I'm not quite as cocky and confident as I was before." And that was putting it mildly.

"You were never cocky, not when it came to the Corps or the Devil Dogs," Elizabeth corrected. She squeezed Ashlyn's hands once in reassurance and then stood. "Is there anything more you can tell us about the mission?"

Ash shook her head. "Not really. If things go as planned, it will be fairly straight-forward. We'll land, get our people and make a few arrests as well as securing certain records. Then we'll return home. It shouldn't be any more difficult than that."

"But you don't think so," Abe commented.

"No, I'm afraid I don't." Not when she considered everything she'd gone through there. "That's why I wanted to be prepared for the worst, just in case."

"You just come home safely to us, Ashlyn. That's all. Just come home."

"I will."

At least she planned to, God willing.

11

———

"They're ready, Mr. President."

President Derek Harper thanked the assistant press secretary and glanced around his office. Waiting with him were Secretary of Defense Klingsbury, Commandant of the Marine Corps, General Helen Okafor, Admiral Tremayne and, looking more than a little discomfited, Brigadier General Elizabeth Shaw. With the exception of Klingsbury who wore a dark suit, the others were in dress uniform. They would stand with the president as he briefed the media on certain events that had, until then, been kept close to the proverbial vest.

A few minutes later, Harper stood behind a podium in the garden outside his office. Reporters filled much of the garden. Their curiosity and concern about the purpose of the press conference filled the air. Shortly after being sworn in, Harper proved to be a much different president than his predecessor when it came to the press. He didn't call a news conference every time he did something. In fact, he rarely spoke directly to the media, focusing instead on doing what he'd been elected to do – clean up the mess and the corruption left behind by the previous administration.

"Ladies and gentlemen of the media." The moment Harper spoke, the garden fell silent. All eyes on the president, they waited, cameras and recorders transmitting into homes and offices around Fuercon. "Less than two weeks ago, our capital came under attack. We were fortunate. First Fleet responded quickly, putting fighters in the air to protect our people and to prevent further incursions by the enemy. The Fuerconese Marine Corps activated its units groundside. They moved in to secure not only the security complex but also the presidential palace. The Devil Dogs, under the command of Major Paul Pawlak, rescued the residents of the Oteri Residential Complex that had also come under enemy attack.

"Military Intelligence, as well as other security agencies, are still working on identifying who these invaders were. We have our suspicions but, without proof, we will not jump to conclusions. In the meantime, rest assured that system defenses have been increased. First Fleet is on-station. There will be no repeat. That is my pledge to you.

"Along that line, the Devil Dogs were an integral part of Fuercon's defense during the last war. One reason why was the leadership of Major Paul Pawlak. Assisting him was his executive officer, Captain Ashlyn Shaw. Together, they kept the Devil Dogs on mission, pressing the enemy and keeping Fuercon and our allies safe.

"Unfortunately, we all know what happened toward the end of the war. Captain Shaw and the survivors of her team on Arterus were charged and court-martialed in what can best be described as questionable circumstances. I made it one of my campaign promises to look into the charges against them, promising to clear their names if the evidence warranted it.

"Some of you have already guessed where this is heading based on a few rumors that came out after the attack on the capital. Less than a week before the attack, Captain Shaw was transported back here to answer questions about what happened. Investigators from the Judge Advocate General's Corps, Military Intelligence as well as special investigators appointed by not only Secretary of Defense Klingsbury but by myself as well, looked into the charges against those brave Marines and determined there was more than enough reason to question not only the evidence presented against them but also the manner in which their courts-martial was handled.

"It would have been easy for Captain Shaw to slip away and disappear into the chaos of the attack. Instead, she risked her life to protect Admiral Miranda Tremayne. It did not matter to Captain Shaw that she had been stripped of her rank and discharged from the Marines. All that mattered was the capital was under attack and a member of the government was in danger. She acted as I expect any Marine would, proving yet again that she would never betray Fuercon or its allies.

"It is my pleasure to confirm on the record that Captain Ashlyn Shaw and those convicted with her," and he went on to name each of them, "have been pardoned of all charges. Further, I have recommended, and the JAG Corps has agreed, that all mention of the charges against them be expunged from their records. They are hereby reinstated to the Marine Corps at their former ranks, with back pay and time-in-grade adjusted.

"As we speak, Major Pawlak, Captain Shaw and other members of the Devil Dogs are on their way to the Tarsus penal colony to free those convicted with Captain Shaw. Captain Shaw has returned to limited duty and has accepted her reassignment to the Devil Dogs. It is my hope her fellow Marines on Tarsus will as well. We need them, and all those like them, helping protect our system and our allies now and in the future.

"I am instructing Secretary Klingsbury, as well as the JAG Corps and other agencies, to initiate an investigation into what has clearly been a terrible miscarriage of justice. If the evidence should show anyone orchestrated what happened, they will be charged and tried. However, at this time, we have no evidence that is what happened. For now, I am simply glad to have this sad chapter over with."

With that, he stepped back and turned, leaving the media to stare at him in surprise. Before any could recover enough to shout a question, he stepped inside his office, Klingsbury and the others on his heels.

"You are an evil man, sir," Klingsbury said with a grin as he moved to pour them each a cup of coffee from the serving tray that had been brought in a few moments earlier. "You've planted seeds of doubt in the minds of those we know responsible for what happened to Captain Shaw and the others. Doubt about whether you know of their actions and doubts about whether any of their co-conspirators have been talking. It won't be long before turn on one another."

"We should be so lucky." Harper accepted a cup from his Secretary of Defense and motioned for everyone to be seated. "I want to keep the lid on the investigation. The last thing we need is for those responsible to flee the system before we're ready to make arrests. Miranda, I'm afraid I threw you under the bus. The media is going to be climbing all over you and your staff, trying to get an interview."

"Then it's very fortunate, for me at least, that I planned an inspection tour of some of the ships assigned to First Fleet, isn't it?" She grinned and leaned back in one of the chairs before his desk.

"Can I go with you?" Elizabeth asked almost ruefully. "Abe and I were ready to start shooting reporters during Ashlyn's court-martial. I don't want to think about what it will be like this time."

"I'll make sure there's a squad of Devil Dogs guarding your place until things calm down," Okafor promised. "I doubt the media will try, at least not more than once, to get by them."

"I won't say no."

"Good." Okafor gave a decisive nod, spoiled only slightly by a wide smile. Then she turned her attention back to the president. "What else, sir?"

"I want to know exactly what the Callusians are up to and how deep their ties here on Fuercon run."

"I'll speak to Rico Santiago about it as soon as I leave here," Tremayne promised.

"Good. Tell him to report to the three of you unless he feels something needs to come directly to me."

"Understood, sir."

"Helen, I want the Devil Dogs to remain in-system until Ashlyn is released to active duty status. Even then, unless something breaks we aren't anticipating just yet, I want to hold them close. The attack on the capital might be making me paranoid, but let's not run any risks."

"I understand, sir. I'll see that it happens."

"Ladies and gentleman, I believe we have our work cut out for us. I want to know the bastards who set up Ashlyn Shaw and her people. I want to know the why of it and I want to know who else might have been involved. Most of all, I do *not* want Fuercon open to attack again. Do I make myself clear?"

"Yes, sir!"

He nodded and dismissed them. As the door closed behind them, he leaned back. Would they find the real enemy before it was too late?

12

"Ms. Moreau, I'm sorry to disturb you but there's a gentleman here who insists on seeing you."

Evan Moreau quickly typed in a command and watched as the vid-feed from the reception area of her office was activated. A frown touched her lips followed almost instantly by a mix of fear and anger. Why was he here? He'd never come to her office before. They had agreed at the beginning of their working relationship that the less direct contact they had, the better. She'd overlooked the way he'd appeared unannounced at her apartment. But this, this was pushing it because there were too many potential witnesses to his being there.

"All right, Keisha. Give me five minutes and then show him in."

Almost before she ended the comm, Moreau was on her feet. She moved quickly to the safe hidden behind one of the several paintings adorning her office walls. The biometric and genetic sensors released the lock and the safe door swung open. It didn't take long to claim the weapons inside.

Next, she input the proper commands into her terminal to block any recording of what might be said, both from inside the room as well as from outside. Then, just moments before the five minutes was up, she returned to her desk, making sure nothing about her or her surroundings betrayed her concern.

"Mr. Kannedy," her secretary said before leaving the office, closing the door behind her.

"I'm surprised to see you here," Moreau said and motioned for him to have a seat in one of the two chairs before her desk.

As he did, she nodded slightly in satisfaction. He'd just confirmed her suspicions. He wasn't nearly as versed in how to control a room as he wanted her to think. If he were, he never would have sat where she'd indicated. He'd have chosen one of the chairs to the side of the office, one that wouldn't have him looking into the light from the window lining the wall behind her. Instead, he'd put himself at a disadvantage. She could see his expression and how he reacted to anything said while the bright light behind her obscured his view of her face.

Fool.

"You screwed up, Moreau." He leaned forward, jabbing a finger in her direction.

She bit down the anger that bubbled up at his accusation. She'd been expecting it. She just hadn't expected him to be foolish enough to come here. God, what if he'd let himself be followed?

"I'm not sure what you mean." She leaned back, doing her best to look relaxed and just a bit concerned.

"You were supposed to take care of Shaw."

"No, I was supposed to make sure no attention was leveled at you or your partners and I've done that."

"You've done everything but that!" he countered.

His hands tightened on the arms of his chair. As they did, Moreau let her right hand drop to her waist where one of her knives rested. If he made a move, he was a dead man.

"Sit still and keep your voice down." She didn't raise her voice. Quite the contrary. She lowered it, speaking softer so he had to lean forward some to hear her. As he did, she noted the way he paled and knew he recognized the warning in her words. Good.

"The only one to put any of us in danger right now is you. First by going to my apartment without giving me a chance to take certain precautions and now by showing up here unannounced. Think about that for a moment and then tell me why you think I screwed up."

She waited, giving him a moment to process what she said.

"You assured me you would take care of everything when we learned Shaw was back in the capital. Instead of having someone slit her throat, you sat back and watched as she was cleared of all charges and sent off to retrieve the rest of her people from Tarsus."

He ran a hand through his hair and she saw how it shook. Interesting. There was more to his unexpected appearance than she'd thought.

"Let me ask you this: has anyone approached you to discuss Shaw or any of her people? Have they come to ask what sort of business you might have had with Sorkowski or O'Brien?"

For a moment, he didn't say anything. Then he shook his head.

"Have you heard tales of FleetCom doing anything more than trying to figure out how the capital was attacked without them having some warning ahead of time?"

"N-no."

"In fact, the attack has everyone focusing on the war again and not on what you and your partners have been up to," she continued. "As for Shaw, consider that there has only been one press release about her and the others and that came after the attack. What did it say? That it has been determined that Shaw and her people weren't guilty of the charges against them and had been pardoned. My sources confirm that all charges against them have been dropped and their records expunged. But there has been nothing – I repeat, *nothing* – said or done to indicate FleetCom suspects they were set up. What happened is being written off as a general cluster fuck that they are now correcting."

"But—"

"There are no buts to it, Kannedy." Now she made no attempt to conceal her derision. "I've done what I said I would. I've made sure certain events happened to protect you and your partners. More than that, I've advanced your interests."

"What the hell are you talking about?" He started to stand but hesitated when she rested her hand, with the knife, on the desktop.

"Everything the government and military is doing right now is focused on reassuring the public that the enemy will not be able to get through the system's defenses again. It won't be long before the president announces that the truce is over and we are once more at war." She watched as he relaxed and leaned back. Maybe the danger was passing. Not that she would drop her guard. "And that is exactly what you and your partners want, whether you admit it to yourselves, much less anyone else. War is much more profitable for people like you and me than peace could ever be. So quit acting the fool and start thinking."

There was more she wanted to say but didn't dare. Not yet, at any rate.

The silence stretched between them. Moreau sat there, her gaze on the man who still thought himself her employer. Well, in a way he was. She'd still accept any money he wanted to give her and do most any job. But she didn't fool herself. He was merely a means to an end. It was his so-called partners she really worked for, partners he didn't even know existed. They were the ones who stood in the shadows, pulling the strings. They were the ones who would make her even richer than she was now and, by the time someone else figured out what was going on, the war would be in full-swing and the balance of power would have finally shifted.

She could hardly wait.

"And what if they start looking at Sorkowski and O'Brien?" Kannedy asked.

Well, she had to admit that was a valid concern and one she'd already considered.

"O'Brien is the weak point, but not one we have to worry too much about. Sorkowski knows what will happen if FleetCom starts looking too closely and he isn't about to let that happen. I assure you he has enough *evidence*—" She made quote marks in the air with her fingers — "to put the entire blame on O'Brien. That will serve two purposes, both good for you and your partners. It will offer FleetCom a sacrificial lamb and it will make them think that what happened was nothing more than sour grapes and jealousy aimed at Shaw. They'll never find out about the rest of it."

She waited, watching to see if he accepted what she said. When he nodded, she relaxed a little. Let him think Sorkowski wouldn't talk as long as it bought her a little more time. All that mattered was she knew the truth. Sorkowski was as much of a liability as O'Brien. At least he'd do everything he could to place all the blame on O'Brien should eyes start looking too closely at what happened.

"You make sure of it, Moreau. It's your head that will roll before mine."

With that, Kannedy got to his feet. She watched as he left her office without a backward glance. Once the door shut behind him, she leaned back and frowned. So, the battle lines had been drawn. He'd betray her the moment he got scared. Not that she hadn't expected it. Still, she was surprised he'd shown his hand.

Well, two could play that game. He just hadn't realized she'd be the winner. But first things first, she needed to let her real employers know what just happened. How long Kannedy remained among the living was up to them – for the moment at least. Then she'd reach out to her sources inside FleetCom to see just what was going on with regard to Shaw and her people.

———

ASHLYN SAT HUNCHED on the edge of her bed, her head bent, her heart racing. In less than an hour, the *Magellan* would enter Tarsus space. Until now, she had managed to keep busy enough that her demons hadn't haunted her. Pawlak understood and made sure she worked until exhausted. But now, knowing how close they were, all the fears and all the nightmares washed over her. She knew circumstances were far different from the last time she had approached Tarsus, but the fear remained. How long until she finally allowed herself to believe the nightmare was over?

A soft *ping* sounded, a welcome interruption. She reached out and activated the comm next to her bed. "Shaw."

"Comms," came the reply. "You have a message, Captain."

"Understood."

She stood and crossed her quarters to the small desk against the far wall. As she did, she felt some of her tension ease. She had no doubt who the message was from or that it had been recorded and downloaded into the ship's comm-bank before they left orbit around Fuercon. A moment later, she leaned against the edge of the desk and watched as the holo display came to life.

Standing before her were her parents. Jake stood between them, his hands holding theirs. Elizabeth bent and lifted her grandson, cradling him on her hip. Then she turned so they faced the camera, making it seem as if they were facing Ashlyn.

"Say hi to mommy, Jake," Elizabeth urged.

"Hi, Mommy!"

He lifted one small hand to his mouth and threw her a kiss. Tears burned in her eyes as Ashlyn reached out, as if to catch it. In that moment, it didn't matter he had done that days earlier. All that did was that he remembered her and thought about her and wanted her to know it. She sniffled once and dragged the back of her hand under her nose.

"Hi, baby," she whispered.

"Ash, we won't keep you. But we wanted you to know how proud we are of you and how much we love you," Abe said as he slid an arm around Elizabeth's waist and pulled her, and Jake, close. "Come home as soon as you can."

"I will, Dad. I promise."

Abe took Jake from Elizabeth and whispered something in the boy's ear.

"Love you, Mommy. Come home soon."

Ashlyn dashed away a single tear as it rolled down her cheek. Then she waited until only her mother stood before her.

"Ash, I want you to remember something. We love you and we are so proud of you, more than you will ever know. But I need you to do something for me. For all of us. I need you to come home safely. So, no matter what you find when you get dirtside, don't do anything foolish. Your life isn't worth it. Promise me that." Elizabeth paused, almost as if she was waiting for Ash to do as she said. "I gave something to Gunny Talbot for you, Ash. He should have put it in her desk last night. See if it's there."

Ashlyn's brow furrowed as she looked on the desk, seeing nothing that shouldn't be there. Then she opened the lap drawer. Resting inside was a small black box. Her fingers shook slightly as she lifted it out. A moment later, she lifted the lid and stared down at a set of dog tags.

"Those belonged to my father, your grandfather," Elizabeth continued. "He asked me before he died to give them to you when I thought the time was right. I know he would be as proud of you as I am. Remember he survived more than four years as a POW. It left him feeling in many ways as you do now. I know that you, like he, can push through this and that you will be stronger, as a woman and as a mother and as a Marine, for it. Now go get your people and come home to us." Tears glistened in Elizabeth's eyes. "I love you, Ash, and am so very proud of you. Come home and I promise we will give Jake the best birthday party any little boy has ever had."

The holo display wavered slightly and then faded away. For a long moment, Ashlyn stayed where she was. Then she removed her dog tags. Carefully, she added her grandfather's tags to her own. As she did, she drew a deep, bracing breath. She would and could do this. She wouldn't let those responsible for what happened on Arterus and afterwards win.

"Comms?" Captain Stefan Carlisle prompted.

"Hail is away, Captain," the young comms officer replied.

Standing behind and to the right of the captain's chair, Ashlyn studied the nav-plot before them. Icons representing each of the orbital defense platforms shone red. As she absently counted each icon, her brows knitted in concern. She wanted to believe the knot of worry forming in the pit of her stomach was due to their close proximity to the Tarsus military prison. One small part of her mind, that treacherous doubting part, still wondered if everything leading up to this moment had been some sort of elaborate hoax and that, at any moment, guards would appear to take her back into custody.

But there was more to it. She knew that. The icons should be glowing green, not red. Something was wrong. But what?

Her sharp intake of breath came at almost the same time as Carlisle's. It was bad enough that the icons shone red, indicating the platforms were offline. Worse was that she counted only nine of them instead of the even dozen there should have been.

Ashlyn's right hand fisted at her side as she fought to remain silent and not demand the comms officer repeat the hail broadcast to the prison. Instead, she stepped closer to the nav-plot. She counted the icons again, praying she had miscounted earlier. But she hadn't. Worse, when she glanced at the comms officer, she could see his concern. He didn't have to tell her no one was answering his hails. For the penal colony to go silent and the defense platforms to be offline . .
..

"No response, Captain," Comms reported.

"Are you picking up any chatter?" Carlisle's voice was even, almost relaxed, but one look at him was all Ashlyn needed to know he was just as concerned about what might be happening planetside as was she.

"Negative, Captain."

Carlisle sat there. The drumming of the fingers of his right hand on the arm of his chair broke the silence of the bridge. Then, with the sudden explosion of movement Ashlyn had quickly come to expect from him when he made his mind up about something, he pushed to his feet. He gave her a nod and moved to stand behind the comms officer.

"Send messages to the XO, Major Pawlak and Lieutenants Marshall and Hrabek to join Captain Shaw and myself in my ready room. Lieutenant Montenegro, you have the conn."

"Aye, sir," the two lieutenants replied in unison as Carlisle moved toward the ready room.

Ashlyn quickly fell into step behind the captain. In the short time she'd worked with him, she found herself surprised on more than one occasion. He'd accepted the Devil Dogs' temporary assignment to his ship with an aplomb many in the Navy wouldn't have. More importantly, he'd smoothed things over with his own Marine CO, Lieutenant Marshall, before they'd come onboard, assuring him the DDs weren't there to take over. Fortunately for all involved, Lieutenant Marshall was confident enough in himself and in his command that he hadn't tried to make things difficult. Either that or he'd realized that the week or so Ashlyn and the other Devil Dogs would be onboard the *Magellan* wouldn't be long enough to cause him any trouble.

"As you know by now, it appears that we have a situation," Carlisle began a few minutes later as the last of those he'd sent for arrived. "Our scanners show the defense platforms are offline. Worse, at least three platforms aren't registering on scanners at all. It is possible they were removed from service for some reason and not replaced but, considering the importance of Tarsus, I doubt that's the case. Add to that the fact we have received no response to our hails and there is no comms chatter being picked up and I think you can see why I've brought the ship to general quarters."

"Captain." Lt. Commander Nicole Underwood's long, slender fingers stroked the rim of her coffee cup. Her dark brown eyes flicked from the tactical display at her elbow to him and back again. "Have we picked up any signs of debris or damage groundside?"

"That's a negative, XO." He shook his head. "I've ordered Tactical to use passive scans only. Since we don't know what's going on, we used one of the drones to hopefully make it appear that we left the system when we didn't receive a response to our hails. It won't work for long, especially not if there's another ship in the system. But it will give us a little more time to try to figure out what's going on. If this is a trap, I don't want to walk into it blindly. Hell, I don't want to walk into it at all."

That was something Ashlyn could agree with completely. She hated the delay, especially when her people were so close, but she knew she couldn't ask Carlisle to endanger the lives of his crew without having at least some idea of what they might be up against. But knowing it didn't make it any easier.

Damn it.

"What are your orders, Captain?" the XO asked.

"I'd like to hear what each of you think. Randy?" He looked to Lt. Randy Hrabek, senior flight officer for the *Magellan*.

"I'd recommend putting our LACs on standby. I'd like to put First Squad in the air, Captain. Let them take a look around, see what they can find. We need to see what's going on groundside."

"I agree with the lieutenant, sir," the XO said, her mouth pulling down in a frown. "I could buy comms going offline at one location but not planet-wide."

"Lieutenant Marshall?" The captain turned to his Marine CO. As he did, Ashlyn had to give him credit. He was according the young lieutenant, who had only been out of the Academy a few years, all the respect he would a seasoned veteran. Not that she'd expected any different after being onboard the last few days.

"I agree with Randy, sir. I've already ordered our Marines to prepare for a drop. Sergeants Hayes and Broussard will hold their units back as possible boarding parties in case we need them. Squads One and Two are prepping now and will bunk in their shuttles until the emergency is over."

Ashlyn nodded slightly in approval. That was exactly what she'd have done in the lieutenant's place. By having the squads bunking in the shuttles, they would be ready to drop at a moment's notice. Good. Maybe the kid wasn't as green as she'd feared.

"Captain Shaw, your thoughts?"

"Sir, you know the Devil Dogs' mission. We're to secure the release of those sent to the military prison on Tarsus with me. However, much as I hate to say it, our priority has to be on discovering why those platforms are off-line. I'm sure Major Pawlak will agree with me when I say the Devil Dogs are at your service and will do as you order."

Her heart broke as she said it but she what else could she do? She wanted nothing more than to free her people. But the safety of the ship and its crew had to come first. Like it or not, she had to accept the possibility that the enemy was in-system. If so, it was the *Magellan*'s duty to make sure the Callusians couldn't advance any further into Fuerconese space. If that meant her people were injured, or worse, that was the price she'd have to pay. Of course, it was also a price she'd exact a hundred-fold from those responsible, not only for whatever happened to her people but from those who originally sent them to Tarsus in the first place.

For a moment, Carlisle didn't say anything. Instead, he looked from Ashlyn to Pawlak where the major sat at her side, his expression serious. Then, as if seeing what he needed to, Carlisle nodded slightly before sitting up straighter in his chair.

"Lieutenant Marshall, no disrespect to you or to your abilities, but I'm going to ask Major Pawlak and the Devil Dogs to take lead for this mission. My grandfather and I might not agree on a lot of things, but there is one thing he taught me that I wholeheartedly agree with: you always put your most experienced Marine CO in charge of your ground forces."

Ashlyn bit back a smile. She noticed the captain didn't mention his father. She'd had the extreme displeasure of serving on a ship then Commander Josiah Carlisle was the CO on. The elder Carlisle was one of those who felt the only things Marines should be used for was cannon fodder for enemy ground troops until the Navy could swoop in and win the day. He'd refused to allow a Marine to do anything more than stand guard on his ships. When the Navy began allowing Marines to pilot shuttles and attack ships, he had been one of those to argue that it would diminish the quality of the Navy.

In short, as far as Ashlyn was concerned, he'd been an idiot. Fortunately, his son didn't show the same tendencies.

"Captain, I agree with you and with your grandfather. I know my limitations and, if we are walking into an ambush, Major Pawlak,

Captain Shaw and the rest of the Devil Dogs have much more experience than I do. I'd be a fool to object to their taking point. Besides, there's not a Marine in my command who wouldn't give his right arm to watch the Devil Dogs in action up close and personal." The young man gave a cheeky grin that left no doubts about his willingness to step aside in their favor.

"Thank you, Captain, LT, but I'd like to make a slight alteration," Pawlak said, waving aside Marshall's objections before he could voice them. "The LT knows his men. He knows who is best to send into any given situation. I'd be a fool to forget that. I suggest we drop the DDs in the first shuttle. We'll secure the landing area and make first entry. The LT can choose the squads to back us up. I'd also like at least two attack shuttles and Lieutenant Hrabek's LACs in the air for support."

"Agreed," Carlisle said and looked once more at the tactical display. "XO, you'll be in AuxCon with your crew. I want you to coordinate our efforts between any groundside targets the major designates unless we wind up in action up here."

"Aye, sir."

"Major, what do you think our first step should be?"

"We know that there are at least three areas dirtside where prisoners are located." He typed in a command and the plot displayed over the table shifted slightly. "The first is the prison itself." A small red dot appeared on the plot. "The second is an ag center used to feed the prison personnel and inmates." A green dot appeared. "This last is the housing area for the prison personnel." A blue dot blipped into existence.

"Captain Shaw, as well as others who have been to the penal colony, have confirmed that prisoners are sent on a regular basis to both the ag facility and a mining area. Unfortunately, we don't have coordinates yet for that last area. I'd like to request your scanners to check for it, Captain Carlisle."

"Done." Carlisle activated his comm unit and issued the order.

"Since we don't have those coordinates yet, my recommendation is that we focus on the prison itself. I suggest we drop the Devil Dogs there. It will be the biggest security challenge. The other two sites can be secured with smaller forces made up from Lt. Marshall's people.

"As soon as we are reasonably sure that there are no enemy ships in the sector, I'd like to drop our people to the surface. I'd suggest live feeds back to the ship. While we are dirtside, I'd recommend the ship remain on alert. Something is going on and I don't like not knowing what."

"I have to agree with you about that." Carlisle paused and studied the officers seated around the table. "All right. Major, I'd like you and Lt. Marshall to remain here for a few minutes so we can build a plan of attack. While we do, the Marines should go ahead and prep for the drop."

"Agreed." Pawlak gave a decisive nod.

"How long until they can be ready to drop, Major?"

"Lieutenant Marshall?"

Ashlyn approved of how Pawlak appeared to be deferring to the younger officer. He wasn't, not really, and they all knew it. What he was really doing was making sure he knew exactly what the ship's Marine complement was capable of. This mission now looked to be much more complicated than they'd expected. That meant coordination of effort was not only necessary but essential. The Devil Dogs could be ready to drop in just a matter of minutes. But the Marines stationed onboard the *Magellan....*

"We can drop in ten, Major, but I'd prefer half an hour or so to brief my people after we develop our plan of attack."

"Then let's say drop will occur at fourteen hundred hours," Carlisle said.

"With your permission, Captain, I'd like my XO to start briefing the DDs."

"Of course, Major."

"Captain Shaw, I'll send specifics to you as soon as I have them. In the meantime, get everyone ready to drop."

"Understood, Major."

She stood and took one last look at the plot. Then, hoping she looked more confident than she felt, she left Carlisle's ready room. As she did, her stomach roiled like it hadn't since her first combat mission. Her nerves were stretched taut and her paranoia was running rampant. The only reason she managed to maintain any control was the fact the Devil Dogs were with her. She knew they'd do everything possible – and then some – to make sure nothing else happen to her. As long as they were present, there would be no betrayal.

Alone in the lift a few moments later, she allowed herself to sag against the far wall. Nightmares had plagued her the previous two nights. Memories of the first time she'd been inbound to the penal colony filled her, bringing with them all the pain and fear she'd felt. Even though he hadn't said anything, she knew Pawlak was aware of how she felt. She'd seen it in his eyes and in the way he kept a close watch on her. But she hadn't let those emotions interfere in her duties. Now that she was so close to her goal, she could manage to hold on a bit longer.

She had to.

———

"Gear up!" Ashlyn ordered as she stepped off the lift into the staging area adjoining the shuttle bay. "Gunny, I want Tank and Hound in heavy armor. Everyone else in light. We now have three groundside targets. The DDs will be dropping onto the prison itself. Unless something happens to change the Major's mind, we'll be going in hot. So be prepared."

"What's going on, Captain?" Talbot asked as he worked to secure the breastplate of his armor.

"I wish I knew for sure, Gunny. All I can tell you is that the defense platforms around the planet are dark. Worse, three are gone. It's like they were never there. If that's not bad enough, there's been no response to our hails from the prison or the other facilities dirt-side. Comms is picking up no chatter either. Captain Carlisle is scrambling LAC wings to scout the area. After what happened back home, he's not about to take any risks with the ship. As soon as he and the Major have drawn up a battle plan, we'll make our drop. So gear up!"

For a moment, no one moved. Faces turned away from armor or weapons to stare at her in disbelief. Every Devil Dog knew their mission. They were there to pick up – no, to rescue – those poor souls who had been sent to the Tarsus military prison along with Ash. None of them expected it to turn into a potential ground fight – or worse.

"Cap," Marino began, his voice harsh.

Ashlyn closed her eyes and forced herself not to react. She knew he was worried. He knew most of those who'd been sent to Tarsus with her. But that didn't change the reality of their current situation. Besides, worried as he might be, it didn't hold a candle to what she felt and if she could hold her emotions in check, so could he.

At least he'd damned well better.

"We have our orders, Sergeant."

If her voice was a little harsh, she didn't care. Marino knew better than to question orders in public. Then, realizing that wasn't what he'd done, she relented a bit. "Look, we've been in this position before. We don't know what the situation is groundside. In all likelihood, there's nothing wrong except for some bit of equipment failure that the idiots groundside haven't gotten around to fixing yet. Honestly, after my time here, that wouldn't surprise me one bit. But, after the attack on the capital, we can't take that risk."

She paused, wondering how much more she could – or should – say.

"But there's something else you need to be prepared for. Some of you saw me right after my return to the capital. You saw the scars on my face and you saw how my tattoo had been *removed.*" She paused, giving herself time to get her emotions under control. But it was hard, especially when she could see how angry the others were as she reminded them what had been done to her. "All of you have seen some of the other scars I still bear and trust me those aren't all of them. That should be enough to let you know that the guards down there don't give a damn about the prisoners. I have no doubts they will gladly sacrifice them if they think it will save their own skins. Because of that, when we hit the ground, we'll need to move fast to secure our people before anything can happen to them.

"I'll be honest, I'm worried the communications blackout means the guards have already done their worst to our people and are on now the run. Even though the guards never let us see much outside the compound – hell, they didn't let us see much inside the compound – I'm pretty sure there were shuttles stationed there and a regular transit schedule of some sort. It was one of the few ways I had of marking time.

"From what I've been able to learn from our briefing materials, there was more traffic to the penal colony than there should have been. My guess is that the guards and administration have been taking part in black market activities of some sort. It's possible they even sold some of the lifers to slavers. That means Coreal and those of his inner circle would presumably have the means to get off-planet if they felt the need. It's very possible when we get inside, we're going to find nothing but bodies. So be prepared.

"But there is another explanation, one we can't ignore. FleetCom isn't ready to confirm the Callusians are behind the attack on the capital, but let's face it. There is no other reasonable explanation for what happened. If we accept that explanation, then we have to consider the possibility that they've done the same thing here. That means we have to be prepared for anything." She glanced around the staging area, seeing the anger and understanding reflected on the expressions of her fellow Marines. "Now gear up. We drop within the hour."

"Yes, ma'am!" the Devil Dogs replied, their voices reverberating throughout the staging area.

She couldn't help it. She smiled, proud to know she was once more a member of the best Marine unit ever.

"Look, there's nothing I want more than to make the drop and discover that my people – *our* people – are all right. But this is one of those times when what we want isn't necessarily what we're going to find. What I need from each of you is to do what you do best. Be

Devil Dogs. Get the job done and no one make any stupid mistakes and get themselves killed."

"You heard the captain, boys and girls. Let's move!" Talbot said.

As he did, Corporals McKay and Gatson appeared, carrying a footlocker between them. Both wore what Ashlyn could only describe as shit-eating grins. Then, as they dropped the footlocker in front of her, she shook her head, disbelief warring with relief. The battered footlocker had seen more than its fair share of combat drops. Not that that was unusual for a Devil Dog's footlocker. But this one was familiar. She knew every scratch and dent. She didn't need to see the name and rank stenciled on the top to recognize it. Her breath caught and she blinked against the tears that suddenly burned her eyes.

"Gunny, would you mind explaining?" If her voice was a little hoarse, none of those close enough to hear let on. In fact, other than the grins they all wore as they watched her, there was nothing about them to show they knew how much this meant to her.

"Well, Cap, Major Pawlak thought you might be needing your gear and contacted General Okafor. She, in turn, contacted your parents. It seems your mother told the powers-that-be at the time to take a leap into the nearest black hole. I've heard a rumor or two that she also told them what they could do while there. Then she took possession of your equipment after your forced *vacation*." His voice turned hard and there were more than a few muttered curses, several of them suggesting things they could do to those responsible for that *vacation*. "After learning we were going to be onboard the *Magellan*, your mother sent it to the major to give to you when the time came and you needed it. Oh, the major did say to tell you everything's been checked and prepped, ma'am."

Grinning, Ashlyn dropped to one knee and ran her thumb over the biometric lock. There was a soft *snick*. A moment later, the top raised and the lower weapon drawer slid out a few centimeters.

"Let's get you geared up, Cap," Gatson said.

She nodded and began laying out her armor. Now, finally, she felt like a Marine again.

———

"Ash."

Pawlak's voice seemed to echo in her head and Ashlyn frowned slightly. It was going to take time to get used to hearing anything coming in over the battle-net *in* her head instead of through her ears. It was a benefit of the implants and invaluable in a battle situation when silence could mean the difference between life and death. But now, as the shuttles carrying the Devil Dogs made their way to the planet's surface, it was a bit disconcerting.

"Sir?"

"Reports from the *Magellan* show that all defenses groundside powered down. But we're not taking any chances. Captain Carlisle has ordered the *Magellan* to stealth and altering orbit until we know what the situation is on the surface."

"Understood, sir."

"We should be making planetfall in less than five minutes, Ash. You are lead shuttle. The rest of us are right behind you."

"Any change in orders?"

"That's a negative. Just keep your eyes open and your head down until we know what we're looking at. Pawlak out."

Ashlyn leaned back in her flight couch and breathed deeply. She couldn't help remembering the last time she made an approach to Tarsus. She'd been on a shuttle then. Instead of wearing light battle armor, her weapons close at hand, she wore the jumpsuit issued to her upon her conviction. Her ankles had been shackled and her wrists secured to the arms of her flight couch. Upon arrival, she'd been freed from the couch, her wrists secured behind her and a hood had been dropped over her head so she couldn't see where she was being taken. God, she'd been so scared that day and so bitter, convinced she'd been abandoned by the very service she'd dedicated so much of her life to.

Now she'd returned, but this time in the potential role of avenging angel. If anything had happened to her people since her return to the capital, there would be hell to pay. For every hurt they'd taken, she'd make those responsible pay ten-fold. She didn't care if it ruined her career. Much as she rejoiced in knowing she was once again a Devil Dog and a Marine, that was nothing compared to what she felt for those who had willingly sacrificed so much to stand by her.

But she couldn't let the others know what she felt. She had no doubt Pawlak had given them explicit orders where she was concerned. At the first sign of trouble, Talbot would more than likely try to get her to fallback to safety. She hoped he realized that wouldn't work. The only way to keep her from being in the middle of anything that happened at the prison was to make sure she never made it dirtside. Since they hadn't managed that, well, they'd just have to accept whatever happened next.

A few minutes later she climbed to her feet and moved into the cockpit. Standing behind their pilot, she studied the displays. The screens were clear of any indication of trouble. It would be easy to assume that meant there was no reason to worry. But the fact they still had picked up no comms chatter worried her. Even if the people dirtside were unaware of their approach, there should be the daily chatter that comes with the coordination of patrols, deliveries and other mundane matters.

Bracing herself against the bulkhead, she dropped her right hand onto the pilot's shoulder. He glanced back at her and nodded once, his mouth set in a grim line. Like most of the rest of them, he was rigged out in light armor. Racked in its place near his seat was his battle rifle. The Devil Dogs emblem was emblazoned on his dark armor. Fortunately. Now that they were facing the possibility of a fight, Ashlyn was even more glad Major Pawlak had included several shuttle pilots when filling out the personnel roster for the mission.

"Anything?" she asked softly.

"That's a negative, ma'am." He shook his head. "If we weren't getting readings from inside some of the buildings to indicate there's someone home, I'd swear the place was deserted."

"All right. Confirm with Major Pawlak and then take us in." She glanced up as Talbot joined them. "Lieutenant, we'll drop in the main compound. As soon as we've cleared the shuttle, I want you back in the air so Shuttle Two can drop. Be ready for anything."

"Understood, ma'am." He banked the shuttle, slowing their speed. "There it is."

Ashlyn closely studied the area below them. As she did, her concern ratcheted up a notch. She hadn't been in a position to see the penal colony on approach when she'd been brought there after her conviction. But, in the time since her return to the capital, she had spent hours studying everything she could find on it. She'd memorized its layout and knew the schedules for prisoner transport and deliveries of food and other goods needed to run the prison and house its staff.

From personal experience, she knew that at this time of day there should be prisoners being escorted between the buildings or working in the yard. But there was nothing. Not a single indication there was anyone living down there.

"Go to infrared scan, LT. Do a flyover of the compound before we drop."

"Aye, ma'am."

"Cap?" Talbot's voice didn't betray the concern she knew he felt.

"Gunny, there should be more than five hundred prisoners and almost fifty guards. And that's not counting the support staff. So where is everyone?" She caught her lower lip between her teeth and studied the scanners as the lieutenant switched to infrared.

Her frown deepened as did her worry. There were pockets of heat showing but not nearly enough. Of course, it could be that many of those sentenced to the prison were far enough below ground that they weren't registering on the scanners. But her gut told her that wasn't the case. Something was going on and they were wasting time, time her people might not have.

"Major," she said after opening her direct link to him. "Are you seeing what I am?"

"I am," he confirmed. "All right. Drop on your next pass, Ash. Weapons are to be hot. I repeat, weapons are to be hot. Secure the LZ and hold position until Shuttle Two drops. We make entry together. Confirm."

She bristled at the order but knew he was right.

"Drop on the next pass. Secure the LZ and hold for shuttle two to drop."

"Good hunting, Captain." He paused and she could imagine him in the second shuttle, his expression impassive even as his mind worked. "Ash, we will get our people – *your* people – out of there. I promise."

"Thank you, sir."

"We're about to make our second pass, Captain," the pilot reported.

"I heard, Ash. Make your drop. We'll be right behind you. Pawlak out."

"Let's do it!" she ordered and turned back to the cabin where the Devil Dogs waited. "Hound, Tank, we're going in hot. As soon as you're down, the rest of us will follow."

"You heard the captain. Get ready to deploy!" Talbot pushed past Ashlyn and moved to the side hatch. "Move it, Devil Dogs, we've a job to do."

"Captain, we've got movement by the front gate!" the pilot called out. The shuttle suddenly veered to one side, sending everyone careening into the bulkhead. "Permission–"

"Lieutenant, do whatever you need to protect this shuttle!" Ashlyn snapped before he could finish his sentence. The fingers of her right hand quickly entered the command sequence to link her to Major Pawlak on the second shuttle. "Sir, we're taking fire. We're going in hot. I repeat, we're going in hot. Recommend you keep your people aloft until we've secured the area," she reported.

"Ready to deploy, ma'am," Talbot reported as Tank and Hound took their positions by the hatch. Their helmets were secured in place and weapons were at the ready. She nodded and, after making sure everyone was ready to follow, secured her helmet, checked her tell-tales and then hit the control panel with a gloved fist.

"Go!" she ordered as the hatch slid open.

Tank lifted his right hand in confirmation and stepped out. She watched as he and then Hound dropped the fifty meters to the ground. The last few meters saw their suit thrusters activating to soften their landing. Small arms fire erupted from one of the buildings outside the prison walls. Ash identified it as one of the maintenance buildings. Projectiles bounced off Tank's and Hound's heavy armor like annoying gnats. Without hesitation, the two turned to the building and opened fire. Their heavy assault rifles tore through the building's walls without trouble. A moment later, flash-bangs were tossed inside, ensuring that any survivors were in no condition to continue fighting.

"All clear, Cap," Hound reported.

"Move them out, Gunny," Ashlyn ordered and took her place at the end of the line of Devil Dogs dropping to the planet's surface.

13

Dante Coreal, commandant of the penal colony, cursed loudly as the attack shuttle opened fire on the maintenance building. A moment later, he watched as armored soldiers dropped to the surface. His guards' weapons were useless against their heavy armor. Without pausing, the soldiers opened fire. Then they tossed several flashbangs inside. As more soldiers dropped from the shuttle, the first two held point, their weapons at the ready. Yet through it all there was no demand for surrender, no contact whatsoever.

"Who are they?" he demanded helplessly.

"Does it matter?" Gavin Haritos countered, bracing himself with a hand on the wall as another explosion rocked the area. "We're dead no matter what."

Coreal knew the guard-captain was right. Even if the invaders should somehow decide to break off the attack, the prisoners were still there. He knew they wouldn't hesitate to kill him if they managed to get their hands on him. He had to prevent that. But he had to be careful. He couldn't kill them outright, not on the off-chance the soldiers gained entry into the main compound. If that happened, the prisoners could be used as a distraction while he and other members of his staff escaped. All he had to do was secure them long enough to see what the invaders wanted.

"Captain, have your people make sure the prisoners are locked down. Barricade the entrances to their cell blocks as well as the underground access tunnels. We can't worry about them right now," he snapped. "Make sure everyone's armed, support staff as well as your people. Then get back here. Maybe by then we'll have a better idea who we're dealing with."

Assuming they haven't already forced their way inside.

————

SHE'D ALREADY DISCUSSED it with Talbot. Not that she needed to. The gunny knew her well enough to understand that she would want blood if they discovered anything had happened to those they'd been sent for. But she'd needed to tell him, to make sure he understood that none of the squad was to do anything they might find themselves up on charges for later. That meant not standing by and letting her do anything foolish. From the mulish look he'd worn as she made him promise, she knew he didn't like it. Hell, she didn't like it, but she wasn't going to let anyone else pay for her actions – not that she could have foreseen the circumstances of simply following orders two years earlier.

"Cap," Talbot began, leaning in close so no one could overhear. "You are to let us secure the area before you go inside that building."

"Gunny, *we* do this by the numbers. I know you want to protect me, but we have a job to do. I promise I'm not going to do anything foolish, or at least nothing too foolish." Seeing that he didn't quite believe her, she sighed. "The only thing I'm worried about right now is making sure the buildings out here are secure and not hiding anyone else who might try to ambush us. Once that's done, the other shuttle can land and we can do what we came here for. We can get our people safely away from here."

"All right. Just remember that, Cap. None of us are going to let you risk yourself." Now he looked at her just as seriously as she had him. "Captain, we weren't able to do anything when the shit hit the fan two years ago. We knew you'd take a dim view of us committing mutiny – or worse – in order to free you and the others, not that we weren't tempted. So now you'll let us do our jobs. If that means tearing this place apart, brick by brick, we'll do it."

"Sounds good to me, Gunny. In fact, I wouldn't mind it one bit if we have to tear this place down." She smiled and then turned her attention to the video feed from the second shuttle.

The video cleared as the shuttle broke through the clouds. Ashlyn blew out the breath she hadn't realized she'd been holding. It was strange looking at the feed and seeing, in the distance, the gray walls surrounding the sprawling penal colony. Walls that were less than half a kilometer from where she stood. Walls that had surrounded her *home* for two years.

Less than two kilometers out was nothing but sand. From her current position, she could see the heat rising from the ground. She remembered it and the grit that always seemed to be present. That heat and the lack of a water source was one of many reasons why no one had tried to escape from the penal colony in years. There was nowhere to go unless the escapee managed to could get to the spaceport and steal a shuttle. They would die of exposure within a day or two, long before reaching any of the more remote facilities or habitats.

Ashlyn swallowed hard and forced back her memories. She needed to focus on the here and now, not on the what had been. That meant securing the landing zone and making sure the outbuildings were clear of any further hostiles.

"All right, folks, it's clear we have a situation here," she said, doing her best not to let her fear for those she'd been forced to leave behind show. "Let's secure these out buildings. Then we'll signal the major that we're ready to make entry into the compound. Dumont, be ready to blow the main gate if necessary."

"Roger that, Cap," their explosives expert replied.

"After we clear the buildings," she reminded him. He really did like his job a bit too much. "We'll knock nicely once and that's it. Something's going on and my gut tells me it is something bad."

"I'll be ready, Cap," he assured her.

"Gunny, I want teams to clear the buildings now."

"You heard the captain, boys and girls," he said, scanning the area. "Tank, you take point. McKay, Gatson, you're in after him. Signal when you have an all clear." He waited as the three moved off in the direction of the maintenance building. "Hound, take Dumont and one other and clear the next building. Same orders."

"Roger that, Gunny." He motioned to Corporal Camille Winstead, their comms officer, to come with them.

"Building One secure, Cap," Tank's deep voice reported over the com-net a few minutes later. "We've got one body in here. Male and wearing prison guard uniform. ID scan confirms him as Piter Nilsson."

Ashlyn frowned, remembering the small, dark man with a sadistic streak she had seen the wrong side of too many times. "Give me a visual." She activated her HUD and waited for that split-second of disorientation to pass as the scene around her disappeared, replaced by the image of the dead man. Her breath caught and she didn't know whether to be relieved or not when she recognized him. What she did know was that it wasn't good, not good at all, to confirm he'd been the shooter. She keyed her comm-link so she could inform Pawlak.

"This is Shaw. We have an ID on one dead so far. He's one of the guards. A sick, sadistic bastard who Satan himself wouldn't want in Hell."

"Easy, Ash." Pawlak's voice was soft.

She drew a deep breath and held it for a moment. Then she exhaled, struggling for calm.

"Is Coreal foolish enough to try to keep us out of the compound?"

She opened her mouth to respond and then stopped. Her first impulse had been to say "yes". She had no doubts the man would do almost anything to save his own skin. But she'd learned one thing during her time as an inmate there. Coreal might be many things, but he wasn't foolish. He knew how to cover his tracks. If he actually tried to keep the Devil Dogs out of the compound, he'd have an airtight cover story to explain why. An ambush them outside the gates didn't fit what she knew of him. She was missing something, but what?

She cursed softly as the only reasonable explanation dawned on her. She could hear him explaining to some review board how the prisoners tried to take over the compound. He'd been forced to deploy the guards to counter their attack. When the shuttles approached, with the penal colony's comms down, he had no idea who they were or why they'd come. He'd done the only thing anyone in his position would have. He'd ordered the compound held at all costs. After all, some of Fuercon's worst prisoners were stationed there.

If that was the commandant's plan, Ashlyn knew none of the prisoners would survive to contradict him. Coreal would even sacrifice some of his own staff to give his tale credence. That meant they had to gain entry into the compound as quickly as possible, before he had time to carry out his plan.

God, let them be in time.

Now she understood why Nilsson fired on them.

"Ash?" Pawlak's voice interrupted her thoughts.

"I don't think so, sir, but it was one of the guards who attacked us." She paused and nodded as Talbot reported that the other building had been cleared. "LZ is clear, sir."

"All right. Go ahead and make entry into the compound. We'll cover you from the air. Once you've made entry, secure the outer area of the compound and the entry to the admin building. I'll join you there. Then we'll decide our next move."

"Roger that, sir. Will you make one last attempt to contact the compound before I have Dumont blow the gate?"

"Consider it done."

She waited, listening as he instructed the pilot to attempt to contact the compound one last time. "All right, Ash. Do it by the book."

"Understood, sir." She ended the transmission and turned to her squad. "All right, let's do this. The Major is making one last attempt to contact the compound. If they haven't responded by the time you have your toys ready, Dumont, blow the gate.

"When we make entry, Tank, you have point. Hound, you're bringing up the rear. All weapons are to be at the ready. Video feed shows the main compound is deserted but don't take any chances."

"You heard the captain. Get moving," Talbot said. "Form up and be ready to move in as soon as the gates are open."

"Gunny, you're with me."

"Glad you realize that, Cap." He grinned and she shook her head. "And I hope you realize that I have my orders from the major to make sure nothing happens to you," he added over a private channel.

"I do. But understand this, Gunny. I will not let anything happen to our people, *any* of our people."

"Understood and agreed, Cap."

"Ready here, Cap," Dumont reported a few minutes later.

"Major?"

"We're seeing signs of life inside, Captain, but no one is responding to our hails. Make entry. I repeat. Make entry."

"You heard the major, Dumont. Blow the gates."

With that, Ashlyn dropped to one knee, her battle rifle held at the ready. Dumont armed the charge he'd placed at the gate and moved back. One hand in the air, he lifted one finger. Two. Three.

The explosion blew the gates from their anchors. Dust flew, filling the air. Ashlyn's HUD instantly adjusted, switching filters until she could see through the smoke and sand. Her lips pulled back in an almost feral grin. Finally, she might actually be able to not only free her people but get a touch of vengeance as well.

"Cap, I'm hurt. We know there are folks inside, but no one seems to want to come play with us," Tank said, amusement rippling in his tenor voice.

Ashlyn grinned and shook her head. Despite the seriousness of the situation, the heavy weapons specialist always found a way to make her smile. "All right. Guess we'll just have to go find the fun, boys and girls." She stood and motioned for them to enter the compound.

————

"Commandant, we have to do something."

Dante Coreal glared at the guard-captain. He knew they had to do something, damn it. The only problem was he didn't know what. It had been bad enough when that damned carrier ship had arrived to transport Shaw back to the capital. Who knew what lies that bitch had been telling since then. Of course, it was quite possible she hadn't said anything. One thing he'd learned about her during her time at the penal colony was that she knew how to keep her mouth shut, especially if she thought by opening it her squadmates might be harmed.

But why had they come for her and could he count on her to keep silent?

Damned bitch.

He hadn't done anything wrong. Not really. The regulations were fuzzy enough to let him get by with most of his *corrective* measures. Still, there had been times when the guards might have gone a bit too far. But who could blame them? The prisoners here would just as soon slit the guards' throats as anything else. By taking a heavy hand with them, the guards prevented future trouble and helped maintain the smooth running of the penal colony.

None of which answered his questions about why there was suddenly a cruiser in orbit around the planet and why they wanted to take possession of the rest of Shaw's squad.

Making matters worse, he hadn't been able to get any answers from his usual sources. He didn't know if FleetCom was simply having them transported back to the capital to handle new appeals of their cases or if new charges were being filed against them or what. But that meant he also didn't know if there was an investigation going on into the daily workings of the penal colony and he was damned if he would let his career be ruined by a bunch of cowards.

But that wasn't the worst of it. The day had gone from bad to worse in very short order. He'd awakened to the sound of the alarms going off. The last time that had happened, some of the prisoners had tried to escape, *tried* being the operative word. They hadn't gotten far before being cut down by perimeter defense turrets. So he hadn't been all that worried as he dressed and waited for a report.

Only he never heard the sounds of the defense turrets firing. Then he realized he wasn't hearing any of the usual shouts or gunfire from the guards. That was enough to cut through the complacency five years as commandant of the most secure penal colony in allied space had built into him.

He listened in growing disbelief a few minutes later as Haritos reported that not only were groundside defenses off-line but so were the orbital defense platforms. No, he didn't know why. Yes, the techs were working on discovering the problem and correcting it. No, he hadn't been able to make contact with the other facilities on the planet. No, they didn't have any idea what was going on.

"Commandant, they've dropped a squad of Marines outside the gate," Haritos reported, paling as he listened to the report coming in through his earbud. "At least two are in heavy armor. You have to do something now or we're going to have real trouble on our hands."

"Are the prisoners secured?"

"Of course," Haritos replied, contempt reflected on his expression. "Neither my men nor I are foolish enough to leave them loose."

"Make sure of it. Until we know exactly who these newcomers are, I don't want to take any chances." Damn it, there was no way out of this mess. Not now. Not unless he figured out a way to kill the Marines who waited to be admitted into the compound and then somehow managed to destroy the ship that had brought them. All he could do was try to buy enough time to cover at least the worst of his tracks. "Get your men in position. I want all guns focused on the gate. Then get your ass down there and get eyes on them. Do not let them anywhere near the prisoners until I say so. If they give you any trouble, deal with them."

"What?" Haritos' voice rose at least an octave.

"You heard me. Remember, your neck is as much on the block as mine is. Now do as I said."

God, some days it just didn't pay to get out of bed.

———

DOING her best not to relive the last time she'd arrived at the penal colony, Ashlyn moved through the gates into the compound. Her hands tightened their grip on her battle rifle and she forced her finger off the trigger. Breathing deeply, she told herself to relax. She didn't need her demons returning to plague her right now. They did enough of that when she slept. Now she needed to keep a cool head. Otherwise, she'd be opening fire on the first guard she came across. Much as she'd love to be able to do just that, she couldn't.

At least not without sufficient provocation and that, she knew, wouldn't happen. The guards were nothing more than cowards who got off on abusing prisoners who couldn't fight back.

Bastards.

She called the schematics for the penal colony up on her HUD and carefully studied them. They weren't complete, not that she'd expected them to be. The admin and support buildings were clearly mapped but the buildings housing the cells were little more than blips on the schematic. No definition and no explanation for what each floor, much less each room, was used for.

"All clear, Captain," Tank reported a few moments later after the initial sweep of the yard turned up no unwanted surprises.

"Gunny, pick three to hold station here until the major arrives with reinforcements. The rest of us will continue on to the admin building. Let's move out."

She started forward, her assault rifle ready, Talbot at her side. As the rest of the unit spread out, sweeping through the open area before the administration building, she scanned the buildings surrounding them. The squad was in the open, easy targets for snipers. Yet no shots rang out. None of her people fell. Had she over-reacted after all?

No. There could be no denying the fact Nilsson had attacked them. He'd never have acted without orders. Whether those orders had come from Coreal or Haritos, she didn't know and didn't really care. The fact that any member of the guard staff was foolish enough to attack the Devil Dogs meant they could take nothing for granted.

"Take cover!" she ordered as the doors to the administration building opened.

"Martino, Dumont, move in!" Talbot added.

Assault rifle ready, stock against her right shoulder, finger resting lightly against the trigger guard, Ashlyn dropped to her right knee. She focused on the doorway, barely daring to breathe. This was it. Would the newcomer come out peacefully or would this become a battle to retake the compound?

"Don't shoot!" a man yelled as he stepped outside, his hands raised above his head.

Ashlyn's eyes went wide and her finger against the trigger guard twitched dangerously as she recognized the guard-captain. Rage suddenly coursed through her. Memories of all the times she'd been his victim filled her. It would be so easy to exorcise those memories now. All she had to do was squeeze the trigger. A split-second and one of the banes of her existence for the last two years would no longer exist.

"Secure him!"

She recognized her own voice. Until then, she wasn't aware of the fact she'd climbed to her feet and secured her assault rifle in its scab-bard across her back. Fortunately, her subconscious had more sense than her conscious did. Besides, there would be time later to deal with Haritos if she found out he'd done anything to her people.

"Cap, you all right?" Talbot asked on a private channel as they waited for Haritos to be brought to them.

"Yeah."

She shook herself, knowing he was worried. Hell, she was too. It would be so easy to fall back into the fear she'd lived with for so long. It would be even easier to grab her gun and start killing those who had hurt her and the others. Perhaps that was why she had yet to remove her helmet. It obscured her identity, giving her the anonymity she'd craved so often while imprisoned here.

Watching Haritos stop just outside the door, his eyes wide with fear as two armored Marines moved toward him, Ashlyn frowned. Something bothered her. After what happened at the front gate, this was too easy. Haritos wouldn't just walk out and present himself to a potentially hostile force, not unless it was the only way to save himself.

"Hold!" she ordered her team.

Instantly, they did as she said, the two nearest Haritos, dropping to one knee and leveling their weapons at the guard-captain.

"Cap?" Talbot asked.

"It's too easy, Gunny." She keyed her visor for infrared and scanned walls surrounding the prison. It didn't take long to pick out several heat signatures and recognize them for what they were. "Snipers and possible assault weapons along the walls. Tank, Hound, Dumont, McKay, on my order, take them out. They'll get one chance to surrender."

"We go to call signs until we have the area secure. I say again, call signs only," Talbot added. "I'll have the skin of the first person to break protocol."

Ashlyn frowned but knew he was right. So far, they had the advantage because Coreal and his people didn't know she was back. But, after what happened at the front gate and after realizing there were snipers waiting on the walls, she knew she'd be the first target if anyone realized she was the team's CO.

"Loco's right," she confirmed. "Tank, broadcast the call for the guards on the wall to toss down their weapons and move into the open. They get ten seconds to comply. Tell them if they fail to do as ordered, we will open fire."

"Roger that, Angel," Tank replied and moved to the center of open area.

As he issued the warning, Ash commed Major Pawlak. "You heard?" she asked without preamble.

"I did and I concur. If you have to blow a few more holes in the prison wall, do it. Keep our people and yourself safe."

"Doing my best, sir."

"Three complying, Angel. We have two more still hunkered down," Tank reported.

"Take out the one at three o'clock, Tank. The bigger the boom, the better. It might convince the other one to come out."

Without a word, the heavy weapons specialist shouldered his RPG and took aim. A moment later, part of the prison wall disappeared in a cloud of smoke and dust. As it cleared, the damage left behind was apparent. The top six feet of the wall was gone and, with it, the hiding place of the sniper. One down, one more to go.

"Go, Tank," Ash said.

He turned to where the remaining sniper still hid. As he shouldered the RPG, a figure jumped up, hands held high in the air. Ash smiled slightly. The example had done exactly as she planned. She listened as Talbot ordered several of the team to secure the snipers who had surrendered. It didn't take long. The Devil Dogs moved with precision and soon the guards were lying face down on the ground, wrists secured behind them, ankles bound. Then, just to be sure they wouldn't be distractions, they were gagged. In short, they were now the prisoners.

Good.

Now to deal with the guard-captain.

Ash keyed her comm for Talbot. "Let's see what he can tell us." She pointed to where Haritos stood, hands clasped behind his head, sweat rolling down his face. "Then we'll go to Coreal's office. When we get there, I want all electronics locked down. Coreal is to be held in the outer office. Make sure he can't communicate with anyone else without my permission or yours. Once that's done, we'll make sure the rest of the compound is secure. Then we will go find our people."

"Understood, Angel," Talbot replied.

She keyed in an open channel to the rest of the squad. "Let's do this by the numbers, everyone. We don't start trouble but we sure as hell finish it. All comms are to be via secured channel until either Loco or I say differently. Now let's keep it tight and keep it chilled."

And I'd best follow my own orders.

"Name?" Talbot snapped as Martino brought Haritos to stand a few feet away from where the gunny and Ash waited.

"Gavin Haritos. I'm the guard-captain here." He tried to pull away as Martino wrenched his arms behind him and, using a pair of flex-cuffs, secured him. Then, before Haritos could protest, he was forced to his knees. Martino's gloved hand grabbed him by the hair and pulled his head back so the gunny and Ashlyn could see his face.

"Report." Again, it was Talbot who spoke.

"Compound is secure. Prisoners are in their cells. Commandant Coreal is waiting for you." Haritos, pale as a ghost, spoke as fast as possible.

"Angel?"

Ashlyn looked around. She knew she should have them bring Haritos with them. But that would divide their attention, even with him cuffed. No, she couldn't risk that. Nor could she kill the man, no matter how badly she wanted to. So she'd do something almost as good. She'd give him a taste of his own medicine. It wasn't what she wanted, but it would have to do.

"Bring him," she said simply and strode off.

Martino and Talbot dragged the now sobbing guard-captain after her as she moved to the center of the clearing in front of the administration building. Almost directly in front of the entrance was an innocuous looking set of metal bars. Two were set securely into the ground and stood almost three meters tall. They were approximately two meters apart. They were spanned by two more bars, one set at a meter above the ground and a second at two meters. The installation had been the scene of her one of her first introductions to prison discipline. That day, she'd been forced to watch as one of her squad-mates had been chained to the bars and whipped into unconsciousness. Now it was time for Haritos to know what fear truly was.

Without a word, she grabbed him by the arm and walked him

forward until he stood before the bars. He began to struggle as she forced him to bend at the waist. With Martino's assistance, she positioned him so his hips were braced against the lower crossbar and his torso was between the upper and lower bars. Without prompting, Martino grabbed the chains attached to the lower crossbar and fitted them around the guard's legs, securing him in place. Once that was done, Martino produced a line from his gear and secure it to the flex-cuffs and then to the upper bar, pulling it tight enough to force the guard-captain's arms upward, forcing him to remain bent at the waist. He wouldn't be getting free of that without help.

Ignoring her suit's warnings that her pulse and respiration were increasing, Ashlyn moved to stand before Haritos and grabbed his hair, forcing his head up. The fear reflected in his eyes was something she'd dreamed of for so long. But it wasn't enough. Not when she thought about all he'd done to her and who knew how many others. Not when she thought about the horror the administration building held for her. Each time she'd been brought through those doors just a few meters away, pain had followed. But she couldn't think about that now. Not yet, at any rate. There'd be time later, after she made sure the others were safe, when she'd be able to get retribution.

Hell, the Devil Dogs would probably help her. Even if they didn't, she was pretty sure they'd do nothing to stand in her way, especially if any of the others had been harmed.

"Angel?" Talbot was at her side, his voice concerned.

"Haritos here is responsible for many of the scars you've seen, Loco, and much more. More than you will ever know," she growled. She relished the fear in Haritos' eyes and the way he tried to pull out of her grasp. It was futile and they both knew it. Even if he managed to jerk free of her hold on his hair, he couldn't break free of his bonds.

"Captain, we need him. At least for a little while longer." Talbot spoke softly over a secured private channel.

She wanted to argue. She finally had the chance to repay this bastard for all he'd done to her. But Talbot was right. They did need him, at least for the moment. But that didn't mean she couldn't drive her point home.

"Look at me," she growled. "Look at me and know your worst nightmare has just come to life. You try anything that might slow us down or prevent us from carrying out our mission and you'll beg these men and women to turn you over to me." She jerked his head right and then left, forcing him to look at Talbot and the others. "These Marines are members of the Devil Dogs. Do you really want to piss them off?"

Haritos swallowed audibly, his eyes fixed on the Marines standing behind Ashlyn.

"Now look at me again and remember who I am and all you and Coreal did to me over the last two years. Look at me and remember the scars you gave me and think about the scars you can't see. I'd like nothing more than to tear you apart, slowly and painfully. So please, give me a reason." Now she touched the side of her helmet with her free hand and the faceplate turned transparent, giving him his first real look at her.

"N-no." His voice wavered and it wouldn't have surprised Ashlyn one bit to look down and find he'd pissed himself. Like most bullies, he was nothing more than a coward. Faced with someone who could stand up to him, he'd quickly turn on Coreal and anyone else as long if he thought it meant staying alive one moment longer.

"I suggest you tell the captain whatever she wants to know," Talbot took up as he stepped forward. "Unless, Captain, you'd give us the pleasure of *questioning* him."

"No!" Tears filled the man's eyes and Ashlyn looked at him in contempt.

"What happened here? Why are the defenses offline and whose blood was it just inside the gates?" she snapped.

"The defenses and comms went down early this morning. We don't know why. I swear."

"The prisoners?" She knew there was more to it. There was something he wasn't telling them.

"In their cells."

Ashlyn released him and stepped back, looking around. There was more to what happened than he'd said. The problem was, she didn't know what. Worse, she had a feeling he didn't know. But experience had taught her that faced with a loss of the security systems, Coreal would have taken steps, possibly drastic steps, to insure the prisoners didn't get the wrong idea and try to break out. If he'd done anything to her people . . ..

"Gag him and leave him here." She forced herself not to reach for her gun. But that would be too quick, too easy. She wanted him to suffer, to be afraid. She wanted to be there when the executioner acted and Haritos breathed his last. By God, she would be there and as a free woman. He wasn't worth losing her freedom over.

But it was so tempting.

"Do you think Coreal has something planned for us, Cap?" Talbot asked over the secure channel a few moments later as they moved back toward the administration building. Behind them, on display much as he'd displayed prisoners over the years, was the gagged and sobbing Haritos.

"I don't know but it wouldn't surprise me." She swallowed hard against her fury. "Gunny, unless I miss my guess, Coreal ordered Haritos and the guards lock down the prisoners. It wouldn't surprise me to know he ordered competing gangs locked down together, hoping they'd kill one another. Coreal wouldn't care if any or all the prisoners died as long as he wasn't harmed."

"From the way that bastard reacted, I think you're right." His voice was as grim as she felt. "And we will make them pay."

"That we will, Gunny. But let's make sure the area is secure first. Once the major's here, we can deal with Coreal and find our people."

"Yes, ma'am." They stopped outside the main entrance to the admin building. "Hound, you take point. Tank, you bring up the rear."

"The major wants this done by the books. So clear the first floor. By the time that's done, the major should be here with reinforcements. Then we'll move up, clearing each floor as we go. In the meantime, Wolf, work your magic and lock down the building. All exits but this one. Loco, two men on the entrance. No one in or out who isn't a Devil Dog."

"Yes, ma'am."

Without waiting to see who he put on guard duty, Ashlyn pushed through the doors, her rifle at the ready. The sooner they cleared the floor, the sooner she'd finally be able to confront Coreal and find out where her people were being held.

14

"What the hell are they doing?"

Coreal sat at his desk, his fingers punching code after code into his computer, trying to bring up any of the numerous security cams in the building. But it was all in vain. Each command code had the same result. A dark screen followed by an error message telling him that the camera was off-line. That left him blind and deaf to whatever the soldiers were doing.

Except they weren't soldiers. He'd seen enough before the video feeds died to know his worst nightmare, at least one of them, had come to life. Fuercon had sent Marines to Tarsus. Marines who would take a very dim view on what he and the others had been doing here. Marines who, if they discovered what had been done to Shaw and the others, would not hesitate to slit his throat.

Damn it!

At least something seemed to be going right, if he could call it that. If he couldn't see what the Marines were doing, they couldn't see what he was. He entered in a new set of commands, watching, waiting. If he was lucky, he'd be able to scrub the data banks before the Marines figured out what he'd done. Then there would be nothing to prove he'd violated regulations. More than that, it would hide other secrets he most definitely did not want to come to light.

Command line error.

What?

He stared at the display, disbelief filling him. Then he typed in the command sequence again slower this time to prevent making a mistake. He waited, not daring to breathe. The screen blinked once and then went dark. A moment later it flickered back to life, mocking him.

Command line error.

Damn it!

Somehow, the Marines had managed to lock him out of his own computer system. But maybe it wasn't them. Maybe that bastard Haritos had done it before going down to meet them. That would be just like that bastard. Well, two could play that game. Haritos might have locked out the system, but he had backups of not only his files but the guard-captain's as well. If Haritos even thought about betraying him, he'd see his neck in the hangman's noose.

But now he needed to be ready for the soldiers. More than that, he knew he needed luck to be on his side. It was obvious they weren't taking any chances. If he could just get them to believe that his people, especially that little bastard in the outer yard, hadn't realized who they were because of the comm system failure, he might just be able to talk his way out of this. He could do this. He knew he could. All he had to do was remind them about the attack on the capital and how he simply couldn't take any chances, not when he had hundreds of prisoners who would do anything to see freedom again.

Even as he began to believe he had a chance to pull it off, the sounds of a scuffle in the outer office reached him. A moment later, the door to his office blew open with a deafening blast. Fear unlike anything he had ever before experienced filled Coreal and he fell to his knees. As he did, he saw the clerk in the office beyond spin in the direction of one of the soldiers, gun in hand. Before he had completed his turn, four shots rang out, cutting him down. Then the

Marine in the lead strode through the ruins of the door, his pulse rifle aimed directly at Coreal's head.

Oh God, why hadn't he followed his first impulse and disappeared somewhere off-planet, preferably out of the system, the moment that bitch Shaw had been removed from his custody?

———

"GUNNY, SECURE THESE PIECES OF SCUM," Major Pawlak ordered as he removed his battle helmet. He tossed it onto the nearby desk before reaching for his comm-link. "Captain Carlisle, Admin's now under our control. As soon as we've secured the commandant's office and records, we'll move to the inner compound."

"Excellent, Major," Carlisle's voice replied over battle-net. "Keep me in the loop."

"Understood, sir,"

As Pawlak listened to the various reports coming in from the Devil Dogs as they secured the floor, Ashlyn never took her eyes off of Coreal. How different he looked as he cowered behind his desk, sweat on his brow and fear in his eyes, than he had all those times she'd been brought to him for discipline. She felt a bitter smile touch her lips as she wondered how he'd react once he realized who actually stood before him. This time she was the one with the power.

God, how she wanted to make him suffer the way he'd made her suffer over the years.

But she couldn't. Not yet at any rate. Pawlak had been clear once he'd joined them. She was to remain at his side until he said differently. She was to leave the talking to him and she was not to remove her helmet. She'd balked at the orders even as she'd understood them. Pawlak wanted her to be able to communicate with him without Coreal knowing. She was his ace in the hole just then, the one able to tell him if Coreal was telling the truth or not.

Her money was on him lying through his teeth.

"Gunny, get him on his feet." Pawlak's nodded to where Coreal continued to try to hide behind his desk.

Without a word, Talbot did as the major ordered. Ash's smile lost some of its bitterness to see how he yanked Coreal upright. The commandant would be bruised from the gunny's manhandling, especially after Talbot slammed him against the desk and kicked his feet apart before roughly searching him. Once he had, he accepted a pair of security cuffs from Ashlyn and bound Coreal's wrists behind him.

"Name?" Pawlak barked.

Ash fought back a very inappropriate giggle as Pawlak looked at Coreal, his expression impassive. If possible, Coreal turned even paler. His mouth worked but nothing came out. Even with her helmet on, she could almost smell his fear. God, was this what she'd looked like when Haritos brought her here? No, she knew better. She had relied on her training not to let him see just how scared she'd been

"Coreal. Dante Coreal, commandant of this penal colony," he stammered out.

Before he could say anything else, the sounds of several people approaching reached them. A moment later, Lucinda Ortega entered with a dark-skinned corporal Ashlyn didn't recognize. Before they could brace to attention, Pawlak waved for them to stand easy. Then he asked for Ortega's report.

"The captain was right, sir. Someone did attempt to scrub the data systems. Fortunately, we'd already locked them down."

"Do you know who?"

"The command sequence came from this office, sir." Even though she didn't name Coreal, Ash knew he'd been the one. From the way Pawlak and Ortega looked at him, they did as well.

"Very good, Captain. Pass the word to the *Magellan* that Fleet-Com's suspicions do appear to be valid and ask them to send the JAG officers down to take possession of the data and to begin the investigation."

"What?" Coreal tried to twist out of Talbot's grasp only to have the Gunny slam him against the wall.

"Easy, Gunny. We need him conscious for a few minutes longer." Pawlak's voice was soft, almost amused. "Coreal, you have a great deal to answer for. But, before we get to all that, let me introduce myself. I am Major Paul Pawlak, First Division First Battalion, Fuerconese Marine Corps. We're better known as the Devil Dogs. You may have heard of us. After all, Captain Ashlyn Shaw is one of our own."

"No!"

The gasp was torn from Coreal and he renewed his struggles against Talbot's grip. The gunnery sergeant glanced at the major and, when Pawlak nodded, he moved quickly. Ash watched in approval as the gunny executed a perfect leg sweep and took Coreal down. The commandant cried out in pain as he fell head first to the floor. Before he could begin to even try to get to his feet, Talbot had twisted a hand in the man's thick blond hair. He dragged the now sobbing Coreal to his knees. Then Talbot bent and told him to kneel there unless he wanted his legs broken – or worse.

"I take it from your reaction that you know exactly who and what we are," Pawlak continued coldly. "Then I'll make this perfectly clear. I don't give a damn if you live out this day. Whether you do or not is entirely up to you. Give us the information we want and you'll live. Refuse and I'll turn you over to your prisoners. I'm quite sure they'd enjoy some *quality time* with you."

Coreal blanched at his words.

"W-what do you want?"

"It's really very simple. Where are our people?" Pawlak spoke softly but the way his hand rested on the pistol at his hip spoke volumes about what would happen if Coreal failed to answer.

"I can't!" he protested. Sweat ran down his face and soaked the front of his shirt. "They are here under lawful order. I can't turn them over to you."

"Captain?" Pawlak glanced at Ortega and Ashlyn watched as her friend checked her datapad.

"FleetCom's orders to him to have the others prepared for immediate transport home were received and viewed a week ago, sir. Included with the orders were copies of their pardons."

"Do you have a death wish, Coreal?"

Ashlyn smiled again. She recognized that musing tone in her

major's voice. It might sound mild, but it meant he was about to become Coreal's worst nightmare.

"H-how was I to know the orders were valid?" Coreal looked around, his eyes wild. "The capital had been attacked. For all I knew, it was a ruse by the Callusians. After all, it was made pretty clear during their courts-martial that Shaw and the others were working with the enemy."

Fury spiked and Ash took a step forward. How dare he! Then, before she could close the distance between her and Coreal, Pawlak stepped between them. The look on his face spoke volumes. He understood what she was feeling. More than that, unless she missed her guess, he was about to let her get a little of her own back.

"Perhaps you'd like to explain to Captain Shaw herself about why her people weren't here, ready for transfer when we arrived. While you're at it, you can explain why one of your guards opened fire on her and her team."

"No-no-no-no." Coreal's protest turned to a moan.

Without a word, Ash reached up and removed her helmet. As she handed it to Ortega, she stepped up to stand next to Pawlak. With a nod to Talbot, she waited as he once more forced Coreal's head up.

"Where are my people?"

Such a simple question and yet so much rested on how Coreal answered. Not just his life but hers as well as those poor souls who'd been sent here with her. There was even more hinging on his answer. For the last two years, she'd been so focused on just surviving and finding a way to free her people that she hadn't let herself think beyond that one goal. But now she couldn't stop thinking about it.

No, thinking about the *why* of it.

Why had so many people taken part in the farce that had led not only to their court-martial but also to their conviction and sentencing to here, the worst prison in the system? It was as though there'd been a conspiracy against them. There had to have been. Otherwise, the case never would have made it to trial. She had to believe that.

But who and why?

And could Coreal shed any light on what happened and who might have been involved?

"Look at me, *Commandant*." She put as much derision as she could into that one word and silently rejoiced to see him flinch in fear. "The Marines are an extremely loyal group of men and women. One of our firmest beliefs is that we don't leave anyone behind. It is even more so with the Devil Dogs. So don't think for a moment that any of us will buy your excuses that you couldn't believe the orders to release our people were valid. We came with one mission – to retrieve our people and take them home. You are preventing that by first ordering Nilsson to open fire on my landing party and then by refusing to admit us into the compound. You've seen just how effective those efforts were.

"But I digress. The major here isn't going to let me do anything foolish, at least not without provocation. However, each and every member of the Devil Dogs will back me when I report that it was with extreme regret that I had to forcibly defend myself when you tried to attack me. I really did try to avoid injuring you, but you were desperate. You knew an investigation into what has been going on here would lead to charges being filed and the very real probability that you'd be sentenced here and that, you knew, would be a death sentence. But no matter what we did or said, you simply wouldn't surrender. You left me no choice. I had to kill you before you managed to injure or kill me or one of my team."

"And my report will back hers up." Pawlak pulled his sidearm and held it before him, carefully examining it. "As will the rest of the entry team. Right, Gunny?"

"Oorah, sir," Talbot replied. "We tried to talk him down, but he wouldn't listen. It was almost as if we were fighting one of the suiciders the Callusians have sent against us."

"So, what's it going to be?" Pawlak asked. "Are you going to give yourself at least a chance to survive?"

Coreal couldn't start talking fast enough.

ASHLYN HAD NEVER BEEN as angry or heartsick as she was just then. Coreal was even more of a bastard that she'd thought. Of the six sent to Tarsus with her, only three remained at the main compound. The others had been moved after her return to Fuercon. Two had been sent to the mines, an almost certain death sentence. But worse was hearing how the Corporal Navarro, the only other female sentenced with her, had been sent to The Residence. Ash's blood had run cold to hear that. She'd never been sent there, but she'd heard the whispered horror stories. The men and women sent there had one duty – to serve their masters in whatever manner they were told.

Fortunately for everyone involved, Ash had turned her weapons over to Talbot, telling him to hang onto them for her. Even more fortunate, she'd done so before they learned about Navarro. That was the only thing that kept her from killing Coreal right then. As if realizing how she felt, Pawlak ordered Tank and Hound to take the man to the courtyard and secure him next to Haritos. Let the prisoners see that the two were no longer in control. Even the JAG officer who arrived shortly after Pawlak's first report to the *Magellan* had agreed it was the best course of action until they knew more.

Her hand shaking, Ash activated her comm and signaled the *Magellan*. Pawlak wanted her to be the one to report what they had discovered so far to Captain Carlisle. When Pawlak first gave her the assignment, she couldn't help wondering if he was setting her up. Then she realized he was doing the exact opposite. By forcing her to act as liaison between groundside and the ship, he was keeping her busy coordinating information. That meant she didn't have the opportunity to do anything foolish. As always, the Devil Dogs were taking care of their own, whether she wanted them to or not.

"How bad is it?" Carlisle asked simply, confirming her suspicions that he'd been closely monitoring their status.

"Bad enough, sir." She leaned back and ran a hand over her face. "We've got the compound on lock-down while we try to bring comms and defenses back up. From what Dumont has said, it looks like the comms system went down due to basic neglect. The same with the defense probes. The JAG is looking at the records now and I have a feeling he'll find Coreal and others have been skimming funds. Nothing else, short of them scavenging and selling parts, would explain why they are missing or off-line."

"Your people?"

"Three are here in the compound. They have been located and are being checked by the medics right now. From what I'm not being told, I have to assume they are the worse for wear." She paused and breathed deeply, reminding herself that she couldn't let her emotions rule. Not yet at any rate.

"The other three were moved from the compound after my return to Fuercon. Major Pawlak has sent teams to retrieve them."

"Captain Shaw," Carlisle interrupted, his expression troubled. "What aren't you telling me?"

"There is a very real possibility that none of the three will be found alive, sir." She closed her eyes, fighting against the anger and pain that filled her. "Sir, two were sent to the mines. That's pretty much a death sentence. Prisoners sent there rarely return. They are worked until they drop or until they are killed by either equipment failures or by other prisoners. At least Coreal was quick to give us the location of mines.

"The third, Corporal Navarro, was sent to The Residence. If possible, that's worse than the mines. Those sent to The Residence have one job – to do whatever, and I do mean whatever, their *masters* say. Rape isn't nearly the worst thing that can happen there."

"All right. Keep me informed." Carlisle paused and Ash could see he was thinking hard. "Tell the JAG that I want updates every two hours."

"Understood, sir."

"What about Coreal and the other guards?"

"Most of the guards have been secured away from the main prison population. The JAG wants to review their records and interview them. But, until he can, he doesn't want them where they can talk with one another or try to escape. Coreal, Haritos and several others I know firsthand to be the worst of the lot are secured in the outer courtyard. They'll be moved to cells later but, for a few hours at least, Major Pawlak believes it will be beneficial for the inmates here to see that those who tormented them the most are no longer in control. Fortunately, the JAG agrees."

"Understood, Captain. Please tell Major Pawlak that I'll send word to FleetCom reporting that you have secured the facility. Are you requesting reinforcements to staff the prison until this mess is cleared up?"

"That's an affirmative, sir." At least he understood that they couldn't just turn the prison back over to the guards, not without insuring they wouldn't be even worse than Coreal.

"I'll send personnel down to assist you and your team ASAP. As soon as the medics clear it, have your people transported to the ship. I'll have the medbay waiting for them."

"Thank you, sir."

"I'll let you get back to work. Next report in an hour. Carlisle clear."

Ash sat back for a moment after the transmission ended, doing her best to get her emotions under control. When she left the office, she needed to be able to do so without heading straight for Coreal to kill him. But that didn't mean she couldn't scare him some. He deserved that and so much more. Besides, if it helped speed up the JAG's investigation and answered some of her own questions, she didn't much care about the consequences.

A slight smile, bitter and twisted, touched her lips. No, she wouldn't go to Coreal. She'd have him brought to her, just as she and so many other prisoners had been brought to him over the years. She had no doubts that by now he realized this was not a dream from which he'd awaken. Good. She'd show him exactly what a nightmare his life was about to become.

"Lt. Liu, would it help the investigation if Coreal answered some of your questions?" she asked the JAG over a secure channel.

"It would, Captain, assuming his attorneys couldn't later claim we coerced anything from him."

"I promise no one will lay a hand on him. Let me run my idea by the major and I'll get back to you." She switched to Pawlak's channel.

"Sir, permission to have Coreal brought up to the office for questioning."

"What do you have in mind?"

At least he hadn't automatically told her no.

"Major, one of Coreal's habits was to bring a prisoner to his office for *discipline*. I learned very quickly to dread those trips. Several ended in visits to the infirmary and more should have. If he finds out that I've ordered him brought up here for a *discussion*, he's going to do whatever he can to save himself. And, before you ask, I've already promised the JAG that I'll not lay a finger on him. It will all be in his mind."

"Do it," he said so quickly she knew something else had happened.

Swallowing hard, she forced herself to speak. "Major?"

"Team One has made it to the mine. They're securing it as we speak. Ash, it's as bad as you warned. As soon as they identify the prisoners, both living and dead, they'll send the roster to us."

"And the Residence?"

"We need the access code to get in. The facility has been locked down and Dumont doesn't want to risk explosives unless he has to."

Anger flared as did fear. The longer it took the team to get inside, the longer Coreal's people had to deal with the prisoners sent there. Ashlyn had no doubt many, if not all, would be dead before the Marines finally made it inside.

"I promise you'll have that information in just a few minutes."

Even if she had to break her word not to lay hands on Coreal.

"Gunny," she said as she moved into the outer office where he and several other Devil Dogs were searching the physical records. "We have a problem. Those at The Residence have locked down the facility and the team can't make entry."

"We haven't found anything here that would help, Cap." His eyes flashed with an anger that matched her own. Good. That meant he wouldn't hesitate to go along with her plan.

She hoped.

"I think it's time to have a chat with Coreal." Now she held up a hand, forestalling the protest she saw forming. "I've already discussed it with the JAG and with Major Pawlak. I'll make you the same promise I made them. I won't lay a finger of Coreal. But we are going to scare the hell out of him."

"That's the best thing I've heard since we landed on this damned rock, ma'am." His grin left no doubts that he'd do whatever was necessary to find and free the last of their people.

"I want you to find the two biggest, meanest looking members of the team you can to go down to the courtyard. As they approach the prisoners, have them taking bets on what they think I'll do if I manage to get my hands on either Coreal or Haritos. Then they are to release Coreal from the posts. Once they have, secure his wrists behind him and shackle his ankles. He is to be told that he's being brought to his office – and have them correct themselves to say it is now my office – for a discussion. Emphasis on discussion. Then hood him and bring him here. They are to continue speculating on what I want and what I'm going to do to him."

"In other words, they are to put the fear of God in him." The gunny grinned and nodded in approval. "Ma'am, remind me never to make you mad at me."

"Mad's one thing, Gunny. He's pushed me far beyond that." She shook her head. She couldn't let herself think about just how far Coreal had gone. "I'll contact Lt. Liu and have him here by the time Coreal arrives."

"One question, ma'am?"

"What?"

"Permission to be present?"

"Of course." If nothing else, he'd make sure she didn't do anything foolish. "Once Coreal is here, I want you to be your biggest, meanest self. I promise I won't touch the son-of-a-bitch, much as I want to, but he doesn't have to know it.

"Understood, ma'am. I'll make sure he's here within five minutes."

Ashlyn nodded and returned to the inner office. It wasn't exactly what she wanted but she'd make the most of it.

Five minutes later, the stage was set. Ashlyn leaned back in Coreal's chair, her booted feet resting carelessly on the desk, scattering his data chips. At her side, looking as intimidating as possible stood Talbot. Looking up at him, Ashlyn grinned. He'd be scary enough glaring at the chained and hooded commandant if dressed in civvies. In his battle armor, weapons close to hand, he'd terrify even the bravest of men. Of course, Coreal wasn't brave. The question was whether he was foolish enough to try to bluff his way with them?

Lt. Liu sat in a chair to the right of the desk. Even though he was the one who would eventually run the interrogation, he'd agreed to let Ashlyn take center stage. At least until Coreal was begging to tell them all he knew.

A moment later, a knock sounded at the door. Talbot called out for the newcomers to enter. A moment later, the door slid open and two of the biggest men Ash had ever seen stepped inside. They each held one of Coreal's arms. Without a word, they moved further into the office. Ashlyn grinned and nodded. The sergeant on the right, Travis Booth, grinned in return. Then he and his partner, Corporal Vincent Cenci, forced Coreal to his knees.

Show time.

With a wink, Ashlyn nodded for Booth to remove the commandant's hood. As he reached out do to so, she wiped all amusement from her expression. She wanted Coreal's first sight of her to be something he'd never forget. Unless he was as scared of her as she had once been of him, she'd have failed.

The moment the hood was removed, Coreal shook his head, blinking his eyes against the sudden light. Then he gasped, his eyes going wide and all the color draining from his face as he recognized Ashlyn. In return, her upper lip curled back and she negligently dragged her boots off the desk, leaving scuff marks in their wake.

"Gunnery Sergeant, has this poor excuse of a human being told us the access codes for The Residence?" she asked as she climbed to her feet. As she did, Coreal blanched. Good. Let him fear her, fear them.

"That's a negative, ma'am." If she had sneered, Talbot's expression all but withered the commandant. "Of course, after his first attempt to pass the blame, he hasn't exactly been in a position to say much of anything."

Oh, he was good. She needed to remember that.

"You're right of course. Maybe that's given him the time he needed to decide if he's going to cooperate or not."

She shook her head and moved around the desk, motioning for Talbot to join her. Ignoring the way Coreal flinched and tried to move avoid her touch, she grabbed his jaw in her gloved hand and forced him to look her in the eye. "I'd have killed you by now if that's what I was after," she said coldly. "Hell, I still might if you don't tell me what I want to know. Or I might just toss you into one of the larger holding cells with a few of the lifers here. How long do you think you'd last with some of them?"

"Captain Shaw, you promised we could have him if anything happened to our people," Talbot growled.

It was all she could do not to look at the gunny in surprise. He sounded like he meant it. More than that, he sounded like he wanted her to do just that.

"Ah, Gunny, I really wish I could. But I promised the good lieutenant over there that we wouldn't do anything to Coreal if he cooperated." She nodded to where the JAG sat, impassively looking on. "Lt. Liu, what are the current charges against the *former* commandant?" Her extra emphasis on *former* had Coreal wincing.

"Failure to follow orders, insubordination, dereliction of duty, fraud, embezzlement, six counts of aggravated assault, three counts of kidnapping, three counts of attempted murder. And those are just the counts that apply to your squadmates, Captain, and doesn't take into account additional charges that will be filed after the strike teams return from the mines and what you called The Residence." His voice was almost bored as he listed the charges.

"And what are the potential charges he faces if the strike teams find my people have been injured or killed?"

"At the very least, he will face additional aggravated assault charges. If any of your people have died, I will personally charge him with capital murder."

"Is there any way for him to mitigate the charges against him."

She heard Coreal gasp and knew he was finally getting the message. Good. She wasn't sure how much longer she could be this close to him and not simply reach out and break his neck. One quick twist was all it would take. Her right hand was already in place since she still had those fingers twisted in his hair and his head pulled back so he had no choice but to look at her. There was no doubt in her mind, she'd be able to kill him before Talbot or Liu could stop her.

"Please. Anything. I'll tell you anything." Sweat steamed down his face and she knew they almost had him where they wanted him.

"What's the entry code for The Residence?" Ashlyn asked. "No tricks. I want the main code. If my people tell me anything goes wrong on entry, I will have your head after I let the inmates here spend some quality time with you."

Coreal swallowed hard and then rattled off the code. Before she could respond, Talbot was relaying it to the strike team. As he did, Ashlyn stepped back, not trusting herself to be near the man who had haunted her dreams for so long. She needed something solid between them before she proved that she was no better than he.

And, damn it, she was. She wasn't a monster even if he had made sure there was now a very dark side to her she struggled to control.

"Lieutenant?"

"I think that's a good place to start, Captain. I'm sure you have more important things to do besides spending one more moment in the presence of this sorry excuse for a man."

Liu looked at Coreal in distaste and Ashlyn realized he had no more use for the man than did she. Good. She might not have much use for the JAG Corps yet, but Liu was doing a lot to prove that most of his section had nothing to do with what happened to her and the others. More importantly, it was also becoming clear that he didn't approve of what happened. Hopefully that meant he'd fight to see justice was done.

"I do." But she didn't leave. There was one more thing to do. "Coreal, listen closely because I'm only going to say this once. If you want to save yourself, you will answer each and every one of the lieutenant's questions. You won't hedge and you won't lie. As you made abundantly clear while I was under your *care*, accidents can happen and I know there are a number of Marines on-planet right now who would gladly see that an accident occurred. More than that, think about the inmates. They have their own reasons for hating you. Reasons they will gladly tell the investigators. So, if you want to save your skin, tell Lieutenant Liu everything, including anything you might know about why my people and I were convicted and sent here."

She moved back around the desk and crossed the office in the direction of the door. Suddenly, she couldn't get out of there fast enough.

"Lieutenant, keep the major and me in the loop. Sergeant Booth and Corporal Cenci will remain here. I'm going to check on my people."

"And me, ma'am?" Talbot asked.

"Gunny, I know you'd like to have a few minutes alone with him, but I need you with me right now. Sergeant, when the lieutenant finishes questioning the prisoner, find a cell for him. It can be in the main population area as long as he's the only prisoner in it. Do the same with the others currently enjoying some time in the yard."

"Understood, ma'am."

"I'll leave you to it then, LT. Let me know if he—" She jerked her head in Coreal's direction – "gives you any trouble."

"Will do, Captain."

Ashlyn nodded and left the office, Talbot on her heels. Once the door slid shut behind them, she blew out a breath. So far, she'd managed to hold it together, but she knew it wouldn't be long before reaction set in. She felt the pressure of it building. All the memories and fear, all the pain and despair seemed to be fighting to return. If she didn't get out of there soon, she wouldn't be responsible for what happened.

"Gunny, I'm going to go check in with the medics and see how our people are doing. While I do, I need you to do me a favor."

"Of course, Cap."

15

Ash stepped inside the shuttle and nodded. After leaving Coreal's office, she'd found herself just standing before the lift doors, wondering what to do next. Pawlak had left her at the penal colony because of her limited duty status instead of sending her to either the mines or the Residence. Even though she'd wanted to argue, she knew he was right. Any doubts she might have had had been erased when she was finally face-to-face with the former prison commandant. She'd wanted to hurt him and it wouldn't have taken much to push her over the edge. If she'd gone with either of the strike teams and found her people hurt – or worse – she would have lost it. Fortunately, the major realized it and was doing what he'd always done best. He was protecting one of his own from doing something they'd regret later.

Later, as she rode to the ground floor, she realized there was something she could do. She could be with the three of her people they had found so far. More than that, she needed to be with them. She needed to see for herself that they were going to be all right and she wanted to be the one to tell them what had happened to bring about their freedom. She just hoped they understood why it had taken so long for her to come back for them.

Now, standing inside the shuttle, she breathed a sigh of relief. Talbot had assured her that the three were going to be all right. She'd wanted to believe him. But the doubts had been there. She understood, and even appreciated, the fact he might be trying to protect her from being hurt. So she'd needed to see for herself.

And, thank God, the Gunny had been right.

Two of her former team were bundled in blankets on flight couches. They watched closely as the medic worked on the third member of the team. All of them bore scars and had that same haunted look in their eyes Ash still saw all too often in her own. But they were alive and, at least at first glance, not too badly injured.

As if sensing her presence, the man nearest her turned his head. His green eyes widened in disbelief and he was suddenly struggling to get free of his blanket. Instantly, Ash reacted, motioning for him to lie still. The last thing she wanted was for him to injure himself trying to get up.

"Captain?"

Lieutenant Michael "Mick" Malloy looked at her in a mixture of hope and disbelief. As he did, the man in the second flight couch turned his head in their direction. The expression on Corporal Edward Harston's face was an almost identical match to Malloy's.

"Easy, LT," she soothed, crouching next to his flight couch. Tears burned in her eyes as she reached out and pulled the blanket about his shoulders.

"Cap, what's going on?" Harston asked.

"The short version is that we're going home, guys. Our convictions have been tossed out and, just to make sure there are no questions, we have received pardons from the President."

"How?" Malloy wanted to know. "And why now, after all this time?"

"There's more to what's happened than I can tell you in a few minutes. But from what I've gathered, the public didn't buy the brass's charges against us any more than most of the Corps did. In the next election, those pols who didn't back an attempt to clear our names and free us were pretty much voted out of office. President Harper took office and immediately began cleaning house. While he did, Senator Tremayne." She grinned in understanding as the two looked at her in surprise. "Yep, the admiral went and turned politician on us. Anyway, she continued working to find out what really happened on that last mission and between what she discovered and what Rico Santiago and his people found, the President issued full pardons for all of us.

"In the meantime, General Okafor took over as Commandant of the Corps and she's been merciless in how she's dealt with those behind our being brought up on charges. The investigation has continued and she's assured me that there will be charges filed for what happened to us."

"You've talked to the general?" Harston asked.

Ash nodded. This was where it could get difficult. Would they understand that she hadn't had a choice in leaving them in this hell-hole? Or would they resent her for being released even a few weeks before they were?

"I have." She thought hard, trying to figure out the best way to explain what happened. "Several weeks ago, I was ordered to assume the *position*. There was nothing to make me think it was for anything but another session with Coreal. I don't know how they treated you, but any time I was moved, I'd be hooded, cuffed and shackled. That's how it was this time."

When they both nodded, she relaxed a little. Maybe they would understand.

"When I realized it was Haritos who'd come for me, let's just say I figured I'd be visiting the infirmary again."

"God, Cap, I'd hoped I was the only one seeing the sadistic side of that bastard," O'Malley said.

"I think it's probably a good bet we all saw too much of him and of Coreal," Harston commented.

"I'm afraid you're right," Ash agreed grimly. "But this time was different. I was taken to a shuttle and transported to a ship that took me back to the capital. I didn't even know where we were going until I was on a shuttle heading dirtside and could see the surface. Even then, no one told me why I'd been returned.

"The only thing I knew for certain was that Haritos had warned me to keep my mouth shut. You, all of you, were the weapons he held. The not-so-subtle threat was that if I talked about what was going on here, you would all die – or worse. So I did as he said."

She paused and rubbed her face, trying to scrub away the memories and the pain. "A lot has happened since then and I'll give you a full briefing after you've eaten and have gotten some rest. Just know that a week after I arrived, I was pardoned and so were each of you."

"Then why—"

Sergeant Caleb Baldwin didn't finish his statement. He didn't have to. Ashlyn had a very good idea what he'd been going to say.

"Word of your pardons was sent here. I've seen the comm and I've seen the acknowledgment of it. We didn't come sooner – Hell, Caleb, we couldn't come any sooner – because the capital was attacked."

That had all three sitting up, their expressions mirror images of outrage and disbelief. Before Ash could explain, the medic was telling Baldwin to lie back down or she'd sedate him. Then she gave Ash a look that left no doubt in her mind that she'd like to sedate her as well.

"Our best guess is that it was a test of our defense systems and response because it was a very limited, one time only attack. But FleetCom pulled First Fleet in and didn't want to strip out even one ship to come here before they were sure the home system was secure."

She held her breath, waiting for their responses. Hopefully they'd understand that she hadn't wanted to wait to come for them. But what choice had there been?

"Callusians?" O'Malley asked.

"That's our best guess."

"Cap, don't look so worried," Harston told her. "You couldn't get here any sooner. We know that. Hell, we know you'd probably have stolen a ship if you could have to come back for us. But you're here now."

"Breaker's right, ma'am." Baldwin nodded in agreement. "All I want to know is if any action is going to be taken against the bastards here." His voice turned hard, harder than Ash could ever remember it being.

Well, that was one thing she could answer and, hopefully, make them feel better.

Without a word, she pulled out her datapad and typed in a set of commands. A moment later, the video feed from Coreal's office came online. She adjusted the angle slightly and then handed the datapad to O'Malley. Seeing the satisfaction light his expression before he handed the datapad to Harston was enough.

"I assume it was your idea to take that bastard to his own office in chains, Cap," Baldwin said as she studied the video.

"And hooded." She gave them an almost feral grin, knowing they'd understand and approve. She took the datapad back and typed in a new command before handing it back to Baldwin. Unless she missed her guess, the sergeant needed to see Haritos chained and helpless even more than she had needed to see Coreal that way.

"Captain, they need to get some rest now," the medic said as she helped Baldwin to one of the flight couches. "You can talk with them again in a couple of hours."

"But—" O'Malley protested.

"He's right, Mick." She carefully stood. "I'll have some fresh uniforms for you when you wake. We'll talk more then."

"Cap, just one more question." Baldwin waved back the medic and sat up. "What about Sorkowski and that rat bastard O'Brien?"

Now Ashlyn could smile, especially at the thought of their former Marine CO.

"Sorkowski has been forcibly retired and, before you ask, General Okafor has assured me that she wants him brought up on any and all charges they can find. Same for O'Brien with one difference. They didn't let him retire. Our beloved Corps Commandant has an evil sense of justice. She had him assigned to escort duty around the capital – escort duty for the children and relatives of VIPs."

For a moment, no one said anything. Ash had no doubt they were

She saw he was worried about her but wasn't sure she could do anything to reassure him.

"I need you to check the records here and see what they did with my belongings after I was transferred back to the capital. I didn't have much but there were a few things, a picture of my son and a book my mother gave me, I'd like to have."

"I'll see if I can't find them."

"Thank you." She closed her eyes and struggled for the right words. "Gunny – Kevin, you've got a pretty good idea how hard today's been for me."

He nodded.

"And I know you will do whatever you can to keep me from making a mistake I'd regret later."

Another nod.

"I can't stay here. I need to get away before I decide to go back in there and tear Coreal apart with my bare hands. So I'm going to go sit with our people and try to reassure them that they really are all right and will soon be going home."

"Cap." He looked around to make sure they wouldn't be overheard. "Ash, the fact you haven't killed that bastard already amazes me. I'm not sure I could have stopped myself if I were in your shoes. Don't you worry. We'll make sure he gives the LT the information we need to close this hellhole down. He's going to pay for what he's done. I swear it and you know a Devil Dog never breaks his word."

She couldn't help it. She smiled, touched not only by the conviction in his voice but by the fact he'd broken protocol enough to call her by her name. She could count on one hand how many times he'd done so and still have fingers left over.

"Now go sit with the others. I'll see what I can find out about your personal effects. I'll join you once I'm done."

"Thanks, Gunny." She clasped his arm and then left the outer office, wanting to put as much distance as possible between herself and Coreal before she did something they would all regret.

too stunned to. Then O'Malley threw his head back and laughed. Soon Harston and Baldwin joined him. Relieved, Ash smiled and turned her attention to the medic.

"Take good care of them and make sure I have a copy of your report as well as Major Pawlak."

"The Old Man's here?" Baldwin's humor turned to surprise.

"He is. He'll be in to see you soon." She smiled again, relieved to know that these three, at least, would soon be going home. "Now do as the medic says before she decides to sedate all of us. I'll be back soon. I promise."

"Well?" Talbot asked as she emerged from the shuttle.

"I think they're going to be all right." At least she hoped so. "The medic wants them to rest for a bit before anything else."

"That's probably for the best, ma'am. I know you want to be with them. Hell, Cap, we all want to be with them. But they need time to adjust to what is going on."

She nodded, remembering her own suspicions and doubts. At least she knew what they were going through and could, hopefully, help ease some of their concerns.

"Gunny, we need to secure fresh uniforms for them and, if possible, their dog tags," she said as they moved across the landing area in the direction of a second shuttle.

"I'll see to the uniforms, ma'am. As for their dog tags, the Major said to tell you they are with your kit in the shuttle. He thought you'd like to be able to return them to our people."

Ashlyn nodded and made a mental note to thank the Major.

"He also left orders for you to get some rest. You're to take a solid four down. I'm to make sure of it. To quote the Major, I'm to sit on you if I have to and, if that doesn't work, I'm to have the medic sedate you."

For a moment, she just looked at him, eyes narrowed. Then she nodded. She had no doubt Pawlak had left orders for her to take some down time. Nor did she doubt Talbot had added the part about sitting on her. So she'd agree, at least to "resting". She doubted she'd be able to sleep but the downtime would give her a chance to review the JAG's report of his interrogation of Coreal as well as check the prison records for her people. Hopefully, by the time the prescribed four hours were up, Pawlak would have news from the strike teams about the others sent there with her.

———

Lucinda Ortega groaned in pain. Rolling onto her side, she drew a shuddering breath. Then she cursed long and hard. Damn it! Ash had warned her not to take any chances. She'd even listened. But she hadn't expected Coreal's people at the Residence to put up any real resistance. She certainly hadn't expected any of them to choose to act as the man who greeted them at the main door had. Fortunately, something warned her not to trust him. Perhaps it had been hearing some of what her former roommate had suffered while on this hell-hole of a planet. Perhaps it was seeing the conditions of Malloy and the others. Whatever it was, she knew things could have been much worse.

She slowly climbed to her feet and scanned the area. As she did, the sensors in her battle armor read out her vital signs. Her helmet's visor shifted through various filters until she could see through the dust and debris filling the air. Pain registered for a moment, but it was incidental, too small to worry about. Besides, her armor would soon dispense any analgesics needed so she could continue carrying out her orders.

"Sound off!" she snapped. As she did, she kicked aside what looked to have been the man's hand. Not that she could tell for sure without looking closer. Strapping a bomb to your chest tended to leave little recognizable behind.

Which was for the best. Otherwise, her squad would want to tear him apart. Hell, she wanted to do so. If he killed any of her people. . ..

As she listened to various members of her squad reporting in, she checked her weapons to make sure they had not been damaged in the explosion. Then, as the count ended, she cursed again. Three had not responded. Before she could order a search of the area, others were there, pulling the injured out of the debris and to safety.

"Status?" she asked as she stalked to where the squad's medic checked the one of the injured.

"Bad but they should recover, Sorceress. That bastard from inside wasn't so lucky."

She nodded. She'd shed no tears over the man. Fortunately, she'd ordered most of the squad to remain under cover instead of following him inside as he wanted. Private Schapper went with him. More accurately, Schapper had started to follow him. Then an explosion ripped through the air and Lucinda watched as Coreal's man disintegrated into nothing but bits of bone and flesh and blood. Schapper flew through the air, landing with a sickening thud on the stone walkway. Windows shattered and then everything had gone silent. Now, looking at the damage, Lucinda shook her head. They had been lucky. She planned on making sure that luck did not run out.

Opening comms to not only her squad but to the second squad stationed at the rear of the building called the Residence, Lucinda knew what she had to do. "This is Sorceress. We have hostiles. I repeat. We have hostiles. Three down after encounter with a suicide bomber. Front entry compromised. Delta Squad, you are to breach the rear of the building. Make a door!"

"Making a door, Sorceress," Lieutenant Travis Houston replied.

"Alpha Squad, let's make our own entry and then teach these sons-of-bitches how foolish it is to play games with the Devil Dogs."

With that, she signaled Tank to take point. The heavy armored Marine shouldered his battle rifle and moved forward. The rest of the squad fell in behind him. As they did, Ashlyn opened a secure line to the attack force's comms specialist.

"Singer, Sorceress."

"Sorceress, go."

"No comms traffic to Angel until either Hammer or I approve it. Understood?"

The last thing they needed was for Ashlyn to find out what happened. Lucinda had no doubt Ash would waste no time getting to the Residence if she did. She knew her friend well enough to realize Ash was holding on by sheer force of will just then. It wouldn't take much to push her over the edge and she wasn't going to risk the captain doing anything that might find her brought up on charges once again.

"Understood, Sorceress. Hammer already issued the same order."

That didn't surprise her. Pawlak, almost as much as she, wanted to do whatever he could to protect their XO – whether Ash wanted them to or not.

Lucinda switched back to the battle-net. "Singer, once inside, get me comms that will carry throughout the building. I don't care if we have to send up smoke signals. It's time they understood who they're dealing with."

"Understood, Sorceress."

"Tank, once we're inside, find yourself a spot to watch our backs. Anyone not in armor – *our* battle armor – is to be stopped. If they refuse, open fire at your discretion."

"Roger that, Sorceress."

"Alpha Squad, Delta Squad, you have a fire order. I repeat, you have a fire order. If they want to make this a fight, we will, by God, show them what a real fight is."

"Ooh-rah!"

Leaving the medic and a guard with the injured, Lucinda nodded at Tank. The man nodded in return. Then he turned to study the building before them. A few moments later, he shouldered his RPG. His voice came over the battle-net, warning them to take cover. An all too brief moment of silence exploded in sound and debris as he fired. By the time her armor once again adjusted helmet filters to let her see through the debris, Tank was moving inside through his newly created "door".

The moment she stepped inside, Lucinda ordered the squad to secure the room. As she did, she looked around. Tank's impromptu door brought them inside what looked to be a formal sitting room of some sort. From expensive wall hangings and art to furniture down to crystal decanters and glasses, nothing about the room said penal colony. Instead, she had a feeling they had discovered where some of Coreal's funding had gone. Her upper lip curled back in distaste as she glanced around, looking for her comms specialist.

"Singer, get me an open channel. These *people* get one chance to surrender."

The comms specialist nodded and, with another member of the squad joining her, left in search of a working comm-unit. Not wanting to waste any time, Lucinda knew what she needed to do next.

"Boomer, Falcon, make sure there aren't any other surprises waiting for us. Toad, Storm, take two others and start searching the front of this place, first floor only. We'll clear room-by-room, floor-by-floor. If you come across anyone, give them one chance to surrender. If they refuse, do whatever it takes to keep you and your people safe and to make sure no prisoners are injured. Understood?"

"Understood, Sorceress."

"Delta, Sorceress. Report."

"No surprises so far, Sorceress. No people either," Lieutenant Houston replied. "We have found access to what looks to be the basement."

"Secure the passage and send eyes down. We're securing this floor, front of the building. Singer is trying to find building-wide comms. I'd prefer to do this the easy way but, after what we've already seen and after what happened at the entrance, we will do it any way we have to. Sorceress out."

As she waited on the comms-specialist, Lucinda monitored the progress of the rest of the squad. Room after room was searched and sealed. So far, no one had been found. That should have reassured her, but it did not. Their greeting at the main entrance proved those inside were not going to give up without a fight. It also meant they were more than likely willing to sacrifice any prisoners they might have – if they hadn't already. So where were they and what were they planning?

Frowning, she keyed her comm and waited for the shuttle pilot to respond.

"Talon. Go ahead, Sorceress."

"Talon, run new scans on the building. Where are they?"

Several moments passed before he answered. "I have heat signature almost directly above you, Sorceress. Three, maybe four. There is a larger cluster below. Be advised, there is now a dead zone in the center of the building, looks to be on the second and third levels. It was not there before you dropped."

"Tank, your thoughts?" Next to herself, Tank had the most experience in the squad.

"That's their hide-a-hole, Sorceress. The other two locations are either false readings or are meant to keep us distracted while the others prepare a breakout or worse."

"Agreed." She switched over to Pawlak's channel. Before she did anything else, she wanted to confer with him. "Sorceress, Hammer."

"Hammer. Go, Sorceress."

She quickly filled him in. He listened closely without interrupting. Only when she finished did he say anything.

"Do you have a plan?" he asked.

"Hit the three targets at the same time. I think Tank has the right of it, but I don't want to risk one of the smaller groups being able to activate a self-destruct. They've had one try at blowing the squad to Hell and back again. I'd prefer not giving them another."

"Make sure you blind them first. Don't let them see you coming."

"Understood. Sorceress out."

With Tank on her heels, she left in search of the comms specialist. The young woman's assignment had just changed.

———

"Where are they?"

An unmistakable note of panic laced the man's voice as he glanced from one monitor to another. He'd been so sure they would be able to hold out against the Marines. After all, the Residence had been built not only as a retreat for Coreal and those he favored but it had also been the one place the commandant made sure would be safe if the prisoners on Tarsus managed to seize control of the prison.

Two squads of Marines, even Fuerconese Marines, hadn't bothered him. With the penal colony no longer answer his hails, he knew what to do. He, along with those with him, would hold out until the Marines were either dead or gave up. Then they, and any of their *companions* who still lived, would use the shuttles secured at the rear of the building to get off-planet.

But now they were blind. Somehow, the Marines had cut the security monitors. That meant they had taken the secondary control center. If that was the case, how long before they closed in on this part of the building?

"Jaegger, bring the prisoners. We'll use them as cover."

The burly man nodded once.

"I want the girl. Let's see if those bastards are as determined when they see my knife to her throat."

He'd make them beg just as he had her.

———

"GET ME EYES IN THERE, SINGER."

Alpha Squad ranged down the corridor and around the corner from their target. Lucinda had to give it to whoever designed the building, the doorway into the *safe* area was almost invisible to the naked eye. If she had not been looking for it, she would have missed it. Now she needed to figure out the best way to make entry. After the fighting they had seen at the other two targets, she had no doubt, those inside were ready to die before surrendering.

Worse, she now knew they had at least a dozen prisoners, including Corporal Navarro, with them. Their search of the building had found others, killed by their captors before the Marines arrived. Each of them showed signs of torture and worse. Anger and fear about what they had done to Navarro pushed at her. She fought it down. She had to maintain control, for Navarro's sake as well as for the well-being of the squad.

A few minutes later, Singer gave her a nod. Lucinda's faceplate darkened for a moment and then she found herself looking at the inside of the room. Her lips pulled back and she ground her teeth in anger at what she saw.

A dozen men and women stood in the center of the room. They formed a tight-knit group. Standing so they each faced out, watching for anything that might warn them the Marines might be about to make entry. Weapons held at the ready, they waited. Even without sound, Lucinda knew they were scared and desperate and that made them dangerous.

Worse was the sight of almost as many others who were very clearly prisoners. Most were women. None were clothed. They all appeared to be bound. Some knelt in front of one or their captors. Others were held against a captor, a gun or knife keeping them from struggling. All showed signs of being beaten and quite possibly drugged.

"Sorceress."

Tank's anger came through loud and clear and she realized he, too, had recognized their squadmate. A few of the others had as well. They shifted restlessly and she felt their anger as surely as if it were her own. Switching once again to a private channel, she inhaled deeply. She was about to violate her own order.

"Sorceress, Angel," she radioed. As she did, she had no doubt Ashlyn would quickly reply. Singer had reported their XO had made more than request for an update already.

"Angel. Go ahead, Sorceress."

"Angel, I'm going to send you a feed. It's bad but I need to know what you can tell me about those you see." She waited, praying her friend didn't do anything foolish like hijack a shuttle to join them.

"Understood."

Something in the XO's voice reassured her. With a nod, she signaled Singer to transmit the feed to Ashlyn.

"Anything you know that will help us diffuse this situation?"

For several long moments, Ash didn't reply. Lucinda waited, wishing she hadn't needed to bring her in on this. If anything happened to Navarro, Ash would blame herself and that was the last thing any of them needed. Lucinda knew it was also the last thing Navarro would want.

"They're not guards. At least none that I recognize. My guess is they are members of Coreal's staff and some of his *friends*."

From the way Ash all but spat out the word, Lucinda knew she'd be asking her about these *friends* once this mission was over.

"Is there any way to gas the room?"

"Not that we've found, Angel. Looks like the only way in is through a door down the corridor from our current position. There has to be a secondary exit somewhere, but we haven't found it yet. I'll be honest, we were damned lucky to find this one."

"Did you find any shuttles or other means of transport?"

"Aye. A single shuttle hidden behind the building."

"The exit will be close to it. However, from the way they're gathered, they either don't have a pilot or they don't think they can get to it." Ashlyn paused for a moment. "You cut their video feeds?"

"We did."

"Then they probably think you are waiting for them there and have decided to make a stand there. My guess is they want to try to bargain. If they are anything like Coreal and Haritos, they won't hesitate to kill one or more of the prisoners to try to make their point. Navarro won't be the first. They'll keep her as their bargaining chip. But they will hurt her. Just as they will the others."

Just as they did you? Lucinda wondered. She knew there was much her friend had not yet told her about her time on Tarsus.

"All right." Now it was Lucinda's time to think. "We're going in hot. Boomer will blow the door. Tank will go in first. His job will be to get to Navarro. We'll save as many of them as we can, Angel. I promise."

"Don't unnecessarily risk the squad to do it."

"We're going silent now, Angel. I'll report in once we've made entry. Sorceress out."

She tapped the side of her battle helmet and waited for the faceplate to turn clear again. She had seen enough. Besides, Singer would continue monitoring the situation inside and would warn her if anything changed.

"Delta, Sorceress."

"Delta here. Go ahead, Sorceress."

"Take up positions near the shuttle you found. There may be a secondary exit the targets will head for. Do not, I repeat, do NOT let them board that shuttle."

"Roger that."

"Alpha, prepare to move on my command. Boomer, I want a controlled blast with lots of smoke on the door. Make a hole big enough for Tank to get through. Tank, you'll be first in. If you can, secure Navarro. Then lay down cover while we take down the targets." She waited, watching as the squad took one last look at the video feed before continuing. "Any questions?"

"Only one, Sorceress," the heavy armor specialist said. "Can we kill those mother fuckers?"

"If they draw down on you or make any attempt to harm their prisoners, I expect you to do just that." Voice cold, eyes hard, she found herself hoping for the opportunity to do just that to the man who held the knife to Navarro's throat. "Boomer, make it happen."

The explosives expert nodded once and moved quickly down the corridor toward the doorway. It wouldn't be long now.

16

Ashlyn stepped inside the shuttle that had become the mobile medbay for the Devil Dogs. This time, the shuttle was filled with Marines needing treatment. Her jaw clinched and she watched as the medics moved between their patients, doing everything they could for them. Fortunately, most of their injuries were non-life threatening.

Most being the operative word. Several of the Marines sent to make entry into the Residence had been seriously injured. Then there were the prisoners, those few Ortega and her squads had been able to save. Fortunately for those responsible, none of Coreal's people survived the initial battle. Fortunate because Ashlyn would have seen them dead for what they'd done to the prisoners who had been taken there, most especially for what they'd done to Corporal Navarro.

Navarro.

The thought of the young woman had Ashlyn glancing around the shuttle. Her mouth drew tight to see the medics treating the corporal. They worked quickly and almost silently, something Ash knew was a bad sign. Much as she wanted to go over and demand an update on the woman's condition, she wouldn't. She didn't dare. She would not risk her squadmate's life that way.

Nearby, the others of her team waited. The two who had been rescued from the mining operation were in worse shape than the three rescued from the main compound, but they would recover. It would take time and they would bear the scars of their time on Tarsus, both mentally and physically. But they would live and nothing else mattered at the moment.

Without a word, Ashlyn signaled for Talbot to hand out the uniforms he had secured for their squadmates. Once he had, she followed. Almost reverently, she handed each one his dog tags. As she did, she remembered what she'd felt when Talbot had tossed her her own tags in the middle of the attack on the capital. Hopefully, having them on again would help her people as much as it had her.

Moving carefully amongst the injured, she made her way to where Navarro was being treated. Without a word, she placed the woman's dog tags on the cot next to her. Then, after an encouraging nod from the nearest medic, she gently wrapped the chain for the tags around Narvarro's hand. She wanted the corporal to know they had been returned to her the moment she regained consciousness.

"Captain, we need to get her and several others back to the *Magellan* once we have them stabilized," the medic nearest her said.

"All right. I'll let the Major know."

She took one last look at Navarro before turning away. As she did, she swallowed hard and fought down her anger. Those responsible – well, most of them – for what happened to the younger woman were dead. The Devil Dogs had made certain of it.

"Cap?" O'Malley's voice was soft, his concern clear.

"They're doing all they can for her." She hoped it would be enough. "I need to report to the major and then see if we can't get off this rock once and for all."

"God, that sounds good, Cap," Baldwin admitted.

The others nodded in agreement.

"Agreed." She nodded to Talbot. "Gunny's going to escort you to another shuttle where you can clean up and change. There's food and drink waiting for you as well. I should be back from meeting with the major by the time you're done."

"Ma'am, are we really free?" Lance Corporal Odell Vickers asked?

"We are, Vickers, and all charges against us have been expunged from our records." She motioned to Talbot who produced his datapad and keyed in a command sequence. Then he handed it to Vickers. "You'll each find copies of all the pertinent documents on there. I promise we'll get you kitted out once we've returned to the *Magellan*. I'll do my best to answer all your questions then."

"Your word's enough for us, ma'am," Harston assured her. "Now, with the Captain's permission, can we get the hell out of here?"

Laughing, Ashlyn nodded and watched as the five carefully climbed to their feet. She knew she didn't need to tell Talbot to report in after they reached the second shuttle. Trusting him to look after their squadmates, she left the shuttle and made her way across the landing area in the direction of the administration building.

"Captain, the major is in with Lieutenant Liu," Hound said as she entered the anteroom of what had been Coreal's office.

"And the prisoners?" She had no doubt he knew exactly who she meant.

"They are secure in their cells. We have constant eyes on them. It wouldn't do for any of them to have an unfortunate accident before they get the chance to answer for all they've done to you and the others."

"Good." And if it was wrong to feel more than a hint of satisfaction to know what Coreal now inhabited a cell similar to the one she had lived in for so long, she didn't care.

She knocked at the door to the inner office and waited until Pawlak called for her to enter. A moment later, the door slid open. As she stepped inside, she was a little surprised to see the JAG seated behind the desk and Pawlak sprawled in one of the chairs situated before it. Then she realized it made a kind of sense. The JAG had been using the office to conduct his investigation. The other member of the JAG Corps had traveled to the mining facility as well as The Residence. From what she'd been told by their Devil Dog escorts, the two weren't missing anything that could be used to build a case against Coreal and the guards.

"Ah, good." Pawlak motioned for Ashlyn to join them. "The LT and I were just going over what he's found so far."

"And?" Ashlyn took the seat next to Pawlak and waited.

"Let's just say it I'd be surprised if either Coreal or Haritos manage to avoid the death penalty, Captain," Liu said grimly. "And I have a feeling a number of the guards here will be joining them."

Ashlyn closed her eyes, not sure whether she should feel relieved or not.

"Ash, it's worse than I think even you imagined," Pawlak took up. "It's going to take months for Liu and his people to sort through all the evidence and talk to all the potential witnesses."

Ashlyn's eyes widened and she swallowed hard. Surely Liu didn't expect her and the others to stay there that long. They couldn't. All of them, herself included, needed to get off-planet and the sooner, the better.

"Don't worry, Captain," Liu began as if reading her thoughts. "You and your people may return to the *Magellan* as soon as Captain Carlisle gives the go ahead. You can dictate your statements and file them from the ship."

"Thank you."

"How are they, Ash?" Pawlak asked.

"Pretty much like I was those first few days, sir. The best thing we can do for them is get them away from here. Seeing the video feeds of Coreal and Haritos in custody helped. But, as I know from personal experience, being away from this hellhole will be the best medicine."

"Then I'll issue orders to get Shuttle Two ready to return to the *Magellan*. As soon as the medics have Navarro ready to move, be prepared to leave."

"Understood, sir, and thank you."

"I'll have my preliminary report, as well as the evidence we've seized so far, ready to transport up, Captain. If you'll ask Gunnery Sergeant Talbot to hand it over to Captain Carlisle for transmittal to FleetCom, I'd appreciate it."

"Of course, Lieutenant."

"Go be with your people, Ash. I'll touch base before you lift," Pawlak told her.

"Aye, sir." She stood, glad to know that soon she would be away from that hellhole and hoping she never had to return.

17

"Sir, you don't have to do this," Ashlyn said as they paused outside the staging area in Marine Country onboard the *Magellan*.

"I need to do this just like you needed to bring them home, Ash." Pawlak looked down at her, understanding and something else reflecting in his eyes.

Seeing it, Ash nodded. She had been touched when he commed her an hour earlier and explained what he had in mind. But he wouldn't do it without her being present. Not that she would miss it. This was too important, to her and to those sent to Tarsus with her, to miss. Even so, she knew how much was still to be done at the penal colony and their CO was taking time away from it for this.

A moment later, the hatch slid open. As it did, Pawlak stepped inside. Ashlyn followed, Ortega at her side. The moment the hatch slid shut behind them, Talbot braced to attention from his post next to the hatch. Before those gathered could do the same, the gunnery sergeant told them to remain at their ease. Since several would have been hard put to stand, much less brace to attention, Ash nodded to the gunny in approval. She had no doubt it was something he had discussed with Pawlak earlier.

"I'll keep this brief," the major began as he stepped forward. "I know I speak for every Devil Dog, every Marine, when I welcome you back. We never forgot you. We knew none of you were guilty of the charges against you. We might not have been able to do anything at the time, but we remembered you. We, along with a number of others, worked to find a way to free you. You were ours and we weren't going to leave you behind to be sacrificed on the bier of political agendas.

"None of us are going to pressure you about the future. Just know that you will always have a place in the Devil Dogs if you want it. We're just damned glad to have you home again. I'm only sorry it took us so long to get here."

He stepped back and, much to Ashlyn's surprise, he motioned her forward.

"Sir?"

"This is for you to do, Captain." He held out a hand and Ortega stepped up. Without a word, she handed him a stack of folders. He gave them a glance before handing them to Ash. Her mouth suddenly dry, she looked down. Tears burned in her eyes as she realized what she held. Each folder, leather-bound and bearing the insignia of the Fuerconese Marine Corps, reminded her of the one she had been presented not that long ago. To be able to give them to those sent to Tarsus with her meant everything. More than everything.

"Go on. You need this as much as they do, Ash," Pawlak said softly.

"I'm not going to ask how the major got these." She glanced to where Talbot stood near the hatch, doing his best to look as if he didn't know what she meant. "I brought these onboard the *Magellan* with me." Her hand lightly caressed the top file.

"You have seen the digital versions of your pardons, of the paperwork not only clearing each of you, of us, of the charges leveled against us after Arterus but expunging our records as well. However, if you're like me, you still have doubts. We learned the hard way that digital records can and have been altered."

Each of them nodded, their expressions grim.

"What can't be altered or faked is the fact that I was present when each of these documents was executed. I demanded to be before leaving Fuercon. I wanted to be able to assure you that this isn't another trick. We've had more than our fair share of those, haven't we?"

More nods.

"These contain the official documents clearing your names. All charges are formally dropped and your convictions have been over-turned. President Harper has added pardons as well, his way of showing his support for our cause. You will also find that you have been returned to duty, inactive status until cleared by the medics and until you have decided whether you want to return to active duty or not. By the time we get home, your back pay should have been remit-ted. In short, you are now and, as Hammer said, always, Devil Dogs.

"There's something else to prove this is real," she continued. "When we leave here, you can send messages to your families. You'll also find messages waiting for you. General Okafor spoke with each of them before the *Magellan* broke orbit, letting them know what was happening. They sent messages and they will be there to greet you when we return to Fuercon."

"Is it really over, Cap?" Navarro spoke softly and Ashlyn saw the fear lurking in her eyes.

"It's really over, Yvonne. At least this part of it is."

"What do you mean, Angel?" Malloy asked sharply.

"Like I said, we're free, our names cleared. But those responsible for what happened are being investigated. It goes beyond Sorkowski and O'Brien. Once we return home, we'll all receive a full briefing." She held up a hand before they could interrupt. "I know. I didn't trust JAG to handle this either. But it isn't just JAG. Rico Santiago, General Okafor, even SecDef are involved in the investigation. They want to know the why of what happened just as much as we do. More impor-tantly, they will make sure those responsible pay and, for whatever it's worth, I believe them."

With that, she handed out the files, pausing to speak with each member of her team. There were tears as well as laughs. If they were bitter, no one blamed them. She certainly didn't. When the rest of the Devil Dogs on the mission filed into the staging area, she shook her head. No one needed to tell her why they were there. They were Devil Dogs and they would make sure their fellow Marines knew they were finally home.

That made all the difference in the world.

"The medics said no booze," Tank said as he stepped forward. "But we figured we could have sort of a party to welcome you home even so."

"That includes you, Angel," Ortega said before she could step back. "You did what you promised. You brought them home. Now relax and let us show you how glad we are to have you back."

"And I'll make it official," Pawlak said with a grin. "It's an order, Captain. You and the others are to relax, spend as much time as you want or need catching up and then each of you is to get a solid eight hours down."

"Gunny, I think it's time to get this party started." Ortega nodded to Talbot.

A moment later, the hatch slid open and several members of the ship's crew entered, bringing with them enough food and drink to satisfy even the Devil Dogs.

"You did it, Ash. Enjoy this. You earned it," Ortega said softly as she pulled her friend in for a hug. "We'll get back to work on putting nooses around the necks of those responsible for sending you here soon enough."

No. Not ever soon enough but it could wait a little while. Lucinda and Pawlak were right about one thing. She needed this time with the others. She needed it almost as much as she needed to get home and spend some time with her family, especially her son.

———

"Brigadier General Shaw is here, ma'am."

General Okafor looked up from the latest reports received from Tarsus and nodded. "Send her in."

She got to her feet and moved to stare out the window. When she issued the orders for most of Alpha Company to go to Tarsus, she'd suspected they would find everything Ashlyn told them to be true. She had even been prepared for it to be worse. But Major Pawlak's latest report turned her stomach. How had Coreal been allowed to act as he had and for so long?

How deep did the cancer run and would they be able to cut it out before the enemy attacked again?

A moment later, the door to the office opened. Without turning, Okafor listened as Elizabeth stepped inside. When she did finally turn to face the woman, she smiled slightly. Despite everything, it was good to see Elizabeth back in uniform. She only hoped the woman agreed to remain on active duty status after hearing what she had to say.

"You wanted to see me, ma'am?"

"Relax, Liz." She waved her guest to one of the chairs before the desk. "I promised you before Ash and the others left for Tarsus that I'd keep you apprised. That's why I sent for you."

Fear lit the woman's expression and she inhaled sharply. Cursing herself, Okafor quickly reassured her nothing had happened to her daughter. At least nothing physically. But what old wounds would visiting the penal colony have ripped open for the younger woman? Only time would tell and Okafor worried time was the one thing they didn't have much of.

"No." Okafor shook her head and dropped onto the chair next to Elizabeth's. "Ashlyn's all right. I'm sorry. I didn't mean to worry you."

Elizabeth blew out a long breath and then seemed to almost shake herself before speaking. "You're sure?"

"I am."

For a moment, the woman said nothing. Then she nodded, her expression easing at least a little. "Then what?"

"I received a new report from Pawlak less than an hour ago. Tarsus was, if possible, worse than we feared."

"Ash's people?"

"Alive and they should all make full recoveries, at least physically."

She closed her eyes for a moment and searched for the right words. Quickly, she relayed what she knew of the situation. As she did, Elizabeth's expression darkened as her anger rose. Even so, not once did the woman interrupt. She listened, occasionally making a note on the datapad she retrieved from her thigh pocket.

"Those responsible?" Elizabeth asked when Okafor finished speaking.

"In custody. The JAG officers, as well as Lucinda Ortega, are souring the penal colony's records. If there is anything there to find, they'll find it."

"You realize this means the corruption goes deeper than we thought." It wasn't a question, more of an observation and Okafor nodded. "My guess is that Coreal has been selling at least some of the prisoners as slaves. We have to find out who he has sold them to. We also need to find out if there is any link between him and Sorkowski or O'Brien."

"Agreed and I will talk to Rico about it when we're done here."

"What do you want me to do?"

"What you've been doing. We are going to war. It isn't a question of if. It is a question of when. I need you to make sure your division is ready. I also need you to let me know how Ashlyn is doing. If she needs anything because we both know she won't tell me."

Elizabeth chuckled softly and nodded in agreement. "When is the *Magellan* returning home?"

"From what Pawlak said in his report, it should be able to break orbit in no more than three days." Now she smiled, knowing at least part of why Elizabeth asked. "Don't worry. Ash will be home in time for Jake's birthday."

Elizabeth didn't try to hide her relief.

"You're going to have to be prepared for the toll this investigation is going to take on Ashlyn, Liz. It's not going to go as fast as she wants. It can't. President Harper has said he wants everything to be checked and double-checked and I agree with him. We can't risk anyone accusing us of acting out of malice because of what happened to Ash and her people. So, before any other arrests are made, we have to have every bit of evidence we can."

"Understood." She leaned forward, elbows on her knees, her chin resting on her upraised fists. "General – Helen, Ash knows this. At least she does on some level. But you're right. It's going to be hard on her and, to be honest, on all the Devil Dogs. The first few weeks after the Magellan returns home won't be too bad. Ash has to report to the doctors and then she is going to have get up to speed on everything that's happened since her arrest. To be honest, it is the Devil Dogs I'm more worried about. We can't risk some of the hotheads deciding to go out and handle this on their own."

"I have a few thoughts about that. We'll discuss them with Pawlak once they are back."

"I may have a few ideas of my own by then."

Okafor smiled slightly. She had no doubt the woman would. "Good. Now, let's put that away for now. I have the latest report from FleetCom concerning the attack on the capital . . .."

18

"How is she?" Paul Pawlak leaned against the edge of his desk. He knew Ortega and Talbot knew who he meant.

Neither said anything. Instead, they looked at one another. Pawlak waited. He knew he was asking a lot. But he was worried about his XO. Over the course of his career, he had seen too many Marines after they'd been prisoners of war. The physical scars they bore were bad enough. But the mental and emotional scars, the scars no one but those closest to them ever saw, were far worse. If they weren't treated, they festered, eating away at the person.

He had seen Ashlyn doing her best to convince not only herself but everyone else that those demons didn't haunt her. He'd let it slide before the mission because he'd hoped coming to Tarsus to rescue the others would help. Now he wasn't so sure. If anything, she seemed closer to the edge than before. He worried something inside of her might break if they didn't do something and soon.

Not that she was the only Devil Dog running on a short fuse. After what he'd seen, he knew how lucky Ash and the others had been to survive their time here. Worse, every Devil Dog on the mission knew. An anger Pawlak hadn't felt from them since they learned Ashlyn and the others had been convicted threatened to boil over. He needed to do something, not only to keep the Devil Dogs from taking matters into their own hands but to keep Ashlyn from breaking.

"Off the record?" Ortega asked.

"Off the record."

At least for now.

Ortega looked conflicted for a moment and then she shook her head, sighing. "She's on edge. None of us can deny that. My guess is she's not sleeping well either." She looked at Talbot who nodded. "She feels guilty not only because the others were sent here with her but because Coreal and his animals hurt them after she was taken back to Fuercon. She looks at Navarro and knows how close we came to losing her. Even though neither of them have said anything, I think it's pretty clear Navarro was raped, probably multiple times and, unless I miss my guess, Ash was as well when she was here."

"Wouldn't knowing our people are safe now and the monsters who hurt them are going to be brought up on charges help?" Pawlak asked.

"It's not enough, sir." Talbot looked uncomfortable and Pawlak understood. None of them liked talking about Ashlyn behind her back. But they had her best interests at heart. They had lost her once and, if he had any say about it, they weren't going to lose her again.

"What do you mean?"

"She knows intellectually Coreal and the others are in custody and will have to answer for what they did. But it's not enough. She needs to see them in the brig, see them in prison garb and chains."

"Kevin's right," Ortega said. "We have to remember that the others are relying on her to tell them the truth about what's going on. They trusted her before they were court martialed and they trust her now. She sees that trust as why they were sent to Tarsus with her. The fear of something going wrong and washing back on them eats at her."

"Then what do we do to help her and them?"

He'd do almost anything short of letting Ash kill Coreal and Haritos.

"She's kept her word, sir." Talbot drummed his fingers against his thigh. "She hasn't gone near where any of the prisoners are being held, either dirtside or on the *Magellan*. It's been hard on her. I've seen her starting to go and then stop. She made a promise to you, and to us, that she wouldn't. But she needs to see them. I think she needs it more than she realizes."

"Lucinda?"

"I agree." She thought for a moment before continuing. "But we don't risk her doing anything foolish. I'll go with her."

"Ma'am," Talbot started.

"Nothing against you, Kevin, but I've known her longer than anyone onboard. She'll trust me to make sure she doesn't do something she'll regret later. Hopefully, she will trust me enough to let some of her walls down."

Pawlak didn't say anything. Instead, he considered what the two said. Like it or not, they were right. Ashlyn needed this if she was going to have any chance of putting Tarsus behind her. Even then, it wasn't a sure thing. But it was something and he was willing to risk it if it meant giving her a fighting chance of moving past what happened to her and her people.

"All right, but let's put this to good use. You're our intel officer, Lucinda. If you see that Ash's presence is impacting the prisoners, use it. Let her know what you're going to do. If she can see they are scared enough of her to start talking, all the better. But this isn't like when we landed. She isn't to make any threat, real or not, at them."

"Understood. Trust me. I'm not about to let her do anything that might come back to bite either of us on the ass."

"Then let's get this set up." He pushed away from his desk. "I'll send for Ash. You two stand ready."

"Hammer?" Lucinda looked at him in question.

"The gunny will go with you." He waved off any objections she might have had. "Ash trusts him and knows he, like you, will not only keep her safe but will keep her from doing anything foolish. But it's more than that. His presence will help convince the prisoners not to do anything foolish. I don't want to risk them attacking the two of you and forcing Ash – or you – to act."

"Understood and agreed." Lucinda stood and watched as Talbot followed suit. "I'll get everything set up while you send for her. We'll be in my office. Let us know when you're ready for us."

He watched as they left his office. Then he blew out a long breath. He hoped he was doing the right thing. Not that he saw any other option.

————

"You sent for me, Hammer?"

Ashlyn stood before Pawlak's desk. She waited as he looked at her. As he did, she fought the urge to squirm. She knew he was worried about her. She couldn't even blame him. There had been too many times since their arrival at Tarsus that she had come close to losing control. She hoped the rest of the Marines hadn't realized it, but she had no doubt Pawlak, as well as Ortega, had.

"I did." He motioned her to a seat.

Her brows knitted in a frown as he moved to the front of his desk. Instead of taking the second chair, he leaned against the battered desk and looked down at her. Wondering what was on his mind, she waited. With each passing moment, her unease grew.

"Ash, I'm going to be honest with you."

"You always are, sir." Sometimes more than she'd like. But that was one of the many reasons he was such a good officer and Marine. He didn't play games with his people.

"I know how hard this mission has been on you. I thought things might be better once we found the others and had them safe away from Coreal and the others. But it hasn't helped, has it?"

She closed her eyes and tried not to let her frustration show. So much for putting on a brave face. She should have known he'd realize how she felt.

"It has some," she answered a moment later as she once more looked up at him. "But I can't get past what they went through because they followed me."

"And that is where you're wrong, Ash. What happened to them

wasn't your fault or theirs. That blame falls primarily with those who put you here and then on Coreal and his people. You all did your duties to Fuercon and to the Corps. The sooner you accept that, the sooner you'll heal. More than that, the sooner you can help them get past what happened."

She looked down at her hands where they rested in her lap. He made it all sound so easy. Unfortunately, it wasn't. Worse, she didn't know how to move on. Why couldn't he understand that?

"Ash, would seeing Coreal and Haritos in the brig help?" He moved to sit in the chair next to hers. "I don't mean on a screen. I mean going down to the brig and standing on the outside of their cells."

She swallowed hard and nodded. "I think it would."

"Then go get out of your workout clothes." He nodded to the shorts and tank she wore. "And into your BDUs. Let them see that your roles have truly changed. You can talk to them. You can ask them anything you want or tell them anything you want. But you can't go into their cells. Do you understand?"

"Yes, sir."

"Then you should understand one other thing. Lucinda is going to be there with you as will the gunny."

She opened her mouth to protest and then snapped it shut. Before she protested, she needed to know why he wanted them there. "Are you trying to protect Coreal and Haritos or are you trying to protect me?"

"Honestly, all of you." He rested a hand on her forearm. "Ash, I know that if our roles were reversed, I'd give almost anything to get some of my own back from those two. I also know they would risk almost anything to keep you from testifying against them. That's why both Luce and Talbot will be with you. Luce is there to ask a few questions herself. Talbot is there to make sure they don't do anything to hurt you or to cause you to do something foolish. If you agree to having them with you, I'll arrange for you to see those bastards without delay."

She didn't hesitate. If seeing the two helped her \sleep at night,

269

she'd do it. Then, if it really did work, she'd do whatever it took to ensure the others got to do the same thing. They'd suffered as much, if not more, than she had at the hands of Coreal, Haritos and others at the penal colony. It was only fair they saw those responsible stripped of their freedom and without hope of ever seeing the light of day again.

"I agree." She smiled and then a quick laugh escaped her lips. "I would agree to almost anything to be able to see those two in a cell, Hammer."

"Then go get showered and changed. I'll let the others know and have them meet you at your quarters in half an hour. Agreed?"

"Agreed." She stood and held out her hand. "Thank you."

"Go. Report back after you're done."

She nodded and left his office. For the first time since they entered orbit around Tarsus, she looked forward to something. Unlike earlier, she was in control. Or at least as in control as she had been since her conviction. Now she had the chance of proving to the two who had done all they could to break her that they'd failed. That would be her best vengeance against them.

At least she kept telling herself that, even as she knew the only real vengeance would be to hold her gun to their heads and fire.

Half an hour later, she entered the *Magellan*'s brig. A few minutes earlier, Ortega explained Coreal and Haritos, as well as several others from Tarsus, were held one to a cell with at least one cell between them. Captain Carlisle had ordered the penal colony's former commandant and former guard-captain held at opposite ends of the brig. Standing at one end of the row of cells, Ash felt the first of hopefully many layers of stress easing. The cell doors were closed, preventing those inside from seeing who might be approaching.

Good. She didn't want to warn them of her presence. Let them know the same fear she had for two years. If that made her less of a person than she'd been, so be it. She wanted – no, she needed – them to understand what they had done to her and to the others.

"Are you ready?" Ortega asked softly as they paused before the second door.

Ashe gave a single, jerky nod. As she did, Ortega signaled Talbot. The gunny reached up and placed his palm against the security screen. A moment later, the hatch slid open. As it did, the soft hum of the security field reached Ashlyn and she swallowed hard. A shiver of remembered fear ran down her spine. She pushed it down and stepped forward. This time she was in control. The past was just that – the past.

A bitter smile touched her lips to see Gavin Haritos sitting on the edge of his bunk. Elbows on knees, head in his hands, he didn't bother looking up to see who was there. Dressed not in the black jumpsuit she had worn upon her return to Fuercon but in the piss yellow jumpsuits the military reserved for those charged with the most heinous of crimes, he bore little resemblance to the sadistic guard she learned to fear.

"Face the door and assume the position!" she barked out.

Haritos started. She heard his soft gasp. When he looked up, fear filled his eyes. His mouth worked but nothing intelligible came out. Perspiration dotted his upper lip and forehead. Even so, he remained where he was. Too frightened to move or trying to prove he wasn't afraid, she didn't know and didn't care.

"I said to assume the position, Haritos. Do it or we'll leave you here and go talk to Coreal. I'm sure he'll be more than happy to tell us that everything you did to me, to my people, was on your own. That he had nothing to do with it."

She waited, wondering what he would do. Then, when he remained seated, she turned. With one hand, she motioned Talbot to seal the cell. Haritos had broken, much as she anticipated. She simply had not expected it to be this soon.

"No! Wait!"

His plea stopped her, and she waved Talbot away from the control panel. As she did, a slight smile touched her lips. She gave herself a moment before turning. She did not want him to see how much this was costing her. If he had any idea how badly she wanted to enter the cell and beat him to a pulp, he would do everything he could to goad her. She would not give him that satisfaction.

"Yes?"

"What do you want? Just tell me what you want."

"I thought I made that perfectly clear." She shook her head, her expression disappointed. "I instructed you to assume the position. At least I'm letting you face the door and see what is about to happen."

He didn't need to know nothing would happen. As Ashlyn had learned during her time on Tarsus, the anticipation of punishment was almost as bad as the punishment itself. She had purposefully phrased her order in such a way he'd assume they were going to do something to him.

With Ortega on one side and Talbot on the other, she watched as the former guard-captain stumbled to his feet. He took two steps forward and then sank to his knees. Breathing in something very close to sobs, he crossed his ankles and then spread his knees. Then, as he sat back on his heels, he lifted his arms and linked his fingers behind his head.

"Up on your knees, Haritos. I didn't say you could sit back," Ashlyn snapped. As she did, she remembered the pain of having to kneel like that, sometimes for what seemed like hours, before the guards would pull her to her feet for whatever they had planned next. "Head up, eyes on me."

Sweat trickled down his face and she could almost smell his fear. To her surprise, it didn't make her feel any better. As much as she wanted revenge, she did not want to turn into the sort of person Haritos and Coreal were. But she had a point to make and, if she did it right, the former guard-captain might be able to give them some of the information they needed to unravel all that had been happening on Tarsus. More importantly, they might finally know if the events there bore any relation to what happened to her and her people on Arterus.

"I hope you've realized you aren't going to weasel your way out of the charges against you." She waited until he nodded once. "However, against my recommendation, the JAG has said it will consider a lesser sentence if you answer, fully and truthfully, Captain Ortega's questions. However, one lie, one misrepresentation, one failure to be totally honest and all bets are off. Do you understand?"

"I want my rep here for this."

"Fine." In fact, she had anticipated that. Haritos might look beaten, but she knew him too well. His ego wouldn't let him believe they truly held the upper hand until forced to. Well, she was about to force him to understand just how hopeless his situation was. "Captain Ortega, you've got your answer. He wants his representative with him when and if he meets with you."

"That's his right, Captain Shaw." Ortega looked at him as if he was no more significant than some annoying insect about to be swatted. "Since he hasn't arranged for representation and he won't be brought before a judge until next week some time, we'll leave him and let him consider his options until then." She nodded for Talbot to secure the hatch back in place. "How long do you think before he's screaming to talk to me?" She grinned and an unholy light shone in her eyes.

"Not long," Ashlyn replied. "He's a bully and a coward. You saw him. He doesn't want to admit it, but he's already beaten."

"More than you think, ma'am."

Ashlyn looked at Talbot in question.

"You two were already turning away as I secured the hatch. You didn't see him piss himself." He shook his head, disgusted. "How do you want to handle Coreal?"

Ashlyn thought for a moment. Somehow, she had a feeling they would frown on her going a few rounds with the man. She also knew he would not be as easy to break as Haritos. Not that it mattered. She had a few things to say to the former commandant. Perhaps that would be enough to loosen his tongue.

"I'm not going to ask him anything. I have something to say and that's it. If he wants to talk after that, it will be up to him." Then, seeing their concern, she blew out a breath. "You don't have to worry. I'm not going to do anything stupid, nor am I going to rant and rave at him. I give you both permission to drag me away if you think you need to. But I have to do this. Not just for me but for the others as well."

They didn't look convinced, but they didn't try to stop her either. Instead, they followed her down the row to Coreal's cell. Talbot used the security panel to open the security hatch. Unlike Haritos, Coreal looked at them, hatred in his eyes. He stood and took three steps in their direction. Before Ashlyn said anything, Talbot did.

"Stop!" The gunny's voice echoed up and down the corridor. "I believe the order is *assume the position.*"

Coreal, dressed in the same sort of yellow jumpsuit as Haritos, stared at Talbot in disbelief. For a moment, he stood where he was. Then he dropped to his knees and assumed the same position Ashlyn had so many times in the past. Defiance radiated from him and Ash knew she had been right. He would be much more difficult to break than Haritos had proven to be.

"What do you want?" he demanded.

"Quiet!" Ortega snapped. "Captain?"

Ashlyn stepped forward until she stood close enough to the security field to feel it dancing along the skin of her arms and face. Looking at Coreal, knowing he would never see another day of freedom meant the world to her. Even so, her stomach churned. She knew first-hand how quickly things could change. That was why she knew they needed everything he could tell them about his operations on Tarsus as well as any other questionable activities he might know about.

That knowledge would add yet another nail in his proverbial coffin. She wanted to make sure it was nailed tight. He could not be allowed to escape justice.

"This won't take long." She made a show of looking him up and down. "I wanted to see for myself how you liked being the one in custody. I promise I'm going to be at your trial. If it is the last thing I do, I'll make sure everyone knows who and what you are. You'll have no secrets by the time I'm done. Everyone in the system and beyond will know you're more than a sadistic son-of-a-bitch who gets off on tormenting and torturing those who can't fight back. They will know you are a traitor and a slaver.

"Coreal, you'll be lucky if the court gives you the death penalty.

Frankly, I hope they sentence you to one of the penal colonies. I think it would be most appropriate if you had to return to Tarsus as a prisoner. Think about it. Some of those you've taken such pleasure in tormenting will be there to *welcome* you."

He blanched at that and she smiled slightly. Good. Maybe he wasn't as sure about beating the charges against him as she thought.

"You know as well as I do that they will be more than eager to show you how much they've appreciated your treatment.

"Think about it, Coreal. Think about being with the same prisoners you took such pleasure in abusing. I feel confident at least a few of them will still be on Tarsus by the time your trial ends. Can't you just imagine what they'll do to make sure you feel welcome?"

"You can't!" He started to rise and then stopped, looking worriedly at Talbot.

"I can't but the court can." She took one last look at him and prepared to turn away. There was one more thing she needed to say first. "Dante Coreal, remember this. You did your best to make my life a living hell while I was on Tarsus. You did so knowing your actions were in violation of the Military Code of Conduct as well as who knows how many other military and civilian laws. Now think about this. I'll be at your trial and, if they sentence you to death, I will be there when you draw your last breath. You are an embarrassment to the military and to Fuercon and the sooner you are dealt with, the better."

With that, she turned and walked off. She had done all she could. The rest was up to the JAG and any others who wanted to lay charges against the man. She'd trust the system, for now, to make sure justice was done. If not, well, she wasn't the woman she'd been before being sent to Tarsus and the new Ashlyn would do whatever it took to protect her people.

19

Ashlyn rolled onto her side and cursed softly as an insistent buzzing work her. She'd gone to bed less than four hours earlier. Whoever was on the other end of the comm-call had better have a darned good reason for waking her. Then, as several possibly explanations – none of them good – hit her, she reached out activated the comm unit for voice only.

"Shaw," she said as she sat up.

"Sorry to disturb you, Captain Shaw," Captain Carlisle began. Something about his voice warned her she wasn't going to like what he had to say.

"What can I do for you, sir?" Much as she wanted him to get to the point, she couldn't. One simply didn't order a ship's captain to do anything, at least not if she wanted to see another promotion.

"We've had a change in status. Report to my ready room in ten."

"Aye, sir. Shaw out."

Worried, Ash climbed out of bed and headed into the small head adjoining her quarters. A much too quick shower would clear her head even if it wouldn't answer any of her questions. A change of status could mean almost anything. The only thing she was sure of was that they weren't in imminent danger. If they were, Carlisle would have brought the ship to General Quarters. But that still left a number of other scenarios.

God, he could have at least given her a hint about what was going on.

She'd just finished dressing when a soft knock sounded at the door. A moment later, Gunnery Sergeant Talbot stepped inside. Ash shook her head and one corner of her mouth lifted in a wry smile to see him. How could he look more rested than she felt? She knew he'd gotten no more sleep than she had because they'd been talking until she was ready for bed. Yet he looked like he had managed a good eight hours down.

"Captain?"

"You know as much as I do right now, Gunny."

She turned to the mirror and quickly checked her appearance. As she did, she drew a deep breath, stilling her emotions. She couldn't let her mind jump to conclusions. She didn't have enough informa-tion about what was going on. But with Major Pawlak, as well as most of the Devil Dogs, still on the surface, she was the senior Marine officer onboard. That meant she had to act the part, at least until Pawlak could catch a shuttle back to the ship.

"All I know, Gunny, is that I'm to report to the Captain's ready room. He said we've had a change in status," she said as she turned away from the mirror. "What are you doing here?"

"The XO sent instructions that I was to accompany you and await any orders you might have after the briefing. Seems I'm senior non-com right now."

Ash smiled slightly. He sounded as disgruntled about being the ranking Marine non-com onboard as she felt about being senior Marine officer.

"By any chance has Major Pawlak reported in since we called it a night?"

"Negative, ma'am."

Ash blew out a breath. She'd hoped their CO could give them at least a hint about what was going on. Unfortunately, she didn't have time to try to contact him either. Not when she was already in danger of being late reporting to Carlisle's ready room.

"We'd better go, Gunny. Hopefully, whatever's going on isn't going to kick us in the teeth."

"Roger that, ma'am."

Barely more than ten minutes after being awakened by Carlisle's comm, Ashlyn entered the ready room off the bridge, Talbot on her heels. She nodded to those already gathered. Then she took the seat Carlisle indicated. As she did, the communications chief brought up a live feed from the surface. It didn't surprise Ash to see both Pawlak and Lieutenant Liu on the screen.

Once his steward passed around mugs of coffee, Carlisle took his place at the head of the table. As he did, Ashlyn frowned slightly. Concern darkened the captain's expression and that, in turn, worried her. Ash had seen that expression before, including in her own mirror before every combat mission she'd led. It was the look of an officer who knew death was on the horizon.

But that didn't make sense. The ship wasn't at GQ and there was nothing about Pawlak and Liu to indicate there'd been any trouble on the surface. Then another explanation dawned on her and she swallowed hard. Had the capital been attacked again?

"Ladies and gentlemen," Carlisle began. "Approximately fifteen minutes ago we received an encrypted message from FleetCom. All ships in the fleet are to go to alert status. This is not a drill." He paused, sipping his mug of coffee. Ash wondered if he was giving them time to accept what he'd just said.

"According to the message, word has reached the capital that Cassius Prime has been attacked. One of our courier ships entered the system while the attack was taking place and managed to get off a transmission, complete with sensor and video data. Unfortunately, FleetCom has since lost contact with it. Even more troubling is the fact that there have been no transmissions or traffic intercepted from the system."

Ash sat back and blew out a long breath. Carlisle didn't need to tell her who the invaders were. She knew the answer. The invasion, break-down of communications followed by what could only be a picket was exactly how the Callusians operated. They'd sweep into a system, target the major defense platforms and, after destroying them, lay siege to the capital or one of the larger population centers. No warning and no demands. Just wholesale slaughter. Then, they would demand the system government's surrender. Failure meant more bombardment from space, followed closely by ground forces with the sole purpose of securing the target and causing the most terror and destruction possible.

What made the attack on Cassius Prime worse was its proximity to Fuercon. Never before had the Callusians struck so close to home. Now the attack on the capital made more sense. It kept the Fuer-conese military focused on the home system while the Callusians moved into position to take over Cassius Prime.

"FleetCom is attempting to confirm what happened to our courier ship as well as trying to obtain more intelligence about the attack on Cassius Prime. In the meantime, all ships are to return their assigned sectors, including this one. We will be leaving orbit as soon as we have personnel shifted between ship and surface to maintain control of the penal colony until reinforcements can be sent out from the home system."

"And the truce?" the XO asked.

"Officially, there is no change. However, FleetCom has said that it expects the President to declare the truce over and to issue a formal Declaration of War just as soon as we have secondary confirmation of what happened and who is responsible."

A ripple of reaction ran around the table. From her place to Carlisle's left, Ashlyn watched the others. Most wore expressions that ran the gamut from surprise to satisfaction. But it was Pawlak's expression that had her wondering what else Carlisle might have to say. There was something about her CO that warned her there was more, much more to what was happening than they knew so far.

"Captain, you mentioned that we would be breaking orbit as soon as we shifted some personnel. Can you elaborate?" the XO asked from her seat opposite Ashlyn.

"Major Pawlak?"

"Yes, sir." Pawlak looked down and Ash wondered if he was consulting notes. "FleetCom included orders for the Devil Dogs with their orders for Captain Carlisle. The DDs are to return to the capital with the *Magellan*. Lieutenant Marshall and his Marines will transfer planetside to relieve the DDs down here. When reinforcements arrive from the home system, the lieutenant and his people will return to the *Magellan*."

"Lieutenant Marshall and his people are preparing to transfer down as we speak," Carlisle took up. "Shuttles should be dropping within the half hour, Major."

"Very good, sir." Pawlak turned and said something to someone off-camera. Then he turned back, his expression serious. "The first shuttle returning topside will be carrying half a dozen more prisoners to transport home. Lieutenant Liu will be returning with them. The other JAG is going to remain here to continue the on-site investigation. Gunny, I want guards on the prisoners 24/7."

"Yes, sir," Talbot said from where he stood behind Ashlyn's chair.

"Captain Shaw, you have command of the Devil Dogs for the return trip home," Pawlak continued.

Ash sat up, her eyes going wide. "Sir?"

"You heard me, Ash." Now he grinned. "Lieutenant Marshall is a fine young officer, but he doesn't have the experience or the reputation to run this prison until reinforcements get here. Because of that, I'll be remaining here until relieved. Take the Devil Dogs home and get them ready for war, Captain."

"Until you get back, sir," she said.

"Have someone collect my gear and send it down with the shuttles, Captain. I'll do my best to brief the Devil Dogs down here but will leave it to you to brief the entire team once you break orbit."

"Understood, sir."

God, what else was going to happen?

"Captain, with your permission, I need to get things moving on this end."

"Of course, Major. The first shuttle will drop in half an hour."

"We'll be ready, sir." Pawlak nodded, his expression calm and confident. "Ash, we'll talk before you break orbit."

"Yes, sir." Before she could say anything more, the video feed ended.

"All right, we have a lot to do. As more information comes in from FleetCom, it will be passed on. In the meantime, get your departments prepared for immediate departure. Dismissed."

Ashlyn waited as the others filed out of the ready room. Then she turned to Talbot, a thoughtful expression on her face. There was so much to do, more than she felt ready for. Not that she had any choice. The major had made it very clear that she was to step up as his XO and make sure their orders were carried out. Fortunately, she knew she could count on the gunnery sergeant to help.

"Gunny, this is going to be a lot like when you were wiping my nose back when I was still a green second lieutenant," she said. "I won't lie. I need your help. You know the team and you are certainly more up-to-date on what's going on."

"Cap, you know what to do," he assured her. "You just have to trust yourself. But don't worry. I'll be glad to kick your rear – respectfully of course – if you start to screw up." His grin did more to reassure her than anything else could have.

"All right, Gunny. Just don't be surprised if I kick back." She grinned in return. Even as she did, she knew he was wrong. The last two years had taken their toll on her and it was going to take time to learn to trust herself and her superiors again. "Go see if you can be of any assistance to Lieutenant Marshall and his people. Have someone pack up the major's things and get them on the first shuttle down. I'll make sure the captain has everything set for the prisoners."

"You need to check in with the CMO as well, ma'am," he reminded her.

She nodded, her expression grim. So far, she'd done exactly as she'd promised Dr. Ahern and had spent time almost every day with the CMO. What she'd learned her very first day onboard the *Magellan* was that Dr. Bischoff had not only read Dr. Ahern's reports on her medical condition and treatment plan but had taken them to heart.

How she would react to Ashlyn having to assume command of the ship's Marine complement worried Ash.

"I'll do that just as soon as I speak with the captain," she promised. "Let's get going. There's a great deal to do to make the personnel shift."

With that, she left the ready room, her mind working feverishly to figure out what her first step should be after talking with Captain Carlisle.

She could do this. She had to.

God, she wasn't ready for this.

———

"The final shuttle just arrived, sir," Ashlyn reported.

She sat in the small office that had, until twelve hours earlier, been assigned to Lieutenant Marshall. Now that he and his unit had transferred planetside, she had formally assumed her role as the *Magellan's* Marine CO. Even though she'd protested that it wasn't necessary, she'd had little choice but to move into the office for the return flight home, especially after Captain Carlisle reminded her that she had an image to uphold as well as a duty to perform.

Part of that duty was informing Major Pawlak that the *Magellan* was ready to break orbit and return to the home system. Close as they were to the planet, there was no lag in communications. Normally that would be something Ash appreciated. Just now, however, she wished there was at least some lag. Maybe it would have given her time she needed to think of a convincing argument for Pawlak to return to the ship. After all, they could leave the Gunny or one of the two staff sergeants with Lieutenant Matthews. That ought to be enough to run the prison until FleetCom got reinforcements out to them.

"Very good, Ash." Pawlak's face looked out at her from the comm screen. "I doubt you will see any trouble on the way home. Still, I recommend you and the Gunny run the team through sims to keep them on their toes."

"Yes, sir."

"I've transmitted my report and my recommendations about what should be done concerning the situation here as well as the prisoners. Be sure to append your report to it as well."

"Understood."

"Lieutenant Liu will also be taking statements from you and those sent to this hellhole with you."

"I'd expected as much, Major."

"Ash." He smiled at her and shook his head, his expression revealing that he understood what she felt just then. "It's just the two of us. So be honest. Are you all right?"

For a moment, she didn't say anything. Then she smiled slightly. She'd answer his question and do it truthfully – and she knew he'd never hold it against her.

"Hell, Hammer, you know I'm not." She shook her head and dropped her defenses, letting him see her worry. If he didn't recognize it, the fact she'd called him by his call sign, something none of them did except on the battlefield or in informal circumstances, should have let him in on just how worried she happened to be. "Just being this close to Tarsus and the penal colony has me on edge. Add in the fact that you've just dumped the team in my lap without warning and I'm looking for a hole to hide in."

"C'mon, Angel." His use of her call sign, given during her first assignment after graduating from the Academy, brought a slight smile to her lips. Back then, she'd been dubbed Angel, short for the Angel of Death, because of her skills as a sniper. "You know me well enough to understand I wouldn't be doing this if I had any doubts about you being able to do the job."

"You knowing it and me knowing it are two very different things right now, Hammer."

"Then trust me, kid. You know I'd never turn the Devil Dogs over to someone I didn't think up to the job." He waited until she nodded, albeit reluctantly. "Use the trip home to run sims with the team. If you do, you'll see that you aren't as rusty as you think you are."

"I hope you're right." She said it softly, not really meaning for him to hear.

"I am." Now he cocked his head to the side, a slight smile lifting one corner of his mouth. "Besides, one of us has to stay until reinforcements get here and you have a young man expecting you home in time for his birthday."

The thought of little Jake was all it took for Ash to nod and admit that she wouldn't – and couldn't – remain behind. There was no way she'd miss another of her son's birthdays.

"You do realize that you're going to have to make it up to him for not being there, Hammer. You are one of his godfathers." Now she grinned, remembering how honored the man looked when she asked him to stand as her son's godfather.

"Of course. Tell him I'll see him just as soon as I return home."

"Will do. Now, anything else I need to know about the team?"

"Nothing the gunny can't tell you." He paused and turned away for a moment and she guessed someone off-screen was talking to him. "I need to run, Angel. I have a meeting with the prison doc that was supposed to have started five minutes ago."

"Watch him, Hammer. He's not necessarily bad, not in the way Coreal and the others are, but he also didn't stand up to them." Memories returned and she pushed them down. "He also didn't do anything that wasn't absolutely necessary to treat my injuries. I'd guess it was the same with any prisoner sent to him. You might suggest to the JAG officer that it wouldn't hurt to look at where the monies budgeted for the clinic went."

"Will do." He lifted a hand, waving off whoever stood off-screen. "That's part of why I'm meeting with him. If things go as I expect, he'll find himself occupying your old cell before the day's out. Now I have to go. Pawlak out."

Ash sighed and leaned back. Like it or not, she was now in command of the Devil Dogs. She just hoped they managed to get back home without anything else happening.

20

"The general sends her apologies, Captain Shaw, but she's running a few minutes late. May I get you a cup of coffee or something else to drink?"

"Coffee would be fine, Corporal Narjang."

The young man nodded and excused himself. Alone, Ashlyn moved to stand before the windows lining the far wall. Looking outside, she watched as men and women hurried through the streets of the capital. Some were rushing to work and others gawking at the damage from the attack. Even though much of it had already been repaired, the worst of it would take longer. At least the fear she'd felt in those she encountered her last visit to the capital seemed to have passed. Replacing it was an anger she understood and approved of.

She'd been back on-planet for almost a month. When the *Magellan* returned, she received new orders. She had ten day's leave and then she had to report to the medical facility. Since the orders had come directly from General Okafor, she knew better than to argue. Before she'd been able to ask for clarification about what to do regarding the Devil Dogs, at least until Pawlak made it back to the capital, she received another packet from Okafor. The Devil Dogs were given a corresponding leave and then they were to begin running sims for both boarding enemy ships as well as groundside assaults. Since Ashlyn's treatments at the medical facility would not take all day every day, she was to review the sim results and give guidance for each day's work.

When she returned home from the medical facility the day before, she found a request to meet with General Okafor waiting for her. *Request.* She smiled slightly at the thought. When the Commandant of the Marine Corps *requested* your presence, especially if you were a Marine, you damned well better present yourself on time and in mess dress uniform unless told otherwise. At least she'd been spared that much. She'd been instructed this was an informal meeting and BDUs were appropriate.

"Here you go, Captain," the corporal said as he handed her a mug of coffee. "The general said you take it black."

"I do."

She nodded her thanks and turned back to the window. Part of her wanted to ask the young man if he knew why the general had sent for her. But another part, the veteran, knew better. Okafor would tell her soon enough the reason for the summons.

Ten minutes later, Corporal Narjang escorted Ashlyn into the general's office. As the door closed behind her, Ash faltered slightly. She had expected Okafor to be there. On a certain level, she'd even expected Major Pawlak's presence. What she hadn't expected was to find her mother and Rico Santiago there as well. More than that, the two of them, as well as Pawlak, all wore rank insignias she hadn't expected.

"Mom?" It was out before she could stop it. "Captain Shaw reporting as requested, General." She braced to attention before Okafor's desk, mentally kicking herself for breaking protocol upon entering the office.

"Stand easy, Captain," Okafor told her. Then she smiled. "And quit looking like you want to find a hole to climb into. I understand what you must have thought when you saw everyone, especially your mother."

"Permission to speak, ma'am?"

"We're not standing on protocol right now, Ash. Speak away." Okafor motioned for her to be seated.

"Am I right in assuming you've finally found a permanent slot for my mother?" As much as it had hurt to be brought up on charges, the knowledge that her mother had been punished as well was almost worse.

"You are and we'll get to that in a few minutes," Okafor assured her. "But there are a few things to get out of the way first." She leaned back and watched as Corporal Narjang appeared, carrying a tray with several coffee carafes on it. He placed one of the carafes on the general's desk and the other on the table in front of the sofa where Elizabeth Shaw and Rico Santiago sat.

"First of all, I've reviewed your report as well as Paul's about what you found on Tarsus. I've also had a chance to speak with Lieutenant Liu. I hope you and your people will be satisfied to know that the JAG is wasting no time in bringing charges against Coreal, Haritos and the others you brought back onboard the *Magellan*. The charges range from murder and attempted murder to misuse of office. I promise they will never see the light of day again."

For a moment, Ashlyn simply sat there. Even if she'd wanted to, she wouldn't have been able to say anything. She'd waited so long to hear those words, or words like them, and she suddenly realized she'd convinced herself that she never would. Even knowing that Coreal and the others had been removed from their positions at the penal colony hadn't been enough to really convince her they'd be made to pay for their crimes.

Then she felt tears pricking at her eyes and blinked them back. That brought another realization. Despite everything, she'd still been waiting for those who freed her and her people to turn around and betray them. She'd known intellectually that they wouldn't, but her heart hadn't yet accepted it. Now, hearing how they were taking steps against their tormentors at the penal colony, she knew she'd wronged them.

More than that, she knew she could finally allow herself to trust them as she once had.

Even if there was still that small voice in the back of her mind telling her that she shouldn't drop her guard just yet.

"Thank you, General."

"There's more, Ash." Now Okafor smiled, a predatory smile Ashlyn remembered from the time she served under the then colonel. It was the same look she'd seen whenever one of their missions worked out exactly as Okafor planned and their Marines were about to spring the trap on the enemy.

"Ma'am?"

"Rico has been looking into the two Marines who were supposed to *take care* of you during the attack on the capital. Rico?" She nodded to where Santiago sat.

"Let's just say those two will soon be out of our beloved Corps with Dishonorable Discharges. Since they didn't actually take action against you, we can't prove they had the intent to do anything. But the investigation into them has given us enough evidence to prove they've been taking bribes from prisoners held in the brig and from others operating on the black market to look the away when certain deliveries come in."

It wasn't enough, not by a long shot, but she'd accept it.

For now.

"Don't get me wrong. We're going to keep an eye on them. If they so much as sneeze wrong, I'll have them up on charges."

"Did they identify who gave them their orders?"

Ashlyn looked at her mother, surprised by the barely repressed anger she heard in Elizabeth's voice.

"Not yet. However, we're continuing to look into it. My people are checking all their comm traffic and we've tagged their personal comps and comms. We'll find out. I promise."

"Sorkowski and O'Brien?" Ashlyn wanted to know.

"We're still working on building a case against them." Before Ashlyn could interrupt, Santiago held up a hand. "Yes, we have enough to arrest them and charge them with falsifying military records, impeding an investigation, perjury and other charges associated with your trial. But ask yourself something, Ash. Why? Why were they willing to risk so much to set you and your team up?"

God, did he think she hadn't asked herself that every day for the last two plus years? She'd wracked her memory trying to find the answers. There were any number of possibilities but nothing that made any sense.

"What do you know so far?"

"It's obvious that they were working, at the very least, with the comms officer. There's no other way all your transmissions, not to mention your personal log, could have been altered as they were. I have some of my best people looking into who else might have been involved. My gut tells me it can't be more than another one or two or someone would have let something slip by now."

She nodded.

"But the closer we look at the ship's logs and Sorkowski's personal records, the clearer it becomes that his ships were always well away from illicit runs made in that sector. From the state of his various bank accounts, it is obvious he had an income source that paid him far beyond what his military pay did. That tells me he was aiding the local smugglers. We're looking for enough evidence now to tell us who he was working with. But we are also looking to see if he had dealings with others, folks worse than smugglers. I can't believe he'd sacrifice you and your team because you were close to discovering what he was up to. It would be too easy to simply make sure you were assigned elsewhere whenever a smuggling run was about to occur."

"I'm not so sure." She almost drawled out the words as she remembered her days onboard Sorkowski's flagship. "He doesn't like anyone rocking his boat. I saw him put a steward on report for serving coffee that wasn't hot enough to suit him. But I also know I'm not the most unbiased person when it comes to the man. I suggest you look at his previous commands and compare them to what happened this time."

"We are doing just that, Ash," Okafor assured her. "And, before you ask, we have eyes on O'Brien. We know he met with Sorkowski shortly after the attack and it was obvious the former admiral did not appreciate the visit. Witnesses said their conversation, while hushed, was very definitely tense. Sorkowski seemed to be in control of his emotions, for the most part, but O'Brien was almost panicked. It's not going to take much to get them to turn on one another."

"And O'Brien is the weak link," Santiago took up. "In fact, that is where you can help us."

"How?" Now he had her attention.

"When we are done here, you and I are going to walk out together. If everything goes as planned, we will run into O'Brien as he is escorting his latest group of visiting dignitaries and their children around the capital. There will also be half a dozen or so of the Devil Dogs arriving at the same time. The good gunny has helped set it up so that O'Brien gets to see that you are not only back from Tarsus but that you are back to duty and once again a member of the Devil Dogs. It will be interesting to see what he does after that."

Ashlyn shook her head, a smile lifting the corners of her mouth. She'd learned a lot during the mission to Tarsus. She'd come face-to-face with her demons and had not only survived but she'd done so without sacrificing her freedom by killing either Coreal or Haritos. In fact, she'd learned how satisfying it was to have their roles reversed. It would never take away the pain of the last two years but seeing them in chains and knowing they would soon be facing trial went a long way to helping her get over what had happened.

Besides, Santiago was right. It would be interesting to see how O'Brien reacted to seeing her once again.

"You are an evil man, Major, and I like the way your mind works." She grinned as she spoke.

"He is and that's why he is so good at what he does." Okafor leaned back in her chair, a look of satisfaction on her face. "And he has a full brief for you that you can share with the rest of the Devil Dogs after you've reviewed it."

Ashlyn nodded. If this was a dream, she never wanted to wake up. After so long doubting anyone would ever believe her about what happened, to know that those responsible for setting her and her people up, those responsible for so many deaths, would soon be brought to justice was almost more than she could believe. But seeing how her mother nodded in confirmation, she knew it was real.

Without thinking, Ash stood and crossed the office to stare outside. The others stayed where they were, giving her the time she needed to accept what had been said. When she turned, she saw the truth in their expressions. They were worried about her but, more than that, they were still out for blood. They wanted those responsible to pay for their actions just as badly as did she.

"General, that is some of the best news you could have given me. Thank you." She rubbed her hands over her face, brushing away the tears she knew none of them would ever mention.

"I just wish I could tell you that everyone responsible for what happened to you were about to be brought up on charges, Ash, but I can't. Not yet. However, you have my word that they will be. It might not give you back the last two years, but it will keep them from ever doing it to anyone else again."

"Me, too." Ash managed a smile that seemed to help the others relax a bit. "Tell me one thing, ma'am. Was Sorkowski simply trying to keep his illegal activities from being discovered when he set us up or was something else involved?"

"What do you mean, Ash?"

"We all know there have been ship's commanders, and even sector COs, who have been on the take. It's not that difficult when you're away from the home system to bypass procedures if you want to. Just as it should be relatively easy for a CO to make sure patrols aren't in an area where a smuggler is going to be.

"But we weren't out on the fringes. Not really and certainly not once the fighting came to us. And that was something that never really made sense to me. Why did the Callusians choose to hit that system? It doesn't have any unique resources to set it apart from any of the systems nearer to Callusian space. Nor did it have an industrial base better than closer targets. So why strike there?"

"Rico will get you the full report." When Okafor glanced at the intelligence officer, he nodded. "But you just asked the same questions many of us asked after the fact. The problem is we were having to deal with information sent back to us by Sorkowski. What we didn't know was that there was a very specific target the Callusians were after, the same target the smugglers had been relying on.

Ashlyn listened in growing disbelief as Okafor and Santiago described what happened to the system after the mission – no, the ambush – that had led to the deaths of so many of her people as well as her own court-martial. Arterus had been primarily an agricultural planet. It had standard industry for a planet of its size but what it had in abundance was a workforce of able-bodied men and women. Men and women who had been taken after Sorkowski had pulled his ships out of the system after the ambush.

"Did he know?" Ashlyn's voice was harsh and she didn't bother to try to hide her anger.

"We don't know for sure, but my gut says yes," Santiago replied. "That is why we are being as cautious as we are about building the case against him. If he is a traitor, we want to know. More than that, we need to know if there are others who might have been working with him."

"And O'Brien, where does he fit into all this?"

"He'd been sent to Sorkowski because no other fleet CO would take him, at least not in wartime. He'd made it through the Academy solely through his family's connections and by bullying others into doing his work for him. That same attitude continued after he was commissioned. I've included his complete service record in your briefing materials. You'll see that he kept getting sent further and further away from the home system and from the prime assignments. That last assignment was pretty much his final hope if he were to ever be promoted again.

"And, before you ask, his accounts also show money he shouldn't have. He hasn't been as careful about trying to cover it up as Sorkowski was, not that it mattered. Your father and others who either know you or served with you have worked tirelessly to uncover and then follow the money trail. I think they're getting close, but they aren't there yet."

Ash closed her eyes and willed herself to relax. Knowing that her father and others who knew her had been working to find out what happened – were still working on it – helped. But now she was home, and, by God, she wanted answers and she wanted vengeance. Neither could come soon enough.

"And I made the mistake of sending you and your team to him, Ash. I'll never be able to kick myself enough for that," Pawlak took up. "I didn't know anything about O'Brien except that he was a political ass kisser. All I knew was we needed a crew out there to keep the sector secure."

"What happened isn't your fault." The last thing she wanted was for him to blame himself. "I should have let you know my concerns about the posting long before I did. But I can't blame myself either. God knows, I've been doing that long enough. The only ones responsible for what happened to us are Sorkowski and O'Brien and anyone else who worked with them."

"We're not going to argue with you, Ash, but we won't let ourselves off quite so easily," Okafor said. "Once we have enough evidence to issue arrest warrants, President Harper has assured me he will release a statement about the investigation. While he won't go into details, he will make it clear that this administration will not tolerate corruption of any sort in the military or government. The investigation will be ongoing because we all want to make sure the cancer has been cut out.

"What he won't say is that we now know that certain members of the military, government and in private industry have been acting against Fuercon's best interest in the war. They manipulated facts and events to make sure the so-called truce was signed, and they worked to keep the former government from investigating the violations of the truce. We are also looking into the possibility that they were behind the attack on the capital."

Treason, betrayal, violation of oaths. What else were they going to reveal?

"God, I don't know what I feel right now." She returned to her chair and sat. "And I have a feeling you aren't done hitting me over the head with surprises." She tried to smile and wasn't sure she succeeded.

"Not so much surprises as further correction of oversights of the past," Okafor said with a smile. "As you noticed when you arrived, some promotions have been made. *Lieutenant Colonel* Santiago is now FleetCom's Intelligence chief. He's proven himself more than capable of handling the position."

Ashlyn nodded, a smile touching her lips. She had no doubts the man could do the job.

"Lieutenant Colonel Pawlak will be moving over to Second Division to take over Second Battalion, the Warlords."

Now Ashlyn knew it had to be a dream. She couldn't imagine Pawlak leaving the Devil Dogs. More than that, she couldn't imagine anyone else in command of them. She opened her mouth to say just that but nothing came out.

"Don't worry about the Devil Dogs, Ash. They'll be in good hands," Pawlak assured her, as if reading her thoughts. "The general will introduce you to their new CO shortly."

"Paul's right, Ash," Okafor replied with the grin she was coming to dread. "But first, let me introduce you to the new CO of First Division, Brigadier General Elizabeth Shaw."

Ashlyn didn't care if it violated every rule of protocol or even if it looked unprofessional. She got to her feet and hurried to where her mother sat. A moment later, pride filling her, she bent and hugged Elizabeth. If anyone deserved a promotion, it was her mother. Better yet, at least as far as Ashlyn was concerned, by being in command of FirstDiv, Elizabeth would be stationed on Fuercon, at least until the division shipped out. That meant she would be there for Jake, something very important to Ashlyn.

"I take it you approve of your mother's new assignment." Okafor's amusement was clear in her voice.

"I most certainly do, ma'am." She grinned at her mother and then looked back at the general. "And I also appreciate it because it means she will be close for my son."

"I'll admit that was a small consideration," Okafor said. "But it was a very small consideration. I offered her the posting because she is the best for the job."

"Have you told Dad?"

"Not yet. I will when we finish here," Elizabeth replied. "Now sit and we'll tell you what's going to happen with the Devil Dogs."

Ashlyn nodded and sat next to her mother on the sofa, a knot of anxiety in her stomach. She'd been more than glad to return to the Devil Dogs while they were under Pawlak's command. She knew him and trusted him with her life. They shared a kinship with the other Devil Dogs that was born from combat. The thought of someone from the outside coming in to take over, the only possibility she could think of, turned her blood cold. Hopefully, the new CO had served with the DDs before.

"She hasn't figured it out," Pawlak said with a smile.

"I told you she wouldn't," Santiago countered easily.

"Be quiet, both of you," Okafor told them, her own amusement shining through. "Liz, it's your division. So you get to tell her."

Elizabeth nodded. Then she turned her attention to her daughter. "Ash, FleetCom needs Paul to take over the Warlords. Second Division is going to be our leading element in the early phases of the war and the general needs him to do for the Warlords what he did for the Devil Dogs. But that means I need a new CO for FirstBatt. The Devil Dogs are our best SpecOps unit and they need a commanding officer who not only knows but understands what it means to be a Devil Dog."

Ashlyn didn't say anything. She wasn't sure what to say. There had been a time when she'd wanted nothing more than to one day command the Devil Dogs. Even now, with all her doubts about her own fitness for duty, she still held that dream. She'd do her best to work with whomever her mother put in as her new CO. She just hoped it was someone who knew what it meant to be a Devil Dog.

"Who?"

"You're not usually this slow to pick up the cues, kid," Santiago chuckled. He fell silent when Elizabeth flashed him a warning look.

"Ash, you're taking over as CO of the Devil Dogs. You'll maintain your rank of captain for the time being. Not because any of us think you don't deserve promotion to major but because we know you won't accept it. However, we need you to accept this new assignment."

For a moment, she couldn't say anything. How could she when she wasn't sure she'd heard right. Then, seeing how they others waited, watching her expectantly, she asked, "Why me?"

"Because you're the best for the job," Pawlak said simply before anyone else could answer. "Don't you think I was doing everything I could to prepare you to take over the unit before that last mission?"

Now that she thought about it, she could see that he'd been doing just that. So, not sure what to say, she simply nodded.

"Paul's right about you being best for the job. It goes beyond training and experience, both of which you have in abundance," Okafor took up. "We need someone who *is* a Devil Dog. Someone who understands what it means to be a Devil Dog and someone the members of the unit will respect and follow into Hell and back. Again, traits you have proven, time and again, that you possess.

"I'll admit there is also a bit of vengeance in this as well, Ash. I want to see those who stood by and watched what happened to you and the others when they realize that their actions, and inactions, won't be forgotten or forgiven."

Ashlyn looked at each of her companions and shook her head. Everything they said made sense. But what they weren't taking into account was her, the changes she'd undergone as a result of the last two years. She wasn't sure those changes made her the best choice for her beloved Devil Dogs.

"Ash, if you decide you don't want the assignment, I'd be more than glad to have you on my staff," Santiago put in. Then, as her eyes went wide and she shook her head, he laughed gaily. "Somehow, that's what I thought you'd say – or do." He grinned as she continued to look at him in disbelief. "But I'm serious. I'll always have a place for you on my staff if you want it."

"Thanks – I think." Once more, she pushed to her feet and walked across the office. "If I accept, do I have any say in my senior staff?"

"Of course," her mother assured her. "I can't guarantee you you'll get everyone you want if they aren't currently with the Devil Dogs, but I will do my best to get them for you."

"As will I and I do, as you know, carry a lot of weight in the Corps," Okafor said with a grin.

"If I'd had any doubt about that, today's dispelled it." Ashlyn smiled now, relaxing more than she had since her arrival. "Under normal circumstances, I'd want Lucinda Ortega as my XO. But with her now a captain, that won't work."

"If that's your wish, we'll make it work," Okafor assured her. For a moment, Ashlyn stared at the general, her eyes narrowed in suspicion. The woman was up to something but, for the moment at least, she didn't want to know what. "Who else?"

"I'd like MJ Adamson back in the unit if she wants to return. She's one of the best NCOs I've ever worked with when it comes to teaching what it means to be a Devil Dog."

"I'll cut her orders as soon as we're done here," Elizabeth assured her. Then, before Ashlyn could say anything, she continued. "She's already contacted the general asking to be reinstated to active duty now that you and the others are back home."

"Hammer, you can probably answer this better than anyone else." Ashlyn turned her attention to her now former CO. She just hoped he understood that, by using his call sign, she was asking him Devil Dog to Devil Dog and not subordinate to superior officer. "Why is Talbot still a gunny? He's too good to have been stuck at that grade for more than two years. It also puts the Devil Dogs at a disadvantage because we don't have a master sergeant or, better yet, a master guns." She'd wanted to ask just that since returning to the Devil Dogs but there had never seemed to be the right time to do so.

"Like a number of the rest of us, Ash, he refused promotion until we got you and the others home. That way we didn't face the possibility of being transferred out of the unit," Pawlak explained. "I've recommended him and some of the others in the unit for promotion."

"And I've already approved Talbot's promotion to Master Guns," Okafor said. "It's unusual to promote two ranks but, with the war back on, I want our best people in the slots they are most needed in and we need him as your senior non-com."

"I have to agree with you there, ma'am." Sitting next to her mother, seeing the four watching her with amused and under-standing expressions on their faces, Ashlyn sighed. She might not feel ready to assume command and her skills were definitely rusty after the last two years, but they were at war. There was no way she could turn her back on her planet or on the men and women who were her military family. More than that, she couldn't turn the Devil Dogs over to someone who might not understand what it was they did or who they were. "I can't see the Devil Dogs under anyone else's command but Hammer's, but I'll give it a try."

"Excellent!" Okafor all but rubbed her hands together gleefully. "Use today to put your staff together. Tomorrow, I'd like to meet with you and your mother to discuss the immediate plans for the Devil Dogs. But don't worry. Unless the war escalates much quicker than we anticipate, the core units of the Devil Dogs will remain on-planet for the next few months at least. That gives you time to knock the rust off and to bring them up to your standard, Captain."

"Yes, ma'am."

"Lieutenant Colonel, I believe the two of you have some things to go over as well."

"We do, ma'am," Pawlak replied.

"I believe you have three days before you ship out to Second Fleet. Will that be enough time?"

"It will." He turned to Ashlyn and winked. "Shall we meet for lunch tomorrow, Captain?"

"Of course, sir." She didn't know whether to brace to attention or stick her tongue out. Maybe she should do both.

"Go get your staff put together, Captain. I'll meet with you and your mother at 0800 tomorrow. Mess Dress uniforms. The two of you will stand with me as I announce your new assignments and give the press information about the investigation into what happened on Tarsus. Now, I believe you and Lieutenant Colonel Santiago have something to take care of. Dismissed."

Ashlyn braced to attention and, after Okafor's nod, executed a perfect about face and left the office. So far, the day had most definitely not started out the way she'd expected.

———

HE WAS IN HELL, his own private Hell in the middle of the capital. It was bad enough he had to act as escort to a bunch of spoiled brats who had never heard the word "no" before. But did they have to scream and run around like a bunch of wild animals? The history museum had been bad enough. Usually he could simply turn brats like these loose and tell them to be back at a certain time. But not this time. His orders had been very clear. He was to keep each and every one of them within his field of vision at all times, no matter what.

Now, as they prepared to tour the Capitol Building, he prayed for something, anything to interrupt them. At least at the museum the brats were interested in the exhibits and there were docents to explain everything to them. But now it all fell to him.

He couldn't take much more of this. If he wasn't reassigned soon, he'd resign his commission. He didn't deserve this sort of treatment.

"Another tour, Major?"

O'Brien glanced at the young private stationed near the doors to the building and fought back a frown. Every day for the last month, the private had asked the same thing with the same oh-so-polite tone of voice. But he wasn't fooled. This snot-nosed private, barely out of Basic, found his current assignment just as funny as everyone else. Well, the day would come when the tables would turn and he'd be back to the sort of assignments he deserved. Then he'd show them all. He had a very long memory.

Before he could dwell too much on how sweet it would be to get back at all his detractors, O'Brien paused. There was something different about the Capitol that day. A sense of excitement, almost electric, seemed to fill the air and he wondered what caused it. Congress wasn't in session for the rest of the week. From what he had seen of the schedule, most of the so-called Honorable Members were away from the capital. That had been another reason why he'd dreaded his current escort assignment. There would be no one in chambers to pawn the little brats off on, not even long enough for him to grab a cup of coffee somewhere.

"What's going on?" he asked. As he did, he reached out and grabbed one of the kids in his group by the arm before he could wander off. "Everyone seems excited about something."

Before the private could respond, three people came into view. For one long moment, O'Brien's world seemed to stop. He didn't breathe. His heart may have even stopped. It wouldn't have surprised him if it had. Then a fury unlike any he'd ever felt before washed over him. He wasn't aware of it, or of how his grip on his pre-teen charge's arm tightened until the boy cried out. That broke the spell and he quickly released his hold. But his eyes never left the three moving across the lobby in his direction.

Suddenly they were before him. One of them braced to attention, just as she had many times before. The others stopped and he knew they were waiting to see what he would do. Well, to hell with them and to hell with the captain standing there waiting for him to acknowledge her.

"Major O'Brien, you seem to have forgotten how to salute a senior officer," Miranda Tremayne drawled, her blue eyes flashing dangerously.

"I don't see a senior officer here." He all but spat it out. How dare they come near him, much less speak to him!

"Then I suggest you report to Medical and have your eyes checked," the senator said. "Because I can see Lt. Colonel Santiago's rank and, unless things have changed recently, a lieutenant colonel outranks a major."

His lips pulled back in a sneer before he forced all expression from his face. Then he braced to attention, resenting every moment he stood there. But what choice did he have? That bastard Santiago would put him on report and, if he didn't, Tremayne would certainly pull strings to get him into trouble.

No, into more trouble.

But none of that bothered him nearly as much as the sight of Shaw standing there, waiting to be put at her ease.

"Stand easy, everyone," Santiago said, humor dancing in his eyes. "I'm sure you'd like to welcome Captain Shaw home, Major. I know she was an invaluable member of your last command."

Damn him! Now that bastard was mocking him. If they weren't standing in the middle of the Capitol building's lobby with witnesses hanging on their every word . . ..

"Shaw."

"Major."

"I'm sure you are also as relieved as we are that Captain Shaw and her people have been cleared of all the charges leveled against them, their convictions expunged from their records and have been returned to active duty." Tremayne this time.

"So I heard."

Did she really expect him to say he was glad that bitch was back?

"Begging your pardon, Lt. Colonel, but we do have a briefing to get to," Shaw said.

O'Brien's blood boiled as she looked at him. No, looked through him. There was no emotion, nothing on her expression. He'd always known she was a cold-hearted bitch. But how could she stand there, knowing that he had a hand in what happened, and not feel something?

Or maybe she hadn't realized what he'd done. That would explain why no one from JAG or CID had come for him yet. Maybe his luck hadn't turned. God, could that be it?

"Good to see you back, Shaw." The words were bitter in his mouth, but they had to be said. If he could convince them he meant it . . ..

"You're right, of course, Captain. Senator, shall we?" Santiago motioned toward the door and the aircar that had just pulled up to the curb.

O'Brien watched as the three moved past him. As he did, he felt the sweat trickling down his spine. He had a feeling if he looked down, he'd see his hands shaking. Then the anger returned and, with it, his ability to think. That bitch Shaw might think she'd won but he'd show her. She'd pay, and so would everyone else, for how they'd ruined his career.

"Major?"

The private's voice broke into his thoughts. O'Brien looked around just in time to see the kid he'd grabbed earlier, starting toward the elevators at the back of the lobby. "Go get him, Private. I have a call I have to make."

Not waiting to see if the young man did as he'd ordered, O'Brien turned and left the building. His charges could all go play in traffic for all he cared. He needed to let Sorkowski know what had happened. Let the old man figure out what their next move should be.

———

FOUR HOURS LATER, Ashlyn leaned back in her chair and blew out a breath. After leaving General Okafor's office, she'd made her way to her parents' estate outside of the capital. On the way, she'd sent messages to first Talbot and then to Lucinda Ortega and MJ Adamson, asking them to meet with her that afternoon. Then she'd sat back and replayed the meeting in the general's office.

Once home, she'd reviewed the data Rico Santiago had prepared on Sorkowski, O'Brien and the others involved in setting her and her people up. She had no doubts they were guilty. Greed might have been the driving force for most of them – although she also realized jealousy played into it where O'Brien was concerned. As a member of the Devil Dogs, she'd already accomplished more than he ever would and it was obvious he knew it and hated it. – not that it excused what they'd done. People had died because of their actions and they had to pay for it. Now, for the first time since being brought up on charges, she was satisfied with letting others mete out justice.

A soft *ping* sounded, alerting her to a new message. She frowned slightly to see it had come from General Okafor's office. The general had already authorized her full access to all files and information pertinent to the Devil Dogs. Past mission reports, personnel files, requests to join the unit, all that and more had been sent to her. So what could the general have sent now?

Assuming it had something to do with the meeting scheduled for the next morning, Ashlyn opened the message. She quickly skimmed it, her eyes going wide. Then she read it again, slower this time, sure she'd misread it the first time.

Swallowing hard, she reached for her communicator. For a moment, she considered contacting her father. He'd know if her mother was still in the capital. Then she changed her mind. That was only putting off the inevitable. Whether Elizabeth was home or not, she was who Ashlyn needed to speak to.

"Shaw," her mother's voice said over the comm unit a moment later.

"It's me," Ashlyn said simply.

"I assume by the tone of your voice that you received the general's message," Elizabeth said and Ash heard the amusement in her mother's voice.

"Did you know?"

"Not until a few minutes ago. But, before you say anything, I agree with it. Hang on." There was the sound of her mother speaking softly to someone else. Then Elizabeth was back. "Ash, I have to go. I promise we'll discuss it when I get home. In the meantime, you'll find a package waiting for you in your room. I suggest you take a look at it before you do anything else. And, Ash, that's an order."

Shaking her head as Elizabeth ended the call, Ashlyn sat back and sighed. She really was getting tired of all the surprises people kept springing on her. Not that this last one surprised her, not if she really thought about what General Okafor had said in their meeting. Still, couldn't they let her have just a few weeks without springing anything else on her?

A soft knock at the door interrupted her thoughts and she called out for the newcomer to enter. The door to her mother's study opened and Marie LeClerc stepped inside. Ashlyn smiled at the woman, a mainstay of her life growing up. Marie insisted on calling herself the family's housekeeper, but she was so much more. Many times, Ash had heard her mother say that Marie was the heart of the family and she was right. Marie had been the one to always been there when Elizabeth or Abe had to be away from home. She'd been surrogate mother to Ashlyn and her siblings and now, for Jake, she was surrogate grandmother. In truth, she was family in every way that mattered.

"Captain Ortega, MJ Adamson and Gunnery Sergeant Talbot are here," Maria said as she moved further into the room. She cast a quick look around and Ashlyn knew she was making sure everything was in its place before showing anyone else in.

Ashlyn chuckled. Her friends hadn't let her down. Even though she'd asked to see them at different times, she'd made a bet with herself that they'd show up together. No doubt they'd been trying to figure out not only why she'd been called to meet with General Okafor but also why she'd asked to see the three of them.

"All right. Show them in." She climbed to her feet and moved around the desk. Then, remembering what her mother had said, she changed her mind. "Give me ten minutes and then show them in. Apparently, there's something in my room I'm supposed to see first."

The faintest hint of a smile touched Marie's lips and Ash fought the urge to sigh. Whatever her mother had planned, Marie was in on it and approved.

"Shall I bring in coffee and snacks?" Marie asked

"Please, Marie." She had no doubts the woman would do so whether she agreed or not. Marie would see it as part of simply being a good host.

Exactly ten minutes later, there was another knock at the door. Before Ashlyn could call out, it opened. For a moment, there was a bit of hesitation, almost confusion, as the three newcomers stood there. Ash fought the urge to laugh as she watched them. Normally, Talbot, as junior to the two women, would be the first to enter the room. But with Adamson technically a civilian, at least until she was formally returned to active duty, protocol was a bit confused, to say the least.

"Don't just stand there. Come in and have a seat," Ash said with a light laugh.

For a moment, the three just stood there, looking at her. Then, in a move that didn't surprise Ash, MJ Adamson gave a decisive nod and did as she'd said. The small blonde moved across the study and took one of the seats before the desk. Following a bit more slowly was Ortega. Ash's former roommate took the middle chair. Then she gave a rueful grin and motioned for Talbot to take the third chair.

"I see the three of you have a problem with following orders," Ash said, fighting back her smile.

"What?"

"Ma'am?"

"I don't think you can order a civilian around." Only Adamson seemed nonplussed by Ashlyn's comment.

Ash didn't say anything. Instead, she leaned back in her chair and lifted her booted feet onto the edge of the desk. She still wore her daily uniform, most of it at least. But, after seeing what her mother had left for her upstairs, she'd stripped off her "blouse", opting for the tank top she wore under it. By doing so, she avoided questions she wasn't ready to answer. Besides, it gave her some time to decide what she planned to do about the general's latest surprise.

"But I don't believe you are a civilian, Sergeant Major, not anymore," Ashlyn said. "Unless you've decided to change your mind and withdraw your request to return to duty."

Adamson's expression spoke volumes. Then she was digging into her pocket for her datapad. Ash watched, barely daring to breathe, as her friend discovered the transmittal from the Office of the Commandant of the Marine Corps.

"I—" Adamson cleared her throat and tried again. "I have a feeling there's a lot you have to tell us, ma'am."

"MJ?" Ortega turned in her chair to look at the blonde.

Instead of answering, Adamson simply handed over her datapad. Ortega scanned the display before returning it to the blonde. The look in her green eyes as she turned her attention to Ashlyn was full of speculation.

"MJ has been returned to full active duty status," Ash explained for Talbot's benefit. "And she will be rejoining the Devil Dogs, assuming she wants to." Now she looked at the blonde, her heart beating a little faster as she waited for Adamson's answer.

That answer was quick in coming. Adamson popped out of her chair and braced to attention. "Master Sergeant Adamson reporting for duty, ma'am!"

"Sit down, MJ," Ashlyn laughed, relieved.

"Welcome back, Master Sergeant," Talbot said. "Let me know when you want a rundown on the unit."

"That won't be necessary, Kevin," Ash said and her smile was, if anything, even wider. "I suggest you check your inbox. In fact, both you and Lucinda should have messages from General Okafor's office."

While Ortega and Talbot quickly reached for their own datapads to check their messages, Marie returned, a tray in her hands. Ashlyn got to her feet and hurried to take the tray, thanking Marie as she did. Then, to give the others a bit more time, she poured coffee for everyone and passed around the mugs.

"Would you care to explain why they look like they've been hit – or worse, transferred to the Navy?" Adamson asked as Ashlyn returned to her seat behind the desk.

"Before I do, there are a few things you each need to know." She waited until Ortega and Talbot set their datapads to one side. "I suspect you each know that I met this morning with General Okafor."

They nodded.

"What you probably don't know is that the meeting included Rico Santiago, Hammer and FirstDiv's new CO. What I'm about to tell you doesn't go beyond this room until further notice. Understood." She waited until they each nodded again.

"Let's start with what, to me, is the most important news. The JAG will be filing a number of charges against Dante Coreal, Gavin Haritos and others from Tarsus, not only for what they did to me and our people but for what has turned out to be a long history of corruption. Between the severity of the charges and the number of them,

Coreal and Haritos will never see the light of a free day again. In fact, they will be lucky to avoid the death penalty."

Ortega sat up, her expression hard. "What about Sorkowski and that bastard O'Brien?" Her voice was harsh, cold.

"That's a bit more complicated. I'm still going through the information Santiago and his people have pulled together. As soon as I've finished, I'll forward it to you. However, General Okafor has assured me they will be charged just as soon as the JAG is sure they have an airtight case." She held up a hand when she saw Adamson about to speak. "After hearing what Rico and Okafor had to say today, I agree. We're talking about something that goes beyond what happened to me and the others. We're talking possible treason, collusion with the enemy and more. They have to be careful not to tip their hand in case there are others involved."

"I always knew Sorkowski was a bastard," Adamson growled.

"Agreed." Ash inclined her head. "If it makes you feel any better, the president is aware of what is going on and wants to know how deep this cancer runs. And, when charges are finally brought, if we are still on planet, I'm going to request that the Devil Dogs escort the JAG officers as they make the arrests."

"I want in on it, Cap," Talbot said.

"You'll have to stand behind me, Gunny," Ortega told him.

"If my request is approved, I have a feeling General Okafor and FirstDiv's CO will select the personnel. I'll let them know of your requests when the time comes," Ash promised. "Moving on, as I said, FirstDiv does have a new CO. She is Brigadier General Elizabeth Shaw." Now she smiled proudly.

"Good!" Adamson gave decisive nod. "Your mother is too damned fine of a Marine to be beached."

"I happen to agree with you, MJ, but she will be a hard taskmaster and she's already let me know that she is only going to accept the very best from the Devil Dogs. Not that we've ever given anything but that."

"Wait a moment." Ortega looked at Ash, her expression thoughtful. "Why did she tell you? That's the sort of thing she'd be telling the unit CO."

"That's the next piece of news. Hammer is now Lieutenant Colonel Pawlak and he's being transferred to SecDiv to assume command of the Warlords. As for the Devil Dogs, well, I've been asked to take over as CO. Our senior non-com will be Master Guns Talbot here." She nodded to where the man sat, shaking his head in disbelief. "I expect he'll bring you up to speed very quickly, MJ. Then I want to meet with the two of you. We are at war and I want to make sure our people are ready."

"Understood, ma'am." Talbot sounded as stunned as he looked.

"Kevin – Loco." She smiled as his lips turned up at the use of his call sign. "Same rules now as Hammer had. Meetings like this, when it is just the inner circle, so to speak, we're informal. First names or call signs are fine."

"It may take some time, ma'am – Angel—" He smiled as he corrected himself. "But I'll do my best."

"I'll make sure he does," Adamson added with a cheeky grin.

"Ash?" Ortega's voice was soft, unsure.

"The rest of it, at least all they've let me in on so far—" She knew her frustration was clear, but she also knew they would understand. – "is simple. Just before you arrived, I received notice of my own promotion to Major. I didn't ask for the promotion nor do I think I deserve it." Now she held up her hand to keep them from interrupting. "But I'm not going to argue because it does allow me to ask one thing. Lucinda, I'd like you to be my XO. I'll understand if you'd prefer another assignment. After all, we've had the same time in grade. Hell, as far as I'm concerned, you've had more time in grade because of my little *vacation*." She didn't try to keep the bitterness out of her voice. Bitterness not at the fact her friend had been able to continue serving with the Devil Dogs while she'd been imprisoned but for the imprisonment itself, and the betrayal behind it.

"In fact, Hammer has said he'd gladly take you on as a member of his staff any time you say the word."

For a moment, Ortega didn't say anything. Then she grinned and got to her feet, reaching across the desk to shake Ashlyn's hand. "I think the four of us have a thing or two we can show the other Devil Dogs," she said. "And as for time in grade, as far as I'm concerned, you more than doubled it by managing to survive what those bastards Sorkowski and O'Brien did to you and the others and then surviving that hell of a prison they sent you to. Okafor knew what she was doing when she tapped you to take over for Hammer."

"I'm not sure about that, but I do know the three of you are the best to help me make sure it never happens again to any of our people."

"So, when do we get started?" Talbot asked.

"Unofficially, right now. Officially, once the announcement is made. Come morning, Lucinda and I have a meeting with our new division CO before my mother and I meet with the general and then stand with her as she announces the changes to the media.

"But, before we get started, let me tell you about my *little encounter* with a certain Thomas O'Brien today."

She leaned back and smiled at the memory. Then she launched into an accurate, if slightly more dramatic recitation of the encounter than it really was, she wasn't surprised to see the almost wicked glee reflected in her friends' expressions. It might take time to get used to being back to duty. It would certainly take time to adjust to being in command of the DDs. But, with these three by her side, she had no doubts the Devil Dogs would continue to do their duty to protect Fuercon and its allies. If, along the way, they managed to get vengeance for their fallen brothers and sisters in arms, all the better.

Duty and honor. Corps and family. That was what mattered. It was all that mattered.

AFTERWORD

I want to thank everyone who has been so supportive of the *Honor and Duty* series. This extended version of *Vengeance from Ashes* is one way of doing so. There is a great deal of new material in the book. That material does nothing to change the story arc. It does, however, give us a better look at who Ashlyn Shaw is and was.

This is the first of the extended versions I'll be doing. But this doesn't mean there won't be more stories in the *Honor and Duty* universe. There will be. Ash and company have many more stories for me to tell.

I hope you enjoyed this, for lack of a better term, author's-cut version of the book. I had a great deal of fun putting it together. Ash and company are some of my favorites and any time I have the chance to play in their universe, I enjoy it.

For more information about what I'm working on, check out my website: www.nocturnal-lives.com.

Until later!

AUTHOR'S NOTE

Vengeance from Ashes is a book that's been a long time in the works. The germs of the story were planted years ago, when I found a battered copy of Heinlein's *Starship Troopers* in a closet at my grandmother's. Another foray into that same closet, which looked like it was where my grandmother stored all the books and records my father and his five siblings had left at the family homestead, yielded more books by Heinlein, early copies of *If* and more.

And I was hooked.

Vengeance turned into a book I had to write. It has had various other iterations. But the basic premise has always been the same – duty and honor and family. Family doesn't necessarily begin and end with your blood relations. It can also be those men and women who are your brothers-at-arms.

It began as the first of what I thought would be a three-book story arc. The current story consists of five mainline books and a prequel. There will be more in the *Vengeance* universe after that. But the first books will center on Ashlyn and her fight to do her duty as well as her need to get vengeance – and justice -- for the wrongs done to her people.